Once in a Blue Moon

Once in a Blue Moon

a novel

Leanna Ellis

PUBLISHING GROUP

Nashville, Tennessee

978-0-8054-4988-4

Published by B&H Publishing Group,
Nashville, Tennessee

Dewey Decimal Classification: F
Subject Heading: MYSTERY FICTION \ ROMANTIC
SUSPENSE NOVELS \ ROMANCES

Scripture quotations are from the Holy Bible, New
International Version, copyright © 1973, 1978, 1984 by
International Bible Society.

1 2 3 4 5 6 7 8 • 14 13 12 11 10

Even youths grow tired and weary, and young men stumble and fall;
but those who hope in the LORD will renew their strength.
They will soar on wings like eagles; they will run and not grow weary,
they will walk and not be faint.

Isaiah 40:30–31 NIV

To Graham and Caroline,
you're the stars in my eyes!

Acknowledgments

It's a conspiracy! That is, any writer who claims to write a book alone. It took a faithful team to get this one completed. So, as usual, I have many to thank.

Gary, you're the best husband ever. You're a better cook than me. You fold laundry wonderfully. And only occasionally do you turn clothes the wrong color in the wash. I love you for always being willing to pitch in and help. I love you because you are always supportive. I love you just because you're you. What a blessing you are!

To Graham and Caroline, you inspire me to be the best mommy and writer I can be. Thanks for always being supportive and loving. I love you both!

To my family who is always supportive and buys books! Mom, thanks for helping out when I go to conferences! Thanks for always buying so many books, too! Laurel, thanks for babysitting! Melissa, what great ideas you have!

Natasha, I'm thrilled to work with you. What a blessing you've been in my life!

The team at B&H is phenomenal! Karen, thank you for all you do! I so appreciate your support and encouragement. Julie, Kim, Pat, Diana, the sales team, and all the rest who do so much for each and every book, I so appreciate each and every one of you! You are the best!

Thanks to so many friends who are so wonderful and supportive and too numerous to name here. I am so blessed to have each of you in my life. Thanks to ACFW loopers who patiently answered questions I desperately sent to the loop. As always, thanks to my prayer partners, Leslie and Maria. I love you guys! Julie, it's been a huge blessing working with you. Can't wait for your book to come out.

And thank you to all the readers who have written me wonderful letters. I treasure each one. And thank you to all the booksellers out there who have been so supportive. Keep doing what you do— selling books!

Chapter One

Here lies obit writer Bryn
She should have stayed home
Instead of jumping in.

It's the story of my life. I often jump before looking, much less thinking. But there it is. My life is an obituary-in-the-making. Scary, huh? It keeps things in perspective. But it's not just me. I see others as potential obits, too. Professional hazard, I suppose. Friends text or e-mail pictures of funny or unusual tombstones. One sent me this yesterday:

The children of Israel wanted bread,
And the Lord sent them manna,
Old clerk Wallace wanted a wife,
And the devil sent him Anna.

On Halloween, to give everyone in the office a laugh, I dress up as the Grim Reaper. Every artist's rendering I've ever encountered of the bleak goon in dark, heavy cloak resembles a tall, skinny scare-crow. That's pretty much me in a nutshell. Minus the scythe.

Today, on assignment, dressed in fairly normal clothes (for Austin's relaxed attitude, but not necessarily Houston's uptight-ness) of jeans, cowboy boots, and T-shirt (which reads, *Dead Men Tell No Lies, but their family will!*), I stand in a long, snaking line of which I can just now see the front, waiting my turn (not necessarily patiently). Of course, my brain wanders as it is prone to do when it doesn't have anything occupying it, my thoughts leaning toward the morose.

Most folks I've talked to this weekend celebrating the fortieth anniversary at NASA have happy memories of the *Apollo 11* landing on the moon. Astronauts, celebrities, and the common folk alike who observe the stars above and dream of galaxies light years away have gathered at the NASA facilities. Their spirits are as buoyed as the gazillion red-white-and-blue balloons floating around the build-ing, some bound together to form puffy rockets and planetary orbs.

Visitors who were alive on July 20, 1969, when Neil Armstrong stepped on the gray surface of the moon, want to share their memo-ries of *the* event of the twentieth century. It's a universal hobby this looking up at the moon, gazing into the depths of space and won-dering if life on Earth is all there is. Or if there is more, heavenward or in the opposite direction, if there are men from Mars, women from Venus or from some other galaxy. The stars spark our imagi-nations. The longer we gaze, the smaller and more insignificant we feel, and a craving to know there is something beyond us grows. "One small step for man . . ."

. . . a giant leap into the black hole of my past. I was just a nine-year-old kid busy with throwing a softball into my glove rather than listening to Walter Cronkite narrate the historic occasion, the night my mother stepped into the hereafter . . . a murkiness of darkness or light, whatever your beliefs might be. Mine bend toward a gray mist clouding over my heart, leaving me most often in the dark. The gravity of my mother's death pulls me down into a mire of sticky emotions I usually avoid. Without even the spin of the simulator I'm waiting to ride, I suddenly feel my world reel and my stomach tilt.

To distract my wayward thoughts, I make up another appropriate obit:

> *Brynda Seymour*
> *Took a turn in zero gravity*
> *She ain't no more.*

"Hey!" The stranger next to me who has been texting with his cell phone for the past thirty minutes leans toward me, "What's that?" He nods toward an orange pail outside the door we've anticipated entering for more than an hour.

"In case we barf."

"What?" His lips thin, and he loosens his narrow, gray tie. He seems the type to choose cremation rather than burial, maybe his ashes sprinkled over some cosmopolitan area on a cloudy day. "Have you seen anyone get sick?"

"Hard to tell. After the ride, victims"—I smile and edit myself—"*passengers* exit a different door."

At that moment the metal door slides sideways. I crane my neck to see around the few guts-or-glory fools waiting ahead of me. Through the doorway ten slightly dazed, pale tourists walk (or wobble) out of the simulator, their eyes glazed, their mouths pulled back in a grimace as if they're still experiencing the full impact of the g-forces. I hold back a laugh. One young woman stutters, grabs a wall, and is shown a wheelchair in which she flutters like a collapsed parachute into the sling seat.

"Not too late to change our mind," the man shuffling along ahead of me says. He's slightly older than I am, maybe full into his fifties from the looks of his gray head. He's dressed in shorts and loafers. I imagine him picking out a plain, no-frills casket for his future use.

"Oh, don't worry. This will be fun," I say. "Can't be worse than HALO diving."

The older man turns, raises his eyebrows, which resemble tufts of gray clouds above his blue eyes. "What's that?"

"High altitude, low opening," the suited guy behind me answers. Definitely top-of-the-line casket required here—piped-in music preferred. He looks me up and down, not checking me out for a pickup, but sizing me up and assessing whether or not he believes me capable of the edgy skydiving. "You've HALO skydived?" Doubt permeates his whiny voice. "You military or something?"

"You mean, crazy? Nah, just a reporter." As if that explains my penchant for the extreme. I'd tell him I'm an obit writer but that might make those in line even more nervous, like I'm scoping out new material.

"Me, too. *Houston Chronicle.*" The lofty tone of his voice sets my teeth on edge. Even though Austin is the state's capital, the larger metropolitan city reporters tend to look down their snooping noses at our smaller paper.

"*Austin Statesman.*" I give a tight smile and skim the warning signs posted outside the simulator room. If you're pregnant . . . If you have back trouble . . . If you have heart problems . . . If you have second thoughts . . . Stay out. "You ever experience g-forces?"

"Once." He's young and fit, close to my daughter's age, with a tanned face and easygoing smile. "Puked my guts up."

"Don't sit next to me then." As I move toward the opening door, my step garners a bounce. The green light above flashes. All clear. It's a go-for-launch.

First, a brief introduction to astronaut training by a grim teenager who looks Vulcan minus the pointy ears, then he tells how Buzz Aldrin puked during training. Next, we're given one last chance to abort this mission. A thin, waif of a woman gives an *adios* and is escorted out of the lockdown area.

"Are you ready then?" Star Trek Wannabe eyes our small group of wary space travelers.

"Let 'er rip!" someone behind me hollers. He, I speculate, will be the first to hurl.

"Okay," Spock's cousin says, "let's blast off."

I roll my eyes and follow the master of ceremonies to my personal docking station. I check the plastic cushioned seat for any unidentified stains or particles. All clear. I climb in, pull down the chest guard, and strap the lap belt in place. "What happens," I ask one of the young workers checking for secured seat belts, "if we get sick during the simulation?"

"Bags are provided in the pouch in front." She sounds as if she's repeated the same phrase a thousand times today.

"No extra charge?"

She gives me a sideways glance, confusion darkening her brown eyes and puckering her forehead.

The older man behind me chuckles.

"Have many been used today?" I ask.

The young woman points to an overflowing trash can. A picture is definitely worth a thousand words.

Sitting quietly for one minute . . . two, I check my watch, tap my fingers against the metal handles latched to a fake electronic board providing lights and buttons for my enjoyment. The hatch descends over my head and clicks securely in place. The simulator jerks forward. A bumpy vibration begins in my backside and rattles up my spine. I draw in slow, regulated breaths, releasing the carbon dioxide in equal puffs. I lean my head back against the headrest and close my eyes. My cheeks begin to tremble and shake of their own accord as they pull back toward my ears in a smile that lacks humor or joy. Pressure against my chest builds like a hand bearing down on my heart.

My mind drifts to those first astronauts. What fears did they face during training, during actual liftoff? Did they want to weep? Shout? Say, 'Look, Mom, I'm flying to the moon!'?

And right then, my pulse starts racing as if passing the speed of light. It has nothing to do with the simulator or the vortex it's creating around me. My eyes open. I look around. The enclosed space seems smaller. Frantic, I hold the metal handrails. My breath comes out harsh, fast—then stops. It's as if I've stepped off the *Eagle* right along with Neil Armstrong onto the lifeless moon, but I'm without my astronaut space suit and air pack so I can't draw even a single breath.

I wasn't watching the television at the moment he set that spongy shoe on the rocky, dull surface, but at my mother. I watched her chest rise and fall with each ragged breath. Soon my world began to spin out of control, out of orbit . . . and it's never stopped since.

Before the contents of my stomach start to rise, the simulator jerks to a stop. I sit there a moment, gather my thoughts back into myself, contain them in a tiny capsule, do a mental check of my body parts—arms, legs, stomach, all still with me even though I feel loose and out of touch. Nothing lags behind, not even the contrails of memories.

When the hatch opens, I hop out quickly, ready to escape my past, and give a forced laugh as my boots clunk on the linoleum floor. A retching sound comes from the simulator next to mine. Discreetly, I glance away from the young man in the suit but can't help looking around me at the other faces, which seem drawn and shaded like the green men of a 1960s sci-fi film. I give a thumbs-up sign to the older man who stood beside me for so long and who now seems steady on his feet. The young reporter crawls out of the simulator, hangs onto the edge, and searches through his pockets. For his barf bag? But he pulls out his cell phone and texts a message. Probably: *Survived.* It sounds more optimistic than his shaky reality.

"Where've you been, Bryn?" Marty Peters, my cameraman, rushes up to me.

"Taking a spin." I thumb back toward the simulator.

He grabs my arm and tugs me out of the simulator room and into a crowded hallway. His camera bag bangs against my shoulder. He wears his Nikon around his neck with a long lens attachment.

We seem to be swimming upstream. Marty's long blond ponytail swings from side to side across his back.

I have an urge to grab the ponytail and slow him down. *Whoa, boy.* "What's the hurry? Where are we going?"

"I've got somebody for you to meet. Might be your next article." Article, not obit. I write inspirational true-life stories for the Sunday paper—stories of life—overcoming, overachieving, survival tales. Ironic, huh?

Marty sidesteps a kid in a wheelchair and veers down a corridor, making me hop, skip, and swerve to avoid getting my toes crunched under wire wheels. "Can't we get something to eat first?" My stomach feels wobbly but not from the ride. "Didn't I hear there's cake?"

"Shaped like a moon. And nearly as big. But later."

"So who is this person? Dead or alive?"

"Oh, he's kicking all right. Could be a Sunday special. I told him about you. Said he's a fan."

"Of what?"

Marty pauses outside a doorway. Inside a crowd jumbles together in the oversized room. The din of voices swirls around me, and I feel nauseated. What's wrong with me? Marty scans the crowd, stretching one way, then the other. "This guy worked in the Mission Control room from *Gemini* to *Apollo 14.*"

"Okay. But I need to eat." I wonder if I should have taken the barf bag and tucked it in my hip pocket for insurance, like carrying an umbrella to scare off rain clouds. I spot the cake across the room and plunge into the crowd, my trajectory straight and determined. "What's he do now?" I toss the question over my shoulder at Marty. "Is he an astronaut?"

"Retired, I think." Marty catches up to me. "He's old." This, from a twenty-something's perspective.

We weave through the crowd holding plastic cups of a lime-green punch. I press a hand against my stomach just as I reach the

table and grab a plate with a square of cake. The frosting is an unap-
petizing pale gray. A bit of red piped frosting bisects my piece. Must
be a part of the American flag. Just as I shove a forkful of sugary
sweetness into my mouth, Marty comes to an abrupt halt. I bump
into his back, barely avoiding slamming my cake into his shoulder
blade. He swerves around and stares at my mouth, giving me a look
that says, 'What are you doing?'

"Brynda Seymour!" A voice bursts toward me like a thrust of a
jet engine. The man, as tall and slender as a flag pole, steps forward,
hand extended toward me. "I'd have recognized you anywhere.
Anywhere!"

I gulp down that bite of cake and shake the man's hand a bit
warily. Who would have heard of me? And why?

"Bill Moore," Marty adds to clue me in.

Should I know that name? An ex-head of NASA or astronaut?
The older man with scraggly lead-gray hair that reminds me of the
professor in *Back to the Future* also sports a handlebar mustache. He
leans toward me, his thick glasses making his eyes loom larger. His
gaze aims at me like a laser. "That's not my real name," he whispers
in a rushed huff, then glances over his shoulder. "But I must be
careful."

Surprised by his confession, I wait for him to explain. He
doesn't. "You were a part of all of this"—I swivel my wrist, indicating all the hoopla around us—"forty years ago?"

Cragged and pockmarked as the surface of the moon, his face
breaks into a smile, his mustache curving upward with his lips.
"I was. I was. Amazing time. Truly amazing." He surveys the room
and from his high-perched vantage point, he should be able to see
just about anything he wants. Suddenly he hunches his shoulders
forward and shoves his hands in his pants' pockets. His casket,
I decide, would have to be extra long. "We should have gone back
before now. So much we didn't do. So much we . . ." He waves
away his statement like it's a pesky fly circling my cake. "I've been

contemplating writing my memoirs. You're on the top of my list of writers. Top of my list."

I arch an eyebrow at Marty. "That's flattering, Mr. . . ." I pause, not knowing what to call this strange man. "What should I call you?"

He glances sideways, then behind him. "Howard," he whispers, his breath a mixture of cigarettes and coffee, puffing across my face and making me take a step back. "I'll explain everything—"

"I'm afraid you might have me mixed up with another reporter. I write inspirational profiles, but mostly I'm an obituary writer."

"Isn't that all a memoir is? A long obituary?" His laughter is strange and awkward, as if he's unaccustomed to the procedure. Casually, he loops an arm around my shoulders, and I give Marty a look telling him through make-believe mental telepathy that he's going to pay for this.

Marty jumps forward as if the point of my boot stuck him in the backside. Unfortunately I didn't have that particular pleasure. "Can I get anyone something to drink?"

I frown at him. If he leaves me alone with this guy—

"Do you know if they have lemonade?" Howard's face scrunches into serious consideration. "Pink, not yellow."

"Uh, I'll check. But let's get a couple of shots of you in the lobby. Maybe with a moon rock or next to that rocket."

"No pictures!" Howard's voice booms like a rocket on liftoff. He shakes his head vehemently, making his mustache quiver. "Thing is, Brynda," he still has a hold on me, "my story needs to be told." His breath puffs against my ear and the hair along my nape rises. I lean as far away from him as I can without tipping myself over, but Howard only moves closer. "It's a shame it hasn't been brought to light before now. But so many here . . . at NASA . . . don't want the real story told. Others are afraid."

I aim my fork at the space between his chin and mine. He backs up slightly, and I fork my cake instead of him. "And why's that?"

"Because *they* know."

"Know what?"

"What was really found on the moon."

I start to laugh, but something in Howard's clear gaze stops me. He's serious. Or else an Oscar-worthy actor. Carefully I slide my gaze toward Marty and assess his reaction. He seems just as baffled. I shove my empty plate at Marty, cross my arms over my chest, and meet Howard's gaze again. "And what was found? No air? A lack of gravity?" I decide I need the last scoop of icing and cake and swipe it with my finger. "A bunch of rocks? Or cheese?"

"A crystal palace," he states lucidly. Or so I presume.

I freeze, finger in mouth, and wait for Howard to laugh first. But he doesn't. Not even a crack of a smile. His features remain solid, serious. The cake thickens at the back of my throat and I choke, cough, sputter.

Howard slaps me on the back and continues as if it's quite normal to believe a crystal palace resides on the moon, like some exotic resort taking reservations for family vacations. Is it an all inclusive resort? "The evidence is quite clear."

"Crystal clear?" I laugh at my own joke, but no one else joins me. I wrangle my humor, strapping it down as best I can. "And who lives in this palace? Cinderella?"

Howard's gaze crackles like broken glass. He pokes his bifocals back into place with his index finger. "Obviously, we don't know. Yet. But don't you think more investigations should have been conducted rather than covering up the evidence?"

I slide my gaze toward Marty. His eyes widen as if to tell me he didn't know Howard was a loon. "Okay, well . . ." I give Howard a careful smile. Time to go. But as with any crazy, I've learned to go slow. "Interesting. Definitely interesting. As you know, I'm not a scientific journalist, Mr. . . . Howard. I'm sure a solid foundation in physics"—or psychiatry—"would be beneficial." Or even a rope to tether him to reality. "Good luck with your . . . um . . . project. Maybe you could get Will Smith to conduct that research for you."

Howard or Bill or Howdy Doody slides a worn, raggedy piece of paper into my hand, pressing it against my palm. "This is my number. Don't share it with anyone." He squeezes my hand, and I get a cold, clammy feeling in the bowl of my belly. "Do you understand?"

"Believe me, I won't."

Chapter Two

"How is she today?"

"We are concerned, Ms. Seymour." The nurse's Bohemian accent pours over me like Icy Hot.

Following her lead, I walk alongside her down the hallway of the assisted care unit, the floors sterile, the air smelling of ventilated oranges. Her Nikes clomp heavily on the linoleum. A sideways glance at her name tag clicks my brain into gear. Beatrice is one of the regular nurses. Having returned from the NASA celebration to Austin, my thoughts churned up with memories of that long-ago day, I need to see my grandmother as powerfully as I need air, food, and water.

"Is her blood pressure up again, Beatrice?"

"It is more emotional upheaval." The young black woman puts a hand on my arm and stops me outside the room.

The door remains partially open. From this angle I see the edge of the television and hear Alex Trebek's voice. Two years ago I moved my grandmother here when Alzheimer's made it impossible for her to live alone or even with me.

"Prepare yourself, Ms. Seymour," Beatrice says, her thick lips enunciating carefully. "She is conducting her own funeral."

"That's a new one."

"I thought you should know." Her lyrical voice soothes me. Her kind dark eyes pinch at the corners as if watching me to see if a storm is brewing.

I nod, swallow back the bitter emotions that erode my insides, and enter room 124.

Cora Agnes Billings Seymour lives in her own world. She doesn't pay *Jeopardy* any attention but stoops over a table. Her flowery housecoat is as faded as she has become. Her ankles are swollen, heels dry and cracked. Her worn feet are stuffed in pink fluffy slippers. I can see years of hard work in the dark outline of squiggly blue veins streaking up her calves. Her stooped shoulders speak of burdens she has long carried. Her hair turned gray before its time. The springy curls are parted and smashed against her scalp where she rested her head on the pillow. The single bed is where she spends much of her time these days.

"Nana?"

She shuffles around. Her steady brown gaze holds no recognition. I ignore the tiny ache in my chest.

"Did you know her?" Her voice is hushed and reverent.

"Who?" I glance at the television, but her gaze shifts toward the rumpled bed sheets. Then I realize she's caught in the funeral Beatrice warned me about. "Oh, yes. Of course. That's why I'm here."

"And you brought flowers!" She hobbles forward and reaches for the daisies. Her hand brushes mine, her skin dry and papery thin, and I long for her to smooth the hair out of my eyes as she used to. To cup my chin, meet my gaze solidly, and say, "It is well."

But it's not. And it hasn't been since I was nine. No matter what Nana said or did, she couldn't wipe away the truth.

"Most folks steal stuff these days."

I blink. "What do you mean, Nana?"

"My painting was stolen! Just look at that blank wall."

"There's never been a painting there, Nana."

"Of course not! They stole it." She blinks and her face softens. "But don't you worry." She pats my hand, breathes in the scent of the daisies. "We'll begin the services in a few minutes."

"All right." I've learned over the past couple of years to play along with her fantasies, whether Nana was dining with Bill Clinton, whom she never even voted for, singing with the gusto of Judy Garland, or picking tomatoes out of her pretend garden, which was actually red glass ornaments on the facilities' Christmas tree.

Two chairs are allowed in her room, one next to the bed and another in front of a television set she rarely watches but is constantly on, day and night. The noise comforts her. I understand the disquieting thoughts that invade one's mind. I settle in the recliner near the television, turn the volume down, and wait for her next move.

I used to attempt to help Nana remember, but that only agitated her until she'd begin to twitch. Our time together would end with one of us losing our patience. She would ask the same questions again and again. "Where's Ginger? How old is she now? She sent me a picture she drew. Where is Ginger? I wonder how old she's getting to be." On and on, ad nauseam.

My daughter, Ginger, traitor to my alma mater, the University of Texas, and now a Junior Aggie at A&M, doesn't visit Nana much. It's too painful. I can't blame her. Patience for me should be easy. I love my grandmother. She took me in when my mother died, raised me, gave much of herself, sacrificed for me. But seeing her this way—where once she was competent and capable—stokes a fire of anger inside me.

I want my nana back, the one I depended on, counted on, relied upon. I need her. Hot tears scald my eyes and I turn away, sniff them back into the simmering geyser inside of me, and remind myself that it doesn't serve either of us for me to engage in conversation unless she leads.

Contentment doesn't come easy, however her puttering around reminds me of earlier days. I watch her, longing to be part of her world again. I wonder if she felt this way as she watched me play when I was younger, if she longed to be a part of my imaginary world where she could forget the responsibilities and heartaches of this life. As she plucks random leaves off the daisies I brought and pockets them, I realize my thumb is thumping against my thigh. Over and over. I slap my other hand over it. I came here to not only check on Nana but to find comfort for the pain that never seems to leave.

"Oh, dear one"—she moves toward me—"don't cry. She's in a better place. A better place." She takes my hand in hers. I look up at my grandmother, hope rising. But she pats my hand as if I'm a stranger. Will I have to walk through her funeral with her now, then again alone? She looks back toward the bed as if it's a casket. "My Jennifer."

I'm taken to another time, another place, another funeral I remember too well. A coldness settles over me, as if I've entered the morgue of my past. *Momma.*

"She should have married that nice man who was so fond of her. What was his name?" Nana looks to me for an answer I don't have. Does she mean my father? Whoever he was? When I asked Momma why other kids had a mom and dad, a full family as I called it, she lifted an indifferent shoulder. "We have each other. You and me, kid. This is the beginning of a beautiful friendship." It wasn't until years later I discovered, watching *Casablanca*, that she'd stolen that line.

"Can you remember, Nana? What was his name?"

"He wasn't my Charlie." She sighs. "Oh, Charlie." Tears fill her eyes, spike her gray lashes. "Did I ever tell you how we met?"

"Yes, Nana."

"He practically scared me to death. I was chasing after my cousin. What a toot he was! Why, Avery could get into more trouble than he was worth. I chased that boy all the way down to the bus depot. He ran onto the bus, saying he was going to join the Army like his daddy. This soldier, all decked out in uniform, came off the bus holding Avery by the scruff of the neck. He looked so official. He looked down at me and said, 'Ma'am, this your boy?' Liked to give me a heart attack. I explained Avery's daddy was a Sergeant and had been sent overseas. Then this big, burly soldier knelt down and spoke directly to Avery, told him he was a soldier on the home front, and he had to follow orders. He melted my heart right then and there. Then he took Avery's grimy hand and placed it in mine. His touch was so gentle." She glances at me then. "Ah, Brynda, I've always prayed you'd find such a man."

For that one moment, she knows me. I reach for her, and we hold hands, connected once again. And though I know this moment won't last, I am both comforted and completely undone.

IT TAKES DIGGING THROUGH all of Nana's boxes, which I stored way at the back of my closet, under the bed and in the attic, to find them. In the process I discover dust bunnies have been multiplying beneath my mattress, a croaked cricket between a pair of black heels I never wear, and one mummified rat stretched outright, flattened and stiff as cardboard, in the corner of the attic. Lovely.

"And what have you been doing?" I ask Elphaba. She twitches her black tail at me, her golden eyes glowing in the dim light. "You could have told me about the rat upstairs."

She jumps into the bathroom sink and pads around in a circle, her paws dainty.

"Do you mind?" I grab her around the middle and plunk her back on the floor. Her guttural response irritates me. With a sigh, I check her water, but the bowl is full. She likes water out of the sink or even out of one of my glasses. It's beneath her to drink from a bowl.

I notice the frame above the toilet has tilted and straighten the photo of Oscar Wilde's tombstone, which states:

And alien tears will fill for him
Pity's long-broken ern;
For his mourner's will be outcast men
And outcasts always mourn.

Once I've taken out the trash, including all the little friends I located on my search, I hook up the boxy machine that has no instructions, fumble with the film I located in the attic, trying not to leave fingerprints, and fiddle with the knobs along the projectors' side. Elphaba settles on the coffee table, close enough to watch me (laugh at me in her cattish way) but far enough away to be assured I can't pet her.

I aim the eight-millimeter projector at a blank wall in my den. An intense longing thrusts down on me, squeezing and twisting inside me, until I feel as if I might crumple beneath the pressure. It's a need I usually ignore or suppress. As a little girl, I'd run to Nana, crawl into her lap, and ask her to read to me. She wasn't much on bedtime stories or fairy tales, so, after a long day of working as a secretary, her knobby, bunioned feet propped on a footstool, she'd unfold the paper and read from the Metro section. Sometimes I'd haul the ladder out of the garage and climb onto the roof, sitting on the sun-warmed black tiles searching for peace. Occasionally in school, when inexplicable emotions would assault me, I'd pick a fight and bloody somebody's nose, or take off running like I'd never stop.

But tonight, there's no running, no escaping, no forgetting. My need is a hungry ache gnawing at my insides. I need to see Momma. I need to remember her smile, the way she tilted her head as if asking a silent question, the way she liked to swing her hips and sashay around a room, singing some little ditty of which she never could remember all the words.

Finally, light spurts out of the lens, illuminating dust particles floating in the air, and opens a square on the wall, a window to my past. The machine flickers and sputters, but then I'm back in 1962, pudgy baby thighs bounce and bobble as they try to get me going in the right direction. A younger looking Nana smiles and laughs. There's no sound, no voices, only the hum of the projector. Then I see a hand. Momma's hand. It's a hand I'd recognize as easily as my own. It's in the frame, then gone just as quickly. I reverse the film and play that five seconds over and over again. Concentrating on the image, as if by force of will I can bring color back to her skin, I try to remember the softness of her hand, her warm, gentle touch.

Many nights I would curl up in bed with her, lie on my side, and she would doodle on my back, making curlicues and zigzags until tingling sensations puckered my skin. She wrote the alphabet in manuscript and cursive. She'd write out my spelling words or a secret message—"Want some ice cream?" Then we'd roll over, face the opposite way, and I'd move Momma's long blonde hair over her shoulder, smoothing down her nightgown's silky material, and write my name across her back, finishing my creations with, "I luv Momma."

"One day"—I can still hear her voice, weighted heavy with the allure of sleep—"you'll go off on your own, discover your own life. But you'll always be here with me, Brynnie. Always . . . you and me."

But she was the one who went away. And it was my fault.

I blink myself out of my trance and press a pillow to my stomach as if it will smother the ache inside.

The movie of my life rolls on, one year into another, my life playing out before me in jumpy starts and stops. My first birthday. Christmas, with me jouncing on a plastic horse. Easter. Me again, this time a wicker basket looped over my arm and throwing me off balance. A trip to Galveston with me chasing waves. I catch only bits and pieces of Momma—her elbow, the toe of her pointed shoe, a lock of hair—as she usually operated the camera. These glimpses are never enough, and yet they have my heart echoing the brevity of beats.

Then Momma walks across Nana's backyard. She was tall and slender, like Twiggy. I grew just like her but never lost the awkward, gangly gait that seems as far removed from her as we are now. She was Audrey-Hepburn beautiful. She carried herself easily, a distinct smoothness in her movements. Watching her as an adult, I recognize jealousy blooming inside me like ragweed. It's a reaction born of unfamiliarity.

I focus on the fig tree (that's what we called it even though it looked more like an overgrown shrub) nestled in the corner of the fence. Momma wears big white sunglasses and a narrow skirt that stops mid-thigh. It's one of those moments where she isn't "on." She doesn't know she's being filmed. She races ahead of my awkward limbs, which are pumping for all they were worth, and picks up a board lying hidden in the grass across my path. Her motherly concern for me awakens a dormant emotion.

Transfixed, I move across my living room, reach for her hand . . . but touch the cold, hard plaster of the textured wall instead. I flatten my hand out, my long fingers reaching for her. So close . . . I stand next to her, wondering if I'm taller, watching her as a curious stranger . . . wanting. My heart pounds in my chest, knocking out my breath. Her image flickers over my skin like butterfly wings. For a moment, we are one. Peace settles over me like a warm comforter, blocking cold reality.

When she turns around, her concern over my safety shifts into a frown. She marches back across the yard, one heel wobbling, her footsteps steady and decisive, aiming straight for the camera—and the screen goes black.

I'm not sure how long I stand there, frozen in time. Longing tightens and constricts my stomach. I lean against the wall and feel the bumpy plaster against my cheek, while the stuttering images dance across me. Memories dart to the surface then scatter and flee. A thumping jars me, and I realize my thumb is knocking against the wall. I curl my fingers into a fist and pound it once, twice, the plaster scraping my knuckles.

With a shuddering breath, I walk over to the projector to stop and back it up so I can watch Momma again. But the film lurches forward. I watch myself toddle around a barbecue cooker. The camera pans the backyard in a jerky fashion. A crowd of people mill around, holding beer and Coca-Cola bottles. They laugh and smile. My hand hovers over the button, hesitating to stop this new image I don't remember ever seeing.

Then a face catches my attention. It's the long, thin face of a man. His military styled haircut is severe. He wears a white shirt and dark narrow tie. In spite of the clean-shaven, younger pock-marked face, I know him. My breath catches, snags on shock. Just as the man moves out of the frame.

But I don't need to back it up to know it was Howard.

Chapter Three

Did Elvis die this way? Kneeling on the bathroom mat? I'm bent over my trash can, pulling out crumpled tissues, a brown toilet roll, and an empty shampoo bottle, rummaging through bits of paper and Q-tips to find the wadded paper Howard gave me. My heart races, pounding in my chest as if it might burst forth. Pushing against the toilet, I stand and clutch the phone number like my last lifeline.

Howard Walters. I read his name over and over. My hand trembles as I dial. Twice I hit the wrong number and have to start over. Finally a long pause precedes ringing.

"Mission control." The deep voice doesn't exactly sound like Howard. "We're busy with a launch. Leave a message. We'll get back to you. Unless . . . you're an alien or Man-in-Black. In that case, please remove us from your calling list."

Through the long beep, I stare at the phone and try to decide how to respond. "Howard? Is this Howard Walters? If it is, please call me . . . uh . . . Bryn . . . Brynda Seymour." I roll my lips inward, one last hesitation, before I rattle off my cell phone number.

After I fold and stick the phone in my hip pocket, I circle the living room, then through the entire house. Nothing to do but wait. I once thought waiting would be the death of me. How many times have I stood in line to check out of the grocery store, to vote, to see a doctor?

"Ms. Seymour?" an imagined nurse might call.

"Oops!" The person who arrived at the doctor's office after me stares down at my body sprawled on the nubby carpet. "Looks like she didn't make it. Can I go in her place?"

When I was young, I waited for Momma to pick me up after school, to put on her makeup—the black mascara thick, the eye shadow a moon blue—to fix dinner . . . to wake up. But she never did.

Then I waited for Nana, the police circling me, watching me like I might spontaneously combust, being overly friendly, their smiles fixed as surely as the guns at their hips as they whispered among themselves. Even while I waited, surrounded by well-meaning folks, I was alone. Forever alone.

It's that aloneness that unnerves me. Redialing Howard's number is tempting, but I resist. Over the years I've learned when interviewing people not to seem too eager. I must distract myself. I head to my computer and Google *Howard Walters*, which provides a long list of articles and blogs. Pages and pages. Ten thousand hits. Web sites. Quotes. Stats. He's even on Wikipedia. Who *is* this guy? Is he famous or infamous? Before I can begin reading the first article, the lock on the front door clicks and I hear the handle jiggling.

"Hey, Mom!" Ginger's voice floats through the house.

"Gin?" I push back from the computer and hurry across the off-white carpet. A furry black streak darts out from under my desk, nearly tripping me. Walking into the living room, I come to a halt at the sight of my daughter nuzzling her cat, rubbing noses.

"I've missed you, Elphie."

"Missed you, too." I move toward her and hug her around the shoulders. Eye to golden eye, Elphaba hisses at me.

"Don't act like that," Gin scolds, but her freckled face breaks into a wide smile. "Elphie still not acting nice?"

"Hates me as usual."

"She doesn't hate you!" Gin rubs her head against her cat's. "She just loves me more."

I glare at the black demon, which utters a guttural cry (for my benefit, I'm sure), swivels in Gin's arms and lunges for the floor. Crouching low, the cat flicks her bushy tail. Such dismissive disdain from a fur ball. "I swear she's planning my demise."

"Should I write your obit then?"

"I'll leave you a rough draft." I hug my daughter again, this time sans cat. A warmth spreads through me, followed by a tiny vibration—that joyous feeling of coming home. "So what are you doing in Austin?"

"Going out with some friends."

"Shouldn't you be in College Station? Or is the night life there getting stale?"

"The grass is always greener."

Her secretive smile gives me a slight pause, but I take the slow route to confrontation. "Are you and your friends crashing here for the night?"

She places the tip of her tongue on her upper lip and rolls her gaze toward me. "If you don't mind having a couple of houseguests."

"Why would I mind? Just don't do anything I would do."

"Oh, you know me, Mom."

I do know her. She's a serious engineering student. "So who else is with you?"

"Just Rachel. She's waiting in the car. I wanted to grab a different shirt. We're running late." She heads toward my bedroom. We've swapped clothes with each other since she matched my height in high school. A minute later I hear, "What's all this?"

Frowning, I follow her voice, find her in the bathroom picking up the mess I left in my hurry to call Howard. I bat her hands away. "Don't worry with that." I scoop up and throw away the trash I inadvertently left all over the rug. Heat suffuses my face. "If you're late, you better get dressed."

Gin stares down at me, her lip curling, her forehead scrunching her bronze eyebrows together. "You okay, Mom?"

I straighten the rug, avoiding her probing gaze. "Sure. Yeah, I was . . . uh . . ." I grab a purple tube of mascara out of the trash. "Have you ever tried this brand?"

She shakes her head.

"Well, don't. It glopped my lashes together and took me three days to wash it off. What shirt are you going to wear?"

She waggles an aqua silk shirt at me, hooks the hanger on the doorknob, and yanks off her T-shirt, revealing a black lacy bra. Not her usual workout variety. The brightly colored shirt makes her eyes sparkle and her strawberry blonde hair shine. A tingle ripples down my spine. My motherly radar flares full alert.

"You two have dates tonight? Or are you cruising?" I wonder if I sound as old as I suddenly feel.

"Oh, you know . . ." She leans toward the mirror and dabs on more mascara. "Don't worry. We'll be quiet coming in."

My chest tightens. I feel the years beginning to separate us as she moves out into her own life, finding herself, and I long for her to be a senior in high school again. Even though there were a few emotional eruptions and the push-pull of mother and daughter, at least then I had her close. I long for the days when she would tell me everything from what her teacher wore to what she ate for a snack. But those days are over. And as I've learned through my life—there's no going back. So I begin my subtly probing twenty questions. Being a reporter, it's one of my specialties. "Must be a special guy for you to drive so far."

She turns and smiles that *Gotcha!* smile. "How are you, Mom?"

"Is he cute?" I persist.

"Haven't met him yet."

"Ah, the infamous blind date." My brow accordions into a frown.

"How's Nana? You saw her today, didn't you?"

"As stubborn as you." We begin the lobbing of questions that usually get us nowhere. "How are summer classes going?"

"One more week." It's apparently deemed a safe topic as she tells me about some theorem from her math class, the subject light years beyond my comprehension. She inherited her gift of numbers (along with her freckles) from her father, not me. Too bad he wasn't half as gifted in relationships. Ever since our divorce when Ginger was two, he's played only a peripheral part in his daughter's life, keeping to the edges of events and milestones. At least he showed up for an occasional swim meet and her high school graduation. But then, I've never been accused of being a relationship expert either. I hope Gin has better luck than I have. And if love isn't reliant on luck, I'm fairly certain she's got more smarts than her mom to handle the till-death-do-us-part type of relationship.

My cell phone sounds off, interrupting Gin's mathematical gibberish. The ring tone she downloaded to my cell is "Touch of Grey" by the Grateful Dead. I freeze, suspecting it's Howard returning my call, wishing I'd set the sound on vibrate. *Now* what do I do? How can I have the conversation with Howard and ask the questions I need to ask with my daughter in the room? For all I know, he could be her grandfather.

"Your backside is ringing, Mom. Aren't you going to get that?"

"Uh . . ." What should I say? *Guess what, Gin? Meet my dad . . . tada! . . . your grandpa! Oh, sure, he thinks little green men are after him, but all families have their quirky relatives.* But I stumble around with another "uh" and listen to my back pocket.

"Mom"—Gin plucks the phone from my jeans—"here."

Before she can flip it open, the song grinds to its death. I snatch it from her as the cell phone beeps, indicating the caller has left a message, I flinch, almost dropping it.

"You sure you're okay, Mom?"

I rub my thumb over the phone like it's a worry stone, thankful it isn't a mood ring that would turn black. A million questions fire through my brain at once. If that was Howard, what message did he leave? What did he say?

"Mom?"

I jerk upright. "What?"

"Are you okay?"

"Sure. Yes, of course. Just snowed under with work. No big deal. I'm fine. Really." I wonder if she believes me, because I sure don't. "Look at the time! What time is this date of yours?"

"Mom—"

"Rachel is waiting. We can talk tomorrow . . . if you're not in a hurry to get back."

Gin makes a face but lets her question go for the moment. "Actually we've gotta head right back. Rachel's got class. And I need to study." She clicks her keys. "But I don't have to go tonight."

"Yes, you do! This guy could be the catch of the century. Now, go. I'm fine. Really. Besides, I may be heading out of town this week." That is, if Howard will meet with me.

"Again? Where?"

"Um, I'm not sure yet."

She tilts her head sideways, eyeing me as if our roles have suddenly, irrevocably reversed. "With Eric?"

Eric Hart. The man who stirs up more questions in my life than answers. I actually hadn't thought about telling him I might leave town. But I better check my calendar, make sure I didn't promise I'd attend one of his music sessions or agree to dinner. With him, most of our dates are last-minute, spur-of-the-moment events of insanity. Besides, someone needs to check on Elphie.

"Why don't you just marry the guy and get it over with, Mom?"

I stare at her. "Where'd that come from?"

"You've been dating, what? Four years?"

"Three."

"So, get on with it."

"Elphaba would kill me for sure." I stretch out my toe to rub her gray tummy as she lounges across the floor like she owns the place. She accepts the attention like an entitlement, Cleopatra being pampered by one of her minions. "Besides, maybe I don't want to get married."

A horn blares three times. Is that the cock crowing for Peter's bald-faced lie?

Gin tips her head toward the door. "Rachel."

"She's waiting."

"Impatient."

I feel the same jitteriness inside my own skin. "I know the type."

Gin puts her hand on the doorknob. "What is it with the women in my family? Nana never remarried. Your mom never married at all. And ever since Dad—"

"Gin"—I stop her dissertation on our family's failings—"Rachel's waiting."

"I guess I'm going to have to be the first one in our family married for fifty years."

I sit on the arm of the sofa, cross my arms over my chest. My maternal instincts perk up just as Elphaba curls her body around my foot and bites my toe. Jerking my foot out of reach, I tuck it under my hip and stick my tongue out at the furry beast. "Do you have someone in mind for this life sentence?"

"Don't you value marriage?"

"Sure, baby. I've been sentenced before. Got out on parole, remember?"

Gin frowns.

"It's just not the be-all, end-all. You're too idealistic."

"Maybe you're too jaded."

Her words slice into me. My first instinct is to lash back with, *"Darn right! I have good reason!"* But I hesitate long enough for recovery mode to kick in as I try to stop the internal bleeding by pressing my lips firmly closed. Reason takes hold and I know she's right. And I don't much like it.

Gin's mouth slides sideways as she contemplates whether or not to continue with the lashing I probably deserve. She flips her keys around her forefinger, her white flag of surrender, and hugs me close again. "Well, be careful, Mom, on your trip."

I breathe in her tangy scent, some new perfume I don't recognize. "Always."

She laughs and pulls away. "Aren't mothers supposed to be the ones to worry about their daughters, not vice versa?"

"New century. New rules."

As the door closes behind Bryn, Elphaba stretches and saunters off, her tail swishing high in the air. There's more working behind those golden eyes than the cat wants to let on.

> *Bryn Seymour died*
> *Quite unexpected.*
> *No one knew why*
> *Except the cat*
> *And she wasn't telling.*

Confident Ginger is off on her night out, I grab my cell phone, dial in to retrieve the message and listen to a long staticky pause. No message. I check the number and hit redial. Immediately I get the same bizarre greeting I heard before. "Howard," I say after the beep, "this is Bryn. I'm sorry I missed your call."

After I leave my message, I pace my living room, waiting for Howard to call back. What if he doesn't call again? What if he thinks I'm playing games? What if he's been abducted by aliens?

Then I might never know the connection he shared with my mother . . . if he's my . . .

I slam my mental brakes on that thought.

The minutes tick away. My mother's high school yearbook snags my attention. It sits on the bottom shelf. A good distraction, which I desperately need. The heavy leather book has thick, slick pages. I locate Howard Walters in the index. Science club. Pimples. Senior. I glance at his picture but linger over Momma's several pages later. Only a postage-stamp size and black-and-white, Jennifer Seymour's picture stands out among the others. I once thought I was prejudiced, but I've accepted as I've grown older that my mother was a looker. No doubt about it. I probably look more like my father, which has me flipping back to carefully study Howard's picture. But I don't think I look like him either. Maybe I am more prejudiced than objective.

Momma's blonde hair was styled in a late-fifties shoulder-length flip. One shoulder dipped forward toward the camera in an innocent yet provocative way. To the side of her picture, her activities are listed—twirler, cheerleader, Home Ec Club. Her high school résumé went with Howard's about as well as jalapeños and wasabi. What was their connection? Maybe he tutored her through Algebra. Maybe she gave him advice about girls. Or maybe—

The key in the lock startles me out of my panicky thoughts. Gin already? What time is it? I glance at the clock on the mantle, an old-fashioned ticker that belonged to Nana. It's too early for college girls looking for fun. Could she be ill?

The door opens slowly. Eric stands in the doorway and gives me his lazy, self-confident smile. His short brown hair is spiked in a bold declaration of independence, which is what originally attracted me. That, and his dangerous edge. "Whatcha doin'?"

"Oh, uh . . . working." I hug the yearbook to my chest, unsure if I'm trying to hide it or if I'm simply unwilling—in a controlling, belligerent, defiant way—to share.

He leans over the sofa, slips an arm around me, and kisses me. My world tilts off kilter. "Time to take a break then, huh?"

The corner of the book digs into my middle, and I shift it to the side. "Wish I could."

He flops onto the sofa beside me. "Whatcha looking at?" He eyes the cover. "Lookin' up an old boyfriend?" He nudges the projector still on the coffee table with his foot. "Strollin' down Memory Lane?"

"Yeah." I toss the book aside and cup a hand along his strong jaw, feel the scrape of his five o'clock shadow.

"What do you need some old fuddy-duddy for when you have a young stud like me?"

"Fuddy-duddy?" I laugh. "Where did you get that word?"

"Probably from my last girlfriend." He winks.

"Which is why I need to line up an older guy . . . in case you dump me."

He slips an arm around my hips and pulls me closer. "That's not about to happen." He nuzzles the slope of my neck and shoulder then moves away. "Mind if I take a shower?"

"Be my guest."

"Join me?"

Although tempted, I feel my gaze drift toward the book.

"I know that look." His voice dips low into the range of disappointment. "Work, right?"

I nod. He heads toward my bedroom, stripping his shirt over his head as he goes. I've never grown tired of that bronze, muscular back. Or any other aspect of Eric. He's a good man, kindhearted. And he's stuck around longer than any other. I'm not sure if it's because he's fifteen years younger or if I'm getting better at picking men. Maybe the human male has evolved. Nah. It might simply be Eric's stubborn streak, which I didn't know existed when we first got involved. Gin's suggestion about marriage comes back to me, and I know the reason I pick the men that I do.

Moving back to the computer, I scan the articles and blogs about Howard. Some revere him. Others blatantly call him a loon. There

are several up in arms about an upcoming lunar probe. Howard
wants NASA to probe a different area, calls them out like a street
fighter. Clicking the mouse, concentrating on following another
link, I startle when strong arms fold around me.

Eric's hair is damp, his ear cold. He smells of Caress and pure
male. "Sure I can't talk you into some recess?"

"You are persuasive." I turn, encircle his neck with my arms.

He dips his head and kisses me, possessing my thoughts
momentarily, taking away all the questions and concerns. Until
my cell phone begins the Grateful Dead song again. I lunge for my
phone, knocking Eric out of the way.

"Important call?" he mutters, rubbing his shoulder.

"Hello? This is Bryn."

A raspy breathing fills my ear for a moment before he answers.
"Brynda? How did—"

"Why didn't you tell me—?" I interrupt and stop short of completing my full question. I glance sideways at Eric who flops into my
chair and I turn away, seeking privacy. The illuminated computer
screen glows eerily like a UFO.

"What's that?" Howard sounds utterly confused.

"That you knew"—I restrain from saying *my mother*—"Jennifer?"

"Would you have been willing to talk to me then?" He doesn't
ask how I discovered his secret. Is it because he doesn't care? Or
because it's about time? When I don't answer his first question, he
asks another, "Are you ready now?"

I walk into my living room, keeping my voice low. "I have to
know about her."

"Can you come here?"

Elphaba rubs against my leg. Knowing what's coming, I sidestep
her before she can bite my ankle. "Where?"

"Ever heard of Marfa, Texas?"

I click through my memory files. "You mean where those weird
lights occur?"

"That's it." His voice is haltingly slow. "Call me when you get here."

How do you ask a man over the phone if he's your father? It is, of course, the first question on my long, growing list. I decide to wait until we're nose to nose, so I can judge if his is growing like Pinocchio's—or if it's way too similar to my own. "I'll be there tomorrow."

A click disconnects the line and serves as his good-bye. For a moment I stare at the phone, teetering between shock and disbelief. It takes a minute for my heart to slow to its usual, steady beat.

"Everything okay?" Eric leans against the doorjamb, watching me. How long had he been standing there?

"Oh, sure." I set the phone on the coffee table. It clatters awkwardly against the glass.

"Some stiff can't wait for you to write about him until later?" He moves toward my bookshelf, scans the books, running a finger along the spines. Our tastes don't seem to intersect; his lean toward comics and sports while I read the nonfiction best seller list, anything from *Marley and Me* to *The Purpose-Driven Life*. Except the now-famous yellow lab seems to have more purpose than I do.

A black streak of fur zips around the corner, then freezes. Her owl-like eyes glare at Eric but he doesn't seem to notice or care. "Hey, Ringo"—my nickname for Eric—"I've got to leave town again. Mind checking on Elphie the next few days?"

He pulls a book from the shelf, glances down at his charge, then slaps the book closed, aiming it at her like a dog's snapping jaws. Elphie bolts out of the room. He grins. "She hates me."

"Well, maybe if you tried a different tactic . . ."

He shrugs a shoulder, a simple up-down motion of disinterest. "I'll outlive her."

"Not if she can help it."

"Come on." He shoves the book onto the shelf, not quite where he found it, and not straight up but on its side and on top of the other books standing like soldiers—not that I notice. His gaze skims over me intimately. "Let's go out."

"I have things to do here." I move back toward the computer, aware of Eric following me. "Go ahead and have fun. I'll call you later in the week."

"You sure? You're not gonna be jealous, are ya?" He snags me around the middle with one arm, nibbles on the side of my neck, working his way up to my ear. His lips brush across my skin whisper-soft. "Wanna have a private party here?"

I press my hands firmly against his chest. "I've got to pack and do more research."

His gaze drops, his hand following along my neckline. "I need to do some research, too." Then he studies me, making me squirm inwardly. "Did I miss something? What's wrong?"

"Nothing." Even I'm not convinced. So I try a different tack by sliding my fingers into the soft hair at his nape and offering my best smile.

His gaze narrows. "This is serious. What did I do?"

Guilt intrudes. I kiss him long and fierce, my form of an apology. "Nothing. I just have this . . . thing."

"You know, you can tell me what's bothering you. Anything."

I place my hands against his chest, tap my thumb in an effort to find the right words. "I know. And I appreciate it. I'm not very good at this."

He waits, glances down at my hand. My knuckles are scraped red, but not bleeding. He gives me a questioning look.

Pressure builds in my chest. *Don't ask. Please don't ask.*

"You sure you're okay?"

"Why wouldn't I be? It's just . . . can't talk about it just yet."

Touching his lips to mine, he whispers, "Say no more." After a quick kiss on my cheek, he heads toward the door. "Don't worry about the cat. I'll fire up the grill while you're gone. Roast a hairball."

Chapter Four

I haven't been inside a middle school since Ginger was fourteen. Not my favorite time of my child's life. It left me predisposed to avoiding places like this, but there's urgency in my footsteps as I mount the concrete steps. "Aunt" Lillie was my mother's best friend growing up. Since she teaches art at Fredericksburg Middle School, I decide to stop and see her for research purposes on my drive to Marfa.

I check in at the school office. Even though it isn't an official school day, there are still students attending summer classes or teachers getting ready for the upcoming school year. With my official media pass in hand, I walk down the long hallway, remembering my own school's cold floors and drab halls. Lockers line the walls. Graffiti mars a few of the metal doors, not-so-polite words have been scratched into the brown painted metal, other words smeared on with permanent marker. Classroom doors are propped open, and I can hear quiet conversations going on in various rooms. For the most part, the hallways are deserted of students and teachers.

The air smells stuffy . . . retro, as if it's pulling me back to a different time. I can almost smell the wet, alcohol odor of mimeograph ink from my own days in school.

Not one of the popular kids growing up, I was a bit of a loner, still trying to get my bearings on life, my seesaw emotions, my loss, my heart. The yearbook staff room became my regular hangout where I learned to sort through my thoughts and put them on paper.

Turning the corner at the end of what the receptionist said was "A Hall," I enter another hallway that leads past a gym and auditorium, past the band hall from which comes the haunting sound of a French horn, then blessed silence. I've never been too familiar with the band or orchestra as Ginger played piano rather than choosing a handheld instrument. Her long fingers were apparently handed down from Momma. She also took art in middle school. She liked to draw abstract designs, her engineering brain at work.

When I was required to take something in the arts, I chose drama, where I could probe the darkness within. The walls and ceiling of the drama room in my school were painted black, the floor gray, except for strips of colorful tape so we could hit our marks. Rodney Kimmel, our eccentric, demonstrative teacher, made us do exercises that stretched our facial muscles and, as he said, "expand your minds." I'm not sure how much you can expand the mind of a fifteen-year-old, but I suppose getting us to think about anything other than ourselves was a major triumph.

He assigned me a scene from *A Moon for the Misbegotten*, which touched a dark place inside me that crumpled me to that cold, gray floor, authentic, salty tears running down my face. Mr. Kimmel dismissed the class early, sat beside me, and put his arms around me, protective, comforting. He didn't offer any words of wisdom. He didn't try to explain why my mother died. Not like Nana had told me: "God needs Jennifer in heaven." I always wanted to know why! Why did God's needs trump my own? Mr. Kimmel simply let me know my turbulent feelings were justified. The emotions I'd fought for so long weren't wrong or invalid. They mattered. I mattered.

Mr. Kimmel died during my senior year in high school. I wrote his obituary for the school paper.

Rodney Kimmel, teacher with a big heart and only a short time to share it . . .

Words had become my refuge, and anger my excuse for inexcusable behavior. From Mr. Kimmel, I learned the power of silence and a warm embrace. Nana wouldn't allow me to miss school and attend his funeral. "If you don't get good grades, you won't get accepted into college, much less a scholarship." It was one of our first big fights. She feared I'd turn out like Momma. Later I received a letter from his parents, thanking me for the sweet tribute to their only son.

I learned the significance of an obituary in closing the door to a life and opening one toward healing. It's a healing I'm seeking today in my journey to west Texas, and it detours into this school where I hope "Aunt" Lillie will have some answers I need to close the door on my past and open up possibilities.

When I reach the end of the school hallway, I step through an opening and onto a concrete floor. My clean, almost new running shoes look out of place among the paint dollops and smashed clay that gives the floor a lived-in look. The walls provide an amateurish museum collection—the untalented far outnumbering the gifted. Pencil etchings, shadings, oil, and watercolors give a variety of styles and colors, depth and insights. A blood-red, livid painting, bold strokes arcing across the canvas, draws my attention. Clay, hand-molded creations and thrown pots (mostly wobbly and dented), some still wet and drying, line the counters. Others have the white-fired casting. Still others shimmer with a gloss coating. In the corner easels lean in a haphazard, precarious way. Throughout the room, row upon row of long tables are assembled with some chairs pushed in and others blocking aisles. The disorder gives me an almost immediate headache.

Humming comes from behind a partially open door and switches to whistling, bouncing back and forth between the two. It's a tune I don't recognize, something ethereal, light, angelic, just like Lillie Martin. When she begins to sing, the notes slip slightly off key. Enya would not envy the mystic quality. The humming returns, expands into what Eric would call just fooling around with notes. But his noodling around on the guitar has more appeal and direction. And manages to stay in tune. Aunt Lillie doesn't seem to be bound by any conventions or constraints of form.

A wedge of light from the doorway points me toward what looks like a cavernous closet. "Hello?"

"Oh, yes! I'm coming!" A flutter of papers follows as if dropped, then a thunk.

"Are you all right?" I set my backpack on a table. Maybe I should go help.

"Yes, yes. I'm coming . . . Now!" She appears in the doorway, like an actress stepping onto a stage, pausing for recognition and applause. She's late middle-aged with long, white/blonde hair, an odd mixture of nappy strands and loose unruly curls that fall way past her shoulders. Her face is wide, smiling, a pinkish color that gives her a youthful charm and innocence. "Hello and what can I—Bryn!"

She rushes forward and embraces me, pulling me so hard against her, my breath leaves with a slight *humph*. I feel myself leaning toward her, welcoming her warmth. She smells of lavender and . . . hemp? She pets my arm as if needing to touch me to know I'm real and not imagined. "What are you doing here?" Her grin disappears and she grips my arms. "It's not your grandmother, is it?"

"No, no, Nana's fine. As well as she can be."

Her concern relaxes back into a wide, gaping smile. "That's a relief. I usually sense things and I didn't . . ." She waves her arm outward, and a wide assortment of bangles and bracelets clatter. Her hands are small, expressive, and match the floor with paint splotches, ink stains, and clay embedded around the fingernails. "Have a seat. Make yourself comfortable."

I pick up my backpack, start to set it on the floor, then rethink that move, sliding it down the table instead, and pull out a chair for myself. Checking the seat first for paint splotches and bits of clay or any other arts-and-craft item I wouldn't want stuck to my backside, I finally sit and notice there's not even a teacher's desk in the room. "I don't mean to intrude on your work."

"Nonsense. I'm just getting ready for the school year to start." Lillie does a quickstep and sashays about until she settles like a butterfly, perching herself on the end of the table, spreading out her white gossamer skirt with an uneven hem that looks like flower petals. "What brings you out this way?"

"I hadn't seen you in a while."

"Life gets busy, doesn't it? I always enjoy your Christmas notes, catching up on your adventures. You look so much like Jennifer. As she might have looked . . ."

My hand involuntarily moves to my face, touches my cheek. I've seen the resemblance in pictures, but I thought it was just hope springing forth, a need rising up in me. And yet, Momma was blonde and I have dark, almost black hair, short and clipped close to my scalp. I'd say it's like Audrey Hepburn's in *Roman Holiday*, but she had more class. Gin calls it boyish. For me it's simply easy. "You knew Momma better than anyone, didn't you?"

"I suppose. Although your grandmother had a pretty good read on her daughter."

"But she wouldn't have talked to Nana. Not about . . . secrets."

"Secrets?" An impish light glimmers in her blue eyes.

"I've never really cared to know." My pulse skips and races ahead. "I mean, it didn't matter. Momma told me I had *her*. She had *me*. And that's all we needed. And it wasn't until after she died, well, I understood everyone has a father. But Nana couldn't talk about Momma, much less . . . she used to sing that song, 'You and Me Against the World.' Remember that?"

"Helen Reddy." Aunt Lillie's wistful smile fades. "So you're asking me who your father is?"

Heat rushes to my face then plummets, leaving me light-headed, the room starting to turn of its own accord. "Yes." Unsure I want to know the truth, I shrug as if my skin suddenly is too tight for comfort. Or maybe it's my heritage that seems too small. "I don't know."

She slides off the edge of the table, moves to a drawing on the wall, studies it for a moment then aligns it with the others. "Did you ever take art?"

"Theater," I say as way of an apology in case she takes offense.

"Art, in whatever form, is the expression of the individual. It's a wonderful outlet for young people when they are dealing with the angst and hormonal changes of youth. Don't you think?"

"I'm not a teenager, Aunt Lillie. I think I'm old enough to handle the truth."

"Of course. And you're a writer." Her smile returns, pride lighting her eyes. "And that is an art as old as the world. Making stories, telling tales. When our ancestors drew on cave walls, they had stories, too. And dance. To be human is to share a need to express ourselves."

Before we launch into a class lecture, I say, "Yes, well, I'm really a reporter."

"You still write stories, lovey."

I cut to the chase, my nerves tangled into restricting knots. "Do you know who my father is?"

She meets my gaze solidly and without hesitation. "I wish I did. I wish I could give that to you. For Jennifer. Maybe after all this time, she wouldn't feel the need for secrecy anymore. But she never even told me."

I chew on the inside of my cheek, wrestle with the next question. "Do you know Howard Walters?"

Her eyes widen, and my breath solidifies in my throat like a hard cubical lump. Before she answers, I know.

"Oh, my yes! Do you? Why, it's been . . . forever since I've seen Howie. Howard Walters." Her tone turns nostalgic. Then she laughs, a tinkering sound like something belonging to a fairy. "Goodness! I hadn't thought of him in years."

Her gaze drifts off as if she's peering into the past before it ping-pongs back toward me. "Is this about . . .? You think Howard is . . . Oh, my!" Her hand touches her face. "Have you met . . . of course not. If you had . . ." She covers her mouth to stifle her laughter and shakes her head with disbelief, her hair fluttering about her like clipped angel's wings. "Howard was a friend. We were all good friends."

"What was he like?" Did he wear floodwater pants or talk about little green men back then?

"Howard was too smart to fit into the regular high school groups. Jennifer and I sort of adopted him, like a little brother. Except he was so much taller . . . and ahead of us by a couple of grades."

"And was he . . . mentally stable?"

"Are you asking if he's crazy?"

"Yes."

"Far as I know. Far as anyone can know that about anyone else." She leans toward me and confides, "I think we're all a little nuts . . . some of us are just better at hiding it than others."

Since I write my own personal obits, I don't have an argument for her. "And you lost touch with him?"

"That happens after high school, I suppose. I see it all the time here as the kids graduate and move on to college and find their way in the world. Howard moved to Houston to work for NASA. See, I told you he was smart as a whip. We'd see him occasionally. Jennifer went to Houston after high school graduation. She wanted a big city for all her big ideas. She didn't follow Howard though. Maybe he'd told her about living there. Or maybe he knew where she could get a job." She touches her forehead. "My memory isn't what it used to be. Been a long time. To tell you the truth, Jennifer just wanted to get away from your grandmother for a while. She wanted to experience life—on her own."

"She got more than she bargained for when she had me so early, didn't she?"

"Oh, you were a surprise all right. But I never once heard Jennifer have regrets."

"Why didn't she go back to Nana's after I was born?"

"And listen to your grandmother say, 'I told you so,' a thousand times? No. Once she made her bed, so to speak, she was staying put."

But who shared that bed? I'd never particularly cared. But something has stirred inside me and suddenly I want to know more. About my mother. And father. Before, fear kept me from digging into the past. I didn't want to think about Momma because memories always ended with her death. Now . . .

I push once more, to make sure there wasn't some secret love affair between Momma and Howard. "But she and Howard never . . . ?"

"Oh, my goodness, no. I believe she saw Howard some in Houston, not romantically, just as friends. NASA was in the news a lot back then, so it was fun for Jennifer to tell friends that she knew someone who worked there. Made her feel important. If she and Howard had . . . well, you know, she would have told me. I'm certain of that. So, no. Not possible."

Relief trickles through my veins, relaxing my tense muscles. Now I can go to Marfa without worrying I'm stepping into a familial mess.

"Howard"—she shakes her head, pinches her lips together—"How long has it been since I've seen Howard Walters? My goodness. He never comes to the reunions. It's getting to be fewer and fewer now who do come. Jennifer was the first to go. So many asked why. Why?" Her eyes fill with tears, making them look like pale amethysts. "I think maybe that was the last time I saw Howard . . . at your mother's funeral. He was pretty broken up over it. Of course, we all were. It was quite a shock. So young. And well, taking her own life that way." She reaches over and clasps my hand, her fingers stronger than I would have imagined, her grasp intense and urgent. "All the harder because she left you. Just broke my heart that day seeing you sitting in that pew, just a young girl . . . and I still remember the obituary you wrote for your mother. I keep it at home. Such a sweet tribute. And already a budding writer back then." Her nostalgia blossoms into a wistful smile.

The sparkle in her eye dims. Her face crimps into a concerned frown, as if she realizes the subject is uncomfortable for me. She settles back on the desk, crossing one leg over the other and swinging her foot back and forth. "Howard Walters." She wrestles the conversation back to the original topic. "Boy, he was a smart one. Should have gone to MIT or something."

I quote the information I found on the Internet. "He graduated from the University of Texas."

"Oh, yes. Graduated early. NASA was just getting started in the big race for the moon." She tilts her head to the side and studies me like a painting. "So why all this interest in Howard?"

"I met him recently. At an event at NASA. I found out he knew Momma. It made me wonder." I run my hands down my thighs as if erasing the crazy thought. "I probably have an overactive imagination."

"Stirred up questions about your mother?"

"I suppose. It's not something I've ever particularly wanted to know." I shrug, my shirt suddenly feeling as tight as the constraints of secrets. But I've gone this far asking if Howard could be my father, so I might as well go the next step. "So, did you know anyone my mother *was* in love with or involved with?"

Aunt Lillie leans back, hooking her hands around her knee and rocking a bit. "Jennifer was funny that way. Oh, in high school, she could flaunt a beau with the best of them. And did. But after high school, well, she kept things to herself more. I personally think she just didn't want your grandmother to know what she was up to. A bit of a rebel in that girl. But isn't that true of all of us at one time or another?"

Lillie slides off the desk and flits around the room, busying her hands. She takes a lump of clay out of an airtight container and begins pressing it, pushing her thumbs in it, working it on the table. "I never did rebel like Jennifer did. And I'm not exactly sure why. Maybe I do in art. My father used to say, 'Do something practical. Who needs art?' So, maybe I am rebelling against him.

"Some people say, 'How can you teach the same thing year after year?' But art is always growing and changing—like we are. Each class is different. It's not the same material at all. It's organic, growing with whatever students I have." She holds the ball of clay out toward me. "Would you like some?"

"Oh, I, uh . . . no, thanks." I wouldn't know what to do with a lump of clay anymore than I know what to do with my own life.

"It's soothing doing something with your hands, molding and shaping it into something. Good for the soul." But her hands still and she glances over at me. She wipes her hands on a damp towel. "I believe I have something of your mother's. Let me go look." She does a half pirouette toward the closet door. "Come."

I follow her into a large room that is more cluttered than Gin's closet. She picks her way around boxes of supplies and canvases. "Over here, I think!"

Finding anything in this room would take a minor miracle. But I make my way over to her. Because of the lack of elbow room, I stand closer than I ordinarily would. Boxes are piled high, blocking the view from one side of the room to the other. I wonder if we need a compass or a Boy Scout to find our way out of here.

Lillie bends over some box, her skirt brushing the floor, her hip bumping me. "We must find this. For you."

From box to box, she pushes further into the room. At first I attempt questioning her but discover each time I ask a question she pauses to answer. A hunger gnaws at my insides, taking over my thoughts and actions. Maybe the desire to know more about my mother has been with me all along, dormant, resting in some quiet place. But it has awoken like a bear from hibernation and is scavenging the countryside for anything to chew on. Even an old letter or scarf, something silly and of little use, matters now to me.

"Ah, ha!" Lillie laughs, and I feel my heartbeat quicken.

"What is it?"

"I had forgotten about this." Her voice lifts into a realm of excitement reserved for squealing college girls.

A tightness forms across my abdomen, and suddenly I can't take a full breath. Her shoulder blocks my view, until she turns. She's cupping an awkward little statue. Is it a horse? A goat? I can't tell. She kept *this*?

"Look at the lines." She runs her fingers along the curve of spine and hip. "Such delicate work."

I try not to curl my lip, but I feel heavy disappointment sink in me like a rock. The statue looks a bit like Tumnus from *The Lion, the Witch and the Wardrobe,* but that requires a broad interpretation. "This was my mother's?"

"Oh, no." She turns it over. "P.L. I don't remember the student's name." She pauses as if trying to remember and I want to hurry her along. I still have a long drive to Marfa.

"Whoever made this, left it here at the end of the school year. I usually throw things like that out. If the student doesn't want it. But I liked this one, saw the potential. Just couldn't get rid of it."

"Uh-huh." I look around for a place to sit, glance at my watch. An unfamiliar exhaustion creeps into my bones and yet the day is still early.

"What were we looking for? Oh, yes. Hmm." She moves a box, resettles it on another, but doesn't open the one beneath. She turns, looks around, then turns back. Finally she goes around a corner and I can't see her anymore, just the hem of her skirt occasionally as she moves or sways or bends over. I hear the soft *wumph* of cardboard against cardboard.

"Do you know"—she peeks around the corner at me—"Willie Banks?"

I shake my head.

"Well, you will. Very talented boy. He's at the Art Institute in San Francisco. See this?" She holds up a sketch of a three-dimensional cube and broken spheres.

"Interesting." I wish she'd stay on task.

"Interesting? Oh, it's much more than that. Much, much more. The perspective is brilliant. From one so young, this is truly remarkable."

I glance at my watch again.

From a portfolio folder she pulls a pencil drawing, stares at it for a long moment as I grow more impatient. But I see in her wide smile, the tilt of her head, gleam in her eye, what makes her such a fabulous teacher. A teacher like Mr. Kimmel. She sees into the heart of her students. She loves to discover raw talent and help pry creativity loose.

Once more Lillie disappears into the cardboard vaults of her past. I watch a tiny spider the size of a pinhead scrabble across the floor. Dirt and dust on the linoleum keep me from finding a seat. So I lean against a box until it starts to move, then reposition it.

"This is it!" Lillie reappears, walking toward me. "I found it." She brushes past me, carrying a rolled paper. "Let's go out in the good light."

Apprehension and eagerness battle inside me. Will something of Momma's help me see into her heart, something I've missed, an answer to . . . I don't know what.

Lillie unrolls thick sketching paper. The edges have curled over, the paper yellowed. It's a pencil sketch of a girl, the side of her head and face and shoulder. She has a short ponytail. She's looking out a window at a meadow, nothing exceptional, nothing extraordinary, just a grassy meadow. But the drawing shows promise in the lines and curves, the shading and delicate touches.

She places it in my hands. The paper is thick—thicker than poster board—rough to the touch. In the bottom corner my mother wrote her name in the curlicue way that most seventh graders write.

"I wanted her to take more classes with me. She was much more talented than I. She had quite an eye. But your grandmother wouldn't allow it. She had other plans for her daughter. Maybe that's why Jennifer headed to Houston after high school. Maybe it was her way of rebelling."

I nod as if I understand, but I don't. A memory lurks in the corner of my mind, then jumps out at me. Momma painting a wall in the den of our apartment. It was a mossy green color. It was one of those moments when I watched my mother as if seeing her for the first time, saw how pretty she was, how delicate and at ease her hands were. It made me wonder what she wanted out of life. But I don't think I ever asked. She reached the bottom of the wall, carefully painting along the edge of the baseboard, then shifted and stood. I heard a clink of the handle against the can then saw the paint can tip over. Green fungus grew and spread outward, soaking into the carpet. Momma cursed, yelled for me to get a towel.

We ruined my beach towel trying to soak up the excess paint. Finally, after scrubbing and soaking the rug with carpet cleaner I found under the kitchen sink, Momma declared it a disaster area. "Guess we know where we'll put the couch now."

I laughed.

She was smiling, but the corners of her eyes pinched into tiny lines of worry. "Oh, Bryn." She put her arms around me. Together, we looked up at the wall she'd painted.

"It's pretty, Momma."

She kissed the top of my head.

"Like you," I added.

She hugged me tighter. "Don't ever be like me, baby. Your momma manages to screw up pretty much everything."

"But the wall is beautiful."

She stared down at the carpet but didn't say anything else. I wrapped my arms around her waist, buried my face against her warmth.

Lillie touches my arm, pulls me out of the past. "It's yours. You should have this to keep."

"Thank you." Emotions well up in my throat, cutting off my air supply temporarily.

"And Bryn"—her blue eyes turn electric, as if she's illuminating my soul—"wherever you're headed, lovey, this is a fork in your journey, a turning point. Be brave enough to face it and move in a new direction."

Chapter Five

The past has died,
Let it lie,
For if you will not
It will bury you alive.

Aunt Lillie's words linger in my mind, reverberate in my heart and fill me with dread. What lies ahead on this long road that seems never ending?

The drive to Marfa stretches into the afternoon, made even longer by my inability to maintain a radio signal. It didn't take too long to convince my editor in chief that a trip to Marfa was necessary for completing the NASA story he wanted. From my neck of the woods—the hill country, a place of lakes and limestone configurations—the twisting, turning terrain that once purported seismic changes flattens into a straight, flat highway stretching into the outer reaches of Texas. Aren't there supposed to be mountains nearby? Didn't I read that on one of the countless Web sites I found online? With an endless ribbon of highway stretched out before me, and less traffic than the moon receives, I rifle through my notes that sit in the passenger seat. Yep, the Davis Mountains should be out here somewhere. You wouldn't think I'd have to hurt my eyes searching for a mountain.

Mountains conjures up the image of the Rockies, where I've occasionally skied. Maybe these Texas mountains are concave or miniscule in comparison. For miles, there is nothing but flat, dry plains. No houses. No wildlife. Not even a billboard to distract me. Why would anyone move to this seemingly deserted place? Unless they were hiding out from civilization. Hunting for black gold, otherwise known as Texas Tea. Or seeking another Area 51.

Situated on the ironed-out plains of west Texas, without a wrinkle or pleat in the topography, Marfa lies east of the Davis Mountains or so I read somewhere. As I near my destination, I spot agaves, ocotillo, and prickly pear cacti populating the sparse countryside of sand and rocks. A rare cow stands all alone in the middle of an empty field. Where are the Texas herds so famous in other parts of the state? Maybe the grass blades, few and far between, can only support one cow per six hundred acres or so. Does anyone besides Howard Walters live out this direction?

Static fills my Prius as I fiddle with the radio. Finally I tune into a local FM radio station. A slow-talkin' Texan, whose cadence reminds me of John Wayne, advertises a truck sale in nearby Fort Stockton. When the current talk show resumes, a clipped female voice discusses the upcoming Marfa Lights Festival, celebrating the weird, unexplained lights that periodically appear near Marfa. When the station goes to a break, they play the chorus of the "Purple People Eater" song, which then burrows its way into my head like that creature from *The Wrath of Khan* and loops continuously through my thoughts as I make the last few miles into this tiny town.

Marfa is as flat as one of Nana's pancakes. The streets are straight and fewer than a short stack at IHOP, so it's easy to find the Hotel Paisano near the courthouse square. It looks like a Mexican citadel, except for the green and white striped awnings. As if the hotel isn't used to visitors (or only aliens), the staff welcomes me like a long lost relative. Mexican tiled walkways lead me through a gallery of gift shops that contain a surprising amount of interest in classic artwork. Does Marta think it's an artist colony like Santa Fe?

One alcove is dedicated to James Dean, complete with a television playing *Giant* and a stand-up cardboard cutout of the ultimate rebel without a cause. I pick up a T-shirt for Ginger with a James Dean quote: *Dream as if you'll live forever. Live as if you'll die today.* The first line suits her as she has big dreams for her future, which she pursues with gusto. But my cynical edge cuts apart that line, and only the last line squares with my life. I've lived each day as if it could be my last. Chances define my lifestyle, not idealistic hopes and dreams. Daydreaming, wishing on stars, seems like a luxury. Time, Dean must have experienced himself, doesn't necessarily permit quantity.

After dumping my suitcase in my room and changing into my usual jeans and boots, I venture back to the lobby. Sitting in a sun-warmed metal chair in the shady courtyard, I pull my cell phone out of my computer bag and dial Howard's number. The six flags that have flown over Texas droop under the heat of the sun and lack of a breeze. A fountain burbles next to me. Window boxes with red geraniums brighten the whitewashed walls of the adobe-styled hotel.

"I'm here," I say without preamble when he answers.

"Who's this?"

"Howard?" How could he not remember I'm coming?

"Yes." Wariness deepens his voice.

My teeth clench. "It's Bryn Seymour."

"Of course, Brynda. Good." He clears his throat. "Did anyone follow you?"

"Follow?" Irritation grips the muscles along my neck. I glance around the empty courtyard and out onto the deserted streets of Marfa, then chastise myself for my gullibility. Who would be following me? "No, of course not." No bright lights in my rearview mirror like Richard Dreyfuss experienced in *Close Encounters of the Third Kind*. No giant disk-shaped flying object hovers over the hotel as in 1950s flick, *The Day the Earth Stood Still*.

I curb my sarcasm as much as possible. "We're all clear."

"Good. Good. Did you tell anyone you were coming here?"

Frowning, I touch the edge of the table, the wrought iron resembling a fire-heated brand wielded by cowboys. He might not want me to tell anyone where I am, but I should have told more, maybe put it in the headlines of today's paper—just in case. "Sure, my boss, my daughter. Why?"

"You have to be careful, Brynda. You can't trust anyone. *Any* one."

This trip was a mistake of universal proportions. What can this man possibly tell me about my mother? A spring in his brain has obviously sprung loose. My jaw aches, and I realize I'm grinding my teeth. All of this is my fault. Once again I took a flying leap off a very steep cliff and like the characters in the movie *Journey to the Center of the Earth*, I feel like yelling, "I'm still falling!" With no end to this free fall in sight.

"Can you be at the fort in two hours?"

I sigh and rub the tension out of my forehead. "What fort?"

"Fort Davis. There's a historic site."

From my computer bag, I tug loose a map of the area and locate Fort Davis. With my pointer finger, I follow the red road west. Only twenty miles. "Sure. I can be there."

"Go to the enlisted men's barracks. Remember, be sure *no one* follows you. No one. And if you see me, pretend you don't know me."

I don't think that will be difficult.

THE NATIONAL HISTORIC SITE sits right inside the town of Fort Davis, an out-of-the-way tourist town at the base of Sleeping Lion Mountain. I wouldn't call the mountain Pike's Peak, but it is bigger than a molehill. And from here on the topography becomes steeper and much rockier than the flat area surrounding Marfa. The temperature cools as my Prius winds into town, and I pull into the long drive and pass over the original *Go West* wagon road that once led to El Paso and beyond. The original frontier.

My gaze drifts upward toward the pale blue sky with sweeping gossamer clouds. Floating in full daylight toward the horizon is the moon. It's pale and mottled with a blue that matches the sky—the next great frontier.

Since I'm early, I scout out the area, paying my entrance fee, checking out the enlisted men's barracks and the officer's quarters. I skip the museum of swords, guns, and Apache clothing as well as the movie narrated by Karem Abdul Jabar, which plays in the small theater. The ruins of the original buildings remain only as low-lying rock walls scattered throughout the green fields.

With ten minutes to spare, I leave the post's hospital, which contains gruesome saws, conjuring up images of Scarlett O'Hara running from the cries of a desperate soldier about to lose his leg. I maneuver my way back across the grounds (nonchalantly, of course), sauntering along what used to be the parade route where the troops rode their horses past the officers' houses for inspection and pretend I have no particular destination. With a quick glance behind me to make sure I'm not being followed, I laugh at myself at my newfound paranoia. Thankfully E.T. isn't waddling along the parade route, only a family of four.

Between Howard's suspicions and Aunt Lillie's odd predictions, I may be certifiable by the time I return home.

I step into the dark wooden structure of the enlisted barracks. Beds made of plywood slats line both walls. Some are empty, but others hold wool blankets, folded uniforms, and cavalry boots. No rails or glass barriers keep visitors from wandering among the antiques. A guard sits in a chair, his shape resembling a puffed up balloon compared to Howard's deflated features. He'll probably require a double-wide casket some day. He gives me a polite nod.

"These look comfortable." I indicate the hard beds without mattresses.

"You can try one out."

"Thanks, but no thanks." I move in measured footsteps along the length of the room, stop to read about the life of a soldier and then move on. Howard doesn't make an appearance. I wait. I feign interest in an old uniform, then a picture of a soldier, even an odd-shaped hat. Still no Howard. Where is he? I check my watch, clench my teeth. He's late by fifteen minutes. Maybe he's not coming. I check my cell phone for messages but find none.

When I reach a small glassed-off area that offers visitors a glimpse into the sergeant's quarters, I blow a few more minutes staring at a wooden desk, a pair of riding boots, and a lonely cot. And I thought my life had become quiet. A tinge of cigarette smoke noses out the musty odor that permeates the barracks. Sighing, I lean my head back and stare at the ceiling, searching for an answer.

Should I leave? Stay longer? Is this the wildest goose chase on record? I puff out a heated breath. A small folded note wedged against the glass and wooden frame grabs my attention. A closer look reveals pencil markings in a constipated manuscript spelling out my name. The hairs along the back of my neck tingle. A glance over my shoulder reveals the guard watching me. Besides him, no one else is in the large rectangular room. Not unless Howard is hiding under a soldier's cot. I give an awkward smile to the guard and try to draw slow breaths, but they come in a hiccupping manner.

When the guard finally looks down at a notepad, I face the window and stretch, pretending to yawn, reaching way up high, leaning to the right. With a last push onto tiptoe, I snatch the note and curl my fingers around it. Years of passing notes during high school taught me to be sly and paranoid about having the teacher snatch it from my hand. Another glance at the guard shows he's not paying attention. I unfold the note, which has been twisted tightly into what looks like something a fourth grader might pass in class. At the sight of more writing, all in light pencil, I refold the paper, unable to follow the pattern of Howard's creases.

His warning comes back to me. *Trust no one.* Not even the guard. So I slide the note inside my hip pocket, then chide myself. I've turned into Howard. Thankfully, I'm not, according to Aunt Lillie, a chip off the old block.

Coughing to cover my movements and mostly my embarrassment, I glance sheepishly at the guard. "Interesting." I thumb back toward the sergeant's quarters. "I like the . . . uh . . ." Nervousness compels me to talk like an idiot. I scan the enclosed area again. "The desk. It's . . . uh, big."

He nods and turns as someone walks into the bunkhouse. Not Howard either. A family shuffles inside, the mother grabbing the youngest of her brood as a grubby hand reaches out to touch a military hat.

"Good afternoon, folks," the guard says. "Take a look around. Try out one of the beds if you like."

I pass the couple and their three kids on my way out of the building. Turning, looking this way and that like Max Smart, I search outside, between the buildings, beyond the ruins for Howard. Hardly any visitors wander the grounds, which should make it easy to spot a tall, gaunt whacko.

I sit down on the wooden steps. Did I do something to frighten Howard away? I pull apart the folded paper and read his note:

> *Brynda, These precautions are paramount. For your safety as*
> *well as my own. Go to Fort D drugstore and have a soda.*

Huffing out my irritation, I crush the paper, squeeze, pounding, compressing it into a tiny ball reflecting the hard lump of anger I feel deep down, and toss it into a nearby trash can. Two points, Gin would say. But at this point in the game, I say, *forget it.* I didn't come here to go on a scavenger hunt. My boot heels clunk against the wooden slats of the walkway as I head for my car. Could Howard really know something about my mother that is worth all of this? Or will his memories be as faded as the activity of this fort?

All of my memories of Momma are from the perspective of a child—small and bright, much like the bold rendition of a painted rainbow, the colors running and merging. And yet, I know there has to be more. More to her. More to her life. Like a connect-the-dots page, I can only see part of the picture.

Nana never could talk about her. And now her memory has shriveled into bits and pieces of unrecognizable mush. Aunt Lillie's memories consist of growing up and high school years. But what of the woman my mother became? The woman I yearn to know? An ache pulses in my chest.

By the time I turn on the ignition, my temper, softened by a tender breeze that accompanies the mountainous area, has cooled. I decide to give Howard one more chance. But finding the Fort Davis Drugstore requires asking a local. I stop at the Rattlers and Reptiles, avoiding looking inside the cages at the snakes. The old man who runs the store spits tobacco juice into a tin cup and walks me down the street, pointing out the hot spots in town. The drugstore has no official sign on the building, so it's easy to understand why I passed it five times.

The double screened doors should keep out the flies but they don't. Inside the soda shop, a bar runs the length of the left side where lunch dishes have been abandoned. Bits of burgers and fries entice many flies. A glass dome covers a dozen ice cream flavors. Framed puzzles of antique Coca-Cola advertisements decorate the walls. Wooden tables and booths fill the other side of the room, and a small area at the front holds gifts of lotion, chili mix, and a chest of wooden swords and guns for souvenirs.

"Are you open?" I call out to no one in particular since no one is within sight.

"We're not serving lunch anymore," a voice from the back hollers.

"Can I get a soda?"

"Sure. Have a seat anywhere you like."

My options are limited unless I want to sit with someone else's used napkins and leftover lunch. Through the jumble of chairs and tables, which haven't been cleared, I weave my way toward the back of the shop, hoping a booth will provide Howard with the maximum cover he so obviously craves. My fingers tap the table, my legs twitch beneath. I check my cell phone for messages, double-check the time, and wait another five minutes before I call out and ask for someone to wait on me.

A slow-moving teenage boy with a mop of red hair and more freckles than there are stars in the sky shows up at my table. I wonder if I've interrupted his kitchen cleaning or more probably a phone call with a girlfriend. "What can I get you?"

"What happened to your crowd?"

"Huh?"

"Looks like everybody abandoned their lunch at the same time?"

"Nah." He scratches his head. "Tommy—the other waiter— didn't show. So I'm here all alone. Did you want something?"

I clasp my hands on the table. "Is this a real soda fountain?"

"Yeah."

"Can you make a lemon coke?"

"Sure thing." He writes it down on a pad as if he might forget. Sure enough, watching him behind the bar, he checks the pad twice before he's finished. I entertain myself by looking over the sparse menu. Burgers—cheese or plain. Fries. Breakfast offers more variety. Eggs—scrambled or fried. Biscuits or toast. Pancakes— buttermilk or wheat.

"Here ya go." The waiter, a loose interpretation of the word, slaps down a napkin and sets a glass of Coca-Cola on it, then slides a paper-covered straw toward me. "Anything else?"

"No, thanks." I rip the paper off the straw, stick it in the lemon coke and stare at the message written on the napkin. Same cramped letters. "Hey!"

The teen turns back, tucking the round tray under his arm.

"Who gave this to you?"

"What?"

"This!" I wave the napkin at him.

"Dunno what you're talkin' about." His gaze slides sideways and I know he's lying.

"Wait!" I jump out of my seat as he walks away and lean back to grab my purse. "Come *back* here!"

His speed doubles and I give chase. I pass the teen and make my way toward the back. "Is *he* in the kitchen?"

"Who?"

"Howard Walters. Howard!"

"You can't go back there." The teen's tone sounds much calmer than my own.

But I ignore his warning and burst into the tiny kitchen, which isn't any cleaner than the counter out front. But it is devoid of help . . . or Howard. A lock secures the back door. Unless Howard is hiding under the sink, then he's made a clean getaway. I wheel around on the teen.

"You know him!" It's an accusation, not a question. And I want answers now.

"Who?"

I force myself to draw a steadying breath. "The guy who wrote this! Howard Walters."

He shrugs a skinny shoulder. "Who doesn't?"

"Well, I don't." I prop my hand on my hip. "So tell me about him."

"I dunno." He props the round tray against a wall. "Same as everybody else."

"Oh, no. Howard is *not* like anybody I know. I don't believe this whole town is made up of people like him either."

He starts scraping plates into a trash bin. "He keeps to himself mostly."

From the looks of the crowded counters, I'm glad I only had a soda. Usually silence gets people to talk, but not this kid. "Uh-huh," I say, trying to be encouraging. When he doesn't continue, I add, "Go on."

"That's all."

Obviously, I'm not going to get any information out of him. So much for his tip. Which gives me an idea. "How much do you want?"

"Huh?"

I dig into my purse for my wallet. "For a tip. How much?"

"Just the regular amount." He scuffs his grimy tennis shoe on the equally dirty linoleum. "Ain't no need for nothin' else."

"Any information you could give me, well, I'd make it worth your while. You could take your girlfriend to the movies, out to a nice restaurant, fly her to—"

His cheeks redden. "Thanks, ma'am, but no thanks."

With an exhausted huff, I walk back to the booth and flop back into the seat. Now what? I finger the napkin, refusing to read the full note. But my curiosity gets in the way of my stubbornness.

> *Brynda—At twilight take 118. Pass Sunset Stables.*
> *At 35 mph, drive precisely three minutes.*
> *Turn onto unmarked road and stop at the gate.*

Perfect. I tap my thumb against the table, stare out the window at a pathway between buildings where a cat lounges on top of a trash can and contemplate my next move. A wet spot forms under my lemon coke and pools outward. I pick up the glass, flop Howard's note face down on the puddle, and wipe it up. Wadding up the damp napkin and message, I leave a couple of dollars plus fifteen percent on the table and toss the napkin on a nearby dirty plate. It lands in a congealed pool of ketchup.

I DECIDE TO SPEND the night in the hotel before returning to Austin. In the mean time, I leave Fort Davis, drive through Marfa and east on Highway 90, and stop at a brown adobe structure advertised as the place to witness the famous (or not so) Marfa lights. I park near a motorcycle, step out of the car, and tug on a windbreaker. Even though it's early August and the Texas summer is not yet at its peak, the temperatures in the desert and mountainous regions around Marfa dip low at night.

Another couple meanders around, vying for a good viewing spot. I read the plaque placed at the entrance telling how a cowboy first spotted the lights in the 1800s and since then many others have witnessed these random luminous orbs that hover and float above the ground. Described as globes about the size of a soccer ball, no known reasons have explained this phenomenon. Some scientists suggested the culprit was swamp gas. Maybe they never visited Marfa and the arid region with cacti and sandy, rocky terrain. Swamps, huh?

Are these weird lights the reason Howard lives here? Is he trying to find out what they are, why they exist? Or does the bizarre attract the peculiar?

"Is it too early?" I peer through the viewfinder.

"Not sure." The man sporting a do-rag on his head and a dragon tattoo on his bicep offers me a beer.

"No, thanks. Have you been here before?"

"We live in Fort Stockton." His date or wife or significant other takes a swig from a dark bottle. "We drive over occasionally to see the lights."

"So you've seen them?"

"Oh, sure!" The woman grins, revealing a gap between her two front teeth.

"Well"—the man dips his head and rubs the back of his neck—"not sure what we saw."

She nudges him in the ribs. "It was like fireflies along the horizon."

"Yeah, I guess, but . . ."

I'll bite. "But what?"

He runs his thumbnail along his jaw as if trying to erase his smile. "We were pretty lit, so who knows what we really saw out there."

"I see." I move over toward the other viewfinder. "Toward the south, right?"

"Yes'm. That's what they say."

I squint through the eyeholes and search the horizon. A few clouds bump against each other overhead. The moon, which was so visible a few hours ago in the middle of the afternoon, plays peek-aboo. A breeze whips through the lonely outpost. Barn swallows warble from their perch in the restrooms. Early evening settles around me in an awkward embrace.

My thoughts drift toward my encounters with Howard. What could he know about my mother? And why do I care? Would I believe anything he might say anyway? I'm not here searching for surprises from my past. Okay, not *big*, outlandish surprises. I don't actually know why I felt compelled to come here to talk with Howard. Maybe it's just that I miss my mother. Maybe more than ever since Nana is no longer a comfort.

With Ginger in college, I feel more alone than ever. Maybe it's just the empty-nest syndrome so many women my age face. But most of the women I know who are dealing with empty bedrooms in their house don't have an empty bed, too. They usually have a husband to turn to in the quiet of the night. Am I reaching into the past for some form of comfort?

I could say I have Eric, but we're not married. We're not engaged. We're not anything, really. Maybe just a convenience to one another, which is not a huge endorsement. And that sad fact makes me feel even more alone. I never really thought I'd walk through life on my own, without a hand to grasp in the middle of the night, a shoulder to lean on, or a sympathetic ear. It's not that

I don't have friends. I do. Plenty of them. But it's just not the same. Fear of being alone has haunted me since Momma died.

I shake my head, remembering Gin's question. Maybe I'm destined to be alone. Momma was. Nana, too. She raised Momma alone after her husband died during World War II. Are we Seymour women cursed? The sins of the mothers handed down, generation to generation, or some such? Or are we too independent? Maybe we're from outer space and can't find our own species here on this planet.

It's not that I never wanted to marry. I did. Dave and I met at the University of Texas and married not long after. He was a good husband, but I wasn't a very good wife. I was faithful. I just wasn't needy enough.

Opening up to others, revealing the hurts and pains, fears and losses has always been difficult for me. So when Dave left me for another woman, I couldn't blame him too much. I knew I hadn't given him what he needed. So I focused on being a better mother than I had been a wife.

Maybe my heart was more open to Ginger's tiny probing fingers. Something about holding a tiny newborn, wet and warm from my own body, pried open the parts of my heart I'd tried so hard to secure. I wasn't the kind of mom who baked fresh cookies. I was too busy at a typewriter, then computer, working on chasing down a story and writing the high points of a life well lived (or not) to focus on imitating June Cleaver. Maybe something about that pure maternal love made me feel complete for a short period of time. But it didn't last. Did reality seep in, as it usually does? The reality of mopping up messes, arguing about clothes, makeup, and dating, holding on and letting go pulled me into the muck and mire of everyday living. The gravity of the mundane and calamity defied the floating, lofty, liberating feeling of love.

Maybe that's the ultimate reason I'm here. That pull of motherly love is like the moon's effect on the tides. It doesn't have to be visible to have the same result.

A smacking sound causes me to glance over at the biker and his significant other. They're making out in the pale moonlight and deepening gray night. Simultaneously feeling embarrassment for my voyeurism and yet curiously detached, I watch them a moment. Then, without witnessing even a flicker of the famous Marfa lights, I walk back to my car and turn back toward Fort Davis.

And an inevitable meeting with Howard.

Chapter Six

What exactly were Howard's precise but peculiar directions? I left them at the drugstore and soda shop. Threw them away actually. Luckily, I make it back to Fort Davis before the sun has completely set, thanks to straight and mostly deserted roads and the speed limit being 80 mph, which causes my Prius to shudder under the strain. If night had already settled over the mountain range, it would be a lost cause trying to find the road leading to Howard's. But the sun hasn't yet disappeared. It blasts out its last rays, making me squint.

Highway 118 leads into the mountains, where the roads begin to curve in a fashion that makes me more comfortable. Signs point toward McDonald Observatory—maybe that's where Howard's spotty directions are leading me. I imagine Ronald McDonald, with red wig and white-painted face, peering through a giant telescope on the lookout for purple aliens circling overhead. In actuality, the observatory is an extension of the University of Texas. This gives me hope that Howard's studies might, by some miracle, be legitimate. That is, *if* he's associated with the observatory.

After taking several twisting turns, I reach Sunset Stables at an ironic time. With the red and orange light slanting right at me, I can't tell much about the place other than notice the white wooden fences. What speed did Howard tell me to go? I check my clock, remembering I'm to drive for precisely three minutes. Or was that three miles? The needle on my speedometer hovers between twenty-five and thirty. My gaze flicks to the clock on the dash. One minute. Two . . . three.

Shadows deepen as my mood darkens. I flip on my high beams to find the road and wish I could find my sense of adventure . . . or humor. I search for some clue, some sign. Just past a bend in the road, a gravel drive hides among the two-foot-high weeds. A headache starts just beneath my compressed brow. Sighing, I slow down and search for a wide place in the road. It's a perfect place for a photo op of the mountain range, the last remnants of sunlight making the hills glow as do my insides, but with irritation. After I turn around, I creep along, prepared for the sudden (and sneaky) turnoff.

I drive at least the length of a football field before I face a ten-foot chain-link fence. Its ominous presence says, "Keep out." A little black box with a speaker and button sits on a two-by-four stuck into the hard ground. I roll down my window and press the button. After a moment or two, when there's no response, I press again.

Surely I haven't come all this way to hit a dead end. I tap the steering wheel in an agitated beat. Where's Howard? Is he hiding? Did he leave more clues, a map, an X marks the spot? He's the one who invited me here! He gave me directions, such as they were— similar to something the Beverly Hillbillies might give—turn at the fallen tree, then again at the fork in the road, if the river hasn't washed it out. Maybe Jethro will show up here in a minute. Should I look for another inconspicuous note? A note that will lead me to another locale? Actually it won't. Because if I find another note, that will definitely be the end of this bunny trail.

The box beside my car crackles. I lean closer. "Hello?"

"Who is it?" Howard's gravelly voice is accented by an odd clicking of his tongue against the back of his teeth.

I lean further out my window. "It's Bryn . . . Brynda Seymour. Remember me?"

No response. Wonderful. I grit my teeth, wait another minute, my thumb thumping against the gear shift. Anger swells inside me like a bloated tick. With a huff, I lean my head back against the headrest, sitting alone in my car, my window rolled down, the car idling. Now what? What should I do? Drive off? I'm not the giving up, calling it quits type. But maybe that's what Aunt Lillie meant, the change I need to make in my life.

I glare at the closed gate. It doesn't budge. Obviously Howard didn't push a button inside allowing me access and my telekinetic powers are on the fritz. Should I climb over the fence? Storm the place? From Howard's modus operandi, he'd probably think he was being attacked by NASA's spies who are to blow his place sky high.

Cool air floats through the car, but I can't chill out my over-heated emotions. I wrap my fingers around the bottom of the steering wheel. Did I really come all this way for nothing? Remembering my sarcastic parting comment to Howard in Houston, I wonder if his wild goose chase has been deliberate, just to bait me, just to get back at me.

"What do you want?" A voice, very close and very deep, startles me.

I wrench sideways, away from the open window. My heart jerks in an erratic rhythm. My hands clench the steering wheel in some weird reflexive move, like I could use it as a weapon (if it weren't attached). Bracing my left leg against the door, I stare at the stranger beside my car. All I can see is a flat torso and, looking upward, wide shoulders. Remembering Howard's tall, thin, frail frame, I know this isn't him. Did I come to the wrong house? Did I somehow fall into *Deliverance*?

Easing my left hand toward the button on the door's armrest, I plan my defensive moves. If need be, I can raise the window and jerk the car in reverse at the same time. The waning sun's deep red rays silhouette the man's head and penetrate my pupils. I shield my eyes, and aim for optimism. "Hello. I'm a reporter. Brynda Seymour. Here to see Howard—"

"Yeah?" His deep voice reverberates with vibrations that seem to crack into his words. From what I can make out, he's wearing a red-and-black flannel shirt, the sleeves rolled up to reveal thick forearms. His hands embrace narrow hips. I restrain my sarcasm from calling this Jethro character "professor" and speak s-l-o-w-l-y in hopes he can grasp my words. "Do you know Mr. Walters?"

"Maybe." Obviously, I'm dealing with a real wordsmith here. This guy is as thick as a concrete coffin. Speaking of which, he'd probably need the type made for NFL players.

"Actually," I say in a slow cadence so I don't lose him, "Mr. Walters invited me here to discuss writing his memoir." Does this redneck even know what a memoir is? "This *is* where Howard Walters lives, isn't it?"

"You that woman he met at NASA?"

A full sentence! There's hope. "Well, yes, we did meet in Houston." If Howard trusted this Neanderthal with the information, considering his usually extreme paranoia, then maybe he's safe. I thrust my hand out of the car window at him. "Brynda Seymour."

Jethro's gaze narrows. "The lady who told him maybe Will Smith could help him?"

Heat fires my cheeks. This isn't the first time my big fat mouth has put me in an awkward position. Unfortunately. I clear my throat and attempt an explanation. "Yes, I did. You see—"

"Howard came home wondering who Will Smith was and how he could help him." Accusation darkens his voice.

"Yes, well . . ." I continue holding my hand outward like the imbecile I originally took him for. But now, I understand his aw-shucks slowness as wariness. "And you are?"

Finally, the man's hand engulfs mine, proving by his size how much stronger he is than I. A teetering laugh bubbles out of me.

This man could squash me. Maybe I should cut my losses and back out now. When I try to pull my hand away, his grip tightens. Not tight enough to hurt, just enough to let me know who's in charge here. Slowly he leans toward the window and peers inside, giving me a slow, insolent once-over that flips my stomach. He has serious, stern features with a sharp aquiline nose that I'm sure he's accustomed to looking down at people. His hair is as dark as his gaze. "Sam"—he pauses, then adds—"Sam Walters."

I catch the recurring last name. "So, you're related to Howard?"

"Well, I'm not cousins with Will Smith."

Could this backwoodsman have a sense of humor? Maybe. Maybe not. I release a slow, cautious breath as he releases my hand. Quickly, even defensively, I pull my hand and arm back inside the car. "I'm sorry about that. Look—"

"You look, lady." He crosses his arms over his broad chest. "I had to explain to Howard that Will Smith is an actor in a stupid movie. *Men in Black*, right?"

I nod, regretting my lack of tact. "For believing in conspiracies, Howard sure is a trusting soul."

"Obviously, he was wrong about you."

His hard gaze makes me swallow any sarcastic retort.

"What do you want, Ms. Seymour?"

"I'd like to speak with Howard . . . Mr. Walters."

"Do you want to make fun of him?"

"Make fun? No! You've got this all wrong!"

"Do you want to write some article to ridicule him?"

"No. Really. I don't want to do an article at all."

"You said you're a reporter. Or did you lie?"

I grip the steering wheel. "I told you I was a reporter, which I am, because I thought it would make things easier." But this time, I realize, it complicated matters. "Look, I just want to talk to him. He—"

"Why?"

"Who *are* you? His bodyguard?" I regret the words the second they pop out of my mouth. "Look . . . Sam, right? I did some research."

"On Cinderella's castle?"

I roll my lips inward and shake my head at my own foolishness. Not only is the gate ahead of my car blocking me from getting information about my mother, but so is this goon. A knot of uncertainty hardens in my belly. My determination solidifies. I'm not about to back down now. "Sam, I'm sorry about those comments. You have to admit, what Howard says is"—Bizarre. Wacky. Crazy. I search for an appropriate but non-inflammatory word—". . . on the unusual side."

He remains silent.

"Okay, well"—I shift into reverse—"you don't have to admit that." For all I know, he's Howard's lab assistant. Or is that Dr. Frankenstein's helper, Igor? "Still, his . . . theories took me by surprise."

"Did you read Landler's book?"

"No." I take a mental note to check it out.

"Then what? Why'd you decide to come out here?"

"I told you. Howard invited me."

Surprise registers on his face. "Why?"

I take a fortifying breath, the kind I need when Nana repeats questions. "He wants me to write his memoir." I speak slowly so he can comprehend. "We met in Houston. After I went home, I watched some old films and—"

He leans in closer, his gaze narrowing on me. "Did you get hold of the originals? Those that weren't doctored?"

"Doctored?"

"The NASA films."

"No, no. These were personal, home movies. Look, just let me speak to Howard. He knows I'm coming. He told me how to get here. How else would I have found this place?"

"He didn't tell me you were coming."

"Maybe you don't have need-to-know clearance." I square off with him, matching him gaze for gaze, stubbornness to stubbornness. "For your information, Sam, since you're so curious, first he sent me to the Fort Davis museum, then for a soda. Each time he left me a note with more instructions. I haven't been followed. So now, here I am." I'm not sure even *I'm* following all of this.

Silence pulses between us while Sam assesses me as if through a telescope like I'm a pulsar or some anomaly in space. Slowly he straightens, takes a step back from my car, giving me some breathing room. It's not till that moment, I realize how my nerves are tangled into tiny knots, restricting my breathing.

"Okay, follow me."

SAM WALTERS OPENS THE chain-link fence, closing it behind my car after I inch through the gate. It isn't until my headlights illuminate the treed area that I notice a camera perched like a bird in the tree limbs. It swivels to trail me as I drive past. Wheels crunch gravel along the drive. The sun has now dipped below the tree line, darkening the narrow roadway, which isn't much more than two tire tracks with weeds jutting up between them.

Sam walks ahead of me. I didn't offer him a ride and I refuse to feel guilty about it. But the further we go uphill and around a bend, the more guilt settles around my neck. Guilt has always been one of my closest traveling companions.

A light glows further up the drive. Wasn't there a scary railroad crossing scene in *Close Encounters of the Third Kind?* Am I about to have a close encounter of some kind, too? Finally Sam reaches a clearing in the middle of a stand of trees. Artificially, the area is lit up like the final scene of Spielberg's lengthy meet-the-aliens movie when the bloated psychedelic spaceship lands on earth. I squint against the brightness as Sam steps out of the way of my car and points me toward some imaginary parking spot.

I brake slowly, put the gear shift in park, but take my time climbing out of the car as I give the area a slow perusal. What have I gotten myself into? My stomach clenches tight.

Another chain-link fence, at least ten feet tall, surrounds a small, unassuming double-wide trailer. If it wasn't for the twenty-foot light poles along the perimeter shining spotlights at the edge of the woods and along the rim of the trailer, no one would think this place was important. But obviously, somebody values what's inside. Did Howard build all of this? Or Sam? Is it a family compound? If so, then I'm definitely relieved I don't qualify to move in.

Questions churn inside my head as I note more cameras, more surveillance equipment. What are they expecting? A meeting of Burglars Anonymous? An *Invasion of the Body Snatchers*?

Before I'm ready, Sam opens my car door. "I'll let Howard know you're here."

"All right. Terrific." My skin puckers in the cool air and makes me wish I'd worn long sleeves. Sam heads off, not toward the house but into the woods, leaving me all alone and in the spotlights slanting across the yard. "Well, thanks!" I call after him, but the night sounds, twittering, chirping and fluttering around, swallow my sarcasm. I flatten my lips. Now what? Will Howard beam down, suddenly materializing like Mr. Spock? I consider climbing back into the car but instead grab my Windbreaker since the temperature has dropped a good ten degrees.

I take a step or two away from the car, leaving the door wide open. Just in case. What do I do now? Wait? Call out? I walk toward the trailer but can't approach the front door because of the metal fencing that resembles Fort Knox. Along the top, razor wiring slants outward. On the gate a giant padlock stops me from even attempting to enter. Are they keeping something in? Or keeping something out? Maybe Howard's discovered Sasquatch is a hairy alien, like Chewbacca.

A crunch of a footstep behind me gives only a second of warning. I whirl, fisting my keys as a weapon—and come face-to-face with Howard Walters. Well, face to chest. He seems nearly as tall as one of the thin metal poles. But of course, he's not. His gray hair sticks out in all directions, but his handlebar mustache is waxed and firmly in place. "Mr. Walters."

"Brynda." He gives a slight nod. "You made it."

Intrigued, I take a slow breath of relief. He doesn't seem hostile toward my previous sarcastic remarks. "Thank you. Your . . . uh, Sam took a bit of convincing. Why didn't you tell him I was coming?"

Howard rubs the top of his head and stares at the ground as if he forgot something. "Don't worry about him."

"Where did he go?" I glance around behind Howard, note his khaki shirt tucked into equally khaki pants.

"Back at the entrance. Waiting. Keeping an eye on things. Can't be too cautious."

"Uh-huh." My gaze shifts toward the razor fencing. "I guess not."

"Let's get inside." He glances over his shoulder, the classic play in the paranoid handbook. "Shall we?"

"Lead the way." I expect him to pull out a set of keys to unlock the giant padlock, then the trailer, and imagine a set of buttons to turn off an alarm. Instead he holds out a black scarf-looking thing.

"If you don't mind."

"Excuse me?" I take the material, realizing it's thicker than I thought.

"Put it on."

I freeze. "What?"

"Like I said, I can't be too cautious. No one must know where the entrance is."

"But this . . . ?" I gesture toward the house.

"You don't want to go through there. Trust me. A squirrel got through last week." He tilts his head and grimaces. "Not pretty." He nods toward the blindfold. "It won't mess up your hair."

"That's the least of my concerns." I offer the blindfold back to him, but he doesn't seem to notice.

He glances up at the darkening sky and sniffs. "It's getting chilly out here, isn't it?"

This may not be the best decision I've ever made. I weigh my need for safety with my desire to know more about my mother. A raw ache pulses near my heart. But before I can make a suggestion that Howard meet me for breakfast in town tomorrow morning, he leans in closer. "You can trust me, Brynda. Jennifer did."

Chapter Seven

I've done a lot of not-so-bright things in my life, but this has the wattage to cause a total blackout across the Lone Star state. Questions swirl through my head and twist my nerves tight. I should walk away from Howard . . . well, get in my Prius and drive away at a slow, careful pace. Or with the rapidity of a comet.

But I don't.

Warnings from childhood pound my brain. Nana, paranoid as any mother who has lost a child would naturally be, used to say:

"Don't talk to strangers."

"Don't go off with folks you don't know."

"Always have a buddy who knows where you are."

Maybe she should have added, "Don't put a blindfold over your head and trot off into the dark forest with a strange (and I don't just mean *unfamiliar*) man." But since she never said precisely that . . .

No one knows I'm standing outside some redneck version of Fort Knox on the brink of entering Sherwood Forest. My daughter only knows I left for Marfa, as does my boss, but no specifics, no detour to Fort Davis or trek into the mountains. There's no trail for anyone to follow. No bread crumbs. Nothing to offer clues to the police where to search for my remains.

I imagine an epitaph that seems as unusual and fitting as this situation:

> *Aliens came*
> *Swept her away*
> *Left nothing*
> *But a tale of a fool untold.*

Aliens could be Howard's alibi. Insanity would be the defense attorney's strategy. Who knows, if crystal palaces are on the moon, then Howard could believe he's an alien from the planet Nibiru (which I heard about on *Coast to Coast*). Maybe Howard thinks Momma is there, waiting, and his mission is to take me to meet her. Okay, let's go. I'm game. We'll build a crystal mansion together and watch three suns rise through its glass walls. Or he could be on crystal meth.

Perfect.

I realize I've inherited (or maybe it's learned behavior) Nana's penchant for melodrama. Maybe instead of writing true stories about real people, I should write fiction. Clearly I have the imagination for it. Howard and I should collaborate on some science fiction fantasy. I give myself a mental shake. *Get a grip, Bryn.* Howard's paranoid in the extreme, but that doesn't necessarily mean he's crazy. I'd recognize certifiably insane. Wouldn't I?

Doesn't matter anyway. The real reason I don't hit the retreating bunny trail this minute is because of his last words: *Jennifer trusted me.*

"How well did you know her?" I'm still holding the blindfold and wishing I could pull reasoning out of it like a magician producing a rabbit from a hat. "My mother."

"Jennifer and I go way back."

"Were you involved?" I'm not about to wait any longer. What if Howard falls down a dark hole and disappears?

He gives me a blank stare, the synapses in his brain definitely not mating. "We knew each other. Met in high school."

"I meant . . . involved romantically."

His face squeezes into a series of lines and creases. "No, no, no."

Three nos. One would be decisive. Two might cause some doubt. But three . . . ? Is it an indication of truthfulness or overblown defensiveness? I don't trust Howard anymore than I could lasso the moon, but trust or no trust, I need to hear what he has to say about my mother, what she was like, what she was dealing with. Standing out in the cool night air, I realize, is probably not the best location for a powwow of this magnitude. It's this irrational need to know more about my mother and the woman she was that causes me to lift the blindfold and secure it over my eyes. At least I can distinguish a sliver of gravelly ground and sprigs of grass at my feet. But then Howard steps behind me and cinches the blindfold snug, snuffing out the crease of light.

"Does that hurt?"

I shake my head. My heart pummels my breastbone like it's desperate to escape. Maybe I should be, too. "No, but—"

Howard touches my hand and folds his fingers around mine. His joints are knobby but the skin smooth. I can smell cigarette smoke radiating from him. Taking my elbow in his other hand, he guides me, turning me this way and that. I get the sense that we circle my car, but I could be wrong. My internal gyroscope is off kilter. If it weren't for Howard's firm hold on me, I might topple right over.

The ground beneath my feet changes, becoming wobbly and uneven, the dirt loose and yielding beneath each footstep. An urge to cling to Howard seizes me, but I push the need away. I keep my steps as slow and deliberate as possible. Howard prods me along, warning of a tree limb here, a hole there. He's almost courtly in his behavior. If he wanted to retaliate against my remarks about Will Smith, then he could walk me into a tree, trip me over a root, or push me off a cliff. But I sense a gentleness in Howard. I just hope my instincts are correct. I refuse to let down my defenses and give into any false sense of security coming from his propriety. There's something patently improper about demanding someone wear a blindfold.

"Whoa." He tugs back on my elbow, turns me to the right by degrees, then encourages me to move forward. "Sorry, Brynda. There was a branch. Wouldn't want it to rip up your beautiful face."

"Me neither."

Night's sounds creep into my awareness: a mosquito hums past my ear, a fluttering of bats overhead as they leave their cave for a nightly prowl, a haunting whistle of the wind through tree branches. The crunch of leaves and twigs along with my disorientation makes me feel like I'm in the *Blair Witch Project*. But this is more unnerving than sitting in my own living room watching the movie with my teenage daughter and her friends while eating popcorn.

Howard suddenly whistles next to me, a shrill sound that penetrates my eardrum and makes me flinch. I dip my offended ear toward my shoulder, and he pats my arm. "Almost there now."

Even in the cool mountain air, sweat collects along my forehead and trickles down my spine. "Do we have to go through this every time someone has to make a trip to the outhouse?"

He remains silent. Is he studying me? Searching for bread crumbs to lead us to his lair? Or did he beam his brain to the planet Kripton momentarily? Then he squeezes my hand and chuckles. "Don't worry. We have facilities."

"That's a relief. I don't understand why you don't use the double-wide. What's wrong with it?"

"It's a diversion."

"From what?"

Once more, there's a long, pregnant pause.

In the forest, one tree fell
But no one heard it,
And no one heeded her scream . . .

I shoot a prayer toward the moon and hope I aimed properly. I admit this prayer thing isn't my regular routine, but then I'm beginning to think I need some help. Unfortunately I kind of expect that God deletes the prayers of total idiots, kind of like e-mail spam. And that leaves me in charge of planning my own getaway. "You know, Marty, my cameraman . . . you met him in Houston, remember? Well, he's expecting me back at the hotel for a late dinner."

Howard grips my arm hard. "You said you didn't tell anyone. You said no one knew where you were. That no one followed you here."

"Look"—I jerk my arm away from him—"you didn't tell me you were going to send me on a wild goose chase all over Fort Davis and then treat me like some prisoner on the way to their execution." I aim to keep the tremor out of my voice and force myself to stop my fictitious blowing of the bugle. No cavalry is going to charge over the hill to rescue me, not even a ghostly Fort Davis search-and-rescue team once capable of facing down Apaches. I've gone far enough.

I dig my heels into the ground and refuse to take another step forward, sideways, or which ways. If I jerk away from Howard, I can throw off the blindfold and make a run back to the car. That is, if I can find my car. Howard's too old to put up any resistance or to catch me if I'm at a full-out run. If need be, I can—

A rustle of bushes from behind stops me cold.

"All clear." Sam suddenly stands next to us.

My one chance for escape vaporizes like the molecules of Captain Kirk as he's transported. *"Beam me up, Scottie . . ."* Too bad that's not an option for me. I shiver.

"You cold?" Sam asks.

"Nah, I'm fine," Howard says.

Rolling my eyes, safely under the veil of the black scarf, I huff out, "Yeah, I am cold."

"Here." Sam's brusque voice echoes in the stillness of the woods. A rustling of material follows, then a blanket of warmth surrounds my shoulders. My windbreaker wasn't thick enough to combat the cold, stiff breeze in the mountains.

"You sure no one followed?" Howard again.

"I hate to tell you guys"—I rip off the blindfold, blink as my eyes adjust to the darkness— but this is as far as I'm going. This little game you're playing—"

My tirade comes to a sudden halt when Sam flicks on a flashlight. The light blinds me momentarily. Blinking, I realize Sam's chest is bare. Obviously, better his than Howard's. His flannel shirt is wrapped around me in a warm embrace. A half-naked man shouldn't bother me. It's not like I haven't seen men in all states of undress. I live ten minutes from Hippie Hollow, a hangout for nudists. But this guy has a chest that reminds me of the Spartan's in *300*, which even the most discriminating woman could appreciate. "Uh, this, uh . . . game . . ."

I distract myself by looking away from Sam's magnetizing chest and stare at the dark sky which is now black as a black hole with a smattering of stars. Which one is the North Star? What is its official name? Polaris? I pull that answer from some stored memory tape of when Ginger was interested in being an astronaut in sixth grade. Maybe it could point me in the right direction.

"It's no game, Brynda." Moonlight filters through tree branches overhead, dappling Howard's face with pale freckles of iridescent light.

Suddenly uncomfortably warm, I whisk off Sam's shirt and offer it back, keeping my gaze slightly skewed from his muscular chest and the two or three white hairs mixed among the swirling dark that deepen the contours of flat planes and firm abs. I chalk it up to hormones. Menopausal hot flashes. It doesn't matter that I haven't experienced one before now. When he doesn't reach to take his shirt, I offer, "Thanks."

He fiddles with the flashlight, making his muscles flex beneath his taut skin as he adjusts the beam, and makes no move to take his shirt. "No problem. Keep it."

"No, really."

Finally he accepts the flannel shirt but only tosses it over his shoulder.

"We should move on," Howard says.

"Where?" Where *now* is what I really want to say but am trying to keep my big mouth shut as much as possible.

"Through there." Sam nods toward a tree trunk. A black scar runs from the length to the base with what looks like a scorching burn from a lightning bolt. The cragged bark looks as old as Texas. "The steps are steep so go slow."

"And watch your head," Howard warns. "I always knock mine on the entrance."

"You guys are crazy."

Sam grins a slow, easy smile that stretches his cheeks. "You think?"

"We're not doing this to scare you, Brynda." Howard's tone is surprisingly kind. "It's for your safety. And ours."

"Really? How's that?"

"Could we discuss it when we get inside?" Howard looks over his shoulder, as if the creature from the black lagoon might be fast approaching.

A rational thought in this absurdity invades my concerns—if they wanted to harm me, wouldn't they have grabbed me, forced me down those stairs, muffled my big mouth? I take a calming breath. "Okay, fellas, but I warn you. I don't understand what I'm doing here."

A wry smile tugs at Sam's mouth, making him more attractive than menacing. I'm not sure if that's a comfort or not. He gestures toward the tree. "I'll go first, show you the way."

I follow Sam through a gaping hole at the base of the trunk, which just looks like a dark cavern but is apparently hiding a stairwell beneath the tree. Aware of his broad bare shoulder, I place my hand on the rough, scratchy bark as I take the first step inward. A flash of a scene from one of the *Star Wars* movies flitters through

my mind—Luke entering an ancient tree, pushing through cobwebs and vines. I brace myself to deal with spiders, snakes, or other
creepy hurdles, but after three steps I feel no wispy cobwebs brush
my skin or tingling spider feet prancing across my back as Indiana
Jones experienced in one of his expeditions. Sam flips on a low-
watt single bulb above us, and the yellowish tinted light reveals a
concrete tubelike stairwell. He points upward. Reflexively, I jerk
sideways, brushing against Sam's bare shoulder, which jars my
senses even more, and glance upward only to find the door frame,
not a snake, an inch from my head.

I'm not usually this jittery. Howard, I decide, has not been a
good influence. The low entrance makes me tilt my head as I take
the next step forward. Howard follows after me at a slower pace.
I place my hand on the cool concrete wall to steady myself rather
than reach out for Sam's shoulder in front of me. There's no railing
to cling to, but that's no surprise. My life has been void of that kind
of stability.

I peer around me. "Where are the roots?"

Sam half turns and looks at me questioningly.

"The tree?" I copy his earlier movement and point toward the
ceiling.

"It's fake." Howard pulls a hatch resembling something that
should belong in a submarine, and it closes with a muffled thud
that makes me feel even more trapped. Each breath sounds harsh
in my ears. It feels like the walls are shrinking in on me like the
trash compactor scene in *Star Wars*. He latches at least half a dozen
locks, rotates a metal wheel, and tugs hard on it until a metallic
click echoes through the chamber. He begins his descent and I turn
back to do the same.

"I had it built about ten years ago." Howard's tone sounds conversational. "Nifty, huh?"

"I'd say. Must have cost a pretty penny."

"I've poured my life savings into this place. But I have donors,
too."

I remember the many Web sites dedicated to supporting or ridiculing Howard. Seems he has as many fans as critics.

Sam waits for me at the bottom of the stairs and tugs on his flannel shirt. But he doesn't rush to button it.

"So you bring all your dates here?"

He winks. "You're the first."

"Lucky me." I glance around the blank gray walls. "Why? Why all this?"

"For Howard's research."

"You don't think it's a bit extreme?"

Sam glances up toward Howard, who descends slowly, suddenly looking every bit his seventy years. Keeping his own thoughts private, Sam steps to the side and gives Howard room to step down.

One small step for man, one giant leap off the Cliff of Sanity.

Together we walk along the concrete corridor which leads to another metallic door. Howard places his hand against a black plastic pad that immediately begins blinking. A series of clicks follows and then a grinding noise. Slowly the door slides out of the way.

"So why all the precautions?" I ask. "Just for research purposes?"

"My research makes some people a little uncomfortable." Howard shrugs as if he doesn't understand it at all.

"I can't imagine why." Sam's sarcasm seems lost on Howard. He steps beside me.

"Makes me a bit nervous myself," I add.

Howard walks through the doorway first but pauses on the other side of the threshold. His treatment of me is more like a guest than a hostage. A good sign. Or so I hope. But then wasn't Hannibal Lector polite? "My research has ruffled a few feathers." His voice ricochets off the concrete walls. "Which is why I had to take extra security precautions."

"Most people who need security get a security system. You know, punch in a code at the door, that sort of thing."

He props a fist on the back of his hip, stares at the floor, and shakes his head, making his jowls jiggle. "Rinky-dink."

"What about guards? Something simpler than all of this?"

Howard studies me for a moment. "Whom do I trust?"

I'm unsure if he's trying to gauge whether I'm trustworthy or not. Or if he's already made up his mind about me. Hence the blindfold. I square my shoulders. "Do you trust me?"

His electric blue eyes meet mine. "You're Jennifer's daughter."

His words slam into my chest. What kind of a relationship did Howard and my mother have anyway? For him to accept me on the basis that I'm Jennifer's daughter is significant. Almost like I have the secret password. It means their relationship couldn't have been casual or simply an old high school friend from biology class. But it also tells me something profound about my mother. She was trustworthy. At least in Howard's eyes. Knowing his level of paranoia, that's saying plenty. That simple acknowledgement by someone like Howard feels like a treasured keepsake.

"Besides," Howard continues, oblivious to the impact his words have had on me, "it's reciprocal, isn't it? You could have run for the cops when I showed you that blindfold."

I laugh. "I almost did."

"And I almost called the cops"—Sam grins—"when you showed up unexpected at the gate."

"Touché. But I *was* expected. Howard knew I was coming. He invited me!"

"I have a bad habit of forgetting unim—" Howard stops himself from saying how inconsequential I am. He averts his gaze, rubs a knuckle against his jaw.

"So why does the idea of a glass palace on the moon make folks nervous?"

Howard pats his breast pocket, pulls a cell phone out, then slides it back inside. "Left my smokes inside." His mouth twists. "It's a long story that goes as far back as NASA. But no need for us to stand in this cool dampness. It's more comfortable inside." He gestures for us to walk on.

Our footsteps reverberate through the corridor, which stretches almost a hundred yards. Have we walked back toward that double-wide and are now underneath it, or have we gone off in a different direction? Even though I'm totally lost, as if I'm in a labyrinth, I'm feeling more comfortable. I rush to remind myself not to let down my guard just yet. There could be a Minotaur around the next bend. "So you're saying government entities don't like the research you're doing?"

"They don't like that I'm alive." His words have the same impact of that first door closing and blocking me from the rest of civilization.

We walk through another three doors in silence, then up a flight of stairs. There we enter what looks like a regular living room with brown carpet, a beige couch, and a wall of televisions. CNN, FOX News, MSNBC, and NASA stations are muted. A desk sits in front of the televisions, piled with random stacks of papers and manila folders. Filing cabinets line the wood-paneled walls. Books and file folders cover most of the floor. It's all a jumbled, disorganized mess that makes me feel claustrophobic. I itch to straighten a stack that leans—a paper Tower of Pisa.

"I tried to make it a little comfortable down here. I have all the regular amenities you'd have in a home—a kitchen, microwave, shower . . ."

"How do you get reception?" I nod toward the bank of televisions.

"A satellite. Everything runs on a generator."

"And what about . . . ?" On the other side of the room a telescope bigger than any I've ever seen grabs my full attention. "How does that work down here?"

"Well, I'll tell you, Brynda, that wasn't easy to construct." He grabs a pack of cigarettes off the desk and taps out one, then lights it. An ashtray full of cigarette carcasses sits at the edge. "And I don't like to give away my secrets. Just know the topside part is hidden but provides direct access to the night sky. I buy time at the observatory. And then there are pictures my sources at NASA send my way. It all keeps me up-to-date."

Sam coughs. His face has compressed into a frown as he watches Howard. I pick up an uncomfortable vibe between the two men. Was the cough a signal of some kind? Or an irritated snort? So what exactly is going on here?

Before I can ask, Howard sweeps through the room and opens an adjoining door. Several boxes are lined up along the wall. The top box is open, revealing a book, the black cover has a large close-up of the moon. *America, We Have a Problem* is the title. Howard's name stretches across the bottom of the cover in a bold font.

I reach for a copy. "This is your book?"

"Yeah." He taps the ashes off his cigarette.

"Who published it?"

"I did." He takes a drag, and as he talks the smoke drifts out of his mouth and nose. "One publishing house backed out at the last minute." He leans toward me. "*They* got to them. Scared 'em away. Psychological terrorism, if you ask me. So"—he puffs again—"I did it myself."

"Can I buy a copy?"

"Nope." Howard snatches the book from my hands, dusts off the front cover, then hands it back to me. "But you can have this one."

I thumb through the pages, flipping through the black-and-white moon shots. "Thank you." I close the cover, leaving my hand pressed against the giant moon surface. "If you wrote this, then why do you want to write your memoir?"

"This is scientific jargon. Most normal folks can't understand it. A memoir though . . . my life . . . well, it needs a professional."

That's for sure.

He snuffs out the cigarette.

I tuck the book under my arm. Why didn't I bring in my backpack? "So"—I turn in a small circle, looking over Howard's cluttered and yet sparsely decorated domain—"is this the complete tour?"

His gaze beams into me for a long moment. Then he walks past me. "I'm hungry. Aren't you?"

"Oh, well, uh—"

"Good idea." Sam's face relaxes and he finally rebuttons his shirt (making me relax), as he inches his fingers downward along the seam of the flannel. But he leaves the hem untucked. "We were about to eat before you arrived. Would you like some?"

"As long as it's not an apple."

Howard's forehead wrinkles into unspoken questions.

Sam laughs. "No poisoned apples. Just chili."

"Good, then I could probably eat." My stomach rumbles, reminding me I haven't eaten since the sandwich I picked up on the drive to Marfa. There's something about realizing I'm probably not going to die immediately that makes me ravenous. "Is it homemade? Or out of a can?"

"Homemade, of course." Sam's face darkens. "My own recipe."

Howard shakes his head. "Sam likes to watch that Food Network."

"When I can get him to turn off C-SPAN. Howard would probably be satisfied with saltines and cold, canned soup." With a careless shrug, Sam leads us into a small kitchenette with a built-in table. It's cramped but utilitarian, having all the vital parts of a kitchen—fridge, sink, and dishwasher. The simmering aromas of spices and peppers fill the room. Sam lifts the lid on a stockpot and stirs the chili, breathing in the steam. "Just about right. I like a good 'throwdown' now and again."

"My daughter likes Rachel Ray." I slide into the narrow booth on one side of the table. "But I'm not much of a cook myself."

Sam's gaze shifts toward Howard. "Neither was my dad."

"So that's your connection, huh?" It's an obvious assumption but I'm just looking for conversational material.

"It is." Howard joins me across the table.

Sam ladles up the fiery red chili into brown plastic bowls. "My cooking is more a function of being a single dad in need of feeding my kids. At least on the weekends when they visited."

Sam sets two bowls on the table and goes back for a third. This time, with paper napkins tucked under his arm, a box of crackers in the crook of his elbow, a hefty-sized ketchup bottle in one hand and spoons in the other, he returns. He pauses only for a moment, looking from Howard to me, then slides into the booth opposite me. But then he snaps his fingers and says, "Drinks. What do you want? Beer? Water? Lemonade?"

I laugh at the odd offerings, wrinkling my nose at the thought of lemonade and chili. "Water is fine."

"It's pink"—Howard stares at me with serious intent—"not yellow."

Then I notice a stack of several boxes of pink lemonade in plastic bottles. "Oh, well, maybe next time."

Sam grabs the drinks from the fridge, gives me a bottle of water, his dad a pink lemonade, and keeps H_2O for himself.

I unscrew the top of the water bottle. "How many kids do you have, Sam?"

"Two. One's in graduate school, the other is out on his own."

"Feels good, doesn't it?"

He meets my gaze curiously, then plunges his spoon into the chili.

"To know you've accomplished that feat," I explain. "They're fully functioning citizens, capable of taking care of themselves now." I shrug. "That's how it feels to me anyway. Except my daughter hasn't graduated yet. Two more years."

Howard gulps his lemonade, slurping loudly from the plastic container. When he draws a breath of air, he wipes his handlebar mustache with the back of his hand then smacks his lips. "Nothing like it."

Sam focuses on his chili, scoops up a spoonful and it disappears. He hisses and gulps his water, his throat muscles working overtime. "Careful. It's hot."

"Forewarned." I take a sniff of the spicy, simmering smells. Steam rises off the thick stew-like mixture. "Smells wonderful."

"Want some crackers?" Sam asks. "Ketchup to douse some of the flames? Tabasco to set the barn on fire?"

"No, thanks."

"Sorry we're not better hosts. Don't get company out here much."

"What? No neighbors drop by, knock on the tree trunk?"

Sam chuckles.

"So how long have you lived like this?" My gaze ping-pongs between the two men, who seem polarized in their looks and demeanor. The only similarity so far is their height.

Before Howard can answer my question, a phone rings and he slaps his front pocket. "That's me." He checks the number. "I must take it. I've been waiting for—"

Sam slides out of the booth, giving Howard room to move out. He snaps open his cell phone and heads toward the door. "Rod! What'd you find out?"

After he leaves, Sam and I look at each other as if we're not quite sure how we ended up alone together.

"That's not Rod Sterling calling, is it?" I ask, hoping to break the awkwardness.

It works. Sam laughs. "You're right, this is a bit Twilight Zone-ish."

He doesn't return to the table immediately. He watches Howard in the next room, stuffs his hands in his back pockets, and shifts his weight from foot to foot.

"Don't worry," I smile at him. "I don't bite."

"Huh? Oh, I didn't think so." He slides back into the booth. Either he's a brave man or a fool. He braces both forearms against the side of the table and hunches over his bowl of chili.

"So, do you live here, too? Or in Marfa?"

"Crazy, huh?"

"I don't know." I glance around the tiny kitchen, notice a pile of dirty dishes in the sink, a few crumbs on the counter. "Okay, maybe. How long have you been living here?"

He grins, and I realize he has a very engaging smile. "A few months. Used to live in Norman, Oklahoma. Before that OK City." He rubs his hands along the tops of his jean-clad thighs. "Let's see . . . Waco. Amarillo. San Antonio. Dallas." He gazes up like there's a map outlined on the ceiling. "But I was born in Houston. That's where I grew up."

"That's some laundry list of places. Makes my staying in Austin sound pretty boring. But I was born in Houston, too."

"We're neighbors then." He tips an imaginary hat. "Where'd you go to school?"

"I didn't. I mean, I was in elementary school when I moved to Austin." I notice his tan skin, the lines embracing his mouth. Laugh lines. Yet serious frown lines run parallel between his dark brows. I clear my throat. "Better give this a try. It sure smells good."

He watches me, making me feel self-conscious until the heat of the peppers singes my lips. I decide a cracker might be a good idea and reach for the box. The crinkly paper inside rattles, like my nerves under this man's steady gaze. "So, what do you think?"

"Spicy, definitely. But good. I like heat."

"A real Texican, huh?" He starts to rise. "I could add more if you want."

I raise my hand to stop him. "Oh, no." My throat sounds raspy. I sip some water, feel my eyes well with tears. "This is great. I'd ask for your recipe but—"

"You don't cook." He smiles again.

"I rely on the generosity of friends . . . and takeout." My cheeks warm under his scrutiny. Must be the chili as I feel the heat of the peppers burning the lining of my belly. "So, why all the moves? For work? You in the Air Force or Green Berets or something?"

His eyes sparkle as if he's about to deliver a punch line. "Preacher man."

That douses whatever flames I might have imagined. I manage to tuck my surprise away like a used tissue. "Really?"

"Yeah."

"Interesting." I avert my gaze.

He laughs. "Most people say *interesting* when it's the exact opposite."

I shrug. Warm from the chili, I slip out of my Windbreaker and fold it onto the seat beside me. "You just don't seem the type. Surprised me is all."

"Why? Cause I'm here in the Hundred Acre woods searching for aliens?"

Laughter bursts out of me. "Could be." Or it could be that I've never had the slightest interest to look twice at a preacher. But I'm not about to tell Sam that bit of news.

He leans back, crosses his arms over his chest, and studies me while I attempt another bite, followed quickly by a cracker and more water. "Telling a beautiful woman I'm a preacher is usually either a turnoff or a challenge."

A beautiful woman? His words wash over me like a sneaker wave, catching me off guard and knocking my feet out from under me. I finally find my voice. "Don't worry. I won't jump you or tempt you beyond your endurance."

"That's a relief. I'm feeling a bit vulnerable lately."

I laugh, but wonder if I should. "So when did your dad move to Marfa . . . Fort Davis?"

"When he left NASA. I was eleven. He's been here thirty-six years. Took him a long time to build this place."

I don't detect much awe in his statement, just a cold, hard fact. I file it away to ask him about later. Maybe. If I'm still here. I glance at the doorway. Is Howard coming back? Apparently not any time soon. His son doesn't seem in a hurry to get rid of me though. Whatever discomfort and defensiveness he exhibited earlier seems to have abated, at least for now. But this cease-fire makes me uneasy. "So you and your mom didn't come with Howard?"

"Their marriage broke up before that. But Howard wasn't what you'd call an involved dad." He fingers the end of his spoon, rolling the metal utensil over and over along the rim of his bowl.

"My ex is that way," I say in my effort to make him more comfortable. As a journalist, it's always been my job to make those I interview relax and tell me all they know. And I want to know more about Howard, which may reveal more about my mother. "It's hard for a man to stay involved in his children's lives, especially if they're living with the mom. I don't know if it's natural but—"

"Don't make excuses for Howard." Sam's hard words resonate in the room, as though his heartache pulses on its own. His laugh lines seem to petrify, hardening into a stone-like mask. He shifts in his seat as if uncomfortable with revealing so much anger and hurt to a stranger.

Before he can close off completely, I throw out another question. "So that's why you're here with Howard?"

"Yeah. Silly I know." The edges of his cheeks redden. But his gaze is solid now, as if he's come to terms with his sins and isn't about to hide them the way I have my own. "Just trying to make up for lost time. My boys don't need me as much anymore. Hate to say that, but it's true. My time with my dad is short."

His words ring an alarm bell in my head, and my heart drifts toward Nana. "Is he sick?"

"He's not well. He works too hard. Always has. NASA didn't have the kind of environment that promoted a healthy lifestyle. They worked long hours, ate fast food, and smoked three packs a day."

"And your mom?"

"She's still in Houston. She found a man who takes good care of her. Same as my ex."

"Pretty hard for a preacher to lose his family."

His mouth pulls into a grim line. Suddenly he stands and scoops his bowl off the table. "Ah, you don't want to hear my story. You're here to talk to Howard. But he could be on the phone for a couple of hours. If you want, you're welcome to stay here. There's plenty of room. And you're safe. From Howard and me. From anything."

"Even aliens?"

"Or the cow jumping over the moon."

I hold up my spoon. "I'll be careful not to let this one get away."

Chapter Eight

The conversation with Sam tilts into an uncomfortable silence. He's polite. But he doesn't know what to say to me anymore than I know what to say to him. It seems we've crossed that invisible, polite first-meet barrier and have said too much. Where do you go from there?

With Howard whispering on his cell phone in what appears to be not only the living room but also his office, I decide to go back to the hotel for the night. Sam escorts me through the labyrinth of tunnels. When we reach the top of the stairs beneath the counterfeit, ancient oak, he turns the lock, his muscles bunching beneath his thick, fuzzy shirt. Determined not to notice anything about this man, I stare at the tiny specks in the concrete wall. The fact that he's Howard's son is a major deterrent. Of course, warning signs never hindered me before. In fact, they usually made me charge forward. Maybe I'm smarter now. Or the opposite.

I'm not quite sure.

I hesitate before stepping through the portal into the real world. "You're not going to insist on that silly blindfold, are you?"

He mutters under his breath and glances back down the way we came as if contemplating going back for it.

"I won't tell." I hold up two fingers. "Scout's promise."

"You were a Girl Scout?"

"Not even a Brownie. But you can trust me."

His jaw hardens. "You're a reporter."

Who knew three simple words could contain such censure? "Reporters go to jail if they talk."

His mouth twists.

I temper my voice to a sugary sweetness. "What if I promise to close my eyes?"

He narrows his gaze on me. His eyes are dark, distrustful. Can't blame him there, because even I know I'd peek. Then he snaps his fingers and pulls a white handkerchief out of his back pocket.

"No way."

"It's clean. Freshly laundered in hot water. Scout's honor. And I *was* an Eagle Scout."

"Bully for you." I frown as he stretches the handkerchief taut between his hands and loops it over and over to form a band. Then he motions for me to turn around.

"No way."

"Then you'll have to stay here."

"Why?"

He releases a long, slow breath. "It's not safe."

I roll my eyes. "Maybe I'll take my chances and find my car myself."

"Good luck." He swings his arm wide.

I take a step even with Sam in the doorway but stop. I haven't a clue which direction. Peering out, the night is as dark as deep space. Getting lost in the middle of the night in a shadowy forest populated by wild animals and who knows what else is not my idea of fun. "Really, Sam, I won't tell a soul. Cross my heart and hope to—"

"I can't take that chance. You might tell without realizing it. Ask the wrong person a question, not knowing the damage you might cause." He waits, poised between us is the white handkerchief, my white flag of utter surrender.

No way. I can do a standoff with the best of them. After all, I had a stubborn, headstrong, smart-aleck teenage daughter at one time. Ginger never cowed me. No way this hulk is going to.

But the longer Sam and I stand on the concrete step, squaring off, meeting each other's gazes, the more I'm drawn to that square jaw and his fierce determination to protect his father. The attraction prickles my skin like a heat rash. Never have I had someone guard me like the archangel Gabriel. A longing wells up in my soul.

Suddenly exhaustion weights my limbs. It's been a long day with a several-hour drive, not to mention the wild goose chase that Howard put me through. With a huff, I present my back to Sam and grit out between my teeth, "Don't pull my hair."

Sam chuckles. His hands are confident, as if he tied many a blindfold for Pin-the-Tail-on-the-Donkey, and firm as if he's not about to let me take off on my own. He brackets my shoulders when he's finished, and I feel his warm breath on my neck. "Too tight?"

A shiver ripples down my spine and I bristle against my reaction. "Would it matter?"

"Yeah." He turns me carefully toward him, making me feel vulnerable and defenseless. "Okay"—I can feel him lean past me to push the door wider—"here we go."

The cool night air rushes in and penetrates to my skin as if my clothes are only as thick as gauze. Night creatures chirp and squawk. Then Sam takes my hand in his larger, callused one. His grip is firm, steadying. "Take a step down." He touches the top of my head with his fingertips and tilts my head forward. "Easy. There you go. Okay. Slight step down. Now hold still while I close the opening."

When he turns away, I tug at the bottom of the handkerchief and peer out from beneath it. Darkness meets darkness, but I can make out the tops of my brown cowboy boots. A hand covers mine again and presses the handkerchief against my face, then he tugs me along. It seems we're making a large circle. Maybe we're going around the tree first. We weave to the right, then the left. Disoriented, I can only hold onto his hand and stumble along behind him, hoping—all right, I admit it: praying—he doesn't walk me into a tree or leave me here alone or punt me off a cliff. He stops abruptly, and I collide with his back, acutely aware of his solidness. He puts a hand on my waist.

I startle. "What—"

"Shh."

His warm breath puffs against my cheek but sends shivers down my spine. He is too close. Did he sense the attraction assaulting me? Has he been waiting for a moment alone when I was defenseless and lost? I jerk the blindfold off seconds before he wrenches me sideways and off balance. I fall against his rock-solid body. Heat rolls off him. My backside scrapes against something rough, which my hand discovers is bark.

I start to swing right, elbows outward in a basketball defensive move I learned from the stands as a cheering mom. "Let—"

"Don't move." His voice tightens and rumbles low in my ear. His body presses the point, keeping me from moving and almost breathing.

"What do you think—"

A shaft of light swings past us and stops me from saying more. It arcs around us, brushing tree limbs, a split trunk, a jagged rock, missing us by inches. My cheek rubs against the warm nook at the base of Sam's neck. More rays of light dance around us like a mirror ball on the dance floor. Pressing my hand against his chest, I feel his heart thumping a rhythm that echoes my own.

"Are those the Marf—"

He settles a finger, firm and insistent, against my lips.

"Look that way!" A deep voice penetrates the darkness. It's hard to distinguish how far or close. But I now understand.

We're not alone.

"I heard something over there." Another voice answers from a different direction.

The lights zigzag, jerking high and low. Footsteps crunch twigs and leaves. After several minutes my body nestled against Sam's, my heart knocking into his, the rustling noises fade and the lights vanish. In the distance an engine catches. Awareness washes over me. Sam and I are alone once more, pressed close, our breath merging. Reasons and excuses muddle into confusion. Before I can act, as I so often have in the past, Sam steps away.

"What was that?" I whisper, not sure if I mean the sparks between us or the intrusion by strangers.

He rubs the back of his neck. "Beats me. But it happens regularly."

Okay, he took my meaning the other way, diverging away from the awareness I have of him as a man. That's good, I suppose. "It's not like whoever was out here are aliens. Why don't you just ask them?"

He grins. "Okay, next time it happens, I'll let you confront them. But you might want to be carrying. Just in case."

"Carrying what?"

"A weapon. What if *they* have one? Or more."

That silences me.

"Come on." He hooks his hand around my elbow and leads me in what seems a different direction but soon my Prius comes into view.

"Is your car locked?"

"I don't think so."

He opens the driver's door for me. My purse sits on the front seat. Another foolish mistake today . . . and counting.

"Better check your wallet."

"Why? Do aliens need cash?" Still, I check it anyway. It's unlatched, but no money seems to be missing.

"ATM cards work better."

"Oh, right." I snap my wallet closed. "Every planet has an ATM machine, just fly up and cash out."

Sam's forehead crinkles. "Might not be wise for you to go back to the hotel."

"Wisdom has never been my claim to fame. Don't worry. I'll be fine. I'm not scared."

"You could stay here."

I squint at him. Does he mean that as a come-on? An invitation? He doesn't strike me as the type to hit on women, but I've been wrong before. I've heard about televangelists who have torrid affairs. Even though he doesn't strike me as that type, I shake my head. "No, thanks."

"Do you want me to follow you back then?"

"I'm a big girl."

"So I noticed."

Okay, maybe I was wrong. An odd tingling in the pit of my stomach distracts me. I jerk my attention back to why I'm here. "Can I see Howard tomorrow? Does he come out of his bat cave? Eat breakfast with mere mortals?"

Sam's mouth pulls to the side in a lopsided grin. "Sure. How about the drugstore?"

"For breakfast?" I remember the dirty dishes lining the counter.

"They have great pancakes and biscuits."

"Okay, high carbs. Nine o'clock."

He nods.

I slide into the driver's seat. "See you tomorrow."

Full and bright behind him, the moon casts his face in shadows. "You want me to come, too?"

"Yeah." My response comes too quickly, and I'm hit with the awareness that I *do* want him to come. I attempt to counter with a casual tone. "Why not?"

But there's a whole list of why nots.

Chapter Nine

The smell of strong coffee draws me into the Fort Davis Drugstore like UFO sightings attract slightly unbalanced citizens. Bleary-eyed from trying to digest Howard's thick tome into the wee hours of the morning, I brush past a group of locals crowding the entrance. It's a happening place with tourists coming and going in the early morning hours. Chattering customers pack the tables, clinking silverware and sipping coffee. The smell of grease, bacon, and buttery biscuits warms the chilly morning air. Grateful for the sweatshirt I had the forethought to pack, I search the patrons for a familiar face.

Toward the back of the drugstore, Sam waves me over to the booth I occupied just yesterday. His eyes are warm, his smile friendly if a bit fuzzy thanks to the shadow darkening his square jaw. He's wearing a college T-shirt and jeans.

When I reach the booth, I wrinkle my nose at the OU on his chest. "Not sure I can dine with a Sooner."

He gives me an equally disdainful look. "You're not a tea sipper, are you?"

"UT's my alma mater. But my daughter defected to Aggie land, so I suppose I can make this one exception." I slide into the booth on the opposite side of the table from Sam and Howard.

"That's big of you." Sam pours coffee from a carafe into a white mug for me then refills Howard's and his own.

Howard glances up only to push the coffee cup away from his newspaper, *The Wall Street Journal*, stretched across the table. He underlines a byline with a blue pen. In the margins are scribbled notes that look like hen scratching. Some of the markings appear to be mathematical formulas, others are miniature drawings of geometric shapes. I need Ginger here to interpret. Or maybe Mr. Spock.

"Sleep well?" Sam folds a section of the paper and slaps it in front of Howard who startles, frowns, then shoves it out of his way again, making more marks on the page.

"Yes, thanks." I pull a paper napkin from the dispenser and set it in my lap. "Am I late?"

"Not at all." Sam squeezes into the booth across from me, next to his father. "We get everywhere early."

"To catch the worm?"

Sam smiles, but Howard grumbles, "Always best to check things out."

I raise an eyebrow.

Sam's gaze shifts toward his father, then back to me. "You never know."

"So you scope things out?"

Sam nods. "We drive around the block a hundred times. Sit outside. Move positions. Walk past the front entrance, then come in through the back."

"I see. At least you didn't send me on a scavenger hunt this morning."

Sam nods to someone across the room. I notice patrons wave to Sam, slide a curious glance at Howard, but don't bother speaking to him. Sam again waves the paper in front of his father.

This time, Howard straightens, blinks like he's suddenly aware of his surroundings, and focuses on me. "Brynda! You all right?"

"Yes, fine."

"No trouble last night, was there?"

"Should there have been?"

"Sam told me about what happened when you two went to your car." He shakes his head. "You never can be too careful. If anything were to happen to you—" He stops himself, glances around, forearms resting on the edge of the table. "You should have stayed at the safe house. Someone could be watching you. Did you check to make sure no one followed you to the hotel?"

I feel as I did when Nana questioned me when I was a teen. "You carrying that maze?"

"Mace," I corrected her. She made me take judo so I'd know how to defend myself. I never told her those special moves came in handy once outside a bar. "Keep a dollar pinned in your bra," she advised, "and a dime in your shoe. Just in case you need extra cash or to make a phone call." I didn't tell her pay phones then were twenty-five cents and are now almost obsolete.

Howard tugs on his mustache, stretching the hairs out to the side of his mouth and giving them a twist. "If they got your information from your wallet—"

"Why? What could they do? What have I done?"

"It's not what you've done."

"Then what?"

His mouth opens, but he doesn't answer. His gaze drifts off like he's just checked out of orbit.

Sam pulls worn paper menus from behind the napkin dispenser and hands one to each of us. "I'm hungry. Anyone else game for pancakes?"

Howard scratches his head. "Didn't we order already?"

"Not yet." Sam holds up a finger and an older waitress smiles and hollers, "Be right there!"

I glance around at the other help but don't see the redheaded teen here this morning. Turning my attention to the menu, I squint at the tiny print. "What are you two having?"

"Pancakes are good." Sam sips his coffee. "But so are the eggs and biscuits."

I lean toward Howard's newspaper. "Anything interesting in there? UFO sightings?"

He folds up the section of the paper, international news, and slides it inside the front panel of his tweed jacket. Beneath, he wears solid khakis again.

A few minutes later Carmelita, or so her name badge reads, takes our order. Her long, peppered black hair is pulled up into a knot at the base of her neck. Her round face is friendly, her features pretty. "And for you, Fred?"

I frown, then realize she's speaking to Howard.

"My usual."

"Si. I remember." She smiles and tucks her pen behind her ear before moving to the next table.

Howard clasps his hands together, his thumbs rubbing against each other. "Your grandmother—Cora—how is she?"

I hesitate a minute too long. This question always stumps me. Nana is basically fine and yet definitely not.

"She's not deceased, is she?"

"No, not at all. She's not herself. But other than that . . ." I've learned not to go into the details. Well-meaning folks like to give all sorts of advice, and frankly there's nothing that can be done that hasn't been done.

Howard nods. "Old age does that, especially for someone so capable. And for someone who needs to control their environment. Cora was always good at that."

"Yes, she certainly was."

"Jennifer surely tested that ability."

"I'm afraid I did, too."

Howard tips his head and studies me a moment. "Another rebel without a cause, eh?"

Feeling Sam's curious gaze, I'm grateful for Carmelita's interruption as she clunks our breakfast plates on the table. She sets Howard's glass of pink—not yellow—lemonade in front of him along with his pancakes, side of bacon, and scrambled eggs. "Anything else, Fred?"

Howard doesn't respond. He shovels in a slab of bacon and rearranges his plates to his liking.

"We're good," Sam replies.

I stare at Carmelita's retreating back. "Did she call you Fred?"

Howard's forehead creases. He glances at Carmelita, who stops at another table. Then he leans toward me and whispers, "My alias."

"His friends protect him here." Sam adds salt and pepper to his scrambled eggs.

Steam rises off the biscuits and gravy, which are not exactly healthy, but I figure a little down-home Southern comfort is needed this week. Howard inspects his pancakes, lifting up each edge with his fork. Does he think someone placed a bug—as in a listening device—beneath the rounds of flapjacks? How far does his paranoia go? Is he looking for aliens lurking under the melted butter and thick syrup? "Something wrong?"

"Huh?" Howard looks up, fork poised midair. "No. I, uh . . . Are you going to the observatory while you're here?"

Carmelita returns and thunks a bottle of red sauce on the table along with a little bowl of jalapeños.

"What would I do without you?" Howard pours the sauce in his eggs, and my stomach rolls thinking of the lemonade combo about to hit his.

"Well," Carmelita drawls, "you wouldn't need to buy no more Tums."

"That's what the lemonade is for." He grins and dumps the jalapenos in his eggs. Forking a large bite, he chews and focuses back on me. "You should see the observatory. Worth the price of admission. Fascinating. They have the Hobby-Eberly Telescope."

He swallows and shovels in more of the peppers seasoned by eggs. If the aliens (or whoever he thinks is after him) don't kill him, then all that indigestion will.

"Sam could take you out there."

I sample the sausage gravy and have to admit it's good. "I don't want to be a bother."

"Only half-an-hour drive up in the mountains." Sam watches me from beneath heavy lids. He doctors his biscuits with pepper and an extra slab of butter.

I doubt he's thrilled his father volunteered him to play tour guide. "I was hoping to be able to talk to you for a while today, Howard." I cup my coffee between my hands and breathe in the heady aroma. "I only have a short time to stay in Marfa since I need to be back in Austin in a couple of days."

Howard pauses and stares at me. One corner of his handlebar mustache droops. "Me? You need to talk to me?"

"That's why I came."

His gray eyebrows come together in a puzzled look. Could Howard be showing early signs of Alzheimer's? Or could he simply be distracted as Sam tends to believe?

I clunk my coffee cup too hard on the table. "I'd like to learn more about what you're researching, your time at NASA . . . even before that. And, of course, what you knew about my mother."

The corner of Howard's eye twitches as he leans forward and speaks in a hushed voice. "That might not be so wise."

"Excuse me?"

He shifts his gaze from side to side, then turns and glances behind our booth before those steely blues bore into me again. "Jennifer knew too much. I don't want you endangered the way she was. Don't go pokin' your nose around where it doesn't belong."

"You're the one who came to me first!"

"It was a bad idea. Bad idea. And after last night, those who were snooping around . . . you need protection instead of me thrusting you into danger."

Heat burns its way to my cheeks. "Believe me, I'm a big girl. I can take care of myself. Besides, how could knowing about my mother endanger me?"

Howard quirks an eyebrow at his son.

Sam grins. "She's no Girl Scout."

Howard shovels in bite after bite of his egg and pancakes. A drop of pepper sauce mixed with syrup rolls down the edge of his chin. "Jennifer worked for . . . well, not directly for NASA." He swipes the sauce away with his hand, then reaches for a napkin from the dispenser. "She worked for a company contracted by NASA."

This news stumps me. Nana never told me anything like this about my mother. She avoided conversations about her own daughter like so many avoid the dentist's chair. I always thought it was too painful for her as I knew the piercing pain of my mother's absence, too. "What did she do?" Since she never graduated from college, she most likely held a secretarial position.

Barely taking a breath or pause between bites, Howard manages to say, "Jennifer trafficked information to and from."

"Trafficked?" A cold sensation settles over me. "What kind of information? To and from whom?"

He shoves his plate away from him, breathing hard from the exertion of sprint eating. "Exactly the kind of question Jennifer would have asked."

To be compared to my mother takes my breath. Of course, I've always seen the resemblance in our height, our long fingers. But other than that, there's been no similarities ever spoken. Nana never said, "You're a good student, like your mother." And she sure never said, "You ask too many questions, just like Jennifer." Never, "You must be like your dad." Not even, "Don't be like your mother," which would have at least been an indirect link.

Maybe Nana feared making any associations. Maybe she feared my life would end as my mother's did.

"It cost her in the end." Howard's statement startles me out of my shock.

"What? What do you mean?"

He gulps down his pink lemonade, his throat muscles contracting with each swallow, then with a heavy sigh he wipes his mouth with his shirt sleeve, twisting the ends of his mustache into fine points. "Go home, Brynda."

"But you're the one who wanted me to come here! And now I want to know more about my mother." I reach across the table and grab his hand. "I need to know more."

A long silence passes, then his startled gaze melds with mine. "She was nice. Beautiful. And she died too young. Too young. I don't want that to happen to you."

My skin prickles. My jaw clenches tight.

Carmelita appears suddenly at my side. She holds a carafe in one hand. Her smile, which seemed to go with her uniform, has disappeared. She slides the check onto the sticky tabletop. Without moving her mouth, she says, "New customers."

Howard snaps his head in the direction of the front door. He doesn't ask her any questions and she doesn't say anything else. She walks to the next table, inquiring how the pancakes are this morning in a bright, friendly voice.

Howard tosses a few bills onto the table, scoops his papers into his arms, and nudges Sam with an elbow to get out of the booth. "It's not safe."

"What isn't safe?" I swivel in my seat, search the crowd, the front door. Just ordinary looking folks stand around the front counter waiting for an open table. The redheaded teen squeezes between two customers, holding a tray of food high overhead.

Howard leans so close to me I can smell the peppers and sweet syrup on his breath. "I shouldn't have invited you, Brynda. I shouldn't have . . ." He shakes his head, his features compressing into regret. "I better go. And you, too."

With that, he disappears into the kitchen. Sam slides back into the booth, his face grim, his mouth flat. He gathers the money his father left, studies the check, then adds more from his own wallet.

"What just happened?" I ask.

"Go ahead and finish your breakfast." He folds his wallet and slips it into his hip pocket. "No hurry." He forks a bite of biscuit dripping with gravy.

"Let me help with the check." I reach for my purse.

He holds up a hand. "It's all right. It's the least we can do."

"But my editor pays a stipend—"

"It's not necessary. I'm sorry you came all this way for nothing."

I stir what's left of my gravy, but my stomach feels just as lumpy and cold. "So what's really going on? Is he schizophrenic? Psychotic? What?"

Sam shakes his head, but I'm not sure if he means it as *no* to my questions or simply a way of expressing his own confusion.

"My grandmother has Alzheimer's."

Sam meets my gaze. I'm not sure if I read questions, fear, or denial.

"I recognize some of the symptoms in your father."

The corner of his mouth pinches into a dimple, but he doesn't comment.

I reach across the table and touch his hand, offering what I hope is understanding and empathy. I've walked this path. I know how hard it is to face reality and how treacherous the road for getting help. "Sam, I know it's difficult to face the truth about a loved one. But—"

He gives a half laugh, his mouth pulling to the side. "If that's the case, then my father has had Alzheimer's since he was seven. Or maybe earlier. He's like the proverbial absentminded professor. He's been focused on his conspiracies for so long he can't concentrate on anything or anyone else."

I pull back my hand, rub away the warmth of his touch, and consider his cold, disconnected tones. "Even his son?"

He shrugs. "That's how it's always been."

"But what about his paranoia? It's a bit extreme, isn't it?"

He pushes away his plate, looks toward the door where Howard left, then back to my plate. "Finished?"

Placing my napkin beneath the edge of my plate, I nod.

"Come on."

Together we leave the restaurant, reach the sidewalk outside and glance around for Howard. When we don't spot him, Sam suggests we walk down the street a ways. "It could be a while before he turns up again."

We end up at a shaded, fenced-off memorial park across the street from the courthouse. A gigantic tree with droopy limbs and lacy leaves that I can't identify shades the area, including a memorial to members of the community who fought and died during WWII. Overgrown grass and weeds try to hide a plaque honoring the man who once took care of this tiny park. I sit on a wooden bench and Sam joins me, bracing his elbows on the back of the bench and stretching out his long legs in front of him.

"Look, Bryn, I know my dad is strange. Radical even. But he believes in this stuff. I came here a few months ago to try to help him, thinking I knew better than he did, thinking just as you are now that he's"—his mouth twists as if he's searching for the right word—"mentally ill. It's hard to explain, but I've seen things that make me doubt my original intent. I don't know if I believe, but it seems someone is after my father, that someone would like to cause him harm."

"Who?"

"I don't know that yet." He shifts, planting his work boots firmly on the ground. He reaches down and plucks a tall blade of grass between us. With his forearms now leaning against his thighs, his back bowed forward, he rolls the green shoot between his fingers. "Believe me, when I came here, I thought I'd be taking my father back to Dallas and placing him in assisted living. Now, I find myself trying to protect him."

As he did the night I arrived. I wait for him to continue, but when he doesn't I ask, "What have you seen?"

"It's not so much seeing something. It's what you don't see." He looks over his shoulder at me and laughs at my expression, which I try to erase. "I know. For most of my life, I've rolled my eyes at his conspiracy theories. I didn't want to hear about his work. Wanted no part of it." He slashes his hand through the air. "Six months ago I would have reacted the same as you are now. I probably did react the same to my father's ranting. But . . ."

"But?"

"You're probably going to think *I'm* crazy now."

"There are worse things."

He grins. "Strange phone calls in the middle of the night. When I pick up there's only static or beeps and blips on the other end. Lights appear in the woods surrounding my father's property. Tire tracks circle the trailer. Cigarette butts litter the yard. Chain-link fences are cut. Letters telling him to stop what he's doing."

"Howard could have left the cigarettes . . . written the letters, even made the phone calls." I argue for what Nana used to say was simply for the sake of arguing. But every stone has to be over-turned, evaluated, catalogued. It's better to ask the tough questions first.

"That's a lot of trouble to go to. And for what?"

"For attention?"

"He doesn't want attention."

"Hmm."

Sam's face darkens "Don't you think I've considered all of the different angles?"

"I don't know. I'm simply trying to help. So what exactly *is* Howard doing?"

"Heck if I understand it all. He's researching the moon and Mars. From what I can tell, he believes ancient civilizations left ruins on both. He's studying photos from NASA and the different missions. Photos that have been erased from files at NASA or doctored. That much I understand."

Intrigued, I lean forward, my shoulder brushing his.

"Howard's putting pressure on NASA," Sam explains, "to explore certain areas of space. He considers it speaking the truth about the secret missions and agenda of NASA. To him, it's a dangerous organization."

"You can't go against city hall," I joke.

"Apparently he believes there used to be a city hall on the moon." His tone remains flat and serious, carrying a hint of embarrassment.

I thought carrying around the stigma of a mother who committed suicide was tough. I reached college before I told anyone, and then only my roommate, Carmen. She was from south Texas. We'd been drinking and the alcohol had loosened my tongue. She reacted with the typical "That's terrible," but then I noticed she became wary of me during the ensuing months, watching me cautiously. After I broke up with a boyfriend, she said, "You're not going to *do* anything, are you?"

"What do you mean?"

"You know . . . like your mom."

I glared at her. Defenses shot up around my heart. I crossed my arms over my chest. "What do you mean by that?"

"I just don't want anything to happen to you . . ." Her gaze fluttered to the floor. "Or to be the one to find you."

"Fine. If I decide to slit my wrists, I'll make sure someone else gets the honor." I moved out of our apartment that night.

Years before, in junior high, though I'd kept it a secret, some kids heard through various channels of gossip that my mother died by dubious means. They thought it was funny to leave a rope tied in a hangman's knot looped over my locker. And to joke that my mother was crazy. But I knew her. She wasn't crazy.

But I suspect Sam has battled doubts and confusion all of his life, not only from friends making jokes about his father, but also from his own perspective. It's one thing to know the truth and keep it to yourself; it's another matter to want to defend your father and throw stones at the same time.

The squeak of brakes makes me jerk to an upright position. I glance toward a brown station wagon with a bad muffler that puffs out black smoke. Howard sits in the driver's seat wearing a low-riding cowboy hat. Together Sam and I walk out of the memorial park and into the street, toward the station wagon.

Howard slumps down in his seat, shoulders hunched, his movements jerky. "Get in."

Through the open driver's window, I grab his elbow. "What's going on here, Howard? What does all of this have to do with my mother?"

"You should go home, Brynda." He shifts to look at his son. "Sam, make her go."

"I'm not going anywhere until I know the truth."

"Everyone said she killed herself." Howard shakes his head. "The police. Toxicology reports. Your grandmother even." Howard's voice cracks. "But Jennifer wasn't like that. She wasn't!" He bangs his palms against the steering wheel. "I *knew* her. She wouldn't have . . . That's not what happened."

His words plunge deep into my soul.

"*They* killed her. They did! I should have stopped it." He clenches his hands on the steering wheel. "If I'd understood . . . if I'd known . . . But I was a fool. Jennifer was so innocent." His blue eyes blaze with intensity. "She didn't kill herself. I let your grandmother believe it was suicide to spare her anymore grief, to protect her . . . to protect you. Jenn couldn't have done something like that." Tears well up in his eyes as if they've been stored for forty years. He looks at me then. "You've got to believe me."

I swallow the emotions that choke me. "I do."

"You do?" His eyes widen as if a new world has opened to him.

"Yes, I've always known my mother didn't kill herself." I keep the reasons I know to myself. It's a secret I've kept for forty years.

I'm not about to confess it now. "But who do you think *they* are?" My voice shakes. "Who do you believe did it?"

"*They*!" The word explodes out of him. "Those in charge. In the know. They're everywhere. They know *everything*! *See* everything." His hand folds over my arm, the pressure urgent. "If you don't leave, then you'll be in danger. You can't be seen with me. It's not safe. I couldn't live if I allowed you to be hurt, too. Go home."

He glances in his rearview mirror. "There he is!"

Chapter Ten

Howard drives off, his back wheels squealing as he takes a corner.

"There who is?" I look around us. No getaway car U-turns and blasts out of sight. No unmarked car chases after Howard. There's not even a bicycle in hot pursuit.

I scrutinize the street, up and down past the café. An old man gets out of a shiny Cadillac. He seems about as menacing as Andy Griffith. A couple of kids scoot along on skateboards, crisscrossing each other's tracks. A woman pushes a stroller out of a store. I can't see anyone who seems remotely threatening to make Howard take off like he's being chased.

Still, his words stay with me, soak deep into my soul, and leave me shaken to the very nucleus of my being. What do I do now? Admit the man needs psychological help? Walk away? Or accept that some back alley conspiracy is really going on?

Howard believes someone killed my mother. His statement—*They* killed her!—sends chills down my spine and leaves my nerves

throbbing. What do I do? Admit what I know? I've never spoken
of my mother's death to anyone. Not even Nana. The possibility
shreds my nerves the way Elphaba once clawed the corners of my
sofa. Maybe it's best if I allow Howard to go on believing in some
far-fetched conspiracy theory. Is it really doing any harm? I stare off
in the direction he took. Does he jeopardize others—innocents—
with his odd behavior?

Not knowing what to do, where to go, how to respond, I walk
away, drifting away from the curb, in the opposite direction of the
café, not even caring where I'm headed. I need to contemplate all
of this, to quiet the concerns pumping through my heart, and yet
I don't want to focus on it. I want to just leave this town . . . this
story . . . my past, behind.

A hand encircles my arm. "It's no use, you know." Sam's voice
sinks like my hope of learning more about my mother. "When he
gets like this, there's no talking to him. He believes there's some
big scheme. A bunch of faceless, ubiquitous *them* running around,
thwarting decent hardworking folks who dare to question or
claim—"

He breaks off what sounds like the beginning of a tirade and
looks down at my hands. My gaze follows. A tremor has taken hold
of me and I can't stop it, even when I clutch my hands together.
"Bryn, are you okay?"

Shaky and tremulous, I can't seem to get a grip on myself. "Yes.
No. I don't know. I just . . . I need to get away from here. I need to
think. But I can't."

He cups my hands between his own as if warming them will
soothe the fear and uncertainty deep inside me. It's an intimate gesture that should make me push away, but instead I want to lean into
him, to absorb his warmth and strength when I have none. Leading
me toward a not-quite-white pickup truck, he talks in a soft, soothing voice. "I'm sorry Howard went on that way. You can't believe
half what he says. Really. Just forget what he said." Mud cakes the
tires and splatters the sides of the truck like a child's first attempt at

painting. He opens the passenger door for me. "Howard didn't mean to upset you. He doesn't think clearly sometimes."

Needing to discuss something, anything else, I ask, "Is this yours?"

"Yes."

"Where are we going?"

"Does it matter?"

I shake my head and heave myself into the passenger seat. The inside is as neat as the outside is dirty. When Sam climbs behind the wheel, I ask, "Where's Howard going? What will he do?"

"Cool off."

"How long will that take?" Because I'm not sure how long it will take for me to recover from this.

"Few hours maybe. But I should warn you, bringing up your mother again will probably end up with the same result—upsetting him." He stares ahead, his hands clenching the steering wheel, before he inserts the key in the ignition and gives it a sharp, quick turn. The engine catches easily. He places a hand on the gear shift but doesn't move it into drive. Instead, he glances over at me. "So you should drop it, Bryn. Maybe Howard's right. Maybe you should go home. Why do you want to probe the past that can't be changed?"

"Because it's *my* mother." I press a hand against my chest, feel my heart pounding. "I can't just leave. I can't. I have to talk to him, find out what he knows about her." I rub the heel of my palm along my jean-clad thigh. "I should tell him."

"Tell him what?"

"I was just nine . . ." The words jam in my throat.

"Look, Bryn, talking about your mother won't help Howard right now. He'll distract himself with research and calm down." Sam puts the truck in drive. No traffic interferes with pulling onto the main street that runs through Fort Davis. We pass the drugstore that looks to have a hearty business this morning. When he reaches the crossroad, he turns into the mountains on the road leading to the observatory.

The sun's glare causes me to reach for my shades, which also thankfully provide a level of protection against Sam's probing glances. Surreptitiously I observe him steering his truck. He's a careful driver, not taking too many risks, but he's not overly cautious. Nana used to brake every few seconds, always making me more nervous than if she'd taken daring turns and crazy risks. Sam seems to take his father's paranoia in stride. Yet I sense a strong emotion bubbling just beneath the surface of his calm demeanor.

"So have you become a conspiracy theorist too while you've been living with your father?"

"If you mean, do I believe all that malarkey about people chasing him and trying to stop his investigations and research?" One shoulder lifts in a shrug. "I don't know. Most of the time I doubt what he says—years of cynicism and hearing the same tales out of him. But like I said, enough odd things have happened since I've moved here that make me question. Not just coincidences, you know? So what exactly is going on?" He lifts a hand off the steering wheel as if ready to grasp some elusive answer that slips out of reach. "What I *do* know is that I don't like seeing Howard all stirred up. Can't be good for him. Or anyone else." He doesn't look in my direction but I assume he means me. "Which is why it would be better if you just dropped all of this and went home."

"Easy for you to say, Sam. It's not your mother. He believes my mother was killed. Killed!" I'm beginning to make the connection that part of Howard's conspiracy theory is grounded in my mother's death. If I told him what happened that night so long ago, the night Neil Armstrong stepped foot on the surface of the moon, then would his speculation and skewed hypothesis burst wide open? Maybe then Howard could live a normal life rather than lurking and skulking around in fear. It's a lot of responsibility to be placed on my shoulders. Something I don't want.

But maybe there is more to all of this—and to my mother's death—than I thought. Was there something else at play surrounding my mother's death, something other than what I always thought was depression? If so, would that help release me from the chains that bind me so tightly to the past? "I can't leave, Sam. Not yet. Not until I know more."

Sam's mouth thins, deepening the brackets in his facial plains. "I know."

The resignation in his voice makes me wonder if he's worried about what kinds of things I will stir up by probing and digging into things he hasn't wanted to face. I also realize Sam has known about my mother longer than I've been in town. "How long have you known his fears and concerns about my mother's death?"

His fingers flex and tighten on the steering wheel. "For as long as I can remember he's talked about Jennifer, the way *they* got to her."

"But—"

"Look, I don't know anything about your mom. Only that he's mentioned her in association with all of this. I'm sorry he put that on you, told you she was killed. I don't know that he has any proof. Consider it the ravings of a lunatic, if that makes it easier."

"Easier for what? To move on? You don't believe he's crazy!"

He gives me a cursory glance before focusing again on the curlicue road ahead. "This isn't a new phenomenon to me, Bryn. It's not senility. I've lived with his ranting my whole life. Would medication help? Psychotherapy? I don't know. It's not like I can haul him into a doctor's office and find out. He'd just think the doctor was part of the conspiracy. The *them*. Maybe he is crazy." His mouth tightens into a hard line. "But then again, maybe he isn't."

I nod, remembering how difficult it was to get Nana to the doctor when I suspected she was losing her memory. For a while I monitored her, keeping tabs on her bills, if she paid the electric and phone company or not. When she didn't, I paid for her. But when she left the stove on and caught a dish towel on fire, I had to act.

When she was diagnosed, I read up on the disease. Events began to make sense. Her paranoia that I was trying to steal from her was fairly normal for this type of patient. With the doctor's help, we convinced her she needed help and that I wasn't trying to steal from her or take advantage of her. She then signed papers so I could handle the finances and get her the help she needed. All of the emotions aside, becoming a parent to the person who raised me was a painful process I would never wish on anyone, especially Sam who has more of an adversarial relationship with his father.

Nana and I had been a team for years, the bonds tightened in some ways by the blame she placed on herself for my mother's death. "I knew my girl was hurting," Nana lamented. "She was depressed. Being a single mother is lonely and hard. I should've made her see a doctor of some sort."

But how do you help someone who doesn't want it or denies needing it in the first place?

Trying to absorb all I've learned today, my mind starts drifting back in time to that night. The full moon shone into my bedroom window with an eerie light that pervaded the room, giving my toys a milky glow. But the light wasn't what kept me awake.

"Hey, look"—Sam interrupts my thoughts and glances over at me—"think of it this way: Howard can't possibly know what happened to your mom that night, can he?"

"I don't know. He lived in Houston, too. He knew more about her circumstances, what might have led to her death. Maybe he knows more than I do." I rub my hands along my thighs over and over as if trying to erase that night from my mind. As much as I want to question Howard, I also don't. "Why do you call your father Howard instead of Dad, Pop . . . Papa?"

"Do I?" He gives a huff. "Hadn't thought about it." He shrugs, not in a way to slough off the question but as if he's uncomfortable looking at himself. "Maybe because for so long he was just that to me . . . Howard Walters. Nothing more. Nothing less. He was never really a father."

"So now you're here trying to build that relationship?"

"I'm a little old to start calling him Daddy, don't you think?"

"Maybe."

"He's still just Howard to me." His comment seems more for himself than me.

"Maybe then you understand why I have to stay, why I need to know more about my mother, why I need to find out all Howard knows."

His mouth slants downward, and he releases a slow breath. "Maybe."

For the next ten minutes we don't speak until we arrive at the observatory, pulling into the parking lot. Despite my protests he pays for our entrance. We wander through the activities set up primarily for children. I focus on reading about scientists who made great discoveries in space. I'm struck by a hearing-impaired woman who catalogued over two hundred fifty thousand stars, her disability helping her concentrate and block out distractions. Looking at the technical aspects of how a telescope works, my thoughts settle back into the here and now, my pulse returns to normal. But my emotions are still jammed in my throat.

In the cool mountain air we walk the short distance uphill and around the bend to the Hobby-Eberly Telescope and view the many mirrors it takes to refract the light from distant stars. Other than a short movie clip documenting the inventors of the telescope and the universities contributing to the building of it, there's not much else to see. We begin the slow descent back toward Sam's truck. At seven thousand feet of elevation, I huddle in my sweatshirt at the coolness of the mountains. Our boots crunch gravel, grinding into my thoughts. Clouds descend over the mountain, turning the temperature down another notch or two.

Despite all the things to observe at the observatory, my thoughts are still mired in the past. I walk beside this preacher, and questions surface. Whether I want them to or not. "Have you ever done something you regret? Something that changed the course of your life . . . and others' lives?"

Sam shoves his hands in his jean pockets and hunches his shoulders against the cold mist. "Yeah."

I wait but he doesn't continue. Regret lines his face so deeply that I hurt for him. Just when I don't think he's going to say anything else, the crunch of my footsteps echoing his and providing the only conversation between us, Sam nods. "Yeah. I turned into my own father."

"What do you mean?"

"He was never home when I was growing up. He worked long hours at NASA. He was obsessed with work. And after he left NASA, he was obsessed with all of this conspiracy stuff."

"Did you go into the family business then?"

He shakes his head, pulling back the corners of his mouth in a grimace. "I was obsessed with making an impact for God. And I wasn't home enough for my kids, who now resent God. And I destroyed my marriage. So, yeah, I have regrets. What about you?"

"Do you know anyone who tried to commit suicide?" I keep my tone casual. This isn't something I usually discuss. Okay, never.

"Yeah." Sam rubs the back of his neck.

"How?" At Sam's confused look, I clarify, "Rope? Pills? Shotgun? Razorblade?"

"A guy in my church asphyxiated himself in the garage. He'd wracked up huge credit-card debts and couldn't see a way out."

"It's a gentle way, isn't it? Like pills. But the rest are more violent . . . less likely someone will stop them, as if an anger burns inside them, as if there's no going back for them."

"You've given it a lot of thought."

I nod.

He slows our pace as we round the bend and aim for the parking lot outside the observatory. "How did your mom do it? Or how do they think she did it?"

"Pills."

"So it could have been accidental."

My throat contracts.

"Or could Howard be right? Was it like Marilyn Monroe? Did she overdose herself, or did someone do it for her?"

I cross my arms over my chest. My thoughts churn into a solid condemnation. "I've tried it myself."

"What? Suicide?" Sam glances over at me but doesn't ask any questions. He maintains a silence as if waiting for me to fill in the blanks. I'm not sure what makes me open this can of bad memories. Maybe it's because he's a minister. Maybe I'm silently asking if I'm beyond help.

"I never slit my wrists or anything." I hold out my hands, shoving the arms of my sweatshirt to my elbows and show him the insides of my forearms as if he wants proof of some kind. Shivering, I slide the sleeves back down to my wrists and shrug. "But I did stupid . . . crazy things. I took chances most people—most sane people—most people who want to live wouldn't think of trying." I draw a shuddering breath. "I don't know why I'm telling you this."

"It's okay."

"Do you get confessions a lot because you're a pastor?"

"I always thought it was because I have big ears."

The sound of my laughter is muffled in the fog. His ears aren't big, but his heart might be. "Maybe it's just that you're good at using them"—I touch my pierced earring—"not just for decorations."

He glances at the building to our left. "Want to get a soda?"

"Sounds good. And maybe a T-shirt at the gift shop."

"They have them. No aliens though. My son wanted an alien T-shirt when he came. Thought that would be cool. But we couldn't find one."

"No little green men, huh?" I laugh.

"Or gray bug-eyed creatures."

Turning toward the observatory, I study the plain brick building. "I suppose the observatory has to maintain some dignity. Why is every rendering of aliens some weird green or gray creature with a big balloon-shaped head and tiny spindly body?"

Sam laughs this time. "Gravity."

I eye him. "Gravity?"

"Sure. It's different on every planet. I would imagine more or less gravity would effect the ol' bod."

"That's an interesting theory. Outside the door I hesitate. Sam takes that as a demand for him to hold the door for me and he jogs around me, pulls open the door. But I need to say this to him, and its too heavy to share during a soda. I swerve sideways and stand beside a dark plateglass window. "My mom died when I was nine."

Sam releases the door and it closes on its own. He walks toward me. "Go on."

I shrug, feeling vulnerable and unsure. "Well, afterward . . . my whole life changed. And I don't know, I didn't worry so much about dying. My mother went to sleep and just didn't wake up. So it didn't seem painful. And honestly I just wanted to be with her." I keep the real reason to myself, not ready to take that step. "Maybe I was defying God or something."

"Challenging the Almighty?"

"Could be."

"But you managed to survive all your thrill-seeking ways. Or are you still bent on destruction?"

"Sometimes." A smile pulls its way out of me. I wait while a family hustles past us and into the observatory. I watch the smallest child being pushed in a stroller. He's a roundheaded blond with cherubic cheeks and pink lips. "What curbed most of my destructive behavior was having a baby." I turn my attention back to Sam. "In a way, Ginger saved me. Suddenly my life changed again. I didn't want to do anything stupid. I didn't want to abandon her. I didn't want to leave her the way—" My throat closes on the rest of my words. I stare down at the concrete sidewalk, notice the butt of a cigarette, and nudge it with the toe of my boot.

"The way your mother left you?"

I reach past Sam for the door to the observatory, but he beats me, pulls it open, and waits for me to enter. I enter the warmth of the building quickly, as if the past is a place I can leave in my rearview mirror and it will disappear over the horizon. "So"—as we flash our stickers to the receptionist, I try to make light of all I've admitted to—"I'm an open-and-shut case, huh?"

"I wouldn't say that." He points me toward a small refreshment area with tables and chairs scattered throughout the open room. "Your reactions make sense. But even if they didn't, you were dealing with emotions that far outweighed rational thought."

I find us an empty table as Sam grabs two sodas out of a refrigerated container and pays at the counter. He sets a plastic container in front of me and settles into the chair on the opposite side of the table. First he unscrews the top of my soda, then his own. A consummate gentleman. My dates, not that this is one, haven't always been so considerate.

After a long pull on his Coca-Cola, his throat working up and down rhythmically, he leans back in his chair and studies me for a moment. "I'm no counselor, Bryn, but I've seen a lot as a pastor. The loss of a parent leads kids to do strange things. Crazy things. Anger can often be the culprit."

"My mother didn't intend to die that night. I'm sure of it." I ignore his raised eyebrow. "So I don't think I was angry at her."

"Everybody goes through the stage of anger at some point. Deep grief causes kids to act out. No explanation is good enough for why a parent dies. It can cause fear, anger, anxiety, all sorts of disorders. But maybe if Howard was right, if someone else was responsible for your mother's death, then maybe you were simply angry at them."

His comment hits too close to its mark. I try to shrug it off. "The ubiquitous *them* again, eh?"

"Maybe." Sam pushes his thumb along the grooves of the soda bottle, concentrating on it rather than me.

"When Ginger was born, I became more cautious. But I also wanted to make a difference. Life is short, or so I learned. And I wanted to make an impact whether I had one year or a hundred.

My mom only had twenty-eight. Her life was too short. But in a way, I thought shorter was better."

"Why's that?"

I sip my Diet Coke and feel it fizz its way over my tongue. Its biting taste makes me grimace as I swallow. "If you're given a long life, then shouldn't you have something to show for it? I don't mean money or a grand house, fame or fortune. I mean, shouldn't you have made a greater impact?"

Averting my gaze from Sam, I lift my shoulders, try to stretch the kinks and knots out of the muscles. Why did I share so much of my fears to this man I hardly know? I roll the soda around in the condensation making the tabletop wet and slick. Nearby a mother slides a straw into a milk box, her impatient child grunting and grabbing for it.

"Much is required of those who have been given much. And time, I'd say, is about the most wonderful gift, isn't it?"

Maybe he does understand. There's something about him that makes it seem as if he identifies with my thoughts, fears, and questions. Sorrowful lines etch his face. And yet he doesn't seem disheartened or miserable. He acts comfortable in his own skin and strangely at peace. It's an odd concurrence, especially with Howard being his father. "But"—I pause long enough to take another sip and organize my thoughts—"what if . . . ? What if . . . ?" I can't manage to push the question out of my mouth. One last try. "What if there *is* an unforgivable sin?"

He mulls the question over for a moment or two, sips his drink, then looks right at me with that penetrating gaze. "Bryn, I stared into the heart of that question myself. If there is an unforgivable sin, then I certainly have committed it." He straightens an arm, making his elbow pop and flexing his muscles. "I only wanted to serve, to do some good. For years I watched my father carry out what he believed to be his mission. But I couldn't see how his mission did any good. It certainly hadn't helped our family. He lost his job at NASA. My mother had to work two jobs to make ends meet. So

I took a different path. I got into the ministry because I foolishly thought I could make a difference and help others. I wanted to be useful. There was a cause greater than me that I could be a part of. But when you can't help your own family . . . well, I got caught up in my mission, too, just like Howard, and failed my family. There came a time when it seemed as if I was only capable of making errors. I never wanted to be like my father, but somehow I ended up just like him."

I cup my hands around the cold bottle and feel a shivering begin inside me. "I don't know enough about my mother to know if I'm like her or not."

"So that's why you're here."

"And that's why I can't leave."

Chapter Eleven

My cell phone rings. The caller ID reveals it's the nursing home. "I have to take this."

Without waiting for a response, I leave Sam drinking his soda and rush outside the observatory into the misty cold. As I snap open the phone, I'm aware of my heart pounding. "This is Bryn."

"Ms. Seymour," a thick, Caribbean accent fills my ear like cotton, "this is Beatrice. Miss Cora's nurse."

"Yes, of course." I walk past a granite sundial in the courtyard of the observatory, my footsteps rushed and clipped. Clouds hover over the building and parking lot, preventing shadows from forming. My limbs suddenly feel as if I've run a marathon. I brace myself for bad news. "Is something wrong? Is she okay?"

"She is comfortable. No need to worry about that. But I thought you should know she is having trouble swallowing."

I stare out at the mountainous terrain surrounding me, the rugged hills and rocky hillsides, sparse at times with vegetation, then thick with it. My thoughts bump along like a Jeep jouncing cross-country. I try to digest the information about my grandmother.

"She choked on her oatmeal just this morning. And last night on her applesauce. Dr. Rodriguez ran a simple procedure to be sure nothing is obstructing her esophagus. All clear there. But frankly, Ms. Seymour"—compassion thickens Beatrice's voice—"this is typical for Alzheimer's patients. Their mind forgets people and events. But their body also begins to forget all those common functions you and I take for granted."

"I understand. And I appreciate you calling." My own throat begins to close. I glance toward the parking lot, calculating how long it will take me to get back to the hotel, check out, and drive back to Austin. "I'm out of town at the moment, Beatrice. A few hours away." A cool breeze brushes against my face. Guilt spreads through me. I'm light-years away from where I should be. I should never have come here on this foolish, selfish trek. What am I doing chasing down the past when there is so little of the present left? "But I'll come home immediately."

"Oh, no, ma'am. Please, do not interrupt your plans. It is no emergency. Miss Cora's resting. She is comfortable. I will be monitoring her carefully. If she continue to not eat, then Dr. Rodriguez will be calling you. Just know you might have to make a decision about a feeding tube."

I squeeze my eyes shut. It's been three years since we took care of all the particulars that Nana's doctor recommended. As if building a dam piece by piece, we prepared the foundational structure, speculated, calculated all the decisions that must be carefully thought through before the moment arrived. That moment when it's too painful to think and the emotions spill over and flood the soul. Nana made her own decisions, planting them in one season of her life. I watched stoically, helping water her wishes, knowing it would make it easier and yet more difficult someday when she entered her final season, and I would have to harvest them alone. "My grandmother made a Living Will before she came to your facility," I explain to Beatrice over the phone. "She requested . . ." The words stick in my mouth, but I have to adhere to Nana's wishes. I can't allow my own emotions to alter the course set before us. "No extreme measures."

"I will be checking her file then for the paperwork. Please do not worry. I will be taking good care of Miss Cora."

Holding the cell phone against my palm, squeezing it hard, I walk away from the observatory, my thoughts trailing behind and racing ahead. It feels as if the fog floating over the sidewalk has penetrated my brain. Nana's slow decline has forced me to wonder if what happened to my mother wasn't better, kinder than the painful disintegration of a once active mind. Momma's death was peaceful. And yet I've reported on other similar events that resulted in vomiting, aspiration, and hospitalization before the body succumbed to pneumonia.

Alzheimer's terrorizes its victims, bombing memories with cruel intent.

Nana once was strong, stoic even. Most of the time concentration and wariness masked her face. Her mouth, thin lips pursed together with fine lines fanning outward, rarely stretched into a smile. She faced life head-on into the wind, bracing herself for what she often considered inevitable heartache.

Maybe the crumbling started when her husband didn't return from WWII. Maybe more blows came with being a single mother, determined to protect her only child. But it wasn't until years later, when her features were creased and set like stone, that heartbreak jackhammered her until something irrevocably broke.

"Does Nana ever laugh?" I asked Momma one afternoon. I'd strapped on my metal roller skates and zipped along the sidewalk in front of our apartment. The skates clanked and clattered as I clomped over to where she had spread out a blanket on the ground and was reading. I wish I could remember now what book. I'd like to know what she read, what she liked, but Nana sold or gave away most of Momma's belongings after she died.

Momma turned the page without looking up. "Not much."

I plopped down beside her, sticking my legs out straight, my once shiny skates scarred from use. I rolled my ankles inward and banged them together, liking the clattering of the wheels, until Momma put a hand on my leg.

"How come Nana doesn't laugh or smile?"

"She just doesn't."

"But why?"

Momma sighed and snapped the book closed, which I now remember had a library sticker and plastic clear jacket over the hardback cover. "Why all the questions, Bryn-who-what-where-why-when?"

That was Momma's nickname for me. I was a reporter long before I majored in journalism. The time I sometimes spent with Nana was quiet. Boring. She didn't like the noise of television. She didn't like incessant chattering or all of my silly questions. She liked to ask occasional questions. "How is school? What grade are you making in math? Don't you have any homework? What book are you reading now?" Her clipped, focused questions highlighted what was different about my life with Momma.

Lots of times Momma would laugh about funny faces and silly dreams. She'd turn on *Laugh-In* and we'd roll around on the floor giggling hysterically. She'd crank up the radio and dance around the apartment to the Beatles's "Penny Lane" or Simon and Garfunkel's "Mrs. Robinson."

But some days Momma's features stretched downward. She barely spoke. She'd glare at the phone as if willing it to ring. And she'd drink.

"Nana just seems sad," I stated on that long-ago day, knowing even then that the same could be true of Momma. I never dared ask her any of my usual questions on those days. I tiptoed around, trying not to be seen or heard, not complaining if Momma forgot to fix dinner or tuck me in bed.

"Nana's had a rough life."

Had Momma had a difficult one, too? Was Momma's silliness her effort to be different from Nana? Maybe sadness was a part of her fiber, the way it was Nana's. Maybe it ran in families like blue eyes and freckles.

"It's made her indomitable."

I tilted up my chin toward the bluish white summer sky. "What's in-dom-i-table mean?"

"Stubborn."

One afternoon I rode home carrying Momma's and my library books in the white wicker basket perched on my handlebars. I cut through the apartment buildings and climbed the concrete steps to the second floor. I opened the door with my key and found Momma in her room, beer on the bathroom counter, red fingernail polish in her hand. My friend Jamie had asked me to play, but with one glance at Momma, I knew she wasn't about to drive me over to my friend's house. And I wasn't allowed to have friends over.

"They give me a headache," Momma said if I dared to ask for a play date.

"We'll be quiet," I once promised.

"No way."

So I quit asking. On this day, slinking into my bedroom, I pulled out my record player, then thought better of it. Momma wouldn't like the noise. So I sat at my desk and doodled, but voices from the den filtered into my room. Sharp, angry voices. Momma's voice was easily distinguishable; I recognized the high-pitched and demanding tones that were often aimed at me. But there was another level to her voice that I didn't recognize. It sounded like pleading, a shrillness that struck me like icy cold on my front teeth.

The competing voice was that of a stranger, deeper and male, brusque and jagged, like the edge of a saw I'd seen Nana use at her house. I crept toward my bedroom door on my hands and knees, the shag carpet rough on my scabbed knees. Pressing my chest flat on the floor, I tried to peer through the crack at the bottom of the door, but I could only see the gold fibers of the den carpet. I'm not sure how long I lay there listening, trying to follow the conversation that went from whispered, heated tones to shrieking and crying. The man mumbled, which made deciphering what he said nearly impossible.

"You don't know what you're asking." He stood close to my door, and I could see the shadow of his shoes.

"I don't, huh? What about me? I'm the last person you consider in all of this."

Then their footsteps, muffled against the carpet, moved away. To the kitchen? Or Momma's bedroom, situated across the den from mine? Maybe I simply wasn't used to listening to that deep bass range that came with the territory of men, since at that time my dealings with men were fairly limited to the principal at school, whom I avoided as much as possible, and the fathers of any friends who came to PTA meetings or Open House.

Then the front door slammed. I flinched, my skin shrinking. Silence resonated, seeping under the doorway and into my room, until my breath filled my ears. It swelled inside the apartment as if the walls would topple under the strain. Suddenly I feared Momma had left me alone.

Scrambling to my feet, I opened my bedroom door. As I came out of my room searching for her, one tiny step at a time, my heart felt heavy . . . too heavy to beat properly. What would happen to me if Momma left?

It's not like I'd never been left alone before. Sometimes Momma couldn't be home when I got off the school bus, and I let myself into the apartment with my own key. "It's like you're a college girl," Momma would say. But I never felt big and grown up during those times. Instead, I jumped at every noise—neighbors calling out to one another, a phone ringing in the downstairs apartment, or the clomp of footsteps on the stairs. Sometimes I called Nana at her work. "Hi, Nana, whatcha doin'?"

"I'm working, Brynda. Don't you have some homework to do?"

I didn't, but I'd say, "Yes," and that would end the call and my lifeline to the outside world until Momma would come home.

So I wasn't sure what to do if Momma had actually left the apartment without telling me where she'd gone or when she'd get back. If I called Nana, she might ask where Momma was and get angry. I'd heard her lecturing Momma at times about being a parent. "You can't just go off and do whatever you please, Jennifer. You have responsibilities. Obligations." And then there'd just be more yelling.

But by the time I stepped fully into the living room, my fears amplified. Momma lay on the floor, her arms and legs stretched outward like some TV show I'd seen where a chalk outline had been drawn around a dead body. My pulse pounded in my ears. I stumbled forward and fell to my knees beside her, clutched at her arm. "Momma!" But my voice only produced a croaked sound. "Momma?"

After what seemed like an eternity but must have only been a few seconds, she lifted her head and turned toward me. Relief washed over me. She was here. She was okay. But her eyes had a strange cast, as if she wasn't really seeing me, as if she wasn't in her body anymore. One side of her face was red and puffy like she'd scraped her cheek over the rough carpet.

"Momma? What's wrong?"

Without answering, she pushed upward, her back flat like when she'd pretended to be a horse for my cowgirl amusement. She rocked there for a moment, as if gaining the strength to get to her feet. Her head lolled between her shoulders. Finally she shifted and staggered to her feet, teetering into the middle of the room. I hovered nearby, not knowing what to do, how to help.

With slow, plodding footsteps, she went to the front door and snapped the lock into place, tugging on the knob to make sure it was secure. She leaned against the door, pressing one side of her face against the wood. Her shoulders started to shake, and I heard a slight gasp, as if she was strangling. She pushed away, her movements halting and awkward, and then lurched into the kitchen. She clunked a glass on the counter, then dragged a chair over, the legs making a scratching noise against the linoleum. She climbed onto the chair and pulled a bottle from the cabinet above the refrigerator. The brown liquid sloshed around inside the bottle and slurped over the edge of the glass, making a puddle on the counter.

Momma didn't bother to clean up the mess. Instead, she opened the freezer, twisted the plastic ice tray, and plunked a handful of ice into the glass. She didn't bother getting ice for the second glass. By the third, Momma's tears flowed freely down her face, and she swiped at her snot sloppily.

I handed her a tissue, tried to hold her hand, to soothe her wrinkled brow that was hot and sweaty. Her mascara ran like dark, murky rivers, pooling beneath her eyes, giving her a haunted, frightened look. "Momma, what's wrong?"

"Go to bed, baby. Just go to bed."

"But it's only six o'clock." That's what the little clock on the oven showed.

"Then watch TV."

News dominated every channel. Walter Cronkite droned on and on about the mission to the moon and what a historical event this would be, but I couldn't concentrate on his words or the interviews he conducted with experts. Even though I sat on the floor, my face turned toward the screen, my gaze slipped sideways to check on Momma with every snuffle and shuddering breath she uttered.

She wobbled getting up from the sofa, grabbed the wall, then the kitchen table, tottered from one to the other like a pinball, and poured another drink. I studied her jerky movements, the way she wavered on unsteady legs, how she spilled the brown liquid onto her white shirt. I already knew she wouldn't be making any dinner, not even macaroni and cheese, and I'd have to sneak into the kitchen later to slap together a peanut butter and jelly sandwich.

"Want me to call Nana?"

"No!" Momma tripped coming back into the living room. Her drink sloshed over the side and made a wet spot on the carpet. She said a word she'd told me never to say. "Bryn! Put your junk away."

But there wasn't a toy on the floor. She collapsed onto the couch, leaning heavily against the armrest, rubbing her forehead. Still, with her other hand, she clutched the upgraded tall glass and drank big gulps. "My head hurts."

"I'll get you something." I ran to Momma's bathroom, pushing aside the blue eye shadow, toothpaste tube, brush, and hair spray spread out along the counter. Searching through the mirrored cabinet, I found a prescription bottle Momma used when she was sad. I poured some blue capsules into my hand, then thought maybe she needed some aspirin. Another prescription bottle hid behind perfume, and I poured some of those tablets out. Loaded down with medicine, I pretended I was Momma's nurse.

She was still weeping when I held out my hand toward her, the capsules beginning to stick to my palm. "Here, Momma. Maybe this will help."

She wiped her hand under her nose. It took a moment for her eyes to focus on the pills.

"I didn't know which ones would help . . . or how many."

Her hand swiped at mine, missed, then she clawed at the pills. A couple fell between the sofa cushions. She shoved them into her mouth and washed them all down with what was left of her drink. Then she patted my hand. She tried to smile, but her face was puffy and distorted, a garish clown with streaks of makeup smeared across her face. "I love you, Bryn-who . . . when—" Her gaze shifted toward the television, and Walter Cronkite intruded on her nickname, making her mix up the words that usually rolled off her tongue. "Who . . ."

Momma's tears eventually dried. I sat beside her, rubbing her temples. Her hand relaxed and the glass tumbled from her fingers. It bounced off the sofa and fell onto the floor, cushioned by the carpet, then rolled a few inches. I picked it up, rinsed it in the sink and dried it. When I returned, Momma slung out an arm toward me. I held her hand as her eyelids grew heavy and she drifted off to sleep.

For a while I went to my room, listened to the Bloody Red Baron song on my gold record player and threw my softball against the wall, catching it with my glove. The *th-thunk, th-thunk* somehow soothed the tension knotting the muscles along my spine. The moon cast a milky glow over my room and toys like fairy dust. I stared up at it through the window and pictured a rocket circling the giant white ball.

When the *Eagle* finally had landed and Neil Armstrong stepped down the ladder of the lunar module, Momma was sleeping and I moved closer to the television, letting the moment crowd out my concerns and fears.

Later I pulled a blanket over Momma so her bare legs wouldn't get cold. I climbed into my pajamas, brushed my teeth, and made a pallet on the floor near her. Her breathing sounded deep and slow, so deep she started to snore, her mouth slanted open. I started to giggle but then stopped myself, not wanting to wake her. Eventually my eyes drooped. With the television still going, I fell asleep on the floor.

Something, I don't know what, woke me.

I jerked up and blinked against the gray dawn. A flickering light came from the television, where an old-time Western with bad guys in black hats and the good guys in white chased each other through swinging saloon doors. The clomp of horses' hooves and the *pop-pop-pop* of revolvers echoed through the apartment. I glanced toward Momma, realized she was still asleep and, not wanting to wake her, I turned off the television. The clock in the kitchen said it was after seven. Hungry, since I hadn't eaten dinner the night before, I poured a bowl of Captain Crunch and ate standing up in the kitchen. I tiptoed around the apartment, waiting for her to wake up.

By the time Captain Kangaroo signed off, I shook Momma's shoulder to wake her, but she didn't move. She didn't roll away from me with a groan and attempt to snuggle back into her dreams as she usually did on Saturday mornings. This time, she lay very still.

Too still.

Touching her arm, her skin felt cool. I jolted backward.

For a long time I stared at her, watched her chest. But it didn't move up and down as it should. I took a hesitant step forward. "Momma?"

Nothing. No response. Fear welled up inside me turning my insides to a cold liquid. "Momma!" My voice unraveled into panic.

I ran to her room, where her yellow phone was plugged into the wall. My hand shook as I dialed Nana's number. It wasn't until the ninth ring that I realized I'd made the mistake of calling her house, not her office. I hung up and dialed again.

"Nana?" My voice trembled when she finally answered, "Cora, Service Department." "Nana!" Panic tightened around my throat like a fist. "Momma won't wake up."

She called the police, who arrived long before she could make the drive from Austin to Houston. I was sitting on the sofa where Momma had been laying when Nana came through the door, her eyes panic-wide, her mouth set in a grim line. "I'm the child's grandmother."

The police officer sitting with me nodded and moved away from us. Then Nana wrapped her arms around me fiercely, protectively, holding me as tight as possible, her hand smoothing the hair down my back. Suddenly all the effort it had taken to hold myself together shook loose. Trembling like I'd never stop, I held onto her as if she were the only solid, steadfast presence in my life. My face pressed against her flowery cotton blouse, the white button pushing into my cheekbone. I can still remember the faded yellows and blues darkening with my tears. "I-it w-w-was . . ." I sobbed, strings of spittle attaching to the corners of my mouth, ". . . an accident."

"Yes, my love, it was. It was just an accident."

The police gathered the evidence—the empty liquor and pill bottles. I heard murmurings. "Did she leave a note?" Long, sad faces filled my vision. Sympathetic eyes gazed down at me. But it wasn't until later, years later, that I understood what they were discussing and hypothesizing.

It wasn't until I became an adult that I could see the event as an accident. I hadn't murdered my own mother. Not intentionally. She hadn't committed suicide, either. Not in the real sense of the word. At least not in my eyes. She wouldn't have died that night if I hadn't handed her all those pills. Instead she would have woken with a bad headache, a fuzzy tongue, and a green stomach.

Did Momma really know what she was doing? Or did alcohol impair her decision? Did she want to die? To leave me? Or did she simply want the incessant pain from whatever or whomever had inflicted it on her to go away? It's an answer I'll never know. But even as my capacity to understand the scope of the situation grew over the years, the guilt never abandoned me. It resides deep inside me like a beacon that draws me back again and again to its pulsing center.

I know now that Nana didn't understand what I was telling her then. She didn't know I wasn't asking if it was an accident.

I was pleading with her.

Confessing.

Chapter Twelve

A soft clearing of a throat brings me out of my past and into the present, where my boots are set solidly on the observatory's stone walkway. Engravings mark each brick, like miniature tombstones, donated in honor or loving memory—another way to memorialize a loved one.

Momma's grave lies in Austin, where she was buried next to her father, whom she never even knew. The granite marker lists her birth and death dates and bears the inscription, "Loving Daughter, Beloved Mother." A preacher read the obituary I wrote the morning after she died. I remember feeling the congregation collectively watching me as my simplistic words echoed throughout the church. The same feeling washes over me now, as if my skin will burst, as I sense more than seeing Sam standing beside me, watching me. "I'm sorry."

"Everything okay?"

I slide the toe of my boot beneath the name on a brick. "Thomas Bently." Nothing else. "Do you know the difference," I ask Sam, not yet daring to look at him, "between a cemetery and a graveyard?"

He rubs the back of his neck. "Did someone die?"

"Most people don't know the difference."

"Isn't a graveyard attached to a church?"

"Did they teach you that in seminary?" My gaze lifts toward the Davis Mountains as I try to pull myself back to the here and now, but my emotions are deep and firmly planted in the grave with my mother. Sam stands so close to me I can feel the heat radiating off his skin. I push my hair back from my face.

"Bad news?"

I glance at him. "What?"

He uses my unfinished Diet Coke that he brought from the refreshment area to point toward my cell phone. "The phone call. You didn't come back to the café."

I glance down at the cell phone still in my hand and slide it into my hip pocket. "Sorry about that. Uh, no . . . yes. It wasn't unexpected."

"Did someone die?" He hands me my drink.

"Not yet."

His gaze focuses on my hand, my thumb thumping against the side of the plastic bottle. As if detached, I watch him tuck the Diet Coke under his arm and in a slow, languid move pull my hand into his. Rough, working-man's hands, calluses lie smooth and thick across his palm, but his touch soothes a rough patch in my soul. Beginning with a tiny circle at the base of my hand, he loops around and around in a way that mesmerizes me, brings me fully back into the present. A quickening stirs deep in my belly. I curl my fingers inward and pull away from him.

He clears his throat, meets my gaze solidly without even a blink of regret. "Are you ready?"

As if awakening from a forbidden dream, I rub my palm against the back of my jeans but I can't seem to erase his touch and its unnerving effect on me. "It was my grandmother," I blurt out as I tap my cell phone. "She has Alzheimer's."

The line of his mouth thins and he nods as if understanding, as if he sees right through the barriers I've erected to my vulnerabilities, my weaknesses. His brown eyes have multiple layers and tones in their depths, like the rugged, ancient bark of a cedar.

I take a step backward, away from Sam. "I need to talk to Howard before I go back to Austin."

"I know where he is."

"Good." I turn away, walk straight for his truck. It's my way of locking away my feelings and hiding my thoughts.

In a quiet awkwardness we drive back down the mountain, passing through Fort Davis. I fix my gaze out the window but the sage brush is only a green blur. When he takes a turnoff which I don't recognize, I glance in his direction. Where are we going? Another joint that requires the top secret password, covert knock, or possibly another blindfold to enter?

With my heart back in Austin with Nana, I can't gather enough energy to worry about my own welfare. Two more turns down deserted country roads, he finally stops at a small cabin. I squeeze the door handle in an effort to pull myself into the present and any danger I might find myself. "Where are we?"

"My place."

I stare through the dusty windshield at the small cabin built with what looks like hand-hewn logs and local stones for a chimney. "But I thought you lived with your father."

"I stay there when he needs me. But I bought the land, built this place to give us both some space. I built it actually." Pride glimmers in his brown eyes. "It's kept me busy for the last few months."

Now I know where those calluses came from, as well as the sinewy muscles along his shoulders and arms. "*You* built this?"

"Don't be too impressed till you see it up close. Besides, it was a kit."

"A kit? Like a model airplane?"

He laughs. "On a slightly bigger scale. And without wings or wheels."

Dragging my gaze away from the cabin, I search for Howard's

station wagon or any other signs—like a crop circle—of his landing nearby. "Where's Howard?"

"He'll be here soon."

"How do you know?"

"It's Tuesday. And almost lunchtime. Which means, it's time for his spit-and-whittle club to meet."

"Spit and whittle?"

He laughs again, a deep-throated laugh that is as warm and toasty as his cabin appears. "You'll see."

"Should I bring my own carving knife?"

"Not necessary. But feel free to spit if you like."

"Great." I step out of Sam's truck and jerk to a stop. A shaggy beast—what looks like a miniature Chewbacca—stands a few feet away from me. Its beady brown eyes narrow on me. But a pink tongue lolls out of its mouth. "Uh, Sam? Is this your . . . uh . . . dog?"

He comes around the back end of the truck. "He doesn't belong to anyone. He's been hanging around for a couple of weeks."

"Shouldn't you call animal control?"

He dips a knee to the ground. "Why?" He pulls a dog treat from his jacket pocket and stretches out his hand. "Here, boy."

The dog whines and sits on his haunches.

"Come on, boy. I won't hurt you."

The dog's tail sweeps along the ground. He crouches low, then belly crawls like an Army soldier toward Sam, who murmurs encouragement.

"Be careful," I call.

The shaggy dog stops, looks at me, then back toward Sam. He sniffs the air, then continues crawling through the brown and red leaves on his course toward Sam. Pushing upright, the dog watches Sam, his eyes worried. He sniffs Sam's palm, snatches the treat, and makes a quick getaway. Once at a safe distance, he chomps on the treat, licking his sagging jowls.

"So what's his name?"

"He's not *my* dog. He'll wander off someday. Move onto some other sucker."

"You carry treats in your pocket. You should name him."

"What would you suggest?"

I study the giant dog for a moment. "How about Goliath?"

Chuckling, Sam stands. "Come on, let's go inside."

I follow him up the porch steps and inside his cabin. The decorations are sparse but it's clean and smells of pine. A living room opens to a small kitchen. Down a narrow hallway are two doors, one of which I assume is his bedroom.

"Howard?"

"We're alone." Sam shrugs out of his jacket and takes mine, tossing them both over the back of his leather sofa. Our jacket arms intermingle and I separate them. "Are you hungry?"

I squint at him. Why did he bring me here? Uneasiness settles into my bones, making my movements stiff. I'm usually the aggressive one in a relationship. "Not really."

He tugs open his refrigerator. "You sure? You didn't eat much breakfast. Want a sandwich?"

Watching him do ordinary tasks gives me a modicum of security, false though it may be. I follow him into the kitchen. "Can I help?"

"Grab the bread, will you? It's in the pantry." He nods toward a closed door.

Closing my hand over the knob, I smile. "And I thought this led to some secret compartment."

"The basement where I keep radio equipment to contact aliens?" He grins.

"Exactly." Instead, I find an oversized container of dog food and giant box of doggie treats. Smiling to myself, I search the neatly stocked shelves with cans of Campbell's tomato soup and boxes of Kraft Mac and Cheese to find a loaf of bread.

"If you want a soda or something, help yourself."

I reach past two boxes of pink—not yellow—lemonade and

grab a soda from a stack at the bottom of the pantry. Sam pulls deli meats, sliced cheese, tomatoes, and lettuce out of the fridge. In a few minutes' time, we have a short assembly line going, slathering mayo on rye and slapping on roast beef, sliced turkey, or ham. My shoulder brushes his arm, and I'm suddenly aware of his physicality—his strong hands, muscular arms. And I remember him shirtless.

A lettuce leaf falls to the floor. Before I can pick it up, Sam scoops it up, tosses it in the sink like an outfielder grabbing a grounder.

"You've done this before. Did you work in a deli?"

"Wednesday prayer groups. Church picnics. Flipping burgers and making sandwiches gave me a hall pass from the never-ending games of Bible trivia." He swings around and grabs two glasses out of a cabinet. "Ice is in the freezer."

As I plunk ice chunks into the glasses and pour the soda, it crackles and fizzes. "Lots of pressure on a pastor to win, huh? I didn't know there was an official game of Bible trivia available."

"Not in a box . . . or not that I know of. Hey, maybe you'd be a good teammate . . . since you know about Goliath."

"That's about the extent of my theological knowledge. So I'm guessing people asked you pesky questions."

"Sure, you know, 'How'd Adam and Eve's kids find spouses and marry?'"

"And you have the answers to these tough questions?"

"I flipped burgers, remember?"

"Did you fail that class at seminary?"

"More likely played hooky." He gives me a wink.

Laughing, I squeeze mustard onto a slice of bread. "So what about those tough questions? How do you . . . I don't know, believe in all of that? If there's so much questioned?"

"There are always questions, Bryn. More than you or I could come up with. You've never made a decision, like inoculations for your daughter's health, without knowing all the answers about if they're safe or not? Or did you go on faith?"

I lean against the counter and watch him add ham and cheese to the mustard-coated bread. "You're not like any preacher I've ever known."

"Have you known a lot?"

"Not in the biblical sense, if that's what you're asking."

He pauses, hands stilling, and his gaze slides toward me.

An electrical current passes between us, and I rush forward, unwilling to acknowledge it. "The preachers I've come across seem to believe *they* have all the answers to life's tough questions."

He shakes his head and carefully folds a piece of sliced ham. "No one knows everything, Bryn." He holds out another slice of bread. "Only God does."

But I hesitate before taking the bread. Several sandwiches are cut and piled onto a plate. "Don't you think we have enough? Or are you planning on feeding Goliath, too?"

Grinning, he washes his hands and cleans the knife. "It's for the spit-and-whittle gang. Remember?" He pauses, cocks his head sideways. "Get the door, will ya?"

Frowning, I wonder how he knew someone was there before they knocked. Does he have bionic hearing? Maybe I was concentrating too hard on Sam, which is more than slightly unsettling. Still, I hesitate before going to the door. "Is someone going to spit on me?"

"Not on purpose."

"That's comforting."

When I pull open the front door, I'm greeted by a short man with bushy gray hair, scruffy beard, and thick Coke-bottle glasses. His magnified eyes widen more as his gaze lifts slowly toward my face. He takes a step back, looks around as if checking to see if he's in the right location. "Who are *you?*"

I smile, thinking birds of a feather—or in this case dinosaurs—flock together. But what do relics do? "You must be Howard's friend. Come on in." I hold out my hand. "I'm Bryn Seymour."

He hesitates, then steps forward and shakes the tips of my fingers as if he's uncomfortable with human contact. "Ralph."

"Hi, Ralph." I pause, hoping he'll supply a last name, which he doesn't. Maybe I could use this impromptu convention of social outcasts for my next weekend lifestyle article. "How are you?"

As if he suspects *I* might do something out of the ordinary, he inches past me.

"Are you hungry? Sam and I just made a bunch of sandwiches."

When he sees Sam setting the plate of sandwiches on the wooden kitchen table along with a bowl of chips, Ralph's shoulders relax and the deep lines across his forehead soften. "Afternoon, Sam. How is it?"

"Good. How you doin', Ralph?"

"Howard isn't here yet?" Ralph scratches the side of his belly.

"He'll be along any minute." Sam points toward the door. "That could be him. Grab a plate and get started."

Grinning, I quirk an eyebrow at Sam. "You heard somebody?"

Without answering, Sam leaves me alone with this odd little man. Warily, we watch each other for a moment.

"So you come here often to see Howard?"

He crams his hands in his front jeans pockets. "Tuesdays. Noon."

His pant legs are rolled up at the ankle, like he belongs in a 1950s' version of *Lassie*. Either he's in a time warp or he's anticipating another worldwide flood. It makes me wonder if Noah's ancient neighbors once thought he was a conspiracy theorist on the edge of the galaxy, too?

"Bryn"—Sam reenters the kitchen—"this is Larry."

No last name again. It's like a rock-star convention. I expect Sting, Cher, and Elvis to walk through the door at any minute. Is the club's membership list guarded? Larry actually looks relatively normal. He's taller than Ralph, yet half the weight. A chambray shirt hangs on his coat-hanger thin shoulders, and his chest looks concave. Balancing a tray of grapes, strawberries, carrots, and broccoli, he comes to a sudden halt. "Where's Howard?"

"He should be here soon." Sam claps Larry on the back. "Go ahead and grab a plate. Bryn?"

"Yes," Larry nods, "ladies first."

Both Larry and Ralph hang back, giving me plenty of room, and I get the distinct impression that neither wants me going first or a tribute to women. Maybe they believe in the ancient kingdom practice of food testers. If I keel over from one of the sandwiches, then they'll know which to avoid. Ralph douses his hands with a hand sanitizer he produces from his pocket, while Larry hoards the fresh fruit and vegetables for himself. Never one to be shy when food is involved, I grab a paper plate, sandwich, and chips.

We settle around the table, and I realize I'm hungrier than I thought. As I munch chips and bite into a thick turkey sandwich, no one speaks. My gaze meets Sam's and he gives me a broad wink.

He chews and swallows a bite of sandwich. "I've got a question for you guys. Something I've been trying to figure out."

Both Ralph and Larry scrunch up their faces with serious intent.

"Which do you think is heavier, a full moon or a half moon?"

Larry snaps off a carrot stick. "Your dad would probably know that better than us, Sam."

Ralph chews and speaks at the same time. "No, no. There wouldn't be any difference at all. It's a perception thing."

Sam's gaze slides toward me. "What do you think?"

I shrug, suspecting a punch line around the corner.

He grins. "A half moon. The full moon is lighter."

There's a long pause. Ralph chews thoughtfully as if calculating some mathematical equation. A snicker slips out of me and suddenly the older men are staring at me.

Ralph shifts his gaze back to Sam. "It's a joke?"

"Not a very good one." Sam laughs, and the other men slowly join in.

Ralph shakes his head. "You got us with that one." He thumbs toward Sam. "He's always trying to put a joke over on us."

Sam's easy manner coaxes conversation out of Ralph and Larry, using the same gentle approach he works on Goliath. With another joke about jackrabbits and cacti, he pulls a hearty laugh from Larry.

I imagine Sam was a good pastor. There's more to leading a congregation than preaching hell fire and damnation. Or so I always suspected. But Nana's church had a dour preacher who was long in the face and short on grace. Nana pressured me to get baptized. For weeks after I moved in with her, we'd sit in the pew during the invitation, Nana watching me, her eyebrows lifted.

"I don't wanna go down in front of all those people," I told her one Sunday after church.

"Why on earth not? Every one has been praying for you. They'll be delighted and rejoice with you."

"Because." It was a typical ten-year-old response, but still it didn't go over well with Nana.

She marched me into the preacher's office one afternoon after school, leaving me alone. In the big leather chair where he sat me, my feet couldn't reach the floor. Over half-rimmed glasses he stared at me as if *everything* I'd ever done wrong was written on my skin like a giant tattoo. I rubbed my thumb over my forefinger, which had ink stains from school.

After several quiet, uncomfortable minutes, he breathed heavily as if it took more effort than he had. "Well, young lady, your grandmother is worried about you."

"Yes, sir."

"She's worried you'll end up just like your mother." His thick lips lifted in a sneer, as if there could be nothing worse.

Anger surged up inside me like an eruption of hot gases. He didn't know Momma! Or anything about her. Momma was good. And kind.

"Do you know what happens to folks who take their own lives?"

Gripping the arms of the chair, I shook my head, swallowed hard.

He removed his glasses, folded them carefully and leaned over his big, wide desk. I could see tiny red veins in the whites of his eyes. "They burn in hell. That's what."

A trembling started somewhere deep inside me. I didn't know if what he said was true or not. But I knew Momma hadn't killed herself. Her death was my fault. Maybe this big burly preacher could see that just by looking at me. If God would send Momma, good, kind, sweet Momma to hell, then I knew what He'd do to me. I ran out of the preacher's office and all the way back to Nana's house.

The next Sunday, gripped by a tummy ache, I stayed home. The following weeks I experienced a succession of headaches, fever (thanks to sticking the thermometer under hot water), and diarrhea. I'm not sure if Nana gave up on me, but she finally quit asking and let me stay home alone while she went off to hear the sermons. She'd often come home and recount them probably word for word—long, depressing monologues of dos and don'ts that made my belly hurt even more. I wasn't sure why the sermons made Nana feel any better. Or maybe telling me eased the weight of her burden.

Even though Nana was pragmatic, she had a softer tone, full of forgiveness and less condemnation. She came home one Sunday when I was twelve and told me Reverend Do-Right had been caught doing very wrong, but I didn't say a word. Nana quit going to church after that, too. Instead, we would go for hikes or bike rides on Sundays together. The outdoors became our sanctuary, a place for both of us to heal.

"What's she doing here?"

The question jerks me back to the present. I glance around the table at the three men.

Sam offers a smile that curves around charity. "Bryn is a reporter. She's doing a story on Howard."

Ralph peers at me through his thick glasses. "She won't reveal our location, will she?"

"Of course not," I reassure him.

"This is important work." Larry bites off part of a carrot. "It should get out. Someone *has* to tell the masses what's going on under their very noses."

"The masses are too dumb to listen." Ralph takes another sandwich. "But maybe you'll do a story on us, too."

I munch on my sandwich, nodding my head and widening my eyes as if I'm open to the possibility. "And what are you working on?"

Larry swallows the rest of the carrot. "I've been gathering documents on the government coup from the sixties."

I tilt my head, thinking back to my classes on modern history. "In South America?"

"See?" He grabs a broccoli flower. "The young people these days are ignorant of American history! They're clueless about what has happened, the changes that have taken place in our very own government." He waggles the broccoli at me. "Just for your information, Oswald did not act alone."

"Here we go," Sam says out of the corner of his mouth.

"I've written a whole book about it," Larry continues. "Seven hundred thousand words documenting what happened in 1963 and since. And you're probably asking what Kennedy's assassination has to do with Howard's work, but they are connected. Did you know Kennedy was making a deal with the Ruskies to collaborate in space forty years before they ever imagined the space station? Why, the whole Cold War would never have taken place if he'd lived. And as it was, the Cold War was a ruse for corrupt politicians to gain more control over us here in America." He pops the broccoli flower in his mouth and chews at least twenty times before swallowing. "The brainwashing that goes on in our schools . . ." He pulls a pen out of his shirt pocket and pushes his chair back. "Paper!"

Sam locates a yellow legal pad in a nearby drawer. "Here."

Larry begins scribbling furiously on his pad.

Ralph pushes his glasses to the bridge of his nose. He pulls apart his sandwich, inspecting each layer systematically and reconstructs the culinary masterpiece, reminiscent of Howard's inspection of his pancakes. "Larry has a bone he can't let go of."

Clandestinely my gaze meets Sam's across the table. He seems tolerant of these eccentrics, maybe from lifelong practice.

"Trans fats." Larry's pen still moves in rapid-fire fashion. "They'll kill you."

"Don't get him started on the medical profession, food industry, and insurance conspiracy." A piece of lettuce falls out of Ralph's mouth. "You'll never eat again."

"I'm beginning to believe that." I focus on Ralph. "And what are you working on?"

"Following Elvis to his grave," Larry says without looking up.

"He is not dead." Ralph points a fat finger at Larry. "And I'm one step closer to proving he is in the witness protection program." His magnified gaze settles on me, and he swipes a hand over his mouth. "You ever heard how Elvis went to the White House to meet President Nixon?"

"I'm not sure." I'm not up on my Elvis trivia anymore than Bible trivia. "But okay."

"Elvis knew everyone in the entertainment industry and how they were pushing stars into drugs. He'd been pumped full of the stuff for years. Stuff to keep him up. To knock him out. To make him gain weight. To lose weight. He knew the toll that stuff took on a body firsthand. And he was gathering evidence."

My gaze shifts almost instinctively to Sam's, just to gauge his reaction. His features have hardened into a mask that manages to hide his emotions. Does he want to laugh out loud at these conspiracy theories? Or do they irritate him the way his father's obsession does? In less than a second, my attention is back on Ralph and Larry as they rattle on about secret agents, mounting evidence, and the connections between all three of their subjects. As much as I want to tiptoe out of this house and call the men-with-white-straightjackets to haul these guys to a hospital for psychiatric evaluation, I realize I'm no different than they.

I want Howard to tell me my mother was murdered by someone other than her own daughter.

Maybe we're all living in Dream Land.

Chapter Thirteen

I told you I have big ears." Sam grins after he announces Howard's arrival. "Like radars sticking out on either side of my head."

I shake my head and chuckle. Sure enough, as predicted, Howard walks up the back steps onto the porch where we settled after pushing back from the lunch table.

"She asks good questions." Ralph thumbs toward me. It's a compliment I've worked hard to earn throughout the afternoon. At first my questions, I'm embarrassed to admit, were more intent on poking fun or holes into their theories. But instead of finding their theories shallow and insubstantial, I found them to have merit. I haven't bought into them yet as I still have my skepticism squarely in place.

The sun has disappeared behind one of the nearby mountains, but the sky hasn't darkened completely yet. The horizon showcases orange and red hues bleeding into a blue sky. Sam refills our glasses and mugs and brings his father a mug of what appears to be lemonade. Settling back in the metal chair, he tips it backward, balancing on two legs.

"Well, she *is* a reporter." Howard salutes me with the mug.

"Then that makes sense." Larry munches on a carrot.

I want to laugh at these men who approach every subject with a logic that defies reasoning. But, of course, I don't.

Larry leans forward in his metal folding chair, bracing his forearms on his knees. "Come with us tomorrow."

"You sure?" Ralph coughs, his magnified eyes widening. "But—"

"No, she needs to come. I think she'd be game."

"For what?" My gaze bounces between the two—what on earth am I in for now?

"Watch out," Sam warns. "They're the original daredevils."

I know a little something about that. "I'm not afraid."

Larry grins a wide yellow-toothed grin as if he's just trapped me. "You will be."

"They're gliders," Howard explains.

"Hang gliders?"

"Light aircraft." Ralph rocks back and forth. "Larry won the competition here in Marfa two years running."

"Ah, that was in the eighties." Larry shakes his head. "But it's still a thrill. I'll take you up. Or Sam can do it. Think you'll like it."

Remembering Nana and other work waiting for me at home, I question if I should just go home. Is there really a story here for me to pursue? Howard doesn't seem to be forthcoming about my mother. Maybe I should just cut my losses. "I should be getting back to Austin."

"Ah, watch out now." Larry chuckles. "She's backing out."

"Scared," Ralph assesses.

"Don't blame her." Howard holds out his mug to his son for more lemonade. "I'd rather strap a rocket to my back and trust the fools over at NASA than to go up in one of those fly buckets with one of you two."

The other men scoff, coughing and blustering.

A quick glance at Sam reveals humor in his dark eyes.

Making an irrational, highly illogical decision, I smile. "We'll see who cries chicken first."

Ralph slams a hand down on the arm of his rocking chair, tips his head back, and hoots.

Howard looks at his son. "Sam, you better go with them. Make sure these two don't get carried away."

"Don't worry." Though Sam is speaking to his father, he's looking straight at me. "I won't let anything happen to her."

A quickening of my pulse unnerves me more than the thought of falling out of the sky. I can take care of myself. Thank you very much. I always have. But a tiny part of me likes the idea that this particular man doesn't shy away from taking charge and wanting to protect me. It's a new phenomenon. And I'm not sure I particularly like it.

TO GET A HANDLE on my strange emotional attachment to Howard's son, I excuse myself from the deck and make my way to the one bathroom in Sam's cabin. It's a tiny space with room for sink, toilet, and shower. No tub. Only a small rectangular mirror above the sink. There's nothing in the tiny space that reveals who this man is. No cross on the wall or picture of Jesus. No medicine bottles on the counter. No toothbrush revealing a favorite color in its stem. I wash my hands, scrubbing at my curiosity like it's a germ and looking at my own reflection in the plain, unadorned mirror. Is this my reporter's nose sniffing out a story or is it something else?

A closer look reveals the mirror is simply that, not a medicine cabinet hiding behind it. A cabinet down below lures me like a fat worm on a sharp hook would a hungry bass. I run a finger along the top of the smooth wooden door, debating with myself if I should probe further or swim away from my curiosity. Fear is my deciding factor. Fear that I will be drawn even more to this man who is not my type and not what I need.

When I return to the back porch, the chairs are empty, the deck abandoned. Then I hear footsteps clomping up the stairs. Sam.

"Where'd everybody go?"

"They had obligations."

"Even Howard?"

"He rented time at the observatory and needs to be in front of his computer to receive the data."

My disappointment must be obvious because Sam walks toward me. "You'll see them tomorrow."

"I think it would be easier to get an interview with Princess Diana than Howard."

"Princess Diana is dead."

"Exactly."

"Come on. I just fed the dog—"

"You mean, Goliath."

He shrugs. "And if you have time, I'd like to take you to dinner."

"You know"—I follow him toward the front door—"the dog is yours. You can't deny that forever."

"I'd say the choice is Goliath's."

RIDING IN THE CAR in the dark with a man I barely know has never been my idea of a smart move. But I've never shied away from it either, though I usually meet dates for dinner at restaurants rather than allowing them to pick me up at home. Maybe that's holdover paranoia from Nana. Maybe it's that I'm a mother protective of my bear cub. Maybe, on some basic level, it's that I don't trust men. Or maybe it's just my own quirk that keeps me from forming deeply intimate relationships.

Even though I've been seeing Eric for a few years now, I still wouldn't call our relationship deep. We have no commitment between us. There's nothing to stop him from seeing someone else while I'm gone. It occurs to me right then that I'm not particularly bothered by the idea of him seeing someone else. I'm not sure that's a good sign.

Thinking of him now, I wonder if I should feel guilty for the thoughts I've had about Sam. But I slough the concern off like sunburned skin. Thinking isn't doing.

Or is it?

Whatever my warped reasoning, I find myself in Sam's truck as it skims along the highway, the headlights pushing back the darkness by only degrees. If there's one constant out here in far west Texas, the speed limits are higher than anywhere else in the state. Antelopes and tarantulas outnumber the cars on the roadway.

We drive back into Fort Davis where Sam takes me to a Mexican restaurant. He knows a few of the folks dining on enchiladas and tacos. Locals chat across the dining room about baseball and the upcoming football season. The dark-complexioned waitress doesn't know much English. She mostly nods and grins. We decide on the buffet, but Sam notices the guacamole bowl is empty. A few minutes later as we scoop salsa onto chips, the friendly waitress brings us our own special bowl of the green stuff.

"My favorite." I dip a chip into the chunky guacamole right away. "So you know a lot of the people here?"

"Not a lot, but I've been around for a few months. Most of the folks know Howard, and now associate me with him."

"And what do they think about him? Do they see him as some scientist?"

He shrugs. "A crazy nut, I'm guessing. But out here that seems to be par for the course. They care about him and protect him from any even crazier fans that might be looking for him."

"Is that who you think was searching the woods the other night?"

He chews for a minute before swallowing. "I don't know. Could be a high school prank. Could be someone who found his theories on the Internet."

"Or could be . . ."

"Government officials?" He asks the question for me. "Or the Men in Black?"

"It's a legitimate question. Sort of."

Smiling, he pushes back his chair. "Ready to get a plate?"

Once we fill our plates with cheese and beef enchiladas, tacos, and chiles rellenos, we settle back at our table across from each other. For a moment or two, we eat in silence but questions fill my head. I decide to take a different tack.

"It seems to me that you and your dad are at odds on a pretty basic level."

"How's that?"

"He believes in aliens. And to me, that's pretty much against what the Bible preaches."

He leans his forearms against the edge of the table, fork in one hand, knife in the other, and pauses, looking at me with mild curiosity. "How so?"

"You don't agree?"

"Not really. The Bible doesn't talk about aliens one way or another. Some people think Elijah encountered aliens. His prophecies talk about some pretty out-there kind of stuff."

"But you don't believe that."

"I don't know if aliens exist or not. You know, at one time, the church thought Copernicus contradicted the Bible when he said the earth wasn't the center of the universe. But we know now that's ridiculous. And I don't think aliens—the possibility that they exist—does either. If the God of the universe could create this planet with all the animals and people, then why not somewhere else? We miss the boat—" He grins.

"Is that Noah's boat?"

He laughs. "That, or the *Titanic*. Whichever, we miss it when we think *we're* the center of God's universe. We're not. He cares. He loves us. But He can and will survive without us."

"So you don't care if there are aliens or not?"

His lips push outward and into a frown. "Not much. Doesn't change what I think about God."

"Or your father?"

He shrugs and pushes away from the table. "Want something else?"

I shake my head and watch him walk back toward the buffet and reload his plate with more tacos and enchiladas. He has an ease about him, and there's something beneath the calm surface that stirs my interest. Convincing myself that it's my curiosity about people that has me fascinated with this man, I focus on my own dinner. But I'm aware of Sam stopping at another table to say hello to a local family. Sam laughs and claps the man on his back, knuckle-bumps the teen, and slowly ambles back to our table. I give him a few minutes of peace before I pounce with more questions.

"Seems like a nice town here."

He mumbles agreement as he continues eating.

"Some place you might settle permanently?"

"I built a house here."

"True." He seems a part of this community, yet separate. "You like living in a small town then?"

"I've lived in big cities and little towns. Both have their plusses and their minuses."

"But which do you prefer?"

He wipes his mouth with his napkin and leans back in his chair. "I grew up in Houston, but I've lived my adult life in several places. The first small town where I had a church—seems like forever ago—it was hard to adjust to everyone knowing everyone's business. Someone would come into my office, tell me something about another congregational member, which wasn't their business. I couldn't quite embrace that mentality. There was a verbal newspaper going around. But then, there is the disconnection in the big city where no one knows you. At first it's nice, but I miss walking into a store and seeing a friend or, like coming here to dinner, bumping into folks. Very Mayberryesque."

"Is Andy Griffith arriving next?"

"Right after Lucy."

"Now *that's* big city living."

He laughs.

I smile at the ease between us. "It's hard to live in black-and-white, isn't it? I've been in Austin . . . in my area long enough to know people when I go to the post office or drugstore. I like a small community, but if I want to buy something personal, I prefer driving across town. If you know what I mean."

He grins. "I do."

"Why do you think your father moved here?"

"Oh, the darkness. Definitely the darkness."

I tilt my head sideways as if that will help me understand.

He grins at my expression. "The better to see the moon, my dear."

"Of course. Makes sense. That ol' blue moon. Once in a . . ."

"Blue moon," he supplies the rest of the phrase.

"If I had my laptop I'd Google it. Where does that phrase come from?"

"You mean other than the song?"

"Hadn't thought of that."

He smiles. "You don't date back to the fifties."

"Neither do you."

"True." He pushes his plate away, leans his elbow on the table, and inclines his head toward me. "It's not something we studied at seminary, but I think it's considered to be a rare occurrence. A second full moon in a calendar month."

"Rare."

"Like snow in Austin."

He smiles. "Being hit by bird—"

"Definitely glad that's rare."

"Okay, how about—the Dallas Cowboys winning the Superbowl."

I nod, having heard the sports writers in Austin complain and deride Jerry Jones's team. "A teenager complying to a parent's request."

He laughs. "Oh, been there! Life turning out the way you planned."

"Or falling in love." I don't mean to say it, but it pops out of my mouth before I fully consider it. My face smolders.

But he doesn't smile or crack a joke. He just nods. "Finding that person who makes you complete."

He glances away, looks off. Is he thinking of his ex-wife, the mother of his children? What might have been? If only . . .

I look down at my plate, twirl a fork through the rice.

"Which brings us back to the song." A smile tugs at the corner of Sam's mouth. "Maybe you're more of a romantic than I thought."

His words fill my head and I look away, make eye contact with the waitress who hurries over. She begins removing our plates, and I'm grateful for the distraction and a moment to refocus my thoughts. While we're waiting for the check, I decide to put a barrier between Sam and me. "I'm not a romantic. Just a realist." I snatch the check from the waitress before she can set it on the table. "This dinner is on me. On work, that is." He starts to protest but I hold up my hand. "No, really. I insist."

"Are you married?"

I try not to let the sudden question throw me. "Divorced."

He nods. "Any significant other?"

Eric is on the tip of my tongue, but beneath Sam's probing gaze I shake my head. Then shake some senses back into me. "Is that why there's tension between you and your father then?"

"Because of my parents' divorce?"

"No."

"Because of mine?" His brow compresses into a frown.

I admit only to myself that my timing is way off. "Because you don't care about his passion? And maybe he's not so interested in yours?"

Sam stares at the table for a long moment. "Could be. My father has always been concerned about things far away from real life. My concern is for the here and now. For what comes after this life."

I feel inexplicably drawn to this man who seems levelheaded and yet full of faith. Sam is comfortable admitting he doesn't know everything, and he doesn't get distracted by side issues that seem unimportant in the big scheme of things. I respect him for wanting to connect with his father before it's too late. It only makes me wish for that same opportunity with my own mother. Melancholy settles over me like a cold, wet blanket.

"You okay?"

How has he grown so in tune to me in so short a time? "Sure."

He cocks his head to the side and studies me for a moment, which makes my skin contract. "You in a hurry to get back to the hotel?"

And be alone with my thoughts? My regrets? My bleak future? "Not particularly. What do you have in mind?"

Chapter Fourteen

Lying on a blanket in the back of Sam's truck, I stare up at the wide expanse of stars. The darkness around us is complete, making the stars brighter and more numerous than I ever imagined. Crickets chirp, sounding like a Morse code sent to alien dignitaries to help with global warming. The ruts and grooves of the metal bed press along my spine, but the view is worth any discomfort. Sam lies next to me, quiet as the night sky. After dinner, he drove me to this secret location on a friend's property to look for the famous Marfa lights.

Why are we way out here in the middle of nowhere and not in some more populated area? "Don't the lights visit the viewing area on Highway 90?"

Sam gives a husky laugh. "Tourists stop there."

"Isn't that what I am?"

He glances over at me. "It's a teen make-out place."

"Something wrong with that?" A smile curls my insides. I might feel safer if I knew we *were* going to make out. "You have a problem with kissing?"

Nana always told me, "That mouth of yours is going to get you in trouble one day." I admit it has on occasion, but I'm feeling reckless tonight, eager to escape my troubling thoughts. I watch Sam's profile. Even in the dark, red deepens the edges of his face.

"Oh, I forgot," I tease, "you're a preacher man."

His mouth twitches at that. "Preacher's like to kiss."

"Shocking!" Rolling onto my side, I prop my head on my hand. "Is that an invitation?"

He juts his chin toward the display of God's finery above us. "You're going to miss the light show."

I let my challenge to him go, but new questions bubble to the surface. Is it me? Is he simply not interested? Or is he uncomfortable with the topic? It's simpler to believe the latter. "Is it a guaranteed appearance?"

"Money back."

"These stars"—I lie back in the dark beside this quiet, private man, feeling the firmness of his shoulder next to me—"are amazing! I've never seen this many. Did they multiply like rabbits?"

His laughter carries upward and floats like a cloud. "City lights block out the view. But here, there's a moratorium on lights. It's why the observatory has such a good view. No highway lights. No street lights. Few houses."

I sit up, staring ahead at a glowing light far in the distance. The tiny, pale yellow beam hovers inches from the ground. My body tenses with an excitement I didn't expect. "Is that one?"

Sam cranes his neck to see. "Nah. A ranch house, I think. Folks confuse the Marfa lights with car headlights, too."

"And *you* can tell the difference?"

"We'll find out, won't we?" He grins, propping himself up with his elbows. "See that over there? The red light."

"Don't tell me you have a red light district here in Marfa."

Chuckling, he wags his head from side to side. "It's an airplane warning light set on a telephone tower."

"So have you actually seen these famous Marfa lights?"

"Not exactly."

I elbow him in the side. "What kind of a tour guide are you?"

"About your only option. My friends swear this is *the* place. But they've also warned it's a random experience."

"Once in a blue moon or just a likely excuse?"

His head lolls in my direction and a flash of a smile is illuminated by the pale moonlight. "No one can predict the future, when the lights will appear."

"Sort of like weather predictions, huh?"

"Exactly." His gaze locks with mine. Our faces are inches apart, our shoulders barely touching, his breath warm and alluring against my skin. "Honestly, I doubt the whole thing. It's another conspiracy."

"What? *You*, the cynic?"

"Yes, ma'am. Born and bred."

"Maybe we'll get lucky tonight."

His gaze smolders but he doesn't comment.

I cough at my indelicacy. I'm accustomed to men who like frank talk, bold advances. Yet I sense Sam is unlike any man I've ever known. "So how do you spring from a guy like Howard, who is so gullible? I mean, he believes in"—I wave my hand trying to find an appropriate word, running through my faulty mental synonym finder—"all of this."

Sam releases a slow sigh and stares up at the moon. "Howard's not the trusting sort either. He's even more of a cynic than I am." He pushes upright, hooking his arms around his knees, his back bowed. His flannel shirt softens the hard edge of his bones and muscles. Even though he's not the type of man I usually fall for, I feel a heady attraction that is probably irrational and foolish beyond measure. "To me, those who believe in conspiracy theories feel helpless and out of control."

I join him, sitting straight, leaning back on my hands, stretching my legs out in front of me. The truck seems to bob in a sea of darkness. It's easy for me to understand that vulnerable, lost feeling. "It provides something to hang onto. Like a lifesaver."

"Or a scapegoat," he tosses out a different angle like a boomerang. "Not only for some horrible event like Kennedy being shot or Elvis dying at a young age, but also like Howard thinking the U.S. should have gone back to the moon. To him, that's equally a tragedy."

"It is?"

"Feeds into his conspiracy. He doesn't think of the government money saved in not returning to the moon. He believes NASA knows what is up there and doesn't want to have to explain it to the naïve masses."

I cross my arms over my stomach. "How can someone as smart as your father—or even Ralph and Larry—believe all of this?"

Sam rubs his jaw and the scrape of his five o'clock shadow distracts me with his nearness. "It compensates for how they perceive their own life."

"That it's someone else's fault if they've failed?"

One of his shoulders lifts in a slight shrug. "That's my theory."

"And you're sticking to it?"

He grins, the corners of his eyes crinkling. "Exactly."

"So do you think Howard is simply reacting to tragedy?" My throat tightens. "Like my mother's death?"

"You mean, *over*reacting. Maybe. Makes sense. Or it could be that his career didn't pan out the way he wanted at NASA. The blame game worked for him. But take it for what it's worth . . . I'm not a psychologist."

"Me neither. Just a nosy reporter." I stretch out my arms in front of me, cross wrists, and lock hands. Then I roll my forearms toward my chest—a gesture I often did as a kid in some sort of a weird backwards praying stance. "So, what happened at NASA?"

"Howard was fired." Sam's tone is matter-of-fact. He flips open the lock on his toolbox that sits beside him, then slaps it closed, as if unsure about opening this Pandora's Box. "That's not how *he* tells the tale though. Still, my mother's version balances out the story. Understandably it's warped by her own bitterness over those years she says she wasted while waiting for Howard to come home. To her, the dinners she worked so hard to make only grew cold. Her excuses for why he never showed up at my baseball games sounded hollow. The pain and humiliation of going to church alone made it unbearable. Like every seesaw, I think the balance of truth lies somewhere in between."

"Life deals some heavy blows, doesn't it?" For a few minutes silence beats between us like a metronome clicking off a long list of tragedies and heartbreaks. Mine give way to someone who suffered even more than I did. As painful as losing my mother was, and its lingering effects throughout my lifetime, the mere thought of losing Ginger proves to me Nana suffered more than I can imagine.

Insect sounds intrude on the silence, and I sigh. "They say the loss of a child is the hardest blow." My words weigh a ton and I feel a heaviness press into my chest. "And yet my grandmother, who raised me, not only lost her one and only child but also her husband."

"She never remarried?"

"Never. Never even dated. She said my grandfather ruined her for any other man. Anyone else would be settling for second best."

"That's a sweet sentiment. But a lonely one."

"It was her choice." My thoughts linger on her choice to be a single mother . . . twice. I've always admired her sacrificial decision, and even made the same choice. It isn't until this moment that I doubt our wisdom. "My mother was a single mom. It wasn't easy in the early sixties to make that choice either. But she was never married. And she chose to have me."

"Brave lady."

"I think so." My chest swells with pride. "She didn't run from her problems."

"You, too," Sam says, his voice tender.

"In some ways I have run away. Or tried to. It's not something I'm proud of." I try to shrug off the weight of my decisions. "Makes it hard sometimes to believe there's a God up there in control of all of this. And maybe my doubt is another type of conspiracy." I laugh but it sounds shallow. I attempt to deepen it. "My trying to blame—" but I stop, unable to continue, the truth too real.

I sense, more than see, Sam watching me. After a moment or two, he says, "My dad wasn't around. I've told you that. But big deal, that's true for a lot of people. And my mom was a single, working mom most of my life. Nothing bad happened to me. I wasn't abused or mistreated. But it was a lonely existence. My friends' dads were at their baseball and football games. Mine wasn't. They had vacations to Mexico or Europe. I never made it outside of Texas. *If* Howard invited me to visit him in the summer, I ended up here in Marfa, where he ignored me while he worked on his theories and evidence for little green men. Or that's how I saw it. No big tragedies. So I glossed over the pain of it all. We all suffer, right?"

"But you found faith in something else."

"I did. People inevitably disappoint, but I learned God doesn't. I needed something more solid and more life changing than men or aliens on the moon. But my kids didn't see my beliefs as any different from Howard's. I made probably the worst mistake a Christian can make. And now my kids resent God." His voice cracks beneath the weight of his regrets.

I wait, wondering if he'll share more, but as his pain resonates between us I have an urge to absolve him of guilt, even when I don't have that power. "How can you be so sure they—"

"Because they've told me." The flatness of his voice makes his words spike. "So that pain that Howard inflicted by showing me I was unimportant to him? I've imposed it on my own sons."

How can he say such things and not run around screaming his head off or preaching repentance to those of us who've done the same? I understand his feelings. I've done the same to Ginger as my mother did to me—deprived her of a male figure. But Sam's calmness causes me to ask, "How do you deal with that?"

"I guess I've always looked at pain and suffering different than most. If our lives were easy, without disappointments or tragedies, then why would we ever need to look for God?" His gaze is steady and even in the dark, pinpoints of hope. "If all our wants are met, what's the point?"

"Maybe there is no point." I shake my head, disbelieving his gullibility. "Or maybe, as you say, God tortures us, so we'll give Him some attention?"

"I didn't say that." Sam places a hand on my arm, the strength of his words like the bands of his fingers. "God *allows* us to make the foolish mistakes that we do, like my dad living and breathing his job and squandering time with his family. The same mistakes I made, too. And He allows us to suffer the consequences. If there weren't consequences, then we'd keep making the same mistakes. It also would prevent us from empathizing with others. To me, our mistakes showcase His greatness, His sovereignty."

I tug away from his grip, rub away the remnants of his touch. "That's some leap of faith."

"So is believing artifacts from some ancient civilization populate our moon. Or that Elvis is in the witness protection program."

"Those are more leaps off sanity's ledge."

He inclines his head toward me as if giving me that point. "But what about the belief that we can manage alone? That we're totally self-sufficient?"

Nice setup. And I stepped right into the trap. I glare at him. "So you're calling *me* crazy now?"

"No, Bryn. But in light of God's plan, it does seem pretty ridiculous to think we're capable of managing on our own." He places his arm around my shoulders before I can protest. It's actually comforting rather than patronizing. "And I only say that because I've experienced it, made the same mistake myself. Even though I was going about doing good, so to speak, I was putting myself in charge. Not God. I decided what needed to get done. That the work was so enormous I should sacrifice time with my own family for God's good—when He wasn't asking that of me at all."

Sam pulls his arm away, taking the warmth I've come to need, as if pulling back into himself. "And that's where I went wrong." He rubs his thumb along his palm. "Now my kids think my belief in God is as wacky as Howard's ancient moon explorers. To think I might have preached to some and planted the seeds for salvation but at the same time hardened the terrain of my sons' hearts so they can't hear the same message—" His voice tightens into a beat of silence. "Sorry. Didn't mean to go there."

My heart pinches with my own regrets and understanding of his. I cover his hands with my own. "I know what it's like to screw up your child's life when your intentions are the opposite."

He meets my gaze but doesn't try to make me feel better by whisking away whatever guilt I might feel. It's a moment of deep, solidifying connection. And it sends a jolt through me.

Silence folds in around us. We sit next to each other, close and yet galaxies away in our thoughts. I wonder if that's why I feel so out of control, eager to blame some mysterious person for murdering my mother when I know who is really guilty. Is that why I'm here in Marfa? Or Fort Davis . . . or wherever I am tonight? Am I searching for some answer to make me feel better about my own life, about my mother's short life, about Nana and Ginger? What am I ultimately searching for?

The slope of Sam's shoulder reminds me he's a man of conviction. And yet conflicted. He's different from anyone I've ever known. Most of the men I've had relationships with were good at excuses or denial or both. Sam's solid in his faith, comfortable not knowing everything, and open about his mistakes. He's inspiring and perplexing at the same time. Usually I can peg a guy, know his limits, and at the same time understand he won't demand more than I can offer, but that may be the crux of my attraction to Sam. I feel a tug toward him as natural as the pull of the moon.

I watch him staring at the full, pie-in-the-sky moon, bright and luminous. He notices my attention and smiles, his gaze shifting back to the giant orb in the night sky. I follow, studying the shades and shapes on the surface of the moon.

"'When the moon hits your eye,'" Sam starts to sing in a robust baritone.

"'Like a big pizza pie,'" I add, feeling sillier than usual.

"'That's amore!'" Our voices blend, and suddenly I feel giddy, lifted from the burdens of regret.

"Do you know how the idea of the man in the moon started?"

I watch him, reveling in the change of conversation and my attraction to him. I smile. "No. Tell me."

"The shadows confused ancient people. Christian lore said a poor man was banished to the moon for some crime and eventually stoned to death. Maybe by that ancient civilization that my father believes used to live up there." He winks. "Anyway, they used some obscure verses in Numbers. Out of context, obviously. But, of course, now we know we're seeing the highlands and lowlands on the lunar surface."

"Didn't believe much in grace back then, did they?"

"Not much. The shades of light, shadows of darkness. Once there was only black and white. Times have definitely changed. The lines have blurred so much that most people can't see anything but gray."

I want to hang onto the carefree moment, but the conversation has slipped back into serious mode. His remorse feeds into my own, and I need the answer to my next question like air. "But do you believe God forgives us?"

He studies me a moment as if surprised by my question. I can't tell him the reason I'm asking, but every beat of my heart is the question repeating itself. "Absolutely. If not, then what would be the purpose of God sending His Son?"

"Why haven't you let Him forgive you then?"

He remains silent for a long time. The corner of his mouth compresses. "Do you always skewer people with your questions?"

"Only if I sense the same in myself."

He dips his head low. "Well, you're right."

"Accepting forgiveness isn't easy." I try to smile. "Even for a preacher man."

"We preachers cling to our guilt, too."

I rub my arms, chafing them as if punishing myself. Feeling the deep probe of his words in my own soul, I manage, "Why?"

"Because it's easier than letting go." He stares up at the broad face of the moon, which illuminates his profile.

Suddenly a flickering light grabs my attention and I reach for Sam's arm. "What's that? A headlight? Another farmhouse?"

"Not out there. No roads."

Together we watch an orbed light bounce around the mesas, moving quickly from my right to Sam's left. Another sphere forms and pulses. Sam reaches behind him for his binoculars, which he told me earlier he keeps in his glove compartment (just in case). After a moment of studying the lights, he hands the binoculars to me. Up close, they are simply brighter, the shapes less round, but still they move in a random, unpredictable fashion.

"What could it be?" I whisper, afraid if I speak too loud the moment will end.

"UFOs?" A smile lifts his voice. "Or little green men?"

"Swamp gas."

When I lower the binoculars so I can watch the full stretch of the horizon and the rosy lights dancing in a spiral formation, I realize I'm still holding onto Sam's arm, clutching his flannel shirt. I lose track of time as we sit there together, silence pulsing between us as we watch the private light show. When they flicker out of view, he covers my hand with his.

"I think," he says softly, "you just got lucky."

I face him, searching for answers I need, yet keeping my tone light.

His eyes are shadowed and dark, but I can feel his gaze, as intoxicating as his touch. "I might have to rethink my cynicism."

Suddenly I need to feel his arms around me. I need him to block out the unrelenting questions in my head. I touch his shoulder, feeling the heat generated through his flannel shirt, and lean toward him. He remains still, unmoving. Without hesitation, I swoop in and press my lips against his. His warmth pulls me like gravity. The kiss deepens, encompasses, wipes out the thoughts crowding my mind, pervading my heart. His breath blends with mine the way our voices did earlier. It's a freeing, exhilarating feeling, the same as when I take a flying leap out of an airplane. I'm floating and falling, tumbling into something I should have considered more seriously. I've taken some crazy chances before, and instinctively I know this one is just as risky.

As I'm opening to this man who stirs a part of me that has been dormant most of my life, I feel his hands encompass my shoulders. His grip tightens. Then he pulls away.

"Bryn . . ."

There's a feverish look in his eyes. I can see the need, the deep want matching my own. We're not children. We're going into this with our eyes wide open. Then a dark cloud infiltrates his eyes. Regret? Caution?

"Look"—I rush forward before he can say what I don't want to hear—"that was crazy. I'm known to do some crazy things, but that, well, uh . . ."

"Bryn, you should know—"

"Don't say anything." Panic charges into my chest. "I'm sorry. Really. That was . . . uh . . ." I scramble out of the back of his truck. "I don't know what I was thinking. Really! I didn't mean anything by it. It was just a crazy impulse. You're not right for me. You're a preacher! You probably don't even believe in kissing or dancing!" *Shut up, Bryn!* But I can't seem to stop myself. I laugh, a nervous twitter that I wish I could swallow back. "And I'm certainly not right for you. Me and a preacher man." I laugh even more, mostly to cover my humiliation. My cheeks stretch with humor but feel as if they might crack under the forced strain. "Really, I'm sorry. Can we still be friends?" I stick out my hand toward him. "I understand if—"

He climbs out of the bed of the truck and stands beside me. "Bryn—"

"I know, now I'm babbling and I can't seem to stop—"

He takes my hand and tugs me toward him. His arms come around me. At first I feel like a two-by-four, straight and unyielding. He smooths my hair, brushing it with his open palm. His heart beats solidly, steadily, but rapidly against my own. The kiss affected him, too. *It affected him.* The truth of that resonates inside me. Slowly I melt against him, my limbs feeling languid, the rush of adrenaline leaking out my fingertips and toes, leaving me exhausted.

"Bryn," his voice is as tender as his touch, "it's not you. Really."

I flinch, want to push away. I want to run all the way back to Austin. But I can't seem to find the energy to move even one foot.

He sways from one side to the other in a comforting, hypnotic way. "Obviously I am attracted to you, Bryn. Granted, you're not my usual type, but I gotta admit there's something about you." He pulls back to look me in the eye, his hands bracketing my face. His mouth curves, and he sweeps the bangs off my forehead. "But honestly, this isn't the right time for me to have a relationship. I'm not looking—"

"Me, neither." I place a hand against his chest and push back. "Really."

But when my gaze is swallowed by his, I know I'm lying.

"And," his voice dips low, "just so you know, I do believe in kissing."

Chapter Fifteen

It looked like a supernova,
Exploding with a force never seen before.
But it was only one foolish, infatuated woman—
Brynda Seymour

The next day dawns; the red orb on the horizon burns with the intensity of my own foolishness. I've learned being quiet and contemplative only adds to my angst. So I kick off the covers and shower. *Keep moving. Keep busy. Keep going.*

As I wait for my hair to dry, kinking along the ends as it usually does, I pick up Howard's book again. The chapter on quantum physics put me to sleep last night and after a few minutes of treading over the same slow-moving, hard-to-decipher language, I decide I need a strong dose of caffeine. As I tug on my boots, the phone rings. The sound magnifies in the confines of the hotel room, and I lunge for it—ignoring the irritating hope that it might be Sam. "Hello?"

A series of squeaks and squawks come over the line.

Frowning, I try again. "Hello?"

A loud beep makes me jerk the phone from my ear.

Easing it back toward my ear, I listen to the static crinkling on the line. "Hello?"

No voice answers back. There's no rhythm to the noises, no pregnant pauses, no rhyme or reason that I can figure. Annoyed, I finally hang up the phone. It's then I remember Sam telling me of the strange phone calls Howard received. Terrific. Now I'm on some alien's call list.

Ready long before the appointed time, I pace the room, then decide to scavenge up a quick and easy breakfast. I scoot my boots a few blocks to a local smoothie joint, my hair drying in the morning heat. In an effort to make me strong and able to resist any more of my wild impulses, I order protein and soy milk added to the mangoes and strawberries.

While slurping my smoothie on the walk back to the hotel— and avoiding thoughts of Sam . . . especially the way the memory of that brief kiss makes my insides curl—I plug a familiar number into my cell phone. I listen to the ring several times, then someone lifts the receiver. There's a long pause, a ruffling sound. "Nana?"

She doesn't answer.

"Nana? It's me, Bryn."

Click. The line goes dead. This isn't the first time she's hung up on me. She forgets what a phone is for, picks up the receiver to stop the incessant ringing, then clunks it back down once the annoying noise has stopped, oblivious that I'm trying to talk to her.

I try again with the same results, then call the nurses' station and ask someone to put Nana on the line.

"Brynda?" Nana's voice is strong and loud as she shouts into the phone.

"Hi, Nana!" I shout right back so she can hear me clearly.

"Where are you?"

"I'm in Marfa on assignment. How are you feeling?"

"Oh, fine. Sure. When are you coming to see me? You never come."

Even though untrue, her jab lands in my solar plexus. "I was there Sunday, Nana. I'll be back as soon as I can."

"Where are you?"

I swallow hard. "I'm in Marfa, Texas." I enunciate my words carefully. "It's in far west Texas. I'm on assignment for the paper. Did you eat breakfast?"

"Breakfast? I used to fix pancakes."

"Yes, Nana, that's right." I smile, but my gaze is snagged by a bald man staring at me, probably irritated by my loud phone call. I turn away and cup my hand over the receiver. "You made animal shapes."

"A cat. That was a favorite."

The memories wrap around me, a comforting embrace. Then I remember Elphaba and hope Eric is checking in on her. "Yes, you're right."

"Where are you?"

I roll my eyes, take a deep breath. "Marfa, Texas." I can't shake the feeling someone is watching me and, sporting some of Howard's paranoia, I turn back—but the bald man has disappeared. "Nana, I'll be home soon."

"Texas. I have a granddaughter in Texas."

"Yes, Nana, that's me. I love you."

Clunk. The receiver hits something, probably the desk. But the line doesn't disconnect. I listen for a few minutes, catching muffled sounds, and imagine Nana shuffling around in her slippers and bathrobe.

I close my phone but then reopen it, turning off the ringer temporarily. I don't want anyone calling when I'm in the glider. When I arrive back at the hotel, I spot Sam's truck parked out front.

"Morning." He leans against the hood in a James Dean stance and holds a Styrofoam cup of coffee. His faded jeans and plain white T-shirt only accentuate his honed physique. But it's his easy smile that locks in my attention. "Ready to fly?"

My heart gives a kick start. He's taking me out to the airfield where we'll go gliding with Howard's friends. "Always."

WE MEET UP WITH Ralph and Larry outside an airplane hanger. The metal building looks like it's been around for at least half a century. But what tightens my nerves is seeing a dismantled plane on the back of a trailer. With the help of Larry, Ralph, and another man in a blue jumper, Sam lifts the plane off the trailer. The weight doesn't even make the men sweat or strain.

"That coffee brewin' yet?" Ralph looks skyward before he and the man in the blue coveralls wander off toward the metal building. Ralph seems distracted. Maybe it's his outfit. Did he dress in the dark? His jeans are rolled up above his tennis shoes, revealing a white athletic sock and a brown dress sock crumpled around his ankles. Over his shoulder Ralph adds, "If ya want some, come on."

Sam walks past me and lifts what looks like a detached airplane wing off the trailer. A slight curl lifts the end upward. He kneels down beside the plane to attach it to the body. The wings look about as secure as a dragonfly's.

"You sure you've got those going the right direction?"

He grins over his shoulder at me. "We'll be flying on a wing and a prayer."

"I know you've got the prayers covered. It's the mechanics and equipment that has me nervous."

"If you're concerned, we could flip the wings and see what happens."

"Sure, go ahead. I'll wait here for you and call 911."

Larry puts a hand on my shoulder. "No need to be worried, Brynda. Sam here is a good flyer."

"Hand me that over there, will you?" Sam asks.

"What?" I hold up a white plastic gadget. "This?"

"Yeah. Perfect."

I hand him the attachment, careful not to brush against his hand, which is better for my frame of mind. Sometime between two and four in the morning, I decided I'm not good for Sam. That's it! I'm protecting him.

Yeah, right. Who am I kidding? "How long have you been flying?"

"Getting nervous?"

I give my arms a shake, like Ginger on the blocks at one of her high-school swim meets, but it doesn't help ease the tension in my muscles. The tin-can airplane isn't what's coiling my nerves into unyielding knots. It's Sam. He's a man who isn't the love 'em and leave 'em type, which is what I usually pursue with gusto. My type of man is the kind who isn't about to settle down. It feels safer for them to leave. Or for me to skedaddle. That's why I should now.

Sam scratches his jaw with his thumb while studying me. "You *are* nervous."

"No. Really. This is nothing compared to bungee jumping off a bridge over ice-cold water in Alaska. But I do prefer a pilot to be . . . cautious."

"So *you* can feel the freedom of being reckless?" His ability to see through me is uncanny and unnerving.

Unable to hold his gaze, I check my watch. "How long till takeoff?"

"Long as you need." He straightens, setting his tools back in a metal box, which I recognize from his truck. Wiping his brow with his sleeve, he squints up at the sky. "Did you want to put it off till another day?"

"Do we need to?" I cringe at the eagerness in my voice.

"The weather's perfect."

"Great." Disappointment saturates my tone. "Actually, I just wanted to make sure I had time to stop at the ladies' room."

"Don't think we have one of those. Just a one-hole wonder." He grins. "We've got time though. Go through the hanger. It's on the left."

Turning on my heel, I walk off, my insides feeling some turbulence already. I sense his gaze following me, and I ignore it, lifting my chin an extra notch and putting a bounce into my step until I realize I'm swinging my backside in a way I've seen a few of Ginger's friends vamp around college-age boys. I deflate my walk immediately.

In the restroom I stare at my reflection in the mottled mirror. I've done some foolish things in my past, but this just might top them all. Not that glider planes are necessarily dangerous. But Sam is. Dangerous to the only part of my anatomy that I've ever tried to protect.

When I return to the aircraft, the boys are standing around, slurping their coffee, kicking the dirt, joking around.

"You ever heard the one about three politicians in a hot air balloon?" Ralph's gaze collides with mine, and he reddens around his jowls. "Can't finish that in polite company."

"Don't worry, Ralph. I told that one last week." Giving him a friendly wink, I lay a hand on the glider plane. "Is the tinker toy ready for liftoff?"

"Yes, ma'am." Ralph explains how he'll provide the aero-tow, hooking a rope to Sam's glider and towing us into the air with his twin-engine plane.

"Don't worry about anything." Larry pours coffee from a green thermos into a Styrofoam cup and hands it to me. "I taught Sam everything he knows."

"And that's not much." Sam grins. "But be warned, this stuff"— he lifts his cup in a salute and taps mine—"is strong."

"It'll grow hair on your chest." Ralph gulps the hot liquid and hisses through his teeth, leaving beads of coffee along his upper lip.

"That's incentive." I sample the stout brew, then down it. "How long will we be up in the air?"

"Depends on the wind and drag." Larry sips carefully from a bottle of water and smacks his lips. "You should be able to go about sixty miles. But there are several factors that can affect the duration."

Sam gives me a tour of his sleek white glider. He explains how the wings are longer and thinner than on a regular plane. He points out ailerons, elevator, and rudder. I'd rather just get on with it, but at the excitement glittering in his eyes I continue on the tour. I remember when I was about to bungee jump, the guide tried to show me how secure the equipment was, but it only made me imagine all the things that could go wrong.

When I glance under the plane at something Sam is pointing out, I notice the wheel. "Only one?"

"Keeps the plane light. Too much weight and we'd never get off the ground."

"But won't that make for a wobbly landing?"

"Not if you hold your breath."

"And," Larry adds, "pat your head . . ."

"And rub your belly at the same time." Ralph pushes his glasses toward the bridge of his nose.

I give them a smirk. Larry chuckles, and the others help hold the glider and keep it from tipping as Sam and I climb inside. We're sitting so low to the ground it feels as if we're about to drive a go-cart.

Sam settles behind me. He points out the lever I'll need to pull to release us from the aero tow. "Just don't release until I tell you."

"Why? What'll happen?"

He gives me a sharp look. "Won't be pretty."

"Gotcha."

Avoid lever. I strap into my seat. "How long have you been flying gliders?"

"A few years. I got interested in an effort to get to know my dad. But it didn't fly to the moon, if you know what I mean."

Unfortunately I do.

"But it interested my son, Josh. He comes here in the summer and we tool around."

"I can't believe we both fit inside here." From outside, the cabin looked the size of a rabbit hutch. Not that it's roomy, but we're not bumping into each other either. Sam sits directly behind me, the back of my seat our only barrier. "You're sure it'll carry both of us."

"At the same time." He catches me looking back at him. "Don't worry, I'll behave." His comment reminds me I was the one that kissed him last night. I wonder what it would be like to reverse that. My stomach dips before righting itself.

"Okay"—I swipe my slightly damp palms along the thighs of my jeans—"let's get this over with."

"Start the engines." Humor fills his voice.

"Uh, Sam, there aren't any engines."

"Pilot humor."

"Terrific, I've got Groucho Marx as a pilot."

WHAT'S THE POINT OF strapping on a seat belt when I'm wedged into a space two sizes smaller than my skinniest jeans? If we crash, no seat belt in the world is going to save me. My pulse is racing, as it usually does when I decide to toss caution to the wind—this time, literally. I throw a quick prayer skyward that I won't leave Ginger orphaned—or Nana either, as I'm more her guardian than my daughter's these days—then I hold my breath and release it in a tiny stream, which eases the pressure building in my chest.

I feel a tiny jolt and Sam calls, "Here we go!"

The twin-engine plane taxis ahead of us, pulling us behind it by a rope. The tail is all I can see at the moment. The runway—only a dirt road with patches of grass—bumps us along. There probably aren't rescue vehicles nearby in case of a botched takeoff or landing. The glider follows behind the tail of Ralph's plane by several feet. It wobbles, dipping right, and I realize we're already airborne, the rope tugging us along like the tail of a kite floating on the breeze. My fingers curl into a nervous fist, and I focus on the tail of the first plane. The hum of its engines fills my ears and a vibration rattles through my body. The tailwinds make the plane dip and weave. It's not bumpy like turbulence, just a leaning here or there, a floating upward.

"We're getting to the good stuff now," Sam says from behind me.

"When do I release the rope?"

"Not yet. Wait till we reach a mile—five-thousand-two-hundred-eighty feet above the earth."

"Look, Mom, I'm flying . . . uh, or is it falling?"

"You're right, it's like a controlled fall."

"That's reassuring."

He laughs. "You're not scared, are you?"

"Not a bit." My stomach wobbles, but my nerves are rock steady.

"Okay, let her go."

"What? The lever?"

"Yeah, pull it."

"You're sure." I glance back and he nods. I pull the lever, and we're loose. Sam steers us in the opposite direction of the twin-engine plane. The window clears, and the view of blue sky, wispy clouds, velvety green grass, and rocky terrain stretches out before me. The sound of the other plane fades into nothing. It's as if I'm weightless, soaring on the wings of an eagle. My breath catches in my chest. I remember a song from my childhood, "The Sounds of Silence." It fills my ears like a warm breath.

Flying reminds me how I've tried to soar above problems that weighed me down, sent me into a tailspin of despair, pulled me to depths from which I never thought I could recover. I always wanted to dare circumstances. Maybe that's why I've never been afraid to risk my life. Only my heart. When it breaks, I know there is no recovery.

The plane dips and swoops low. The ground rushes toward us. I make out boulders and the straight ruler of a highway. Then the plane swerves upward, taking my stomach to new heights.

"How can you do that without an engine?"

Sam chuckles. "Thermals give us lift."

"What's so funny?"

"You are definitely a reporter."

"Why do you say that?"

"Most people just enjoy the scenery, the view . . . but you have a million questions. Is that what gives you stability in your life?"

"You have a good amount of questions yourself."

"It's how I pretend I'm in some sort of control. You, too, right?"

"What's wrong with wanting to know how something works, why . . . when . . . how?" I stop myself, remembering my mother's nickname for me.

"Don't forget who and what. You know, Bryn, no amount of answers can satisfy."

The plane plunges forward, the ground rushes toward me. Then the plane lifts as if on a rush of air. I swallow the lump lodged in my throat. "Are you preaching again?"

"Not at all, but this might be a great way to do so. I could stick an unbeliever in your seat and say, 'So where do you think you're going when you die?'"

I laugh. "That might win a few converts."

"But not you?"

"I already believe." My words surprise even me. In that one tiny second I first acknowledge a belief in God. It may not be the angry God of Reverend Do-Right, but I do believe. Now the question I'm afraid of is this: what do I do with that belief?

Sam aims the plane for Sleeping Lion Mountain.

"You gonna scare me into becoming a nun?"

"Not likely. Not the way you ki—" He stops, but I know exactly what he was saying. My insides fire like a jet engine. I close my

eyes and breathe deeply. In the small confines of the cabin, I can
smell the cool, clean fragrance of his aftershave mingled with the
husky scent of male. Awareness of him magnifies. The weight of his
admission seems to pull the plane downward, as if we're drifting
into uncertainty.

"You should go back to preaching."

"You might be right. I told you I wasn't good at relationships."

"If flirting is—" I stop myself this time. There's another long
pause, and my words fill the inside of the glider, making my heart
pump wildly.

"So what do you think?" Sam asks as if he didn't hear me. "How
do you like the view?"

"You mean, am I about to throw up all over your nice clean
plane?"

"If you are—"

"I'm fine and it's . . ." My mind can't take in the vastness spread
out before me. Below, I see an antelope munching on grass. The
plane dips right, turning and plunging low again.

"You still okay?"

I nod, breathless and out of words.

"You didn't finish."

"It's . . . beautiful." That word seems lacking in describing the
landscape, sky, rays of sunlight slanting downward through lacy
clouds.

Sam doesn't respond, so I swivel and turn. He grins at me, like
a boy riding his first bike, and a part of me feels as if I'm plunging
again. Or soaring. Twirling around in a spiral formation. If I didn't
know better I'd think we were doing a series of barrel rolls. I feel
upside down and topsy-turvy, confused and thrilled. I turn back
and focus on the rocky terrain below. It's steady and solid and
reminds me of which way is up and which is down. What's possible
and what's not. But even the spectacular view can't replace the
impact of his smile.

Like a bird falling out of the air,
Crippled and unable to soar
Bryn fell from the sky
Tumbling through air
Weight dragging
Gravity acting
Splat.

But for some reason I can't explain, I feel safe with Sam behind the controls, which doesn't make me feel safe at all.

Chapter Sixteen

No air bags activate. No oxygen masks deploy. No foam covers the tarmac.

Of course, there isn't a tarmac or runway to speak of, just a grassy field. It looks smooth from this height, but the closer we get the more indentations and rocks I can see. Pressing back into my seat, I watch the ground rush up to meet the plane and brace myself for a jolt or lurch, skid, or crash. But no safety precautions are needed—except maybe a defibrillator as my heart momentarily stops, then picks right back up where it left off—as the plane's one wheel glides smoothly over the relatively flat meadow. Immediately Ralph, Larry, and Howard surround the plane and offer congratulations. Smiling with relief and the exhilaration that comes with survival, I wave back.

Ralph holds a plastic bag and hands it to me as I climb out of the plane. "Feelin' poorly?"

I start to reach for the bag, then realize what it's for. "No, I'm fine. Ready for a big breakfast." I pat my stomach, then tap my head, which makes Larry laugh.

"That a girl!" He claps me on the back and nods toward the plane. "Get on over there and I'll take your picture."

I pose with Sam, his arm around my waist, my shoulder wedged in the crook of his arm. "You did good," Sam says with a proud smile. "You're now one of the gang."

"Do I have to actually spit or whittle?"

"They don't. Not on purpose anyway."

"Smile!" Larry calls. "One . . . two . . ." He fiddles with the lens while my smile congeals. "Hang on."

I glance up at Sam. He smiles down at me, and something inside my chest turns several degrees. Then the camera clicks, and the flash snaps.

"You weren't looking," Larry chides. "Smile at *me*. Will ya? Not at that big goofy pilot of yours."

"No more flirtin', you two," Ralph adds.

His words give me the jolt I expected on landing. "We're not—"

"Definitely not," Sam adds. Our gazes shift away from each other as we both inch apart. It's barely perceptible, more a shifting of attention. A denial. And it feels like a hole in my side, like in childhood when a tooth loosens and falls out, and the tongue presses into the empty space expectantly.

Ralph ignores our denial. "We gotta get on with the ceremony."

"Ceremony?" The flash erupts again, this time nailing me in the retina with sharp light.

"Not 'till we get this picture." Larry frowns at me. "You ready this time?"

With the picture finally acceptable to Larry's standards, I borrow the camera to take a photo of Larry and Ralph in front of Sam's plane, just in case I get that article finished. "Howard? Will you join them?"

He shakes his head and takes one step back, then two. "No pictures."

"Ah, c'mon," Larry hooks his arm through Howard's. "Who's gonna see it?"

With his face screwed into a decided frown, Howard snatches a dull, gray baseball cap off a guy wearing blue coveralls and pulls a pair of aviator glasses out of his breast pocket. Camouflaged, he tilts his chin away from the camera and keeps to the edge of the frame while Larry and Ralph smile.

Afterward, they usher me into the weathered hanger. We pull out metal folding chairs and form them in a loose circle. Larry hands out an odd assortment of mismatched mugs. He's the first to lift his. "To Bryn! A good ace."

We raise our mugs, then everyone slurps. I give my coffee a mere sip and feel my eyes immediately widen. My throat burns. I choke back a cough. "What—" my voice rasps—"did you put in there?"

Ralph chuckles. "Won't hurt you none."

Larry pats his abdomen. "Cleans out the ol' system, too." He leans toward me. "I think he puts castor oil in it."

"Another conspiracy to look into, right?" I smile but only pretend to sip from then on. Still, my stomach warms and my limbs tingle. For the first time I notice Ralph is wearing a wedding ring. "Your wife allows you to make this stuff?"

"Allows it?" Larry laughs. "Why, she showed him how!"

Ralph nods. "She was a good egg." He sips his drink slowly this time. "She sure was. Better than I deserved."

"Any woman is better than we deserve," Howard mumbles, holding a pad of paper on his lap and jotting notes about who knows what.

"Amen to that!" Larry lifts his mug.

Ralph places a hand on his rounded knee and nods toward Larry. "He's the ladies' man in this bunch. The bachelor all the women in town are after."

"Oh, I bet you're all pretty popular with the widows knitting league." I smile, thinking there might be a female countergroup to the spit-and-whittle.

"I don't have time for that nonsense." Howard's ballpoint pen pokes a hole in his paper, then he aims it at me. "You're divorced."

I bristle at the accusatory tone in his voice. "Yeah, so?"

"Your mom had trouble with men, too."

My skin tightens. Someone to my left shifts, but I stare back at Howard with full-wattage intensity. "She wasn't ever married."

"Could have been." Howard slides his pen against his scalp, leaving it hooked behind his ear. "But she had trouble trusting men, I think. Or trusting herself. She always went for the bad boy, the one that caused her trouble. She'd jump into trouble sooner than jumping to safety." He leans back, folds his arms over his chest. "I have a theory."

I feel my skin turning red hot. "What's that?"

"I think she inherited it. Cora, your grandmother, never remarried after her husband died. Why? She had opportunities."

"She did?" The idea of Nana being courted surprises me. Isn't she living a life handed to her? Or is it more complicated than that? Did she choose to be alone? Because of the responsibility of raising a daughter and then a granddaughter? Do we all choose our lot in life, even if it feels as if someone else is in control?

"Sure." Howard nods. "She was a young widow. Attractive." He takes hold of his pen and begins marking on his paper again. "But all these years, I've kept up with you, Brynda. Watched you take crazy chances yourself. Just like Jennifer. But never one where you'd find safety."

My heart thunders in my chest. I count each beat until they slow to an even rhythm. "Maybe safety didn't seem safe. Or maybe it was boring."

His eyebrows narrow to a sharp point. "Do you know what Einstein said about falling in love?"

"Albert Einstein talked about falling in love?"

"Yes." Howard leans back, looks up at the metal ceiling of the hanger and taps his fingers on his thigh. "Gravitation can't . . . isn't responsible for people falling in love. How on earth can you explain in chemistry or physics terms a biological phenomenon like first love? If you put your hand on a hot stove for a minute, it seems like an hour. If you sit with that special girl for an hour, it seems like a minute. That's relativity."

Sam stares at his father. "That's the most romantic thing I've ever heard you say, Howard."

"Well, I don't usually whisper sweet nothings to you, now do I?"

The group laughs, and Sam chuckles at himself. But I'm caught off guard by the simplicity and depth in that simple quote. Then by the way Sam glances in my direction.

Ralph coughs. "Einstein was one smart fellow, but I'm more like your grandmother, Brynda, or so it sounds. I ain't interested either in the opposite . . . well, you know. I'm just waiting for my time to be over so I can see my Maggie again."

His sentiment tightens my chest. I want to reach out to him, but he doesn't seem the type to welcome sympathy. I sense Sam watching me and intentionally keep my gaze diverted. "What was she like? Your Maggie."

Ralph shakes his head, making his beard brush against his orange flannel shirt. "Words can't do her justice."

"She had eyes only for Ralph," Larry says.

"You should know, you tried to get her attention a time or two," Howard adds.

Sam laughs. "Larry tries to interest *any* woman."

Larry pats the air. "Come on, you guys. There's a lady here who—"

"Brynda ain't interested in you," Ralph says.

"Even I can see that!" Larry places a hand against his concave chest. "Her interest definitely lies elsewhere." His gaze shifts slowly and decisively toward Sam.

My pulse lurches. What is this, some kind of conspiracy? Again, I manage not to look toward Sam. Instead, I scramble for something other than my love life to discuss. "So what do the women in your lives think of all these conspiracies?"

Larry tips his chair backward a couple of inches, his long legs providing counterweight. "Well, I've never been married, but the women in my life—"

"And there have been many," Ralph interrupts.

"—find it intriguing."

"At least for a date or two."

Larry scowls and kicks Ralph in the calf. "What about Maggie?"

"She said we all needed a hobby. But she had her own conspiracies. About grocery stores."

"Really?" I lean forward. "And what was—"

"Maggie wasn't like other women." Howard scratches his head, making a tuft of hair stick upright. "Sam's mother didn't understand what my work entailed. She resented it. But . . ." He pinches his lips closed and gives a slight shake of the head. "She's happier now." He clunks his mug on a nearby table and stands. "Don't you all drink too much of that brew. It'll pickle your brains." He heads toward the hanger's wide-open doors.

I start to rise and follow, but Larry grabs my arm and pulls me back into my seat. "Don't take offense to Howard there. It's not that he don't appreciate women."

"He told me once," Ralph adds, "that he loved only one woman his whole life." Through his thick glasses, he looks at Sam. "Don't mean nothing against your momma, but it was before she come along."

Sam's gaze slams into mine. A shiver ripples down my spine.

"But Howard said he and my mother—"

"He loved Jennifer," Sam says, his voice firm, "but that doesn't mean he and she ever . . . well, you know."

"He's not my father," I blurt out.

Sam grins, and a mixture of relief and exhilaration flashes through me. My gaze drifts toward Howard as he leaves the hanger and turns left toward the impromptu parking lot. An ache pulses in my chest for him and his lost love . . . and for Sam, who knows his mother meant less to his father than some other woman. "I'm sorry. I didn't mean—"

Sam covers my hand with his. "It's okay. I'm glad he's not your dad."

Ralph snorts. "Well, that'd be a corker, wouldn't it?"

The party winds down and Sam escorts me back to his truck. A comfortable silence settles between us. Even though we've only known each other for a short time, it feels like much longer, maybe because single moms and dads understand each other's guilt over our shortcomings as parents. Or maybe the problems and pain we've suffered with our parents bonded us. But there's something else between us . . .

Something that manages to illuminate pieces of our hearts and crackle like static electricity at the same time.

Considering how awkward it was between us when we first met at Howard's gate, he seems friendlier and more relaxed now. Of course, I had to push it to another level. Why do I do that? Why do I have to push situations or people? Not wanting to delve further into my own warped psyche, I give a surreptitious glance sideways at Sam and remember his kiss, his smooth lips, roughened cheek, solid curve of his shoulder beneath my palm. A flush overtakes me. *Cool your jets, Starfighter.*

There's a major problem with this crush. The boy's not interested in the girl. Well, he is. He's simply not playing this round. My mind works something over and over, like a worry stone. That's my trouble, never able to let go of something till I've analyzed it to death. But I think I finally understand why he's not interested in a relationship.

Strapped into the passenger seat of his truck, I offer an apology. "I'm sorry, Sam, about . . . well, what my mother meant to Howard."

"No apology necessary. You were hardly to blame."

"Still, it must be like a slap, it coming up again and again."

"It's okay. And it's not your fault. Howard can't let go. It's his problem, not mine."

I fold my fingers together. "Maybe he was afraid to love again after my mother died."

"Maybe."

"Is that what you're afraid of?"

He glances over at me with an impenetrable look, then focuses back on the road, which is pencil straight and about as interesting.

"Of living, risking it all again. Your heart, I mean."

His hands flex, tightening on the steering wheel, making the veins running up along the solid bones of his wrists and disappearing beneath his thick muscles bulge. "And you're not afraid?"

"I take risks all the time."

"Uh-huh. And why is that? Can't you feel alive unless you're risking your neck? Or are you running away from something that frightens you more?"

Self-analysis was not my intention here. I cross my arms over my chest and prop a booted foot on my knee. What did I expect? For Sam to fall on my proverbial couch and let me analyze him? "I wasn't talking about me."

"Sure you were. You want to know why I'm scared of a relationship. Because if there's a good enough reason, then my rebuff of your kiss wasn't about *you*. Then it's because of my wounded pride or ego or whatever." A tick in his jaw pulses, and I realize I hit a nerve. A raw one. "Right?"

I cup my hand over the arch of my boot, feeling the worn leather beneath my palm. "Maybe."

"Well, you're right. It wasn't about you. Does that make you feel better?"

I worry my lip, my heart oddly weighted. "No."

His cheek compresses into a dimple as his mouth stretches into a smile that coils my insides. "The answer is simple, Bryn. I ruined my first marriage. That doesn't exactly inspire confidence that I won't do it again."

"But—"

"No." He shifts gears forcefully. "That's why it's odd to you. You don't worry about throwing yourself into a bad relationship or off a cliff or out of a plane."

I sense the speed of his truck increasing and lean toward my left to check the speedometer. "Uh, Sam, the speed limit is—"

"What are you afraid of, Bryn?" He slaps his hand on the seat between us and steers with only his left hand. His gaze remains on me a beat or two longer than it should before he finally focuses again on the road. "Why do you take chances? Are you defying death?"

I flick my gaze from the road, the scenery a brown and green blurry haze, to Sam. My heart hammers. I lick my dry lips.

"Are you challenging God?" He doesn't look my way this time. His profile remains straight as the road. "Are you trying to see if God really cares about you?"

I shift in my seat, bracing both feet on the floor as if preparing myself for impact. Maybe his father's crazy ideas have rubbed off on him. Maybe he prefers challenging instead of being challenged. "I'd really like it if you slowed down, Sam."

"Why don't you answer my questions, Bryn? What are you afraid of? Do you think God doesn't care because He allowed your mother to die when you needed her most?" His words feel like darts thrown right at my heart and come way too close to hitting the red center.

"Because I don't deserve to live." The words slip out before I have a chance to grab them back. I've never voiced my fear to anyone before.

Sam gives a quick look in my direction, then jerks the wheel, pulling the truck to the side of the road. The shocks jounce over the ruts along the shoulder. Once the truck is in park, he hooks his arm on the back of the seat, twists his body to look at me straight on. No avoidance, no compromise. His brow scrunches together.

Trapped, I clutch my hands in my lap, squeezing hard until the tips of my fingers turn white.

"Why would you say that?" His tone gentles.

I can't meet his steady, probing gaze. My breath comes hard and fast.

"Bryn," he says, his voice whisper soft, "why?"

"Because—" I place my hand over my heart where the guilt throbs even now—"I . . ." The words jam in my throat. I jerk on the door handle. It's locked. I pluck at the metal peg, missing once, twice, then thrust open the door and stumble out of the truck's cab. Dazed, I stagger until I come to a boulder. Where to go? What to do? I lean against the cool, jagged granite and steady myself, try to breathe. Even though the sun is up and the temperature's rising, I feel cold, chilled . . . as if my heart has stopped beating. And yet I hear it pounding in my ears, exploding in my head.

The crunching of gravel behind me tells me Sam follows. I want to crawl under the rock. I wish it were dark, not broad daylight. I feel as if I'm walking along the roadside buck naked, like the Jeff Bridges's character in *Starman* learning to live, breathe, and move with strange bones and new flesh.

"Bryn." Sam speaks in that kind of voice someone might use to a cornered, frightened deer. "There's nothing you could ever do that God can't forgive."

That's not what Reverend Do-Right said about my mother. He condemned her and he didn't even know her. He didn't know how she gently detangled my long, straggly curls. He didn't know how she read me stories, changing her voice for each character. He didn't know how she made me dinner when she was dog tired. Or how she drew pictures on my back for hours on end just because I liked it. He didn't know her. He didn't know anything about her. And yet, he—

"Everybody has things in their past they're ashamed of or wish hadn't happened. Sometimes things happen—to innocents. Through no fault—"

"You don't know what you're talking about, Sam! Drop it. Take off your preacher hat with me. I don't need it. I don't want—"

"Maybe you do." His voice remains calm, reasonable, where I feel as if I'm coming apart at the seams. "Maybe I do, too. Bryn, sometimes we make mistakes, but does that mean we can't try to fix it or—"

"There is no fix! I wheel around on him. Don't you understand?"

His eyes are gentle. "That may be true. But that doesn't mean you have to carry the guilt forever. You can't work it off writing your inspirational stories or with anything else."

"Oh, yeah? You're such an expert, are you?" Blood rushes, pounds in my ears. Hot tears streak down my face. All the anger, fear, and loss I've experienced over the years churns to the surface.

"You know anyone else who killed their own mother?"

Chapter Seventeen

The salty brine of tears stings my face. Each breath lurches out of me, jagged and rough. Crumpled from my confession, I look to Sam, but he doesn't react. His features are locked in place, his feet remain steadfast, and his arms stay at his side, not crossing in self-defense or making the sign of the cross as if to ward off my wicked presence. Either would be normal reactions, but there's not even an eyebrow twitch. The corner of his mouth doesn't flinch.

Is he simply stunned? Or is he tempering his emotions for my protection? Or his own?

My fingers trace the rough edges of the boulder. What would happen if I told Nana? I've imagined her falling back, clutching at her chest. Tears would flow with relief that her daughter didn't commit suicide. But what of my culpability? Would resentment and anger flash in her eyes?

Reverend Do-Right would puff up, eyes popping wide, mouth twisting with condemnation. But the condemnation he would fling at me would be no harsher than what I've spoken to myself time and again.

And Ginger . . . sweet, loving, accepting Ginger. I want to imagine her reaching for me. She never knew my mother, so she wouldn't feel empathy for the deceased as much as for the living—her own mother, who only meant to do good. And yet I managed to cause such destruction.

Eric's reaction is a giant blank in my mind. I've known him for more than three years, and yet I can't imagine what he'd do or say. Look surprised? Shrug because I was a kid and didn't know what I was doing back then? Tell me I shouldn't dwell on it? Write a bluesy song about it? He might even know someone already in jail for a similar crime.

But Sam's nonreaction surprises even me. Is he so schooled at hearing appalling confessions that he doesn't even blink? Or maybe my crime isn't as bad as other confessions he's heard.

Actually, he's probably trying to figure out a way to get as far away from me as possible without being a total jerk and leaving me deserted on the side of the highway.

"Sorry." I put a hand out to ward him off, just in case he decides to move toward me. "I . . . I don't know what I was saying. Really stumped you there, didn't I?" I shake my head in an attempt to spin what I've just revealed.

"Bryn." He steps toward the boulder, leans a hip against it, all the while watching me. "Don't pull your armor back on."

Uncontrollable trembling takes hold of me, rattling me from the inside out. Maybe that's what this is, my life slammed into Sam's. For what purpose? Why, after forty years, did I feel compelled to tell this man my darkest secret? "Really, you don't want to hear the sordid details."

"Bryn," his voice is whisper soft, "I think you need to tell it more than I need to hear it."

Like a school girl standing in the principal's office, I take a shuddering breath and begin. "The night of the landing on the moon. That's when it happened." My thoughts are twisted and contorted, and it takes a moment to sort them out. I can't meet his gaze, but stare at the tops of my boots. "Momma was upset. Not about the moon landing. I'm not sure why, but she was crying. She did that sometimes. And she was drinking. She did that, too. I-I just wanted to help her."

"Of course you did."

I slide my hand into my hip pocket, roll one foot inward, trying to find the words, the answers hidden deep inside. "She had this cabinet in the bathroom. You know, one with a mirror on the front." My gaze skitters toward Sam long enough to see him nod, then skirts away. "Inside she kept her toothpaste, deodorant, and . . . brown bottles of pills." In my head I picture the cabinet, a stray blonde hair of Momma's lying along the plastic shelf . . . her green toothbrush, the bristles worn. "Sometimes when she was upset or crying, she took some of those pills.

"I couldn't remember which ones. I tried to read the labels. Jennifer Seymour. Typed so neatly. But all the bottles looked the same. I snapped off the lids and poured some pills from each into my hands. They were different colors and shapes. I thought she'd know which one to take."

Suddenly I feel as if I'm standing in the living room of our apartment, next to the sofa. "'Momma,' I said. 'Here.' And I held out my hand to her." I hold it out now toward Sam. Even though my hand is larger now, the fingers longer, I remember the pills sticking to my sweaty palm. Fine lines run like highways on a road map across my palm. Should it be stamped, branded *M* for murderer? "Momma snatched the pills away from me." My hand curls inward as I remember the red mark one of her nails made. I rub my palm against the back of my jeans, as if I can erase the stain of guilt.

Then I look straight at Sam, not wanting absolution, not expecting it, just hoping he'll understand in some small way. He's close to me, not too close to crowd, but the perfect distance to listen and yet offer support. His head inclines just so. His eyes are moist with what I imagine are tears for my mother.

"Momma took all of them. And"—I lift a shoulder reflexively—"she never woke up." My voice sounds as if I'm recounting someone else's story rather than my own tragedy. "The police said she committed suicide. Nana always claimed it was an accident. I couldn't tell her it was my fault. I was scared. Scared she'd hate me. Scared I'd go to jail or something. I was just nine. I didn't know what to do."

Sam's gaze is steady and solemn, not flinching from the horrible truth. "So you've been living your life with this fear."

A breath of air rushes out of me in a huff. "Jumping out of airplanes seems easy, I guess, compared to what I live with inside."

"Jumping into bad relationships is what you think you deserve."

I stare at the ground again, feeling exposed to the elements, shivering with undeniable truth but unable to find the strength anymore to cover myself. "So there you have it."

I'm so glad he doesn't say, *"It's not your fault. You didn't know what you were doing."* I've told myself that very thing, over and over. It never helps.

He doesn't even say, *"You're forgiven."* As if anyone saying that could take away the mark of guilt.

Instead Sam moves toward me and wraps me in his strong arms. His chest is hard and sure. His breath puffs against the top of my head.

Tears I haven't shed since I was a little girl cowering in the dark of night come pouring out of me as if they will never ever stop.

WHAT'S TO BE SAID after all that? Without another word, Sam hands me a clean handkerchief from his pocket.

I stare at it a moment, feeling the embarrassment of my confession burn within me and try to make light of the situation. "You're not going to blindfold me, take me out, and execute me, are you?"

His mouth tightens to a firm line as he presses the soft white

material into the palm of my hand and turns away to give me a
moment of privacy. I wipe my face, blow my nose. My eyes feel
grainy and swollen, my throat raw. Sam rolls his shoulder, swiping
his own face with his T-shirt and sniffs. Then he reaches for my
hand and clasps it in his, providing a lifeline, secure and stable, as he
walks me back to his truck. Maybe he thinks I might totally crack
up or apart. For whatever reason he opens the passenger door and
I let him. He waits for me to climb inside, then brushes his thumb
across my cheek to catch a stray tear.

I don't think to ask where he's taking me. I can't think at all.
My brain feels waterlogged. The countryside whips past in a blur
of greens, browns, and yellows. Sam turns the radio on, and a
George Strait song about letting go floats inside the cab. It feels as
if I just let go of everything that I'd been hiding. It's a free-floating
sensation, like the first time I jumped out of an airplane, my arms
and legs splayed outward, the rush of wind and ground, terrifying
and exhilarating, a scream trapped and burning in my lungs. Every
molecule in my body vibrated. Released from all that has been holding me back, I'm free now to fall . . . or fly.

When Sam turns down the street that rams right into the
courthouse, he swings the truck into a parking space outside
the hotel. "Come on. Let's get you cleaned up, and I'll take you to
an early dinner."

I twist my hands in my lap, replaying my confession. My blood
vessels fill and expand with each heartbeat. "Maybe I should just
go home."

He pauses before shutting his door and looks at me across the
width of the cab. "It's too late to go anywhere but to dinner." He
comes around to my side of the truck, opens the door, and holds out
his hand. "Bryn, you're safe."

Am I? His hand waits for mine, open, steady, calm. My hand
trembles as I dip my fingers into the cleft of his palm, feel the
warmth of him soak into me, soothe my nerves like a balm. He folds
his fingers over mine, lacing, grasping, solidifying a hold on me like

a parachute strapped onto my back before it arcs over me, blanketing and lifting at the same time.

Together we walk through the side entrance that leads through rooms of souvenirs and displays of *Giant*, a movie filmed in Marfa during the fifties. The film crew stayed in this very hotel, and the establishment has drilled it for all its worth, putting up pictures of Rock Hudson, Elizabeth Taylor, and James Dean. It's a friendly hotel. The manager, a Hispanic lady with a short bob and warm smile, welcomed me personally when I first arrived. Since I'm not a celebrity, I assume she does this with everyone. With Marfa being an out-of-the-way town on the outskirts of nowhere, maybe hospitality is a lure to bring folks back year after year.

The manager greets us now in the lobby. Standing behind the wooden counter where countless customers have checked in over the hotel's tenure, she calls me over. "Ms. Seymour?"

Surprised she remembers my name, I detour from the elevator to the front desk.

"I thought you should know, a man was here looking for you today."

"A man?" A woman, I suppose would be just as surprising since I'm not expecting anyone. If my editor sent Marty to take photos, he would have called. Confused, I glance at Sam. Could it be Howard? One of the spit-and-whittle gang? The guy Howard was running from? "For me?"

She nods, her lips pressed together. "Dressed in black."

As if the clothes would tell me who it was. "Sure he wasn't green?"

Sam hides a smile by running a hand over his jaw.

The manager tilts her head. "Excuse me?"

"Sorry." I refrain from asking if he had antennae sticking out of his head.

Leaning across the wooden counter, she whispers, "He looked a bit dangerous."

"Oh, well, um . . ." I glance toward Sam, whose forehead

compresses. Clearly he didn't like the sound of that. "Did you tell him I was staying here?"

Her eyebrows launch toward her hairline. "Ms. Seymour, I assure you, we never give out information about our guests. We do not confirm or deny anyone staying here." She lowers her voice. "We've had many celebrities as temporary residents, and they like their privacy. We never give out room numbers."

"Of course." I wasn't accusing, but she certainly took offense to my line of questioning.

"A woman traveling alone—" Her gaze shifts toward Sam, one eyebrow remains in launch position. "Well, I thought you should know. So you can be careful."

I can't say I'm concerned. More curious, really. "Yes, I appreciate that. Thank you."

Sam leans his elbow on the counter, his gaze following the manager as she retreats into the inner hub of the hotel. "She thinks you picked me up."

"Didn't I?"

"Nope, the other way around." He winks then swivels me around toward the stairs. "Come on, I'll walk you up."

"But—"

"I know. You're not afraid."

"Of Men in Black?"

"Humor me."

I rub my forehead. "I can't think of a joke."

"That's a first." He opens the stairway door.

"How come you seem to know your way around this hotel so well? You being a preacher and all. You haven't frequented—"

His thumb presses gently against my lips, and his fingers caress my jawline. "Shh." He peers behind the door, then lets it slam shut on its own. We stand in the stairwell, silence echoing around us. He leans over the stairwell leading to what I can only assume is the basement, then cranes his neck up the stairwell to see beyond the turn. "Come on."

We climb the concrete steps. I allow Sam to continue holding my hand, leading and directing me. It's a first, and for the moment I find comfort for the exposed part of me. He cracks open the door on my floor a half inch, peers out into the hallway, then swings the door wide. Together we walk down the carpeted hallway, passing closed doorways. A tray of food sits in front of one room, a newspaper in front of another. *Do Not Disturb* signs dangle from a couple of knobs. I wonder if those residents are unavailable if I scream. Sam glances over his shoulder.

I roll my eyes. "Who do you think could be following us? The concierge?"

"You can never be too careful."

"Warning, Sam Walters, you're beginning to sound like your father."

He doesn't respond, and I wonder if I wounded him. To compensate for my sharp tongue, I try to boost his ego a bit. "Are you acting out some James Bond fantasy?"

"That's it. And it's Bond . . . James Bond to you, ma'am."

"Terrific. You're living out your adolescent fantasy."

"Who said it's my *adolescent* fantasy? Could be my current one." He winks as we turn the last corner. "Haven't you always wanted to be a Bond girl?"

"Not really. They never got their man, did they?"

"Ah, but they enjoyed him while they had him."

I punch him in the arm.

He comes to a stop, putting an arm out across my middle—a steely barrier.

"What?" Then I see the door to my hotel room standing wide open. A metal cart overflowing with towels and toilet paper sits in the hallway. "It's the maid, Sherlock."

"You're mixing up Doyle with Fleming." His voice is hushed and serious, despite the wacky subject. He grabs hold of my arm, not letting me proceed. "You can't be too careful, Bryn."

I fold my arms over my chest. "Fine. Go ahead. I don't want to get between you and saving the day from gothic doom."

"Good." He grins. "Stand back." He slides past me, pausing at the door, and scrutinizes what he can see inside the room. A noise makes my pulse quicken. Sam leans inward. "Who goes there?"

"I finish here soon," a thick accented voice responds. "Few minutes."

Sam whips his wallet out of his back pocket.

"What do you have there?" I ask. "A microchip?"

"A payoff." He pulls out a few dollars and hands it to the maid who stuffs it down the front of her uniform. "Thank you. But you can stop now. Don't worry. We won't complain to management." He shoos her out of the room. After she pushes her cart to the next room, Sam checks the closet, behind the shower curtain, and under the bed.

"You're forgetting something." Amused, I watch him stalk through the room like some television actor with a fake handgun.

"My mind?"

"Yeah, besides that. The curtain. There could be a man behind the curtain."

"Not a Bond film, but okay. I'm flexible." He flexes his bicep then edges toward the window like a cat stalking its prey. He pounces on the curtains, yanks it back. Nothing. Or I should say, nobody. Just a lovely view of the street. He stands at the window a moment, staring down at the parked cars and lack of traffic.

"You gonna check the drawers? How about the phone for a wire tap?"

He fists the curtains closed. "Pack your suitcase."

His statement surprises me. "What?"

"You can't stay here."

Walking over to the window, I glance down at the street, expecting to see an unidentified car or maybe a UFO hovering over the sidewalk. Instead, an elderly woman walks a little bug-eyed dog with a red coat strapped around its barrel-rounded middle. "Why not? You afraid of the infamous Men in Black? Maybe Tommy Lee Jones is having a convention here for secret agents and unemployed actors in Marfa. He lives in Texas, you know."

Sam grabs my suitcase and tosses it onto the bed.

"Or maybe there's a *Star Trek* convention in town. Has Spock arrived yet?"

But he ignores me, unzipping my suitcase and opening the drawers inside the armoire.

"Cousin It inside?"

He loads up his arms with my shirts and pants, jeans, and socks.

"Hey!" I step forward.

When he gets to my underwear, he pauses, clears his throat. Clearly this is not in the preacher's handbook on appropriate protocol. He pinches a thong between thumb and forefinger and lifts it slowly, his neck reddening. His morals collide with the *Live and Let Die* mentality of 007.

"Give me that!" I snatch my panties from him. "What's the matter, preacher? Scared lookin' might be a sin?"

He turns away.

"James Bond wouldn't hesitate, you know. Neither would Captain Kirk."

"I'll keep that in mind." He throws the comment over his shoulder as he stalks toward the bathroom and comes back less than a minute later with a handful of shampoo, deodorant, toothbrush, floss, and a Listerine bottle that leaves a damp spot on his T-shirt. He shoves it all at me, forcing me to take it or let it drop to the floor. I'd rather not let my toothbrush hit the floor where strangers' bare feet have walked.

"Why are you doing this?"

"Because someone is asking questions about you. I told you—"

"I know, I know. It's dangerous." I hum the music to *Twilight Zone*. "Spooky. So you're not only afraid of relationships but of what goes bump in the night, huh?"

"I'm not afraid, just cautious." Sam scoops a T-shirt off the floor and tosses it into my suitcase. "Someone doesn't want Howard's story told."

"But I don't even know what that story is!" I plop my shampoo on top of the other clothes in a jumbled, messy pile giving me an odd vision of Richard Dreyfuss building a mashed-potato mountain. "I don't even want to know anymore."

"Fine. But *they* don't know that. And wouldn't it be better to be safe?"

I pause one second too long, reaching instead to fold a pair of jeans.

"You may not care about your safety, Bryn, but I do." He slams down the lid to my suitcase, zips it, and yanks it off the bed.

"And so now I'm supposed to drive back to Austin tonight?" When all I can think of is falling on the bed and sleeping for hours and hours. My eyes hurt, my head aches.

"I wouldn't let you drive so far tonight."

I bristle instantly. "You wouldn't *let* me—"

"You're staying with me."

"That's not seemly, Preacher."

"I'm not a preacher anymore." Carrying my luggage, he walks to the door and waits for me to join him.

"I've got more items in the bathroom."

"Get 'em. Or forget 'em. You can borrow my soap."

"And razor?"

He doesn't blink, but a rosy hue sneaks up along his neckline.

I meet up with him at the door. Standing only a foot away from him, I match his stare, feel a smile curling my insides. "So, you really care, huh?"

The suitcase thunks to the floor. Suddenly my back is against the wall, and Sam's mouth slants across mine. My senses ignite, and I kiss him back, matching his intensity. He whispers my name, his tongue caressing the contours of the letters. My fingers curl into the hair at his nape, pulling him back, opening to him in a way I'm more comfortable with than bearing my soul. This arena fools me into thinking I have some sort of control, like humans taming fire before it consumes them.

A knock at the door jerks us apart. Keeping a hand on my waist, Sam looks through the peephole, rolls his lips inward, and shoves a hand through his hair. Releasing a frustrated breath, he jerks open the door.

"I forget to leave fresh towels." The maid again.

I can see a sliver of her through the crack in the doorway, as I'm wedged into the corner. Smiling, I straighten Sam's T-shirt, smoothing a hand along his muscular shoulder. I resist sliding my fingers into his hair, the memory of its softness tempting.

"Fine. Great." He takes an armload of towels and shuts the door. Tossing the towels on the bed, he gives me a heated look. "Satisfied?"

"More like hot and bothered."

His skin turns a dark, mottled red. He grabs my suitcase, opens the door, and escorts me to his truck, my fate apparently sealed.

Chapter Eighteen

Sam's culinary talents do not exceed his fiery hot chili. Avoiding the frozen pizza, I suggest omelets. While I chop red and green peppers, purple onions, and mushrooms, he scoops dog food into a bowl and places it on the back porch.

When he returns, I ask, "How's Goliath?"

"A bad habit." He cracks an egg into a bowl.

Out the kitchen window Goliath lurks from shrub brush to tree, working his way toward the food, sniffing the wind, flinching at any slight sound. "Maybe you should call him Darth Vader?"

"Why the interest in bad boys?" A smile lurks at the corner of Sam's mouth. A wicked smile, I decide.

"Doesn't everyone have a dark side? You wanna be Bond . . . James Bond. Not exactly a choir boy, is he?"

He nods but doesn't say anything else. I begin to wonder myself, thinking through a long list of boys and men I've dated over the years. All had an edge of danger. But Sam is the most dangerous of them all. And for a totally different reason.

We manage to avoid brushing against each other in the small kitchen. I don't know about Sam, but I'm as aware of him as I would be a fire crackling in the corner of the room, warmth emanating and drawing me toward it. At first the tension between us is palpable, as if we want to retry that kiss again but are afraid to even think of it. So we dance around each other, like gawky teens barely moving, out of sync and rhythm.

I reach into the cabinet for plates. "Butter?"

"Door of the fridge." He whips the eggs into a froth with a fork rather than whisk, his method swift and sure.

I divert my attention with unwrapping a block of butter and pretend not to notice his biceps bulging with his quick, focused effort.

"You're not afraid of butter?"

I pause. "Afraid of it?"

He shrugs. "All the women I've known, well, okay . . . the one . . . my ex-wife sprayed the pan instead of using the dreaded butter."

I smile. "Was she always on a diet?"

"Yeah."

"If you're gonna eat, I figure you ought to enjoy it. Not all women are like your ex, Sam. Have you dated other women since your divorce?" I tell myself I'm only curious, even though I can feel my jaw clenching.

"A couple."

With a knife, I slice through the yellow rectangle. The blade makes a clinking noise against the glass container. "Oh?" I attempt a casual tone but don't fool myself. "What happened?"

"The first made my ex-wife seem tame." He rubs the back of his neck. "And the second . . . she dumped me."

"Ouch. Sorry." But I'm not really. "Why?"

"She said it was because I was still married in the eyes of God."

I imagine him dating a Bible-toting innocent who knows all the right phrases, how to pray and sing hymns in the shower. "Do you believe that?"

He quits beating the eggs, resting his hand on the edge of the bowl. "I believe God forgives us for our mistakes. My ex-wife has moved on. She married again. And I've moved on, too."

My eyebrow lifts, a quiet, subtle question.

"Moving on doesn't mean I have to be married. That's not proof of anything."

I lean back against the counter. "If you had the chance to marry your first wife again, would you?"

He reaches past me, pinches a slice of butter, and places it in the hot pan. As the butter pools and spreads outward, beginning to bubble on the outer edges, he grabs the pan and swivels the melted butter around, then pours in half of the egg mixture. "If I knew we would both try to make it work. But I honestly don't think that's possible. Even without all my mistakes . . . I don't think I could have pleased her."

"Even if you'd devoted more time to your marriage?"

"It wasn't time she wanted necessarily. It wasn't even money. It was some nonentity." He shrugs. "I hope she's found whatever she was looking for."

"And what are you looking for?"

"My spatula." He grins, pulls it out of the drawer, and eases up one end of the omelet. "You ready with those veggies?"

"Yeah." I scoop up a handful and sprinkle them across the omelet's gooey middle. "Want some cheese?"

"Is this mine?"

"Doesn't matter."

"Are you scared of cheese?"

"I'm not scared—" I catch myself before I say *anything*, as I recognize the lie. Covering, I add, "Not of cheese, not of butter. Not of green eggs or ham." I smile back, catch myself leaning toward him and pull back. "Only little green men make me kinda nervous."

His grin relaxes me further and yet winds desire inside me tighter. "Green eggs would make me wary."

The smell of buttery eggs fills the kitchen and I breathe in the warmth and comfort here. I realize I'm relieved I didn't stay at the hotel. I would have been plagued with doubts from my confession. But here, with Sam, I have no doubts, no fears. Not exactly. "So, what do your boys think about all of this? Their grandfather's theories?"

Carefully Sam flips the omelet. Bits of cheese fall onto the stove, and he scoops up the cheese and dribbles it over the top of the omelet. "Josh thinks it's cool. He listens to Howard talk endlessly about it all." He folds over the omelet and slides it onto a plate. "But Jared is more reserved. He doesn't say much." He holds out the pan, and I drop another slab of butter on it. "He basically calls his grandfather a loon."

"My daughter says as much about her great-grandmother."

"Is she?"

"Alzheimer's patients aren't crazy. But before I came here, Nana was imagining a funeral, acting it out in her room." My throat tightens. "The staff thought it was her own. But when I talked to her, I realized it was my mother's."

Sam reaches for me, and my gaze slips toward his mouth.

I turn away and grab a plate. "That butter is going to burn."

AFTER WE EAT, I meander through Sam's cabin, checking out pictures of his sons. Handsome and tall, with tan faces and white smiles, they look hearty and good-natured. They have their father's eyes and the angle of his jaw. Each photograph entails some outdoor activity: snow skiing, biking, hiking. I run a finger down a baseball bat lying on the hearth over the fireplace. "Yours?"

"Jared's. His skis are in the guest room closet."

"You don't get that much snow here, do you?"

"I wish. Mostly he stores his equipment here, which is on the way to the mountains."

In the corner of the room, a guitar leans against the wall. I pick it up and run my fingers along the strings. It makes a discordant sound. "This your son's, too?"

"Mine actually. Comes in handy for a preacher."

"Play me something?" I hold out the guitar toward him, pull it back before he takes it. "You won't play 'Kumbaya,' will you?"

He laughs. "I'll try to think of something else. Maybe the Hallelujah Chorus."

We move to the back porch of Sam's cabin, which gives a distant but lovely view of the Davis Mountains. The metal dog bowl is empty, the plastic one half full of water. Sam settles on a chair and lays the guitar across his lap. His hands move gently but assuredly over the strings as he tunes it. "Haven't played in a while. So I might be rusty." His thumb plucks a note several times until he's satisfied. "Here goes . . ."

He begins to play. His voice is soothing, a rumbling baritone with more heart than ability. It's a countrified song, the words unfamiliar until he hits the chorus of "It's a Great Day to Be Alive." He squints out at the setting sun as he strums and sings with a natural, confident ease. As the notes to the song fade off at the end, the sun drops behind the mountaintops, turning the sky an array of burnt orange and dusky red. The temperature dips lower, and a chill puckers my skin.

"You're cold." He swings the guitar off his lap, propping it carefully against the table. He leans over and chafes my arms.

"Thanks."

"For what?"

"The song. This." Our gazes lock. A ripple of desire rolls through me.

He smiles and stands, locking his hands behind his back. "I'll get you a jacket."

"That's okay."

But he returns to the cabin. I rise and move toward the banister, looking out at the beautifully haunting landscape. A brown rabbit sits very still, its ears twitching, its beady eyes searching. I wonder where Goliath is and if he'd chase the rabbit as nature dictates. But the dog seems to have disappeared. At the sound of the sliding glass door closing behind me, the bunny jumps and disappears in a patch of bushes. Sam settles a leather jacket on my shoulders. I offer him a smile, intending to tell him he has a nice place here, nothing fancy, but there's a gentle peacefulness here. But when my gaze meets his, the words evaporate on my tongue like moisture in the heat of day. I lick my lips, feel a bubble of laughter well up in me. I'm not sure where that comes from. Sam rubs his knuckles along my jaw, sending tingles rippling down my spine.

"Are you okay out here? Or is it too cold? We could go inside."

"No, it's lovely."

It feels like an emotional dance, one step forward, two steps back, as if we can retrace our steps to get to the place before the kiss or leading up to it. I clear my throat. I'm not sure it's wise for me to stay in his cabin. Just the two of us. But the alternatives are the hotel room and my wild imagination or Howard's bizarre home, which worries me even more. But I remind myself I'm a big girl. I can handle temptation. I can handle an attraction to Sam. I can! Sam I am.

"Here comes trouble." His gaze shifts, his words startling me, making me wonder if he read my thoughts, but he lifts his chin toward the back steps.

The stray dog creeps up the wooden steps one at a time, his nails clicking against the wood planks. His ears lay flat against his head. His eyes dart toward me and back to Sam.

"You sure he's safe?" I remember a story I did about a kid who had to endure rabies shots.

"Pretty sure." He keeps his voice low. "When I get him to trust me more, I'll take him to the shelter."

"Why?" I whisper back.

"It's a no-kill shelter. They'll find him a good home."

"Hasn't he already found one?"

"I'm not set up here for a dog."

"Looks like the perfect spot for a dog. And you and Howard could use a watchdog with all the visitors coming and going at his place." I prop hand on my hip. "What do you have against dogs anyway?"

"Nothing." He moves slowly and carefully toward the shaggy Goliath, and the stray sniffs his knuckles. Ever so gently, Sam brushes his hand against the dog's head. Goliath's jaw drops and his tongue lolls out of his mouth.

"He looks part lab . . . or is it bear?"

"Part trouble."

"He likes you."

Sam jams his hands in his front jeans pockets, hunching his shoulders forward. The dog settles down at his feet, looking up at him expectantly.

"Bryn?"

"Yes?"

Sam clears his throat. "About this afternoon."

Here it comes. The kiss. He's going to explain it was an accident. A mistake. Wrong. It was no accident. Sorry, my lips bumped into yours. The kiss was a bit more than a bump. Was it a mistake? Probably. Could there be a future with Sam and someone like me? Probably not. But it was fun. I brace myself for his excuses, for the probability of him saying I'm not his type. Unfortunately I'm beginning to think he might be mine. "Okay," I say, ready for him to get it over with, "go on."

"I think you should know, I won't tell anyone."

That's good. He's not the kiss-and-tell sort. No tabloid headlines in my future. Not that anyone would care about a headline about an obit writer. Still, I say, "I'm relieved."

"But I think you need to share it with Howard."

That stumps me. "The kiss? You think Howard needs to know we kissed?"

He rubs his jaw. "That's not what I meant. What you shared about your mother. About her death."

His words slam into me. Somewhere deep inside I begin trembling, and it spreads like a virus all over me. He walks forward, tips his head toward me, and gives me a light peck on my lips, which feel frozen in place. I can't even manage a response.

"Bryn?"

"N-no. W-why would you ask me that?"

"Because he believes some conspiracy was responsible for Jennifer's death. Shouldn't he know the truth? He won't tell anyone, but it might help him to look at all of these conspiracy theories more realistically. Sometimes the simplest explanation is the right one."

I'm shaking my head and can't seem to stop. "How can you ask that of me?" I back away from him. "You of all people should know how hard it was for me to tell you! This isn't something I want to go around telling everyone."

"I'm not asking you to tell everyone. Just Howard."

"You don't know what you're asking." I glance around, searching for . . . what, I'm not even sure. An escape pod? "I have to go." I drop his jacket to the weathered wooden floorboards, move toward the sliding glass door. "I have to—"

He grabs my arm, pulls me against him. "You're staying here." His arms fold around me, hold me fast. It feels as if an earthquake rocks through me, and I cling to the security he offers as if he is the only solid, steady foundation in my life. "It's not safe out there." He smooths a hand over my hair and settles his palm along my neck. "It's okay. I won't force you to tell Howard. Just promise me, Bryn"—he lifts my chin and meets my watery gaze—"you'll think about it."

Like I could do anything else.

Chapter Nineteen

I grab a book off the shelf and plop onto the sofa. My finger taps against the edge of the hardback. I close the cover, read Tom Clancy's name across the jacket, and try again. But after half an hour, the words and story are unable to penetrate my thoughts. The words hold no meaning for me, as if they're written in a foreign language. My mind continues to turn over Sam's request, and I compile lists of reasons to support why his idea is bad. And my insides simmer.

Sam moves around the kitchen, putting things away, cleaning up, then he grabs the keys off the kitchen table.

"Where are you going?"

"To Howard's. I go every night, just to check on things. On him. I'll be back soon." He pauses, swirls his keys around his forefinger. "Want to come?"

I close the book, all too eager to do something . . . anything . . . other than contemplate my life, this situation, or even my mother. "Sure."

We drive into the dark silence, like a black hole that distorts and narrows my view, stretching and compressing my focus onto Sam, as I become aware of each breath, every movement. It's not simply an awkward pause in the conversation between us; it's a barrier that seems thick and great as the asteroid belt, needing careful negotiation. I keep bumping my head against it as I do any problem in my life. Usually I try to look at the different angles, the other side even, but this time the wall of Sam's request is impenetrable.

Why would he ask me to tell Howard when it should have been obvious it was painful enough the first time? It's a selfish request, one meant to help his relationship with his father. I can't solve their problems. Even though Sam promised not to tell Howard, can I trust him?

I should have left my secret buried, never to be exhumed. Glancing sideways at him as he concentrates on driving, I convince myself it was his profession that made me believe he was trustworthy. And I'm not sure why. Ever since Reverend Do-Right, I haven't exactly held preachers in high regard. So maybe it wasn't that. Maybe something about Sam defies categorical description. Since I'm not anxious to delve into that possibility, I'm more inclined to think it was just time, like Old Faithful, erupting when the pressure within me built to a climax.

The silence between us ticks with certainty. I wait for him to apologize. Surely he knows he should. What idiot couldn't figure that much out? But he remains silent, which rockets my anger into the stratosphere.

He shoots a glance in my direction, as if just realizing I'm sitting beside him. "You nervous?"

An odd question, considering. "No." I sound like Ginger at age sixteen . . . okay, fourteen. "Why?"

"You're tapping your thumb." He nods toward my hand on the door.

I look sideways. Sure enough, *thump, thump* . . . I stop.

"I could take you back."

"What?" My tone doesn't improve. "Why?"

"If you're worried we might run into whoever was searching for you—"

"I'm not worried." But I am clenching my teeth. "Okay?"

"Okay." He stares straight ahead at the road, and we go back to silent mode without even a song on the radio.

The truck eventually slows as we approach Howard's drive. Shocks jounce over the ruts in the road, and I brace a hand against the seat. Headlights illuminate a few feet ahead of the truck, but the darkness out the windows is thick enough to put in a bowl and serve. Sam idles the truck while he jogs toward the gate, unlocks it with a key he pulls from his pocket, then returns. We inch forward into darkness.

But something is wrong. This isn't as I remember it. I straighten upright, my forehead crinkling. "How come the lights around the trailer aren't on?"

Sam shrugs. "Howard might be looking through the telescope."

"Maybe he's not home."

Sam shakes his head. "The pine cone was on the gate."

"What?"

"It's our code."

"Oh, like 'do not disturb, I'm entertaining.'"

His mouth curls into a smile. "In a way. But trust me, Howard's not entertaining." After parking the truck, he pulls his cell phone from his hip pocket and punches a couple of buttons. "It's me. You okay?" He pauses and listens. "Okay. I'll lock the gate on the way out." He snaps the phone closed and opens the door to the cab. "This won't take but a minute."

A humming noise precedes a clicking sound above the truck, then the bulbs flicker and grow brighter, flooding the area with an eerie light. I squint and shade my eyes. Flying insects zoom into the light as if it holds a hefty supply of food. Sam walks around the trailer, checking locks on gates, peering into the woods, disappearing into the thicket, then reappearing. He comes back toward the truck and slides into the driver's seat.

"All quiet on the western front." He squints at his rearview mirror. "Uh-oh, visitors." He keeps a hand on the key but doesn't turn on the ignition.

I swivel around and stare out the back window as a black truck rumbles up the drive at a fast pace. It passes Sam's truck as if we're invisible. The bed of the truck overflows with teenagers.

"Oh, boy," I breathe. "They're not going to TP Howard's fence, are they?" I imagine Charmin strewn around the razor wiring, shredded and lying on the ground, bits matted by dew. Will that convince Howard no one is after him? Or will he take it as some sort of threat as if a toilet paper bomb exploded in his yard?

Sam settles back in his seat, releasing the key in the ignition. "Let's see what their plans are. I don't think they realize we're here."

"Hey!" one of the teenage boys yells toward the trailer. "Mr. Man in the Moon!" The horn blares in an annoying staccato beat.

"That's Randy Rogers." Sam nods toward the tricked-out truck. "I know his dad in town. Nice family."

Another boy stands up in the bed of the truck when it comes to a halt. He wobbles a moment like a bowling pin nicked by a ball. "How you like these moons?"

The boys in the back end of the truck jump up and turn around, bending over and revealing their lily-white backsides. The truck starts to move, driving around the trailer, horn blaring. Teens bobble and stumble, falling over each other. Their laughter turns to curses as the driver must have forgotten to pause long enough for them to pull up their pants. Then with a puff of exhaust, the truck disappears down the drive.

I glance at Sam. I'm not sure which of us begins laughing first.

BACK AT THE CABIN, I'm not sure what's expected. Do I curl up on the sofa and chat or turn in for the night? I try to gauge Sam's mood as he rummages around the kitchen for a snack.

"Want an apple?"

"No, thanks." I watch him wash, dry, and cut the apple. He holds the slices in the palm of his hand. "Are you obsessive-compulsive?"

He stares at me, his brow furrowed, like I just punched him and he's battling the urge to hit me back. "How do you mean?"

"You focused on your career, your ministry, for whatever reasons. And you let everything else in your life fall by the wayside."

"Yeah, tunnel vision."

"Exactly. And now, aren't you doing the same thing? Focusing exclusively on your relationship with your father? So you can't have a relationship with anyone else while you pursue this time with your dad?"

He props a fisted hand on his hip. "I don't know how long I have with him."

"Yes, but don't you see, you don't know how long you have at all. With anyone." I realize how my words might be interpreted, but it's too late to crawl back in the plane once you've jumped.

"Balancing is difficult."

"That's just an excuse for not doing something." I reach over and grab an orange off the table, then another and another. I cup one against my palm, weighing it. I balance the three in my hands, then toss one in the air and begin juggling. "It's like saying juggling is difficult, but never trying it or even practicing. The only way to get good at juggling is to juggle. The only way to get better at balancing is to balance more than one thing in your life." I toss him an orange but miss one arcing downward, and it falls to the floor.

He catches it with one hand, but he doesn't take me up on my not-so-subtle offer. He scoops up the one on the ground and places both oranges back in the bowl on the table. "G'night. If you need anything . . . just let me know."

I need something all right, but I don't think Sam is willing to provide.

I settle into the tiny guest bedroom and pace its length over and over, like a caged animal. Unable to sleep, I decide to take a hot shower. Grabbing my pajamas and shampoo, I step into the hallway, listen for Sam. Instead of footsteps I hear the chirp of insects coming through the open sliding glass door. He must be on the back porch. I tiptoe across the hallway to the only bathroom, which is tiny, almost as big as my shower back home. I stand under the hot spray until my skin glows red from the force and heat.

Decked out in polka-dotted boxers and T-shirt sporting a pit bull with giant pink lipsticked lips—from the Palin phenomenon—that Bryn bought me but I can't wear in public around Austin, I pad out into the hallway. My thick socks skid along the slick wooden floor.

"Everything all right?" Sam calls out.

I zip back into the dark guest room, closing the door as I respond. "Yes, fine. G'night."

The bed is comfortable, but I feel like the Princess and the Pea, unable to settle down, tossing and turning. A real pea is not my problem; it's the pod of an idea hard inside my thoughts, keeping me awake. I jot notes about the story I'm writing for the paper on Larry and Ralph, but end up scratching out more than I keep. I open the blinds and peer out at the full-figure moon. The shadowy purples and grays across the surface make faces at me. I can barely decipher the edge of the railing along the deck and wonder if Sam is looking up at the moon, too. What is he thinking?

Leaning my shoulder and temple against the wall, I watch the moon, the glittering stars, and locate the Big Dipper the way my fourth grade teacher taught me, following the two stars that point to Polaris. Unfortunately I'm not sure where this trip is leading me. Aunt Lillie said I was headed to a crossroads. A decision. But what? Should I forget trying to learn more about my mother? Am I destined to make a decision about Sam? His protection this afternoon at the hotel made me feel secure and safe, something I'm unaccustomed to, and yet I joked about Sam being paranoid when we heard someone was asking for me. Why did I do that? Maybe to overcome the out-of-the-ordinary feelings Sam stirred inside me. What if someone *is* watching me? But who? Is there some connection with Howard and my mom? Could we all be in danger?

A shiver ripples down my spine.

I tug on the cord and close the blinds. The four walls of the room begin to close in on me. I climb back into bed, pulling the covers over me then pushing them off. Pale moonlight seeps through the slits in the blinds and slants across the floor and edge of the bed. Shadows form around me, my imagination pawing at me, eager to romp. The night feels forever long as my eyes remain wide awake, as unblinking as the moon. Flipping over, punching the feather-soft pillow, I flop onto my back and stare at the ceiling fan stirring the air over me like a soft caress. Sam's caress.

Enough! I throw off the covers and swing my legs out of bed, then grab my purse and dig for my cell phone. When I flip it open, I see I've got several messages. I turned the sound off and forgot to turn it back on. Worry jerks my nerves. I check the listings. Chip called. Probably wondering about the article. Eric called three times. I sigh and click the phone closed. No calls from the nursing home, none from Ginger. Peace reigns. Anything else can wait till morning.

But I pace the end of the bed, my thoughts tangled and snarled around these strange emotions concerning Sam. Is it simply something physical, like a head cold to get over? And what about Eric? I've known him for three years, and yet I knew from the beginning it wasn't right. Yet that's exactly what kept me with him. I didn't *want* Mr. Right. He probably called because he forgot I'm out of town. Did he forget about the cat, too? She'll be all right. She's self-sufficient, and I left out enough food for a week. But it always eases my guilt if Eric looks in on her. But what will I say to him when I see him? How do I actually feel about him? It's probably significant that

I haven't thought of him since I've been here. Not once. Not even with regret after my kiss—*kisses* with Sam. Unfortunately it may be more of a poor reflection on me than him. I slide the phone back into my purse and resolve to call him later. Tomorrow. Maybe.

Forcing myself to look at my scribbling, which can't be called an outline of an article, I end up doodling. It's what I often did as a kid in class, on homework papers, in spiral notebooks on the thick paper covers slapped onto my school books. Before I was allowed ballpoint pens, I liked the scratchy sound of the pencil scraping paper. Now I use roller balls. I'm probably as obsessive-compulsive as Sam. But I like the feel of my pen, the swooping lines, fine sharp shapes, thick dots. Remembering the drawing Aunt Lillie gave me, I sketch a ponytail, a long swooping line, and then a girl's profile. Long past midnight my eyes droop with fatigue.

I see my hand . . . a younger version, drawing a picture with a brand-new box of Crayolas. The carnation pink lies in the wicker trash can. My favorite color has always been pine green. I'm working at the desk Momma and I painted white. She let me attach giant orange, yellow, and purple flower-power stickers all over it. It didn't match the pink-and-green checked comforter on my bed in the tiny bedroom of our apartment, but I still loved it. Sometimes I practice my name, twirling the capital *B*, swirling the loop on the *y* in case I end up famous one day. I try curlicues and a smiley face at the top of the *y*.

I glance at the door to my room. Momma is in her room. She wants time to herself as she paints her nails. Since I don't like the smell, I stay in my room. She's in one of those rare moods, distracted, giddy and energetic, a whirlwind of energy.

A loud knock sounds at the door. It echoes through the apartment. It seems to rattle the door on its frame. I race for the living room. Momma is a few steps behind me but catches my arm before I reach the doorknob.

"Go to your room, Bryn."

"Who is it?"

"The postman."

"But the—"

She curses, her lips tight as if she tried to hold back the word but it forced it's way through like when I played "Red Rover, Red Rover, Let Bryn Come Over" at school, and I ran for all I was worth and plowed through my friends' linked hands. Momma glares down at her thumb, the red polish smeared.

"Go!" Momma's voice has an exasperated edge to it.

Turning, I scuff my feet against the shag carpet, taking my time back to my room. I glance over my shoulder and see Momma waiting for me.

"Close the door. And stay in your room."

With an angry sigh, I shut the door with a loud bang. But then curiosity gets the best of me, and I turn the knob as quietly as possible and peer out into the living room as Momma opened the door. A stranger pushes his way inside. His face is dark. Not black or tan in color. Just shaded, shadowy. He wears a black suit, white shirt, and narrow black tie. A man in black.

I jerk awake, sit straight up in bed, my heart thumping so hard I press my hand against my chest to keep it from bursting forth. My skin is slick with sweat; my breathing comes in hard gasps. Cool air chills me like a last breath hovering nearby.

It was a dream, Bryn. A bad dream. But somehow I know it's more than that. It's as if a memory has split open, like a seed that's been hiding dormant in the darkness of my soul.

My hand presses hard against my forehead as I try to rub the images away. Diverting my attention, I check my cell phone for the time: 2:14 a.m. I crawl out of bed. The window beckons me. I split open the blinds with two fingers and search the darkness. Clouds hover overhead. Wind shifts tree branches. Shadows lurk at the base of trunks and around bushes. Hiding places. It's ridiculous to think anyone would lurk outside, watching for me, wanting to find me. I don't believe in little green men or Men in Black . . . purple or pink polka-dotted.

The stillness of the cabin weaves my frayed nerves back together. I lean against the wall, reorienting myself to the present and pulling my thoughts out of the past like broken threads. After a few moments, restlessness presses into me. I tiptoe out of my room, check the door across the hall. Sam's room. It's closed. A black swathe lines the bottom of the door.

I edge out of my room, check the shadowy corners around me, and move into the hallway, past the bathroom and toward the kitchen. The refrigerator door resists, and I tug harder until the sucking sound makes me pause. Light bursts forth. I stand in the glow as if it were a pleasant rain shower, absorbing its brightness, soaking up its warmth. If only it were so easy for my soul. Rummaging at the back of the top shelf, I locate a soda can, pop the tab, and suck down gulp after greedy gulp.

"You okay?" Sam's voice sneaks out of the darkness.

I bump my elbow against the door, spill Coke down the front of my pit bull T-shirt. "You're up."

"Yeah. Couldn't sleep. You?"

"I'm, uh . . . um . . . thirsty."

"Sorry I startled you."

I close the refrigerator and darkness folds over us. Usually I wouldn't mind flashing a come-hither glance, especially when it might lead to something that would block my chaotic thoughts or banish nightmares, even temporarily, but there's a change in me. One that surprises me. Shadows merge with grayness and my eyes slowly adjust. I don't hear Sam approach, but suddenly I sense him more than see him standing only inches away. He has a sudsy clean scent of Irish Spring along his skin, as if he just stepped out of the shower, underscored by an intoxicating fragrance of pure male. If odors had colors, his would be green. Deep and powerful, subtle and vibrant all at the same time. I breathe him in, feel myself lean toward him. He touches my cheek, lifts my chin toward him.

"Bryn . . ." He tastes my name, sampling it. His fingers tease my jawline. His breath brushes against me, stirs me.

I anticipate his kiss, need it like sunshine and water. But I refuse to rush it this time. Yet, as I wait, I sense we are hovering on the edge of some precipice. It's my nature to take the leap. But it's not Sam's. I'm not sure how long we stand there, so close, yet apart, the question hovers between us, tender as fine hairs, invisible to the eye, but soft to the touch. Heat radiates off him. His shoulder is so close, so irresistible. I reach toward him, knowing when I touch him something will ignite between us. I might be consumed. And yet, I don't care. My hand hesitates one second too long.

And then he's gone. He enters his bedroom and closes the door. Firmly. Decisively. And I know a part of me is lost to this man.

He holds my heart, and I cannot escape.

Chapter Twenty

A dull gray dawn hovers at the brink of day with tight curls of cooling air. I start Sam's truck, cringe at the noise, and glance back over my shoulder at the cabin. On the kitchen table I left a note for Sam, telling him I borrowed his truck and promising to return it later this morning. Nothing stirs. No light. No door opening. No dog barking. I don't even see Goliath creeping around the side of the cabin. I resist switching on the headlights until I am down the dirt road and turning onto the main one leading to the highway.

To fill the yawning silence I flip on the radio. The station is set to country music, which stirs up memories of Sam strumming his guitar and singing to me out on his back porch. Rock music is Eric's forte and the mainstay of his band, and yet I can't remember him ever singing for me. Maybe a wink during a song as he looked down from the stage. Maybe a thumbs-up as he walked on stage, or once he aimed his guitar at me and plucked a twangy note for effect. I never felt slighted that he didn't dedicate a song to me, so why do I get a catch in my throat now at the memory of Sam offering up a song to the stars for my benefit?

Punching the radio settings, I settle back on the country station as some male singer croaks out, *"How do you like me now?"* Hmm . . . would Eric feel that way if he suddenly made it big and began touring the states? Over the past year I've felt him edging closer, trying to deepen our relationship, and yet something holds me back. Is it fear? My past? No. It's more . . . disinterest. With Sam, fear is definitely the obstacle.

Inside his truck I notice the clean seats and dashboard, all devoid of debris or even dust particles. In the change box sits some quarters and a few sticks of gum. Memories fasten onto my emotions, jam up my reasons for leaving, my need to stay. Misty rain gathers on the windshield, and I slash it away with the wipers.

Using the notes from my notebook, I follow the directions to Howard's trailer and find it without one detour or U-turn. A fishhook holds the pinecone in place as it dangles, twisting and turning in the slight breeze. I pull the key Sam left on the kitchen table out of my pocket and unlock the padlock. Outside the trailer I park, then slip my cell phone from my purse and dial Howard's number. It rings several times without answer. Maybe he has the ringer turned off. Maybe he's asleep. But we have some things to discuss that I can no longer put off. I doubt he has a meeting this early in the morning. So how do I gain his attention? It's not like I can ring the doorbell. I don't want to stumble around in the woods and search for some hidden entrance. I wouldn't recognize that tree if its root tripped me. Knowing Howard, there could be booby traps set up in the woods where the ground caves in or a rope snags a foot and catapults the trespasser into the air.

I open the truck's door, cringe at the creaking noise, then glance around on the ground before stepping out. I locate a smooth rock, rub my thumb along the worn edges, feel a cracked groove running its length as if it could be split in half. Exactly how I feel.

Now, what was it Sam mentioned about a squirrel breaking into the trailer's inner sanctum? I toss the rock once in the air, catch it, then lob it over the razor-wire fence.

Lights flare. Sirens blast, exploding like a bunch of firecrackers thrown on a bonfire. But I don't flinch or retreat. I stare at a camera set high in a nearby tree, wave, and mouth, "Hello, Howard. We need to talk."

It takes a slow, ear-piercing minute for the lights to flicker out and the blaring sounds to *whoop* a sudden finish. My ears throb with the silence, and red spots cloud my vision. I wait, a hand on the truck's door handle. It takes less than five minutes for a rustle of leaves along the ground, then stomping footsteps through the trees. Howard pushes through the brush in blue button-down pajamas and brown slippers that have seen quite a bit of use.

"What do you think you're doing?" Anger blanches his face.

"Pick the place." I slam the door to Sam's truck. "It's time you were straight with me."

"Haven't I always been?"

"I don't think so."

He blinks at me beneath thick, wiry brows. His gray hair is smashed on one side, sticking upright. Defeat rounds his shoulders as he turns and heads back into the woods.

I follow.

I CLOSE MY HANDS together on the top of his kitchen table and wait for him to put on a pot of coffee. He scuffs around the kitchen in his slippers, scratches his backside, then pulls two mugs out of the sink. He rinses them but forgets to use soap or a towel. He remains silent, not even asking about my use of Sam's truck. When the percolation is complete, the bubbly sound softening to a slow, methodical drip, he pours coffee into my cup and pink lemonade into his and sits across from me at the table.

Suddenly weariness from a long sleepless night and fear nipping at my heels settles over me. The moment of truth has arrived. I stare down into my mug, notice some coffee grounds floating on top, and take a quick sip for fortification. "A man came to our apartment the day my mother died."

He sips his lemonade, his lips pulling back and his cheeks compressing into grooved lines. His gaze remains fixed on me.

I embrace the mug with my cupped hands. In spite of the warmth, I feel a raw cold bite into my bones. "It wasn't you."

"No."

It wasn't a question. I know he's speaking the truth, because the face in my dream didn't resemble Howard. "Who was it?"

"I don't know. What else can you tell me, Brynda?" He says my name in a familiar way, as if we're family, as if he knows so much about me. Maybe he does. Or maybe he only thinks he does. Whichever, I shift in my chair uneasily.

But this is my one chance to piece together my past and figure out my mother's state of mind, even if it means looking my mistakes straight on. I square my shoulders and peer back into the depth of my dream. "He wore a suit. A black suit."

He nods, not knowing, simply encouraging.

I waver. I want to know who the man was and why he was at our apartment. I want to know what my mother was doing. I want to believe something else happened that my nine-year-old eyes didn't see. More than anything I need to know or hope that I didn't kill her. My heart thumps heavily in my chest, as if it weighs more than it should. "Was my mother . . . was she involved in all of this?" I wave a hand at his office in the next room. "This conspiracy stuff."

He sighs as if he carries his own burdens, taps his thumbs together three times, then looks at me, pinning me with his blue gaze. "Jennifer worked for a man who had a defense contract."

"So?"

"Defense contractors work with NASA."

Am I missing something? I slurp the thick coffee and manage not to choke. Maybe the caffeine will help me follow what Howard is trying to tell me. "Okay. But . . ."

"She was acting as a spy for him. Finding out information from NASA."

My skin tightens. I lean forward. "For who? The Russians?"

"You're thinking in the way you've been taught, Brynda. That the Russians were against us. Originally Kennedy made a deal with the Russians. A deal to share information about space. But someone didn't want that to happen."

"Who?"

"Well, that's the million-dollar question, isn't it?" He settles back into his seat. "When Kennedy died, the deal they made did, too. Of course, the Russians saw it as us going back on our word. Kennedy's word. And the real space race began."

I drink more coffee, feel the grit of grounds against my teeth and swallow as I try to absorb all he just said. "So how did my mother get involved?"

"I introduced her." He rubs his thumb along the seam in the table. "She came to see me one day at work. She needed a job. This was before you came along. I wanted to introduce her to someone who might be hiring. She ended up working not for NASA as I'd hoped but for the defense contractor." He leans forward, peers at me over the rim of his coffee mug. "Brynda, what did you see the day Jennifer died?"

"Nothing." I wrap my hands around the mug, clinging to the warmth, the sturdiness, as if it will hold me in the here and now, not let me fall back to that day.

But I see the door to my memory opening, just as that stranger pushed open the door to our apartment so many years ago. The shadowy face, the dark suit looms in my mind. My mother's angry face mottled, eyes bulging. I only wanted to please her. To help her. Angry voices penetrated my bedroom door.

"*Please . . .*" My mother was pleading about something. Begging. A rush of apprehension flooded me. Finally the crack of a slap, hand against cheek. My memory darkens and I'm unable to see past that door to what I fear. I can't open it. I can't stop it. Today nothing would keep me back. No door. No strange man. I'd storm into the room and demand to know what is happening, how he dare touch my mother. But, then, I was only a wide-eyed nine-year-old, frozen in place by cold fear.

The memory of the slammed door yanks me back to the present. I attempt to swallow the scream lodged all these years in my throat. My muscles resist, and I lift my chin a notch. I press my thumbs together, the nails turning white with the pressure, as if I can still the trembling inside. "Momma was crying. She went through spells like that. She stared at nothing for hours. She drank heavily."

"Jennifer wouldn't commit suicide." He forces the words through tight lips as if I'm lying.

"If she was involved in all of this—Russians, NASA, defense contractors—then she was probably in over her head. Maybe she was confused, scared, overwhelmed . . . even threatened."

"I told your grandmother it wasn't suicide at the funeral." He clunks his mug on the table. "I didn't believe what the forensics report concluded."

My lips flatten together withholding the truth that I cannot speak.

"Brynda, did the man come back? Later? Did he leave something for your mother? Give her something to take? Some pills? Something to drink? Maybe he gave her a shot of something?"

"No." The word is but a hoarse whisper.

Silence pulses between us for several minutes. Howard sits in his seat, his features tight. In light of all I know, his conspiracy theory seems as fragile as blown glass and my truth could easily shatter it. But I can't tell him. Nothing good ever comes from confessing.

"Would you recognize him if I showed you his picture?"

The question surprises me. "I-I don't know."

"Let's try." He pushes up from the table. With determined steps, I follow him into his office. Desks and tables are covered with stacks of folders and papers. "Let me think." He digs through stacks of books, finally locating a thick tome with a blue frayed cover. He flips open the book and starts turning pages.

I glance down at the mug of rank coffee that seems glued to my hand. Automatically I lift to drink but then stop at the sight of grounds stuck to the side of the mug. I amble around the cluttered office, noticing and yet not. It's a whirl of paper and words that are meaningless to me. With every solid beat of my heart, I hear, *Tell him. Tell him. Tell him.*

"Here we go." Howard steps back from his desk, swivels the large book toward me. "Take a look here. Do you recognize him?"

On one page is an 8x10-inch photograph of an older man, maybe in his fifties or early sixties. On the opposite page is a grouping of smaller photos with events, dates, and subjects listed below each. I feel Howard watching me, gauging my reaction.

I nod toward the book. "That's him."

Howard's brows climb. He sticks a stubby, crooked finger on the large photo of the obviously important man. "This one?"

But my gaze is drawn to a smaller photograph on the opposite page. Three men stand together. It's the man on the left. I recognize the hooked nose, the thick-framed glasses, and the smoothed-back hair. "No. Here." I try to read the tiny print beneath the picture but the words are blurry. I lean away from the book to try to make out the names. "Who is he?"

"The man I was telling you about." Howard's face creases into a frown of sorrow, maybe even regret. "The man your mother was working for. Barry Munson."

I stare at his pale, fleshy hand, imagine it flying through the air and striking my mother across the face. "W-why would he hit her?"

Howard's gaze moves from the book to me. "What do you mean?"

"The day Momma died, he came to our apartment. Momma made me go in the other room. I heard them arguing. It sounded like he hit her. He did. I saw the red place along her cheek."

Howard's features twist. Is he tormented as much as I am in his own effort to help my mother?

"Let's look this guy up on the Internet." I move toward Howard's computer. "Can I borrow yours? Maybe we can figure out where he lives and have a talk with him."

"Brynda—" Howard's soft tone makes me pause a heartbeat— "Barry Munson is dead."

ONE THING I'VE LEARNED as an obit writer: just because someone dies doesn't mean you can't learn more about him. And so my pursuit of Barry Munson begins. It starts with reading his obituary online. He left a widow and three children. There wasn't a funeral, just a graveside service before interment. I confirm that he worked for a company that held a defense contract in the 1960s and 70s. In late 1969 he moved from Houston to Washington, DC, where he lived until his death in the early 1980s. He was only fifty-eight. The death certificate on record shows he died of a heart attack. No foul play. I search for any mention in the newspaper, but the story of his life fades.

"There's always a paper trail," I explain to Howard.

"What?"

"Look, if a guy is involved in secret dealings, he's not going to leave all that paperwork, if there is any, at the office when he retires. Is he?"

"Probably not."

"So then, maybe he took it home. Or had a secret office. Maybe a lockbox."

"He could have burned it."

"Maybe. But a man who died as suddenly as he did in the prime of life might not have taken that kind of precaution." I click away at the computer and find his widow is still living in the Washington, DC, area. She hasn't remarried, and I calculate she must be in her eighties by now. "Shall we?"

"What?" He pulls back. "Call her?"

"You think she'd talk to you or me over the phone?" I shake my head, answering my own question. But a plan is hatching in my brain. "We don't want to give her the heads-up." I click to print. "Can I?"

He studies the computer screen, then nods. "Sure."

"We want to surprise her. If given the chance, she might shred any papers he might have hidden at home. Or even throw away a mysterious key. Where would that leave us? So we have to go to DC."

"We?" Howard turns from the computer to look at me as a paper slides out of the printer.

I grab it and click off the Internet server. "Yep. You and me."

He shakes his head, the skin along his neck jiggling. "Not a good idea. No, no, no. Don't you understand? It's not safe."

"Howard." I place a hand on his arm to emphasize my point and feel him trembling, which triggers a similar reaction in me. It's the kind of shakes I usually get when I'm writing a story and uncover a new piece of the puzzle. An integral piece. A piece that could change the story entirely. "This is something *we* have to do. You and me. *We* have to lay my mother to rest. One way or another. It's time we both learned the truth surrounding her death. Now I'm going to Washington." I stand. "Are you?"

The blue of his eyes darkens. "I guess I'll have to."

Chapter Twenty-One

I pull Sam's truck up to his cabin. Most likely he will want to fly to Washington, DC, with us. If for no other reason than to keep an eye on his father. I actually find myself hoping he will come, but I avoid analyzing the reasons. Before I reach the top step, the front door opens. Sam stands in the doorway, wearing running shorts and a UT T-shirt, which hugs his fit frame. His hair is rumpled as if he just rolled out of bed, but his skin has a sheen of sweat. He greets me with a slow, "Mornin'."

"Hi." I hold out his keys. "Hope you don't mind that I borrowed your truck."

"Not at all." He doesn't ask where I went or why I'm in my pajamas with tennis shoes. "Want some coffee?"

I place the keys in his open palm. "Sans grounds?"

"That's usually how I make it."

As I pass by him entering the cabin, the rich coffee aroma inviting me, I touch a finger to the appliquéd UT on the front of his shirt. "You didn't tell me you were a fan."

"I don't like to brag."

With the sun barely at tree line, a chill permeates the air even inside the cabin. He closes the door, and I amble toward the kitchen, noticing the coffeepot is full. I pour two mugs, slip off my tennis shoes so the cool air can reach my toes, and follow him out onto the back porch. His fingers brush my hand as he takes a mug, and I ignore the way my heartbeat quickens. We sit in silence a few minutes, just the sunrise and questions between us.

Finally, with the coffee warming my belly, I confess. "I talked to your dad."

"I know."

My eyebrows lift.

"You took the gate key. You drank his coffee, notoriously filled with grounds."

"You're good at math, putting two and two together. But don't jump to conclusions. I didn't tell him. Not what you wanted about my mother." I can't meet Sam's gaze. I focus on my thumb circling the rim of the mug. "But I told him about the night my mother died. About a man who came to visit her that day."

"Someone significant?"

I nod. Goliath trots up the back steps, loops around the porch to avoid me but settles close to Sam's chair. Sam reaches down a hand and pats the dog's head. "Your father knew him. He was my mother's boss. I'd suppressed the memory of him, I guess. It came to me last night."

Sam leans forward, his hands cupped around his mug. "Where is he now? Can you go see him? Maybe talk to him."

"He's dead." My thumb taps the mug's handle once, twice. "I'm going to track down his wife. See if she has any old papers, something that might tell me what Momma was doing for him, what was going on the day she died."

A banging at the front door interrupts our conversation, almost makes me spill the coffee. Goliath looks up, utters a gruff bark.

"Who could—?"

"Stay here." Sam sticks a hand out toward me, but his gaze is fixed on the front door. Goliath lopes down the back steps and disappears around the side of the cabin. "Go to the bedroom. Lock the door."

"What? Why? I'm not afraid."

Sam walks into the cabin. "Someone followed you yesterday, remember?"

I trail after him, and he secures the back sliding glass door. I stand toe-to-toe with him in the den, and his size clearly intimidates. Here's hoping whoever is outside is equally impressed. But I lift my chin and throw out my doubts. "That doesn't mean anything. It could be UPS or FedEx."

"Yeah, and it could be the Avon Lady."

I start to laugh. "She rings the bell."

"Go on." He nods toward the hallway leading to the guest bedroom. Whoever it is bangs on the door again. Sam stalks through the cabin, grabs a baseball bat propped against the hearth, and heads toward the front door. No peephole or side window allow a sneak preview of our visitor.

I lean into Sam, pressing against his shoulder, and whisper, "Maybe it's Howard."

"He'd call first." Sam closes in on the front door and wraps his hand around the knob. "Who is it?" His voice dips deep to a dangerous, threatening level.

A male voice responds, but I can't decipher the words.

"Did he say Captain Kirk?"

I shrug, denying the trigger of fear that fires through me. What if it *is* a dangerous sort? Someone searching for me? For Howard? But why? I slip around the sofa, searching the room for a weapon, something besides Sam's guitar or an overstuffed pillow.

"What do you want?" Sam asks through the closed door.

This time, the guy says my name. My skin tingles. My heart strikes my breastbone. I move into the kitchen, consider grabbing a butcher knife. Instead, I lean across the sink, slide the curtain aside and peer out. The visitor is out of view, but my gaze lands on a black Harley parked near Sam's truck. I release a pent-up breath. "Eric."

Something must be wrong. Why would he be here? Is he the one who was at the hotel asking questions yesterday? Why didn't he just call me? But he did. Three times. I rush through the kitchen and put a hand on Sam's tense arm holding the bat. "It's okay. I know him."

Sam gives me a questioning glance.

My fingers are already fumbling with the lock. "Really. It's okay. It's—" I yank open the door and lock eyes with a startled Eric. "Hi."

He greets me with hands braced on his narrow hips. His hair is wind whipped. "Do you know what I've been through trying to find you?"

My heart pounds even harder. "Is it Nana?"

His brow scrunches into a frown. "No."

I lean against the doorjamb. "Did Ginger send you to find me?"

"Why didn't you answer your cell?"

Sam clears his throat.

I turn toward him. His arms are crossed over his chest, the baseball bat resting along his side. Pushing the door open wider, I introduce the two men. "Eric, this is Sam." I indicate the other man in my life. "Sam . . . Eric."

The men eye each other, nod tersely, but refrain from shaking hands.

"What are you doing here?" Eric continues his line of questioning, his gaze more intense this time.

"Who's checking on Elphaba?" I fire back.

"The cat from—"

"You didn't just leave her, did you?"

"She can take care of herself. But I fed her before I left. And I'm going back tomorrow." He shoves a handful of hair out of his eyes. "So are you going to tell me what you're doing here . . . with this guy?"

I feel the heated gazes of both men on me like a branding iron. "I'm on assignment."

"You're on assignment, staying at a strange man's cabin?" Eric's insinuation strikes quick and hot.

"Well," I laugh, trying to diffuse the tension, "Sam is strange, but not to me."

Sam shakes his head and steps toward Eric. "Hey, look. Bryn and I are . . . friends."

It's that slight pause that gives credence to doubt and proves to me he thinks otherwise. My heart flutters. His gaze collides with mine, and I sense the suppressed questions rising up like smoke. Guilt brands me. I should have told him I was seeing someone. Does he now see me like his ex-wife?

Eric moves forward, challenging the threshold, looking Sam up and down, assessing the situation. "Bryn's never mentioned you."

I expect Sam to say, "Ditto," and brace myself.

"That's understandable." Sam doesn't give an inch to Eric's attempt at intimidation, but neither does he challenge Eric's turf. "We only met recently. Bryn knows my father. She came to Marfa to see him."

"Howard Walters, Sam's father"—my face flushes like I'm under a truth-telling lamp—"knew my mother, Eric. He *knew* her." My words I realize may not contain the impact I intend since I haven't mentioned my mother much to Eric. "They went to school together. But also they knew each other when we lived in Houston." That might be the most I've ever shared with Eric about my past. He knows my mother died when I was young but nothing else. Nothing about the suicide cloud that surrounded my family and haunted me for years. Nothing about what I saw, what I did, and the guilt that holds me like chains around my heart. A crinkle forms between Eric's slanted eyebrows, and I shift the conversation in a diversionary tactic. "Did you go to my hotel? Ask questions about me?"

Eric's mouth pulls sideways. "You didn't answer your cell phone. You didn't call me back."

I'm so relieved I start to laugh and meet Sam's gaze. So, no Men in Black are following me. We should have known a simple explanation could have erased our paranoia. And yet the quiet, knowing look between Sam and me feels more intimate than anything I've ever shared with Eric.

Sam slings the baseball bat up to his shoulder. "That explains it then. I'll have to put away my Walther PPK."

"And your secret-agent card." I notice Goliath loitering several feet behind Eric, watching us with those wary brown eyes.

Sam aims a smile and wink in my direction, then sticks his hand out toward Eric. "Come on in."

Eric narrows his gaze and slowly reaches forward to clasp hands with Sam. I notice his knuckles tighten, his fingers tensing..

"Want some coffee?" I ask in my most perky tone, ignoring Eric's darkly caffeinated glare. "There's some great dark roast I can brew." But Eric's dark glare changes my mind. Forget the dark roast.

Decaf will be much wiser.

AWKWARD DOESN'T COME CLOSE to describing the cozy get-together. With my nerves tangled and tripping up my tongue, I retrieve a mug, feeling Eric's gaze on me as I reach into the cabinet without hesitating. Okay, so I know where Sam keeps his coffee mugs. I refuse to feel guilty. After all, what have I done? Nothing. Well, not really. Besides Eric and I may have an understanding between us, but there's no paper document proclaiming our undying devotion.

The men settle in the den. Eric sits on the couch, his arm stretched across the back as if saving me a seat next to him. Sam lounges in a leather chair with a foot propped on the coffee table. They both watch me, as if my choice of seats makes another, more significant choice.

"I'm going to take a shower." The words come out before I fully contemplate the way they sound. I hesitate, wonder if I should explain why I'm here at Sam's rather than the hotel, then decide to let the unasked questions go unanswered for now.

When I return a few minutes later, dressed in jeans and a light sweater, Sam stands as I enter the room. Eric pushes up from the sofa and slips an arm around my waist. I can't help but compare the possessive feeling that makes me squirm with the way Sam's arm comforted me.

"Let's get something to eat." Eric's tone is tense. "I'm hungry."

"I know a couple of places in town." My gaze shifts toward Sam.

He stands. "Might want to avoid the drugstore. Different cook on Wednesdays."

"Good to know. Want to join us?"

Eric gives me a hard look, which I ignore.

"Nah," Sam walks toward the kitchen and sets his mug in the dishwasher. "I've got some things to do here."

"I should probably take my suitcase." I move away from Eric and hover near the door. Is this good-bye? Maybe it will be just Howard going to D.C. with me. I push away the painful pang. "I mean, now that we know no one is chasing me."

"Makes sense." But Sam doesn't move to get my suitcase. And neither do I.

"I can't carry a suitcase on the back of my bike." Eric tugs on my hand, moving me toward the front door.

"Yes!" I curb my enthusiasm. "You're right. I forgot about that."

Sam lays a hand against his flat belly. "I could bring it to the hotel."

Is the offer for me as well? Or is he simply being nice?

"Why don't you do that?" Eric claps Sam on the back, like he's some lackey. "You can just leave it at the front desk, ol' man." He opens the front door and waits for me to join him on the porch.

"But, Eric, we shouldn't put—"

"He doesn't mind."

I glance at Sam, struggle to find an excuse.

"It's no trouble. Glad to do it."

Eric pulls me toward his Harley, but I resist and yank my hand away. I take a step toward Sam. Not knowing what to say, I stand before him. It seems in the last couple of days that we've shared so much . . . we're far more than strangers now. We're friends. And yet . . . more. "Thank you."

Then I throw my arms around him, hug him for only a second, then let go and move away. Going with Eric, staying with him is easy, safe. Sam is the dangerous one now. Dangerous to my heart.

But then, danger has never been a deterrent.

I watch Sam retreat back into his cabin and close the door. Goliath sits on the porch watching me, his head tilted sideways as if wondering why I'm leaving.

Eric hands me his stowed helmet. I reach for it, then hesitate. At the corner of the cabin, Goliath watches us. He sits on his haunches, his eyes shaded beneath a mop of black hair.

"Wait a minute." I have the distinct feeling that I've been pushed into a corner and I don't particularly like it. "Let's go for a walk."

"What? Why?"

"I just need to walk . . . think."

He gives me a look I recognize, the one where his will stands off against mine. "I'm hungry."

"It won't take long, I promise."

With a heavy sigh, he unhooks his helmet and props it and the spare on the seat. He glances around. "Where you want to walk to?"

I take off toward the road and he falls into step with me. With a glance behind, I take note that Goliath is following us, keeping his distance but keeping track at the same time. Ahead of us, low on the horizon, the moon hovers in the pale morning sky. It always strikes me as odd to see the moon during daylight hours. But there it is. The contours and shades look like a face. Sam's maybe? It feels as if he's walking along with us, watching, listening. We walk all the way to the fence line before I come to a sudden stop.

Eric remains silent, but I can sense his irritation, his eagerness to head into town. "You're not hungry?"

"Not really." I slide my hands in my back pockets and study the tops of my boots. His fingers slip through the hairs at my nape and cup my neckline, tipping my head backward. I look up into his brown eyes . . . and before he can lean forward and claim a kiss, I place a hand on his chest.

He pauses, his brows crinkling, then he pulls away. "So that's how it is?"

A hard lump congeals in my throat. "Eric . . . it's not anything . . . really."

"Then what?"

"I don't know." I nudge a rock at my toe. It rolls into a sparse patch of grass.

Clarity brightens his eyes. "This isn't a work trip, is it?"

"Not completely, but it's not what you think either. I'm hoping to get a story out of it eventually. But I had to come for more personal reasons. I met Howard when I was in Houston for the NASA celebration. I learned he knew my mother. I didn't want to go searching down memory lane"—I shrug—"but here I am."

"Yeah, here you are." His features harden.

"I know you don't understand, but it's something I have to do."

"You've never told me much about your past. Your mom."

"It was too hard." I shake my head to loosen the tightening in my throat. "It isn't you, Eric. It's me."

His mouth compresses, pulling the corners back and dimpling his cheeks. "It's more than that. Isn't it, Bryn."

It's not a question, because he knows the answer. And he's right. I just don't have a better explanation. "Look, when I get back to Austin—"

"Bryn, stop." He crosses his arms over his chest, hunching his shoulders forward as if accepting defeat. "Let's not make promises we can't keep. We've always been good about that." His gaze slides toward the black paved road. "Let's just recognize the end of the road when we see it."

Tears well up in my eyes, blur my vision. I don't have an argument. I've never been the sort to plead or grovel, and I'm not about to start now. Because I recognize the truth when I see it.

I search for the words that seem lodged deep in my heart, words that convey my feelings, my regrets, my gratitude for Eric, and all I've probably put him through during the past years.

He reaches out and touches my lips. "Let's not say things we'll regret." He steps away, turns, and walks back toward the cabin. I trail behind him, but stop a few feet from his Harley as he climbs onto the seat, tugging on his helmet. "Long drive back to Austin."

"I'm sorry." It's lame, but it's true.

"Me, too." Moisture glistens in his eyes before he slides his shades into place. "I'm sorry I couldn't be what you need." He tilts his head toward the cabin. "You'll be okay here?"

I nod. I'm beginning to think it's the place I'm supposed to be. After almost fifty years of searching for that place, it's unnerving and peaceful at the same time to finally find it.

As Eric's bike roars to life, Goliath barks and trots toward me. He sits close enough for me to see those serious eyes watching me and yet far enough away that I can't pat him. I look toward the horizon where the moon lingers.

I'm not sure if it's there as simply a warning, an anomaly . . . or a promise.

Chapter Twenty-Two

Sam opens the door of his cabin a moment after I knock. His hair is wet, and he's now wearing a stiffly ironed button-down—hastily buttoned, seeing as one collar juts higher than the other—and faded jeans. His dark eyes widen briefly before his features fall back into neutral. "Where's your boyfriend?"

"He's not . . ." The denial is quick on my tongue, but I stop before a full confession flows out of me. Not anymore anyway, but I keep that bit of news to myself. This is my chance to let Sam know I'm available, yet fear holds me back. I avert my gaze toward Goliath, who lies down on the planks of the porch, his chin resting on his fat paws. I feel like an awkward teen, but I'm not sure why. With Sam's penetrating gaze on me, I shrug. "Eric left."

"His decision or yours?"

"Mutual. I needed time to take care of things here. Without distractions. He needed to get back to Austin."

"So you'll be seeing him when you return home?" Sam leans against the doorjamb. Before I can tell him no, he asks, "There a reason you like the wrong sort of fellow?"

"What makes you think Eric is the wrong sort?"

"What makes him so right?"

"You know, since you're not willing to stick your own neck out for a relationship, I'm not sure you're the one who should be criticizing others."

He studies me for a quiet moment, his eyes dark with hidden emotions. "You're not so brave either, Bryn, since you're not really risking anything."

This definitely isn't the way I imagined this scene. "I don't know what you mean." I start to turn, not knowing where I'll go, but Sam stops me with a hand on my arm. Goliath sits up suddenly, tense and alert, then scratches his ear with his hind leg.

"Sure you do." Sam's not backing down. "You're not really risking your heart with that guy, are you?"

I meet his gaze solidly, squarely, but feel my heart thumping like an injured thoroughbred. "You don't know anything about me."

His right eyebrow lifts, and I know my accusation echoes false. His grip softens, and he releases my arm, but I still feel the imprint of his fingers on my skin. "Did finding you here at my cabin cause problems with what's-his-name?"

"Eric. Why should it?" I fiddle with the edge of my sleeve. "That's not why he left, if that's what you're implying."

He covers my hand with his, making my nerves leap. I pull away. "Did you tell him"—his voice gently probes—"about your trip to DC?"

My head snaps up to meet his gaze. "How did you—"

"Howard told me."

I lift my chin a notch, daring him to tell me not to go.

But he doesn't. Instead, he smiles. "I'm going, too."

It's the answer I anticipated, even wanted, and yet it makes my pulse hammer against my temples. "It's not necessary. I'll take care of Howard."

He steps forward, closing the gap between us, yet he doesn't touch me. "But who'll take care of you?"

I bristle. "I can take care of myself." My words sound hollow. Why am I fighting against him, resisting the urge to lean into him? "I don't need a bodyguard. James Bond can stay home."

"I don't know about that." His gaze warms. "And with the way you look . . ."

I thumb his shoulder, and he shrugs it off. But he doesn't back away. His nearness overloads my senses, overwhelms me. I move toward Goliath, reach out a hand and let him sniff it before I ruffle the thick hair on top of his head.

"So, what time are we leaving?" Amusement brightens Sam's eyes.

Patting the dog's back, I think of all the details that must be taken care of before we leave. "I have to make plane reservations."

"I can help." Sam moves closer, leaving the door to the cabin wide open. He rubs Goliath's ear. The dog sits between us, his brown eyes shifting back and forth, studying us.

"I'm staying at the hotel tonight." I blurt it out, sounding more and more like a silly, frightened school girl. "I mean, there's no need . . . now that we know Eric was the one following me."

"You're probably safer at the hotel. But . . ." He pauses, looking down at our hands, just inches apart.

"But?"

"If you want to stay here at the cabin to make your plans, I'll take you back to the hotel any time you say. You can even use my computer."

"I have a laptop." Excuses come easily but are wafer thin.

He grins. "But you don't have the best guacamole north of the Rio Grande."

I cross my arms over my chest in one last bid of self-defense. "As good as your chili?"

"You'll have to make your own conclusion. I'll fix you dinner. Later, I can drive you back to the hotel." He raises two fingers. "I'll be on my best behavior."

"Too bad." I reach forward and start unbuttoning and rebuttoning his shirt to make the buttons align. But he stops me, pulls me closer, his shirt gaping open and my hand resting over his heart. His gaze burns as hot as the summer sun. I blurt out, "You can't go to DC."

"Why's that?"

"Goliath." It's the last excuse I can think of. "What will he do? Fend for himself?"

"I would imagine he's used to doing that. But I have an idea what to do with him, and I could use your help."

Excuses fall away like a cleansing rain. A solid reason has presented itself, and I latch onto it like an umbrella, holding it tightly as if a stiff wind might rip it out of my hand.

"MRS. MUNSON?" I ASK when the woman on the other end of the phone picks up the receiver and says in a polite but loud voice, "Hello?"

"Yes," the wavering voice says.

"Sylvia Munson?"

"Yes."

"You were married to Barriman Munson?"

"Who is this?" Her voice hardens like an icicle forming, sharp and pointed.

"I'm a reporter from Austin . . . *The Austin Statesman*?" My voice arcs into a question, as if I'm unsure of the paper I work for, but in reality it's attributed to Sam watching me, making me nervous. "I've recently been doing a story on those involved with the NASA space flights, especially the landing on the moon." I turn my back on Sam and try to concentrate, pacing back and forth across the living room, my cell phone in hand. "I learned about your husband through one of the NASA experts and was hoping I could interview Mr. Munson."

"You didn't do your homework. He's dead."

"Yes, ma'am. I'm sorry. I learned about his death while searching for him. I don't mean to stir up more grief for you, but I thought he might make an interesting subject for an article about genuine American heroes who—"

"When will you people learn?" Her abrupt tone silences me.

I glance at Sam. What is this woman talking about? "Excuse me?"

"I've told you people over and over to quit calling here."

"This is my first—"

"And don't threaten me. I'm not talking." A clunk of the phone into the receiver precedes a long, irritating beep.

"This may not be as easy as I'd hoped."

Sam's frown mirrors my concern. "What happened?"

I prop a hand on my hip, my reporter's brain clicking into gear. "Why wouldn't a widow want her husband portrayed as a hero?"

He shrugs. "Maybe she knew he wasn't."

"Maybe. And what people keep calling her?"

Sam quirks an eyebrow. "Now that's a good question."

RALPH ARRIVES IN A seen-better-days Cadillac, pulling up to the side of the cabin and walking around to the back steps. He's wearing the same outfit as yesterday, but I figure his new companion won't care what he wears.

Surprisingly Howard steps out of the passenger side. "Been showin' Ralph around so he can keep an eye on things while we're gone."

"I've got something to show him, too." Sam welcomes his father with a pat on the back, and Ralph with a friendly handshake.

Ralph grins. "I'm gonna have to start chargin' you for all these services. You know I have a full schedule."

I offer to get the men some coffee, and when I return with a tray of steaming hot mugs, they've settled into the chairs and are discussing reasons the alarm at Howard's might be tripped and how to turn it off.

"Nothing at the cabin is as complicated." Sam takes the tray from me and offers me the chair next to him. "But I've got a situation that I've been trying to figure out how to handle." He glances toward me, and I nod encouragement. "For the past few weeks I've had a friend hanging around . . . and well, I was hoping he might stay with you while we're gone."

"A friend?" Howard frowns, his eyebrows forming a fuzzy *V*. "Who you talking about?"

Seeing Sam hesitate, I smile. "Goliath."

Both men give me confused stares. Howard's eyebrows arch upwards. Ralph tucks his chin down toward his chest and peers over his glasses. Around the corner of the cabin, Goliath trots, his pink tongue dangling. He's scruffy but cute, and I hope Ralph will take to him.

"There he is." Sam stands and calls the dog over. "Here, boy!" He whistles and the dog's ears twitch, his pace accelerating. The dog's fur ruffles in the slight breeze as he bounds up the stairs.

"What on earth is that?" Ralph stares, wide-eyed.

Howard steps backward, pushing his chair toward the railing. "Is that a bear?"

"It's a stray dog." Sam pats his leg and the dog trots toward him. "He's very gentle. Really."

Ralph edges forward. "Looks like he eats a ton. Even more than I do."

"He'd make a good companion," I add.

Sam coughs, and I realize I misspoke. He turns back to Ralph. "I'm not asking for a permanent situation. I want him back. He's a good dog. Makes a good watch dog."

"Didn't hear him bark once when we pulled up," Howard protests.

"That's the best kind of watch dog. Just the sight of him will be a deterrent to others with mischief on their minds. Still, he's gentle as a teddy bear."

"Looks like one."

Sam reaches a hand toward Goliath and rubs his head.

"I don't know about this . . ." Ralph scratches his jaw. "Looks like he'll be an awful lot of trouble."

Goliath barks and then leaps upward, placing his big furry paws squarely on Ralph's chest. The two of them stare at each other for a moment, then Goliath licks Ralph's scruffy beard. I hold my breath, waiting for Ralph's reaction. It's slow in coming, but finally a laugh rumbles out of his chest. He pats the dog along his side. "Well, maybe he won't be so bad."

Before we know it, Ralph leads Goliath toward his car, telling him about the bath he's gonna get and laying out the ground rules.

"I'm not sure how he'll ride in a car or if he's ever been in one," Sam warns.

"He'll be fine. Don't worry about a thing."

"He probably should go to the vet, get whatever shots he needs. I'll be glad to pay—"

A car pulls into the drive at that moment, overriding Sam's offer. Goliath tenses, his hair spiking along his spine. A low growl rumbles out of him.

Sam studies the dog. "Well, I'll be. Now, he's feeling protective."

I smile. Of course he is. He's found a home. "Who is it?"

"Don't know." Sam squints toward the gray four-door. "Howard? You recognize our visitor?"

"Saw him in town yesterday."

"Maybe we should talk to him," I suggest.

Howard shakes his head. "Dangerous. Following me."

"That's enough for me to know they're up to no good." Ralph puts a hand on the dog's neck. "Goliath," he pats the furry rump, "go get 'em!"

Without hesitation, the dog lunges into action. He races down the drive, his gait rolling like that of a grizzly bear.

The four-door brakes, sits there a moment as Goliath approaches, then begins a rapid descent, z-ing back and forth along the drive as it travels in reverse. Goliath stops before the gate, sits quietly while the car turns around on the highway, then he trots back toward his new master.

"Good, boy." Ralph ruffles the shaggy fur along Goliath's back. "Sure we're gonna get along just fine. How do you like chicken fried steak?"

I glance toward Sam to gauge his reaction, to see if he regrets giving away his solid companion. But he grins. "This might be the beginning of a beautiful friendship."

Chapter Twenty-Three

Since I want to drive to Austin and check on Nana, our options for airline flights narrow. With the tickets purchased, I begin focusing on the details of the trip. I decide it would be good to get a neighbor to check on Elphaba while I'm gone three more days. I make that call well aware of Sam across the room reading the local paper. I'm not sure why I withheld from Sam that Eric and I broke up. Maybe it's a defense mechanism. Maybe it's a barrier to keep Sam and me apart. Even when I know that's not what I want. Confusion apparently clouds out reason.

Piling three people and their luggage into my Prius is not the easiest task either, but Sam has a gift for organization. Even in the dark of the early morn when I deem the car full, Sam manages to squeeze in my laptop, Howard's overstuffed briefcase, and his own guitar. Weighted down as we are, my little Toyota still gets up and goes, maybe not to the 80 mph allowed on the highway but fast enough.

"We could have taken my truck," Sam suggests for the first time as his knees bump the dash. He looks like it required a shoehorn to work him into the passenger seat.

"Better to take her car," Howard pipes up from the backseat. "Not safe to take our vehicles."

"Why?" I glance from the road to the rearview mirror.

"His station wagon and my truck have been spotted by UFOs," Sam mutters under his breath.

I shoot a sideways glance at him. Has the poor man reached his limit on this cloak-and-dagger operation?

"What are you complaining about?" Howard fires back. "You've got more room up there than I do back here."

"Imagine what it was like"—I verbally step between father and son—"for those first astronauts. There was barely room in the space capsule to breathe."

Sam remains silent. As does Howard. I meet his gaze briefly in the rearview mirror. "Have you ever spoken to any of the early astronauts? What did they see on the moon? Anything that made them think—"

"They were hypnotized." Howard's insertion halts my line of questioning.

Sam sinks lower in his seat, if possible, forcing his knees higher against the dash.

"Hypnotized?"

"Those in charge wanted every miniscule detail of the missions revealed. So they said. But the irony is that they could have blocked the astronaut's memories while they were under hypnosis, so they *can't* remember. They wiped the slate clean."

I tap the steering wheel with my index finger. "Is that documented? That they were hypnotized?"

"Sure. Everybody knows that. And any astronauts I've talked to don't like me pointing that out. Curious, huh?"

Sam turns on the radio, which is tuned to the coast-to-coast radio broadcast. The host George Noory is interviewing some guy about a nearby solar system that seems to have an impact on the planet Earth. I can almost hear the *Twilight Zone* theme song superimposed but restrain myself from humming it. I glance back toward Howard via the rearview mirror, only to see him scribbling on a notepad and not paying attention to the broadcast. For Sam's sake, I change to a country station playing Carrie Underwood's "Just a Dream." Even though the song is about a woman who loses her husband in a war, it makes me think of each of us—Howard, Sam, and me—and how each of our lives turned out differently than we ever dreamed.

With only one stop for a late breakfast, we make it to Austin by early afternoon. We unload my car, dumping Sam's and Howard's luggage into Ginger's room. I strip the bed where my daughter slept the night before I left, which seems as vague as a year ago now even though it's only been a few days, and replace the sheets with clean ones. Elphaba, as usual, hides, but I spot her golden eyes under the bed skirt. I change the litter box and water and put out more food.

Howard and Sam make themselves comfortable in the den with newspapers and a laptop open when I grab my keys off the table. "I need to check on my grandmother."

"Mind if I come with you?" Sam closes a book and slides it back onto my bookshelf.

"If you don't think you'll be bored."

Leaving Howard with C-SPAN for company, Sam grabs his guitar and we head toward the retirement center.

A SOFT, PUTTERING SNORE greets me as I enter Nana's room.

She lies on her back on the single bed, jaw slack, mouth open. I glance back at Sam, but he's a few doors away chatting with an elderly gentleman in a wheelchair who is examining the guitar. Quietly I enter Nana's room, not wanting to wake her and yet wanting her to open her eyes, see me, and whisper my name. It's the hope I always carry in my heart, and yet I prepare myself for the confusion muddling her gaze, the stress crease forming between her feathery gray eyebrows, the question "Who?" on her parched lips.

I edge closer to the bed. Her eyelids look translucent, the tiny blue and red veins like delicate ribbons. I sit beside her, cover her hand with my own, which is much larger than hers, my fingers longer and more like Momma's. Nana was always small but formidable. She never said, "Where did you get your height?" but I would catch her looking at me, as I outgrew clothes by the truckload, and imagine her wondering about my father.

It's not that I haven't thought of him through the years; I wonder sometimes if he knew about me, if he cared. When I was a teenager, scenarios ran through my head: Momma pregnant and scared, deserted by her boyfriend; Momma pregnant and defiant, not telling her boyfriend. Momma pregnant and unsure who the father might be. None of the situations imagined were ideal, and they tended to spin from one to another, like a pinwheel, depending on my shifting feelings for my mother.

Nana snorts, coughs, and struggles to swallow, her chin thrusting forward.

My heart jerks unsteadily. "Nana?" I glance around for the button that calls the nurse. "You okay?"

It takes her a moment to focus on me. She doesn't speak, but I read the question in the depths of those blue eyes.

"I'm Bryn." I quit asking "Do you remember?" a long time ago. "Can I get you something?" I stand, reach for her glass. "Some water maybe?"

She nods, and I help her take a sip, holding the back of her head and pressing the glass against her dry lips. Water dribbles out the side of her mouth, and I dab it with the corner of the sheet. Words well up in my chest. There's so much I want to tell her, so much I want to say. Not a clearing of my conscience, just a thank you for the sacrifices made.

But she wouldn't understand now.

"Just rest." I pat her hand then refold the sheet across her chest. I can't seem to sit still. I need something to do, say. "I've just come back from Marfa." I use the words to fill up the strange silence between us. "Did you ever go there?"

Her eyes follow me as I move about her room, tucking the sheet under the corner of her mattress, readjusting the pillow in her chair, but she doesn't respond.

"I'd heard of the Marfa lights," I continue, just something to fill up the silence, "some pretty weird phenomenon. We . . . I saw something but I'm not sure what it was. It could have been head-lights for all I know."

"But she met some mighty strange folks there." The masculine voice gives my heart a pleasant jolt. Usually I don't like intrusions, but this time I'm grateful to see Sam standing in the doorway, gui-tar in hand. He smiles that easygoing smile that tugs a note from my heart. "Can I come in?"

"Please." I motion him in. "Nana, this is Sam. Do you remember Howard Walters? He was a friend of Momma's way back in high school. Well, Sam is his son. We met in Marfa this past week. He showed me around, protected me from aliens."

Nana blinks as if taking it all in and yet not quite understanding.

Sam sits on the edge of her bed and slants his guitar across his knee. "I just met your neighbor, Ernie Rodriguez, down the hall. He liked my guitar. I played him a song he remembered, and I thought maybe you would like to hear something."

I look to Nana, hoping she will respond, but she acts like a china doll, locked in a porcelain frame. "Would you like to hear some music, Nana?" I shift my gaze to Sam. "She always liked Johnny Cash. And Loretta Lynn."

"Oh, sure." Sam strums the strings of his guitar, pinching the neck with the other hand and producing a melodic sound. "Can't get better than Johnny and June. Or Loretta and Conway."

"Helen." Nana's coarse voice surprises us.

Sam gives me a questioning look.

Her one utterance takes my breath for a moment. I nod, my throat working to control the emotions that threaten to overwhelm me. I pat her hand. "Of course." My gaze meets Sam's. "Helen Reddy."

A panicked look comes over his features, making his eyes hawkish. "I can't sing 'I am Woman.'"

I laugh. "Oh, come on. I want to hear you roar."

"I prefer howling at the moon." His gaze burns into me and I feel myself flush.

Focusing on Nana, I smooth my hand over hers. "We used to sing 'You and Me against the World.'"

Sam's fingers stroke the strings, plucking out a few notes. "Good song. It's not in my usual repertoire, but I'll give it a try."

The song emerges slowly from the guitar strings, a bit haltingly and yet predictably, pulling up memories of Nana taking me fishing, showing me how to pinch the edges of a pie shell, and sharing a shake at a drive-in. At first I try not to think of the words, try to block the emotions they stir, but then I let the song flow over me as a tear trickles down my cheek.

Sam doesn't sing all the words, just a few lines here and there along with part of the chorus. Nana watches him, her eyes wide, and her hands begin to soften and relax. Only moments before her hands clutched the sheet, but now they rest quietly, one over the other. Her forefinger begins to tap in a clumsy rhythm.

Sam alters the tempo and begins another song without even pausing. It's not a tune I recognize. He sings in a deep, tender voice about a feather-soft heart with the strength to weather storms. Sam looks straight at Nana as he begins, but as his voice takes us on a journey of admiration and discovery, he closes his eyes. His voice cracks on the final notes of "Eagle When She Flies."

Nana reaches forward and touches Sam's hand, causing a discordant strumming. "You were singing that about someone. Who was it?"

His solid blue gaze is calm and steady. "My mother."

Nana nods as if understanding his words, his sentiment, his love. My heart swells.

"She was a single mom, just like you, Mrs. . . ." He hesitates.

"Cora," I supply.

"Miss Cora." He looks her in the eye, "Not easy to be a single mom, but so much to admire."

"We should go." I stand and swat away the moisture on my face.

Nana doesn't look at me. She keeps her hand on Sam. "Stay a moment longer."

After placing a kiss on Nana's wrinkled cheek, I leave them alone while I wait in the hallway. A nurse scurries away and makes me wonder if she was hanging out near Nana's door. Another nurse doesn't hesitate to ask me, "Who is that?"

"A friend."

She dabs at her eyes. "If he wants to sing for the residents sometime . . . well, I know it'd be appreciated."

"I'll tell him."

Her eyes pinch at the corners, and I wonder if she wants to deliver that message personally. But before Sam emerges, she's paged. "If I don't make it back," she says, moving down the hallway, "you be sure and tell him now. Okay? He's welcome here anytime."

"Ms. Seymour?"

I turn toward a caramel-skinned nurse. "Beatrice. How is my grandmother doing?"

"Fine, ma'am. If she eat slow, then no problem swallowing. Still she choking some. We give her soft foods to make it easier." She edges closer. Her skin is so smooth it looks like frosting poured over a warm cake. "You should know, she been accusing staff of stealing from her."

My mind flickers through the arrangement of knickknacks in her room, the photograph of Momma graduating from high school, and me in black cap and gown, my college diploma in hand. "I didn't see anything missing."

"No, ma'am. I think it her imagination. She say we take the painting off her wall. But there was no painting that I see."

"A painting?" I rub my face and release a sigh. "It's okay. I'll take care of it. I'm leaving town again tomorrow but I'll come see her before I head to the airport."

She nods and smiles. "You bring that nice man with you again, too."

A few minutes later Sam walks through Nana's doorway, guitar in hand. His face is solemn. I want to ask what they discussed but I also fear knowing. "We need to go before your fan club finds out you're available."

He gives me a quizzical look.

"Some nurses listened in when you were serenading Nana."

We walk down the hallway together. Sam tells Mr. Rodriguez good-bye, then glances back toward Nana's room. "She's a special lady. I'd like to come back and visit her sometime. If you don't mind."

"I think she'd like that."

Sam's thoughtfulness comes from a kind, unselfish heart. No wonder Nana is so drawn to him. She's not the only one.

Not by a long shot.

Chapter Twenty-Four

Your mother must have been a strong woman," I say on the drive back to my apartment.

Sam holds a bucket of the Colonel's chicken in his lap. His guitar, safely tucked inside its case, resides across the backseat. "She was. But aren't most moms?"

I'm quiet on that one. It strikes at the heart of so many questions I have concerning my mother. Was she doing some sort of subversive work, which caused her problems, maybe even caused her death? If so, would that make her brave? Or foolish? Courageous? Or selfish?

When Ginger was born, I realized my propensity for taking crazy chances had to be tamed, and for many years I didn't jump out of planes or go off with strange men who I'd never met before or see again. My life became more valuable only because of Ginger and her needs. Because of that, I wonder about Momma's view of her own life once she became a mother. Was she so depressed that she couldn't think about anyone but herself? Or did the depression

. . . or fear . . . or whatever she was experiencing make her believe I'd be better off without her? Or was what she was working on so important that it usurped even motherly love?

Because I lost my mother at a young age, when Ginger came along I knew any mother—good, bad, or indifferent—was better than no mother at all. And even though I was certainly not the best mother, I was all Ginger had. I determined to be there for her through the good and bad times. But what was my mother thinking when she took those pills from my hand? Did she want to die? Really die? Was her situation that dire? Did she want to leave me alone, an orphan? Was she thinking or simply feeling? Or was her overdose a mistake caused by the whiskey she'd consumed that night, which blurred her thoughts and twirled her maternal compass out of orbit?

What frightens me is that I so desperately want to believe Momma was working on something of national consequence, which puts me in the same seat as any conspiracy theorist.

"Your grandmother is a strong lady, too." Sam interrupts my chaotic questions, to which there are no definitive answers.

"Yes, Nana is. She dealt with a lot in her lifetime. The loss of a husband and a daughter. She was a single mom twice."

Sam lifts the lid on the bucket of chicken and the greasy goodness fills my car with a tummy-rumbling odor. He grins at me like a kid.

"You can wait." I turn the car onto a four-lane road that will lead us back to my house.

Securing the bucket's top, he sighs. "My mom was a single mom before and after my parents' divorce. Dad was never around to help out with diapers or early morning feedings, trips to the ER—" He points to his thumb. "Broke it playing football on the front lawn when I was seven. Mom took care of me. Can't sing her praises highly enough, I suppose."

"Literally."

He grins. "Pretty corny, I know."

"Not at all." My voice deepens and cracks. "It was moving. So many times people blame their moms for all their pain and suffering. But in all honesty, and I can say this as a single mom myself, we are just doing the best we can with what we have." I rub my hand over the steering wheel, debate for a full minute if I should say more or not, then take the plunge. "I used to blame my mom until I became one. Then I liked to think I understood her." I shrug, my hands still firmly on the steering wheel. "Any mom is better than no mom. None of us is perfect, but our kids need us."

"They do. They need their dads, too."

I glance at him. "I never had a dad."

"That may be why you don't think you need a husband. Or God."

My hands tighten on the bumpy, plastic wheel. "Excuse me?"

"Do you think about God?"

"Why? What does that have to do with anything?" I slide the car into the next lane and a loud honk makes me jerk my car back. I glance over my shoulder at a minivan. Apologetically I glance over at Sam then back at the road, braking as the car in front of me does. "Maybe I have missed out on something."

He watches me, not asking anymore questions, just waiting. I've come to realize that's his modus operandi.

This time I turn on my blinker and move into the right lane. When we reach the corner, I turn, then twice more until I'm on the street where I've lived for ten years. I follow the parade of mailboxes, going slow as I know there are many young kids on my block. "There's something about you, Sam. You seem so calm."

"It's not me then." He pats the sides of the Colonel's bucket, his thumbs pumping out a rhythm. "That song, 'You and Me' . . . It's deeply spiritual. But then I tend to see everything through a spiritual lens. When everyone turns their back on you . . . like my family did, and my father. My church didn't want a preacher who was divorced . . . It was a lonely time. But God never turned away from me. He was always there. And I know God was always there for you, too, even when your mom died."

"If He was, then I wasn't aware of it." I brake for a kid on a bicycle.

"God's never intrusive, Bryn. But He's there when we turn toward Him."

His words seep into my soul, and I think back on those events, on the people who came into my life and then drifted away. Was I being protected? Prepared? Or was it all just chance? Is there a rhyme or reason to why I'm still here, and my mother isn't? Is it the consequences of bad choices? If so, then that doesn't make sense, because I've made plenty of bad choices in my own life. Was I given a second chance?

More like a million.

"I'm amazed at what women can do." Sam leans against the car door and angles a look at me. "Raising children. Working. Cooking. Cleaning."

"Confession time: I can't fry chicken."

"You don't need to. There's enough to feel guilty about in life without tacking on inconsequential stuff."

"You're right. I've always joked with Ginger that she'll be in therapy in a few years dealing with her wacky mother."

"My kids have already been in therapy," Sam says quietly.

I turn into my driveway, brake, and turn off the ignition. I turn toward Sam. "I'm sorry."

"Don't be. It was my fault."

"So what is your mother like?" Maybe refocusing the conversation will help us regain the footing we had earlier, before I stuck my foot in my mouth.

"Pretty typical of housewives in the sixties and seventies. She ran my Boy Scout troop, set dinner on the table every night at six sharp, and kept the house clean and me on track. Her father was a preacher, as was his. My grandparents were married sixty-two years, so when her marriage with Howard ended, she took it hard.

She felt like she'd not only let down her entire family but also God. And me. I'm not saying the divorce was only my dad's fault. It's not usually one-sided. After all a marriage is a relationship with two people. Takes two to keep it together and two to tear it apart. Still, Mom is pretty amazing. She went out and got a job as a secretary in a law firm, worked her way up, convincing her boss to pay her way to law school when I was in junior high. So now she's an attorney who helps women who don't have a voice or many options. Took her life falling apart for her to find her purpose. Funny how it often works out that way. Maybe that's how it's supposed to be."

I think of Momma curled on the couch, her eyes red rimmed. Was that a sign of weakness? If I hadn't given her the wrong medicine, would she have found the strength and her own purpose as well? And with her, how would that have changed my life?

Did I not just end my mother's life . . . but also my own?

AFTER DINNER, I CRAWL up into the attic. The picture Nana was accusing the staff of stealing has been here for three years. It's shrouded in a sheet. Maybe she needs to see it. I decide to take her the picture Aunt Lillie gave me, too. Maybe it will soothe Nana in some way.

I pack them in the car and then settle on the sofa to read Howard's book . . . or try to. I'm not sure my brain has the capacity to wrap around quantum physics. Kind of a leap for me. Howard is talking on his cell phone in Ginger's bedroom, and Sam is channel surfing from *The Hunt for Red October* to an NFL game—a blue team vs. a white.

"Have you read this?" I keep my voice low as I close the book over my finger to keep my place and show Sam the cover.

"Three times."

My eyes widen.

"Howard had me check for punctuation."

I glance at the spine, I don't recognize the publisher. "A vanity press?"

He shakes his head, not understanding.

"Did he self-publish this?"

"Of course."

I open the book and locate my place, then pause again. "Did you understand it when you read it?"

"Some. Some not so much." His answer is evasive, but purposefully so? I flip forward to the chapter on hidden symbols at NASA, then give him a sideways glance. Only his wrist and thumb move as he pushes the button on the remote and changes TV channels every five seconds. "So what did you think?"

He keeps his eyes focused on the television. "You mean, is it true?"

I nod, catching in my peripheral vision Elphaba slinking into the room, lurking around the corner of the sofa. Earlier I refilled her bowl, but she acted disinterested, giving me a cursory glance that said, "Get lost." There's a lot of skulking around with Howard's conspiracy. So far some have simply been misunderstandings. But is there something more substantial here? Some deep secrets at a high-up level? Or is it all an illusion? "Yes, Sam, do you believe it's true? Or some figment of your father's imagination?"

I realize then how difficult it must be for Sam to look this situation squarely in the proverbial eye. Would you rather your father was fighting for some great cause? Or that he was delusional? Or is he protecting and defending the truth? Maybe we're the delusional ones?

Sam sighs heavily and clicks off the television. "That may be the question of the century."

"Right after who shot JFK."

"And J.R." He winks.

I laugh.

Sam pushes up from the sofa and peruses a conglomeration of photos on the wall of my den. *"That's all folks."*

"Mel Blanc's gravestone. Man of a thousand voices."

Sam shakes his head and smiles simultaneously. "Okay, what about this one . . ." He looks over the bank of photographs of famous and not so famous tombstones. "*Steel* . . . something . . . *Blade Straight.*"

I smile, remembering the cragged cross. "Sir Arthur Conan Doyle."

"Patriot, physician, and a man of letters, it says."

"It does."

Sam looks back at me. "You don't find this a bit morbid?"

"No. Do you?"

He shrugs. "I guess we all end up the same. Have you given your own tombstone any thoughts?"

"Occasionally," I hedge and look back at Howard's book. "What about you?"

"I'm not ready to write mine. Maybe I'll just let someone else do it. You, maybe. You're an obit writer. What will I care by then?" He turns back to the framed photos and chuckles. "You're kidding."

"Which one?"

"Al Capone's."

I laugh. "Ironic, huh?"

"Very. Someone else must have written it for him." He moves past the photographs and peruses my bookshelf. He's quiet for several minutes, pulling out a book, then sliding it back into its rightful place.

"What do you like to read?"

"Anything. Everything. My mom always said I'd read a cereal box. And it's true."

"Sorry, I'm out of Cheerios. But I might have some oatmeal in the pantry."

"He grins and grabs a thriller off the shelf, cracks the book wide.

"You like mysteries?"

"Research." He waggles the big hardcover at me and plops back onto the sofa.

"Are you contemplating a crime?"

"Lining up options for how to outwit the bad guys."

"And the bad guys are . . . ?" I ask.

"If you figure it out, let me know. In the meantime, I'll have to wait till one introduces himself."

We both focus on our books, and I reread the paragraph I've read half a dozen times and still don't understand. With each page my eyes grow heavier and heavier. Until the book bobs and I jerk awake. "Maybe I should—" I stare at Sam like he's grown antenna. He's stretched out on the couch, his sock feet propped on the coffee table, one hand idly stroking Elphaba as she languishes beside him. *How* did you manage that?"

His brow furrows. "What?"

"The cat . . . Elphaba hates everybody—except Ginger, my daughter."

He shrugs and rubs a hand along her back. "Guess I'm just good with animals."

And people, too. Is there anything this man can't do? And yet I know he has enough regrets in his life to fill a boat and sink it. "You want a cat to replace Goliath?"

He laughs. "Oh, no, you can't relocate a cat."

"What do you mean?"

"That's what my grandmother used to say." He scratches behind Elphie's ear and the cat closes her eyes as if entering an altered state. "Cats don't like to be moved."

"So what do you do? Leave them?"

"Old wives' tale, I think. You're not moving, are you?"

"Don't have plans to, no." It's another clear barrier between Sam and me and any possibility for anything more to happen. He has his life. I have mine. They might run perpendicular, but not parallel. This juncture will end and we will part. At one time in my life I would have seen that as a positive. But this time . . . not so much.

"Well, then"—he glances down at the cat—"Feels good, huh?"

"Is she *purring*?" I put the book down and ease toward Elphie, and consequentially Sam, careful not to startle her or to scare off Sam. I simply want to be near him. A low rumbling emanates from the cat. "What a stinker! She's never purred for me. And I'm the one that feeds her!"

Sam's warm grin draws me closer, nearer, and at the same time questions arise within me. "At least now I know there's another side to her personality. She's not totally wicked."

"Like the rest of us?"

That's definitely the truth. I think I must be wicked to think such thoughts about a preacher man. And to wish there might be a possibility beyond today.

AN INCESSANT RINGING TUGS at me, pulls me out of a dream that doesn't want to release me. *Phone.* The word clicks into my brain. What time is it? The clock shines 2:54. Foggy dreamland falls away and fear takes its place. Ginger? Nana? I snake an arm out of the covers and snag the receiver. "What's happened?"

"Ms. Seymour?" A muffled male voice.

Struggling to sit up, I push off the sheets tangled about my legs and flip on the lamp beside my bed. My heart plunges like it suddenly filled with lead. I can barely draw a thin breath. All I can think of is Nana. My voice wavers when I answer, "Yes?"

"You don't know what you're getting yourself into. Stay in Austin. Stay out of all of this."

"Who is this?"

"Do you understand?"

"Who *is* this?"

A click is the only response. For a long moment I stare at the buzzing receiver. Then I search for the return number on Caller ID. Wonderful. *Private caller.* Which means it can't be redialed.

I lie in the dark, waiting for my heart to calm to a regular, steady beat. The strange voice repeats in my head—and I realize it was a robotic voice, inhuman. Terrific. Now I'm being called by aliens.

"WANT ME TO COME with you?" Sam asks as I carry my suitcase to the door.

Part of me doesn't. But part of me does. He's calm and sincere and just maybe he can help. "Sure. That would be nice."

We leave Howard scribbling in the margins of the newspaper at the kitchen table, and I remind him we need to leave for the airport by 10:30. "Don't forget. We'll be back to get you."

He nods without looking toward us.

When we reach the nursing home, Nana stands outside her room. Her body is rigid, her hands clenched at her side. She reminds me of when I was a teen and came in way past my curfew. Nana was mad, but she didn't say a word. She met me on the porch and hugged me fiercely. "You're safe. G'night."

I followed her, all those years ago, into her bedroom, watched her strip off her robe and climb into bed. "Nana," I started, hesitant, guilt snapping at me like the electric typewriter clicking off each offense. "I'm sorry."

She didn't answer me.

"Nana? Can't you forgive me?"

"Forgive you?" From the dark, her voice came out hoarse. "Brynda, honey, I lost your mother. Every day I think about her . . . remember, question what I could have done to save her, to protect her. And now I don't want to make the same mistakes with you. And I fear I'm slowly losing you, too."

"But I'm not—"

"You're growing up, moving beyond my ability to protect you. And it terrifies me that I might fail with you, too."

I never quit my irrational behavior, never quit taking stupid risks for no reason other than to feed my crazy desire to experience life in the extreme. But at that moment I began to protect Nana from knowing how stupid I could be. Our positions began to reverse.

A friend once told me, "You're like a wolf that has to howl at the moon." She was used to seeing the ER fill up on the night of a full moon when there would be more shootings and crazies going . . . well, crazy. And she pegged me right. But Nana didn't have to know.

So now I approach Nana as I would a wounded animal. "Hi, Nana." I move toward her cautiously. "Everything all right?"

She looks at me, her gaze roaming over my face as if trying to find something familiar. She reaches out a hand and I clasp it. "They stole my picture. Stole it!"

"It's all right, Nana. Come on, let's go sit down." I help her turn around as she leans heavily on my arm, and together we retrace her footsteps into the room. She settles awkwardly in her recliner. It's not facing the television anymore. *Wheel of Fortune* plays softly in the background. Pat Sayjak spins the giant wheel. "Can I get you anything, Nana?"

"My painting."

I'd hoped to distract her until Sam arrived with the painting, but since I haven't I play along. "Do you know who took it?"

She squints her eyes at me. "That woman. I bet it was her! She's always in here, snooping around."

"Beatrice didn't take it. She's here to take care of you, to help you out."

Nana puffs out a breath. "You can't trust them."

I wonder who *them* is—nurses, orderlies, or more Men in Black? Aliens? Another conspiracy theory being birthed?

"Better not turn your back," Nana warns.

A knock at the door makes me turn. Sam leans in the doorway. "Can I come in?"

"Please." Seeing the framed picture in his arms, I turn back to Nana, smiling. "Nana, guess what? We found your painting."

"You did?" She twists in her seat and watches Sam carrying it. She holds out her hands, opening and closing them like a small child. When Sam carefully places the frame in her lap, I pull off the covering sheet. Nana studies the painting for a long time. It hung in her bedroom for many years. Shades of blue blend and flow into each other. The ripples of lake water undulate along the bottom of the canvas, highlighted by a shaft of moonlight. Above is an almost, but not quite, full moon. Her fingers graze the outer edges tenderly. "Oh, Jen," she whispers, her voice cracking. "Oh, my Jen."

I glance at the bottom of the painting for the artist's signature but find no name. "Did Momma give this to you?"

"She painted it in high school."

"Oh, Nana. You never told me." I touch the top of the frame.

She slaps my hand. "Don't take my painting!'

I jerk my hand away. "Nana, no one stole your painting. I've had it at my house with all of . . ." No. Better not mention her other possessions. She might want all of them returned, and there's no room here in the nursing home.

She points her finger at Sam. "He did!"

"No, ma'am." He doesn't back away from her accusation. "I just carried it for Bryn. It's kind of heavy. Want me to hang it up for you?"

She wavers for a minute before trusting him to lift it off her lap. While he locates the hammer and nail we brought and pounds it into the wall, she watches him carefully.

"See"—I kneel beside her chair and pat her hand—"no one is taking anything from you." But part of me knows that isn't true.

And then she begins to cry.

Chapter Twenty-Five

Hey!"

Howard is not at all happy when a security guard at the Austin-Bergstrom International Airport dares to touch his briefcase as it slides through on the conveyor belt. Without removing his shoes, Howard marches through the metal detectors.

Like bees on an intruder into their hive, several guards swarm to Howard.

"What are you doing? I'm an American!"

Sam rushes forward, hobbling, with one socked foot and his other shoe half on. "It's okay. Sorry, sir. He's sorry. He didn't know. It's been a long time since he's flown."

Son takes father by the arm and guides him like a two-year-old through the security process. "You have to take your shoes off."

"Why?"

With a look toward me, Sam rolls his eyes and uses the oldest excuse in the world: "Because."

When we finally reach Dallas, we race through the terminal to change planes. At long last, we land in DC I rent a car, one slightly larger than my Prius, to the relief of the tall men traveling with me. They packed light, and it doesn't take long to load the suitcases, briefcase, guitar, and laptops into the trunk.

"Want me to drive?" Sam holds his hand out for the keys.

"Sure. That would be—"

"Uh-oh." Howard looks behind me across the parking lot. His forehead folds like an accordion.

The parking lot is a sea of gray, blue, white, and black cars, stretching out like an ocean of waves arcing from tall minivans to economy size, the sun shimmering off the metallic paint. A family with a screaming baby and two rowdy children piles into a van, the father wrestling the baby's car seat into place. He bumps his head on the doorway and curses. His wife snaps at him.

Sam pauses before settling into the driver's seat. "What is it?"

I see nothing suspicious either.

Howard turns abruptly toward the car. "That man, over by the check-in building. Black shirt. Dark glasses." Howard scratches his head and ducks down as much as a totem pole can. "I saw him, remember? Back in Fort Davis. You were there."

I glance from the man in question toward Sam, who squints, shading his eyes. Shifting my gaze back toward the man, I watch him start walking in long strides toward us, his fisted hands pumping at his sides. Sam takes a step toward him, his features hardened and determined.

Remembering the strange call in the middle of the night, I pull him back. "What do you think you're doing?"

Sam stares down at me.

"It's not safe."

His gaze narrows. "How do you know?"

"I got a phone call. Like you told me about." I watch the man start to run, reaching behind him as if pulling something . . . a gun maybe?

"When?" Sam demands.

"Let's get out of here!" Howard lunges into the backseat like his backside is on fire.

I don't need any further motivation. I run around the trunk and dive for the front seat. Sam takes the driver's side, jerks the car into drive, and peels out of the parking space, wheels squealing. He follows the signs out of the parking lot, big arrows leading us toward a gatehouse posted by a guard.

"We're good," I say. "No need to stop."

But a bar is across the drive. Sam swerves into another lane but slams on his brakes only a couple of feet from pointed daggers sticking out of the asphalt at our tires.

"Great," Howard grumbles. "They're probably going to make us take our shoes off again."

"This is crazy," Sam says. "We should just talk to the guy."

"Not safe," Howard mutters. I almost expect him to say, "Remember, Jennifer," like "Remember the Alamo."

I place a hand on Sam's arm. "He could be armed."

He glances at me, then jerks the car in reverse and pulls behind another rental car to be released from the lot. Tapping the steering wheel with his thumb, he glances in his rearview mirror while I peek over the backseat out the back window. All clear. How long will this take? The driver ahead of us must be asking for directions from the guard, who points toward what I assume is the highway.

Behind us, another rental car pulls up. It's the family, not the man from Fort Davis. But another car squeals to a stop behind the family's van.

"Hurry!"

Sam's jaw clenches. "I can't jump the—oh, here we go." The car lurches forward, then slams to a stop beside the guard. The automatic window rolls down.

"Your paperwork and license?"

I hand it to Sam, who hands it and his driver's license to the guard. Two cars back, a driver's door opens. A man in black (Okay, a black T-shirt) steps out of his car and begins to walk toward us.

"Have a good stay." The guard punches the button to make the barrier rise in front of the hood.

"Go!"

Sam punches the car forward. He takes several turns, not only losing whoever is following us but confusing me as well. I turn around the map the rental car attendant gave us when we signed all the required paperwork, searching for where we are. I look from map to street and back. "Where are we?"

"Not sure."

"I know." Howard crouches low in the backseat. "Turn left at the light."

Sam turns on the street Howard recommends. "What phone call were you talking about?"

"Didn't you hear the phone ring last night? About three?"

"Nah, I sleep hard."

Like most men. "It was weird. Sort of a computerized voice. He asked for me by name. Then told me to stay in Austin and forget all of this."

"All of this what?"

"He didn't say. When I asked who it was, the call disconnected. I tried to redial but it said it was a private number." I stare out the side window, remembering my fears rising up to greet me. "I should have asked more questions, but I thought the call was about Nana. Or Ginger."

Sam's mouth twists.

Tilting my head toward my hand, I rub the tension gathering at my temples. "I don't like this any better than you, but I think we have to be careful since we don't exactly know what's going on here."

"I can tell you."

I swivel in my seat and wait for Howard's answer, but Sam murmurs under his breath, "But then he'd have to kill us."

Howard's gaze is fastened onto the side window. "The less you know the better. We should get to the hotel as soon as possible. Keep a low profile."

Sam nods but then takes us to dinner while rush hour is heavy. His only concession is that he parks the rental on the back side of the building. After dinner and rush hour has died down, he takes us on a tour of the nation's capital. It's postcard perfect as we drive through Capitol Hill.

"Don't look over there," Howard warns.

Of course, I do. It looks like any old building, nondescript and plain. No quotes on the outside of the building from a founding father. No flag flying. No tourists gathering. I attempt to read the sign as we pass, but Howard shakes his head. "That's just what they want you to believe."

"So what is it?"

"Secret stuff. Agencies most Americans don't even know exist."

"More of our tax dollars at work." Sam brakes for a pedestrian.

We pass the white marble Capitol building, Supreme Court, and Library of Congress in such quick succession that I can't absorb it all. So much history in such a small space. I'd like to spend a week or two just wandering around, but I know that's impossible this trip. Sam doesn't seem inclined to linger and Howard keeps telling us not to look at that building or over there or any place I want to view. Tired of being at their mercy, I suggest we park and stroll through the grassy pedestrian Mall punctuated by national landmarks.

"Not a good idea." Howard shakes his head, still crunched down in his seat as far as he can. "It's not safe."

"Security is tight here." I point out a parking space but a motorcycle hides between two vans. Finding parking is about as easy as finding the answers to all these conspiracy theories. "Security has been escalated since 9/11. We'll be fine."

"That's not the kind of safety I mean."

Sam sighs and with a muffled snort he hunts for a parking space. But it takes nearly an act of Congress to find one. He stalks a family of five walking along the street, the children scuffing their tennis shoes along the sidewalk, one parent tugging on their hands, the other carrying the smallest child, until they come to their minivan. We wait for several minutes while they change a diaper. When they finally pull out, Sam whips the rental car into the parallel parking spot, and together we climb out of the car. I lean back inside. "Come on, Howard. Or are you going to stay in the car?"

"I'm coming." He grumbles and unfurls those long, lanky legs.

Darkness begins to creep in around us, as if it's stalking us, the shadows lengthening, stretching out its fingers toward us. White lights illuminate the monuments turning them a gilded hue. We pass the reflecting pool, and along the outside edges on the great expanses of green grass, crowds have gathered for softball games. I pause, thinking of all those who have walked, marched, protested along these hallowed walkways, carrying out the American tradition of independence and forthrightness. The forefathers these surrounding statues represent are equally as important as the ghosts of those who've stood up for what is right, marched for those who couldn't, shouted to be heard by the heads of state who had the decision-making powers.

We head up the stone steps like a million other tourists have before us to see the Lincoln Memorial. Many others mill around the seated statue of Lincoln, clicking pictures, talking on cell phones. It's a solemn place, and I read the words of the Gettysburg Address which I memorized in the eighth grade, the words still impact me and I realize that Howard is living out those words, trying to get the truth—as he believes it—out to the American people. I read the words slowly, ". . . that from these honored dead we take increased devotion to that cause for which they gave the last full measure of devotion—that we here highly resolve that these dead shall not have died in vain."

Lincoln's words have been hailed and cherished in the almost one-hundred-and-fifty years since he spoke them at the bloody Gettysburg battlefield. *That these dead shall not have died in vain.* Is that what Howard is doing? Is he honoring my mother with his work?

I watch him wandering around the memorial, studying the bits and pieces of Lincoln's quotes and speeches carved into the walls. My heart softens and opens, and I think I finally understand him.

Slowly we gather again at the top of the steps and begin the descent. Howard stops only a few steps down, wobbling a bit. Sam reaches for his father's arm, steadies him. Despite the disputes and degrees separating the men, I know the son loves his father.

"This is where Martin Luther King gave his 'I have a dream' speech," Sam says. "The history here is overwhelming."

I look out over the walkways and reflecting pool, thinking of the dreams we each hide inside our hearts. Howard wants to prove his theories, to prove Jennifer didn't die in vain. Sam wants to reconnect with his father. And me? What do I want? What do I want out of all of this? What am I expecting to find here, from some employer of my mother's?

I turn back and stare at the cragged face of our sixteenth president. The hardships he knew proved his character. A documentary I once saw about Lincoln revealed how he dreamed he would die in office. Still, he stayed. He didn't run away. He didn't quit living or believing through the loss of his beloved mother and son, through the hardships of the war. He stayed the course.

Lincoln lost his mother when he was nine years old. Just like me. The thought resonates through me, spreading outward and pulsing at my center. It wasn't his only loss in life. He had many. If one only looked at the bullet points of significant events in his life—lost mother at nine, too poor to attend proper school, his son, Willie, died at age twelve, at age fifty-six Lincoln was killed—it seems like a sad life. But Lincoln had a great sense of humor. He had a strong faith. And he accomplished much.

I can't say I've accomplished much in this life other than my daughter. But maybe that's because my faith has been weak. Or nonexistent. Maybe Sam is right. Maybe I've been afraid to believe in God, to believe He had a hand in my life or a plan for it. It never made sense to me, how God could use my mother's death to accomplish anything good or right. And maybe it hasn't or won't. Maybe the death of Lincoln's mother and son didn't either. Maybe it was a test. Maybe it was just a consequence of something terrible. Who can know?

"Howard"—I turn my gaze toward the night sky, the smattering of stars, the layering of clouds that obscures the moon, drifting across it like a gauzy shawl—"do you believe in God?"

He stares down his nose at me, and I expect some scientific disdain.

"When you look out there"—I gesture toward the sky—"through your telescopes at the stars and moon, the planets . . . the vastness of space. Does it make you wonder?"

He clears his throat, avoids his son's steady gaze. "Sure, yes." He nods as if confirming his own statement. "I believe."

Sam remains silent, but I recognize the "You do?" knotting his features.

"There's order out there, not some randomness." The corners of Howard's mouth pinch tight, then he steps down one stone step, beginning the slow, inevitable descent.

I feel Sam's gaze on me, and I turn to him and smile. He reaches out a hand, and I take it, enjoying the way his fingers fold over mine. Maybe this is what I've been searching for.

"Look!" Howard jerks his chin. He stares down the memorial's vast steps to the pedestrian Mall. "That man again!"

Sam's head snaps in that direction. In one quick moment, he releases my hand and takes off down the stone steps, leaping over the last few. The man stops, wavers, then turns and runs in the opposite direction, apparently deciding that following Howard is hazardous to his health.

"He shouldn't do that!" Howard grasps my arm as if I can stop Sam, then he wobbles, unsteady on his feet. "He'll get hurt." The pained look in his face reveals more love for Sam than the son has probably ever seen from his father.

"Sam can take care of himself." I put a hand on Howard's arm to steady and reassure him. "He wants to help you, you know."

"Well, he could get himself killed that way. Then where would that leave me?"

From our vantage point, we watch Sam gain on the younger man until he overtakes him, knocking him down. They tumble over each other, rolling across the sidewalk and onto the grass. Families and visitors move out of their way. Some stay to watch the commotion. Others turn to leave. My heart pounds away like I've been running right along with Sam. He's the first one on his feet and hauls the other man upward. Nose to nose, except that Sam has to bend down to get in the shorter man's face, they exchange words. Sam finally releases his grip on the man's shirt front. The younger man steps backward and pulls something out of his hip pocket and shows it to Sam.

"What are they doing?" Howard asks, as if I have the answer. "What are they discussing?"

"I don't know."

Howard pats my hand, which I realize is clutching his arm. "He's okay now."

"Oh, sorry. Did I hurt you?"

He smiles. "Nope. Just hope you won't hurt my son."

"What do you mean?"

"Don't break his heart."

Shaken by his statement, I turn back to watch Sam.

The two men look in our direction and begin retracing Sam's path at a much slower pace. Sam's face looks as solid as Abraham Lincoln's, but he rubs one elbow. The younger man's face is damp with sweat.

"Come on." I urge Howard down the steps, keeping a hand on him. "Let's go find out who is he."

"Not gonna do any good," Howard grumbles. "Like he's gonna tell the truth?"

"You never know."

We meet along the wide sidewalk leading from memorial to memorial. Sam has a scratch on his forehead. He's sweaty but calm. The younger man has a few more cuts and bruises, his shirt has a mass of wrinkles, fanning outward like a sunburst, but he seems to be with Sam of his own accord and not under duress.

"Howard"—Sam gestures toward the stranger—"this is Peter Wallis."

The younger man sticks out a hand to shake Howard's, but the older man holds back.

"He's a reporter for the *Wall Street Journal*."

Howard snorts. "A reporter!"

"I saw his press pass."

Howard's mouth pulls sideways, as if contemplating his next move. Finally he takes the younger man's hand and shakes it.

"Good to finally meet you, sir. I've been trying for months to get in touch with you—ever since I read your book."

"You read—"

"Yes, sir. I believe it's a story that needs to be told. If you'll cooperate, we can do a series on your findings. An exposé, so to speak."

"I suggested to Peter," Sam interjects, "that you might meet with him tomorrow morning, while Bryn and I drive south for her meeting."

Howard rubs the back of his neck, the way I've seen Sam do. "Well, I suppose I could. If"—he looks toward me—"you don't think you'll need me."

"I'll be fine." I touch his hand, trying to tell him in my own way not to worry about Sam. "You need to do this."

Chapter Twenty-Six

The next morning we leave Howard at the hotel with the eager young reporter while Sam and I drive south. Just inside the Virginia border, we locate the Munson's antebellum home. It's a stately manor with white columns and cherry trees along the drive. My stomach tangles into knots as we park and walk up the steps. We ring the bell and wait. Doubts assault me, knotting my stomach.

"What if she's not here?"

Sam takes my hand, massaging the flesh between my thumb and forefinger. "Then we'll wait for her."

"But what if she won't talk to us."

His gaze is soft. "She'll have to."

"How?"

"You're a resourceful reporter—"

"I'm an obit writer. People I write about don't usually complain."

He laughs but stops almost immediately as the sound of footsteps approach the inside of the door.

"Yes?" The wavering voice from the phone. "How can I help you?"

"It's Brynda Seymour, Mrs. Munson."

"What?" The lock clicks and the door opens. An elderly woman with steel gray hair and eyes to match a pasty complexion greets us with anything but a welcoming Southern hospitality. She looks like a serious puff of wind might disintegrate her into a pile of ashes. Definitely the urn type. She looks me up and down, then turns her abrasive gaze toward Sam. "Who are you?"

"I'm the reporter who called you the other day, but I'm not here in the capacity of—"

"I told you—"

"Yes, ma'am." I remember how Peter addressed Howard, full of respect. That worked with Howard, but I'm not sure it will with Mrs. Munson. "I appreciate your hesitation, but honestly I'm not here to do a story. My mother worked for your husband. Her name was Jennifer Seymour."

The woman utters a tiny, almost inaudible gasp, but it stops me cold. Her hand remains firmly on the door handle.

"You recognize my mother's name?"

The skin around her jaw sags and is answer enough for me.

"Would you mind if I asked you some—"

"I knew this day would come." She pushes the door wide. She's wearing a gray skirt and blue silk blouse buttoned to the pulse point at the base of her neck, which is long and graceful but showing signs of age. "I told Barriman this would happen. Of course, he didn't believe me. Or didn't care, more like it." The last is uttered under her breath. She turns and walks away from us, her old-fashioned, orthopedic shoes silenced by the carpeting as she enters the private area of her home.

I glance at Sam. He gives a succinct nod and we follow her inside. The flocked wallpaper along the foyer gives way to pale blue walls in a sitting area. Even though the décor seems to be from some previous decade or century, the home is immaculate, as if she's been waiting for company. Oil paintings of oceans and cliffs, meadows and hillsides decorate each wall and make me wonder if I'd recognize the artist's name if I peered closer. Heavy mahogany tables and bookshelves gleam. Sofa and chairs, trimmed in mahogany, are cushioned with velvet. Delicate knickknacks give the room a distinctive feminine flair. A mothball odor filters through the room and makes me want to pinch my nose. It's like the doors and windows have been closed for decades in an effort to preserve the integrity of the home. Or of this woman.

Sylvia Munson takes command of the room like Queen Elizabeth I. She settles in a chair—more like her throne—and indicates with a slight wave of her hand that we should find a seat. The sofa is more comfortable than it looks. I perch on the edge, but Sam is more manly in his approach, making the furniture groan and creak as he plunks down. He freezes, inches forward, until he is also on the edge. We sit, side by side. I wonder if anyone has sat upon these cushions for years.

"I hope you don't mind if I don't offer refreshments for this occasion."

"We're not here for—"

"What *do* you want?" Her tone is cold and blunt.

"To know—"

"A check? Will that suffice? Is that what you came for?" Without taking her eyes off me, her hand probes a drawer in the round table. She pulls out what looks to be a checkbook and a bundle of papers. "I would prefer for this to stay out of the court system and, of course, the papers. I want to protect my children from scandal."

My forehead compresses, and I glance at Sam then back to the oddly prim woman. "Excuse me?"

"I think you have us confused with someone else," Sam offers.

"I know exactly who you are. I thought I would have heard from you a long time ago. I've been prepared. Every time the doorbell rang, I expected to find you or your grandmother demanding money. I had our attorney draw up these papers years ago for you to sign. You'll find them fair . . . considering. But the terms of the agreement are firm."

"My mother worked for your husband. Why should I—"

The woman begins laughing, cackling really, in a most unlady-like way. She ends it with a snort and presses a finger against her lips. "Jennifer never worked a day in her life. Not the way you imagine. She was a call girl. A hooker. A prosti—"

"What?" My heart jolts and I steel myself to sit upright, not fall back against the cushions. My face burns as if I've been slapped. Hard.

Sam presses a hand against my arm.

"Oh, come, come, my dear, surely you haven't been fooled all these years into believing the false virtues of a young woman who died so young, have you?"

"My mother wasn't perfect but—" I give myself a mental shake to alleviate the cold icy fog that has settled over me like a shroud. "She worked for your husband at . . ." I struggle to remember the name of the defense company. "His company had an alliance with NASA. And—"

"Barriman used the company to front his dalliances. But no, Jennifer was never on the payroll. She was considered a *consultant*. But her expertise was not the defense industry. It was my husband's baser needs." She begins filling out a check, her hand slow and laborious, the pen making a scratching sound against paper like its etching hard grooves permanently in my heart. "I didn't know about Jennifer for years. If I had, I would have stopped it." She gives me a quick glance, a steely gray look that tells me she wouldn't have had any qualms killing to do so. "But by the time I knew, you had been born and—"

"Are you saying . . . ?" My head feels like it's done a Linda Blair turnaround. I can't get my bearings and place a hand on Sam's knee to orient myself to the here and now.

Sylvia stops writing, lays her pen flat against her checkbook, and stares at me. "You didn't know."

I shake my head. "So your husband was . . . is my—"

"If you didn't know all of this"—she carefully closes the checkbook—"then why are you here?"

"To find out more about my mother. I was told she worked for your husband . . . in the defense industry. With NASA." It takes great force and restraint to make the words come out in an orderly procession, but they sound clipped, like the footsteps of soldiers on the march. "Howard—Howard Walter's, a friend of my mother's who worked for NASA—thought she was a spy of some sort."

The woman starts to laugh again, but stops herself, steely determination evident in her features. She shakes her head, reopens the checkbook, rips the check from the leather folder, and holds it out to me. The thin paper flutters between us. "Well, I suppose you have learned more than you bargained for then. For that I can sympathize with you. There was a day when I was innocent, too." She nods at the check she still holds between thumb and forefinger. "Take it. Jennifer earned it, I suppose."

Staring at the thin check, at the blue veins showing on Sylvia's knobby hands, I shake my head. I manage to stand, my legs feeling wobbly. Sam is right beside me, his hand cupping my elbow, lifting and pulling me against him, his arm slipping around my waist. "I'm sorry I bothered you, Mrs. Munson."

Slowly, as if treading through a glass museum, we move toward the door. The antiques around me aren't as fragile as I feel. As if I'm floating, expanding like a hot-air balloon, I wobble through the foyer.

"Wait just a minute!" Sylvia Munson's tone demands obedience. She is clearly a woman accustomed to getting her way. "Come back here! There are papers you must sign."

Without a backward glance, Sam opens the front door. I notice bits of blue glass are welded into the windows, which run parallel to the wooden door. Light catches the blue, magnifying and scattering the light into fragments on the marble floor.

"Come on." Sam leads me out the door.

"Is it more money you want?" Mrs. Munson has followed us to the doorway.

Drawing in big gulps of air into my lungs, I walk with stiff legs down the stone steps, back toward the rental car. My shoes slip on the pebbly drive, but Sam is there to catch me. His arm around the back of my waist is solid and firm. When we reach the rental car, I lean against the warm metal as Sam opens the passenger door.

In the doorway of her mausoleum, Sylvia flaps her precious papers at me. "You must sign this! If you don't accept this check, you'll get nothing else. Do you hear me? Nothing!" With halting footsteps, she moves out to the edge of her porch, tucks the papers and check beneath her arm, and points a finger at me. "If you so much as dare speak to any tabloid paper—or any publication for that matter—I will sue you." She doesn't yell this last bit, but her words manage to cross the wide expanse. "I will *not* have my family dragged through the muck of your mother's sins."

When I don't respond, she turns, enters her house, and slams the door.

I slump into the passenger seat, and Sam secures my seat belt for me. He watches me for a few minutes, as if trying to decide what to do, what to say. Thankfully, he says nothing.

What is there to say anyway?

I'm not sure how long we sit there. It feels as if all sound is muffled through a gauzy material. Like my emotions, bound up, mummified. Is this woman right? Did she really know my mother? Was Howard wrong for all these years? Did he love my mother so much he couldn't see her faults?

A tapping on the window startles me, and I jump sideways toward Sam. A Hispanic woman with gray hair woven through the thick black stands beside the car. Her gray dress looks like a maid's uniform.

"What now?" Sam lowers the window next to me. "Who are you?"

Her black eyes bulge for a moment. "I not important." She reaches her hand forward and touches my shoulder. "But I hold something for you." Her accent is thick as a wool poncho. "I work for the Munson family all these years. I move here with them in 1985. Mrs. Sylvia means well. She had hard life. Mr. Munson was not—how I say—kind. But I remember your mother. He call her Jenny. I take messages back and forth between them sometimes. She sent him many notes. Which I save out of trash can each week. You want?"

"You have notes my mother wrote?"

"Si."

I blink, trying to absorb this new information. "Where are they?"

"Stay here. I get for you." She walks behind the car and disappears around the side of the house.

I turn a wide-eyed look to Sam. "Can you believe this?"

"This could be the proof you need if you ever want to take the Munson family to court, sue for your inheritance."

I shake my head. "I would never do that! The people at fault are dead now. It's time to move on. For me . . . for Mrs. Munson. I wouldn't want to cause her any more pain."

"Why? She didn't care about hurting you. She didn't even try to soften the blow of the news about your mother."

Sighing, I slide my hands down my thighs. "Don't you know me better than that?"

His mouth thins, pinching at the corners and forming a Kurt-Russell-size dimple on one cheek. "I do . . . or thought I did. But I also know that pain can trigger vindictiveness."

"Stories from your divorce?"

He shrugs. "I'm proud of you. Of the way you're handling this. It can't be easy."

"I'm not sure I can fathom what's actually happened. May take me a while to process." I place a hand on his arm. "Thanks for being here with me today. I know this is awkward and . . . well, I wouldn't have wanted it to be anyone else."

"Me, too.

The woman appears beside the car again, this time with a shoebox in her hands. It's an old box, slightly smaller than normal, as if made for a child's shoe, with the manufacturer's logo across the top—Hush Puppies. She pushes it through the open window. Her hand covers mine for a moment, and in those work-worn fingers I sense warmth and compassion. "I wonder if I ever meet you some day. And now . . . Your mother was sweet."

"Thank you."

"I wish I collect all her letters. I didn't start until I realized her . . . relations with Mr. Munson continuing for long time. Then I think maybe she want letters some day." She taps her heart. "Sentimental."

I swallow a lump in my throat and nod. "Thank you."

"You tell Jenny hello. She probably not remember me, but I remember her all these years."

The second I debate telling her my mother is dead seems eternal. Should I smile and say, "I will," holding back the truth? But withholding the truth is what caused us to be here today, the sun shining and yet not warming. "My mother . . . Jenny. She died."

"Oh!" Her eyes round and fill with tears. She reaches forward and clasps my hand again. "I am sorry. She a good girl. Bad situation, not so good man. We all make mistakes. Yes?"

I nod, unable to speak.

She pulls away, keeping her gaze locked with mine for a long moment before she walks away and disappears around the corner of the house. I feel Sam watching me but I don't have the courage to meet his gaze. If I read sympathy or empathy or anything tender in his brown eyes, I'll lose it.

With my heart thundering, I flip open the lid of the shoebox. Inside is a row of letters stacked against each other. The stationery is canary yellow, mother's signature color. I run my hand over the tops of the envelopes and imagine her licking the sticky back, sealing each one with hope. "I'm not sure I can read these."

Sam sits quietly behind the wheel, letting the engine idle. "When you're ready."

I nod and he puts the car in drive. But we don't get far. "Pull over."

Sam complies, stopping the car on the side of the highway. Before he can shift into park, I jump from the vehicle and move a few feet from the paved shoulder into the weeds and wildflowers that have taken over. My stomach lurches, but I manage to swallow back the bile that rises to the back of my throat.

Sam reaches my side. "You okay?"

I nod but feel light-headed, and a rush of heat as if a geyser has erupted inside me.

"Lean over." Sam advises, putting his hand on the back of my neck and pushing me forward. "You're pale."

Bracing my fists on my knees, I feel his steadying hand move to my back. Each breath scrapes across what feels like jagged pieces of glass in my throat. After a moment or two, the hard lump in my belly softens. I shove back the hair from my forehead and glance up at Sam, backlit by the sun. "I wasn't expecting this."

"I wouldn't think so."

My gaze shifts from his understanding to the rolling fields of yellow flowers. "I wanted to believe Momma was doing something noble, something of value."

He nods but remains silent as the stout oak pressing into the fence line, its branches stretching outward in an umbrella of strength and protection, unbending in the breeze.

"I was deluding myself, wasn't I?"

"It's human nature to hope for the best."

"And now what?" Tears burn my eyes as if my internal geyser's juices are spewing. "What do I believe about Momma? Myself? Did I ruin her life? Was I just a mistake?"

Sam cups my jaw, stilling the questions. His eyes probe deep but once again he doesn't offer pat explanations or presumptions that attempt to brighten the situation. But I need guidance, a light to point me in the right direction, something to banish the stalking dark thoughts and shadowy guilt.

"What do I believe now?"

Shifting from one foot to the other, his hand still warming my skin, his thumb brushing my bottom lip, his gaze flickers from mouth to eyes, a brief interlude that expands hope inside me. He draws a deep breath. "I've always believed God wants to turn our ashes into something beautiful. In fact, He specializes in raising the dead to life, the hopeless to hopeful. He can take our rainfall of failures and turn them into a rainbow of possibilities." He pulls away from me, rubs a hand along his own jaw. "How's that for a sermon?"

I take his hand and hold onto him. "I have no doubt you inspired your congregation." Our hands meld together, fingers linked, palms pressed flesh against flesh. "But now . . . does all that pretty talk apply to the ashes of your dreams?"

He lifts our joined hands to his lips and kisses the back of mine. "It does."

BACK IN THE CAR, somewhere along the drive back, I gather enough courage to tug one letter out of the box. There is nothing special about this letter, and I'm not sure why I start in the middle. But I pull the thick stationery, out of the envelope, notice the four-cent stamp in the upper right corner. The return address is our old apartment on Riverside. Seeing Momma's handwriting, its precise slant, perfect formation, very schoolgirlish, makes me smile—and yet tears collect in the corners of my eyes. I press my hand against the top of the folded stationery, unsure what I'm hoping for. A secret code? Something to corroborate Mrs. Munson's story? Microfiche would be good, but nothing like that falls out when I open the letter.

Barry,

I waited until three for you to come but then I had to pick up Brynnie from the babysitter. She charges more if I'm even a minute late. I'm sure you got delayed at work again. I understand. Your job is important.

Brynnie is sure growing. Talking up a storm, too. Guess she gets that from me. But every time she smiles, it's obvious who her daddy is. I hope you'll think about seeing her. I hate thinking of her growing up without a father, the way I did. I want so much more for her life. She's the best thing that ever happened to me. But I'm not so sure I'm the best for her. She deserves so much more.

By the way, I got the check and cashed it. I'll plan on seeing you next week. Same bat time. Same bat channel.

Love, Jen

Chapter Twenty-Seven

We reach the hotel in virtual silence. Sam turns off the engine and, before he can exit the car, I put a hand on his arm. "I have to talk to your father."

"But you—"

"He has a right to know, Sam. He *needs* to know."

Strain shows in the crevices of his face. "I don't know how he'll take it. What will it be like for a man to learn his whole life is a house of cards?"

"You're the one who wanted me to tell him about the way Momma died."

Nodding, he stares down at his hand looped over the bottom of the steering wheel. "I know. And now I'm not so sure."

"It's time we all face the truth."

Sam looks deep into my eyes, as if probing gently inside my heart. "Are you sure you're ready?"

I shrug. "As ready as I'll ever be."

We walk into the hotel together, my mother's letters tucked under my arm. We locate Howard and the reporter in the coffee shop. Breakfast plates are piled to the side along with three empty glasses, pink liquid congealed at the bottom of each. Deep in conversation, each leaning forward over the table, Howard and Peter don't see us approach. When we're standing beside their table, Peter leans back in his chair, his eyes alight with the look I've seen in the newsroom before—pure delight at nailing down a story.

"You're back!" Howard glances at his watch as if surprised at the amount of time that has passed. "How did it go? Did she have any papers? Any proof—"

I place a hand on his shoulder. "Would you mind if you and I took a walk, Howard?"

"Sure. But . . ." He glances at the reporter.

Peter closes his notebook, slips his pen and microrecorder in his shirt pocket. "No problem. We can finish this later. I have some work to do, and then we'll schedule a taped interview. All right?"

"That's fine." Howard actually smiles, which I don't think I've ever seen before. It's a small, tight smile, awkward and yet filled with delight.

"I'll see you out." Sam claps a hand on the reporter's back. The two men walk out of the coffee shop together.

I wait for Howard to gather his papers, which he then deposits in his room. When he returns to the lobby, we head outdoors into the sunshine.

"Not too warm today."

He waves his thumb over his shoulder. "That fellow read my book. He gets it. They're going to go national with this. Maybe now we can pressure NASA to probe the areas of the moon they've been resistant to photograph for too long. Peter is also working to get shots from the space probe India sent up last year."

"That's terrific."

He slides his hands in his back pockets and glances sideways at me. "But I take it things didn't go so well with your meeting with Barry Munson's wife."

"How about the park?" I indicate the tree-shaded park across the street.

We settle at a picnic table. Bits of crust from what looks like a peanut butter and jelly sandwich have been left by some picnickers next to splashes of white bird droppings. The trash can nearby overflows with soda cans and fast-food sacks, bees buzzing around the opening. I trace my fingers over the grains of wood along the tabletop, trying to find a place to begin.

"So did Mrs. Munson give you a hard time? Call the cops? What?"

I reluctantly meet Howard's gaze. "I haven't always been honest with you."

He tilts his head to the side and waits for me to continue.

"You see, I didn't want to face what happened to my mother. I've been running from it my entire life. And when I met you . . . and you were so convinced my mother was some sort of spy . . . well, I think I wanted to believe that. There's something intriguing and somehow special thinking she gave her life for her country or to preserve national security." I stare down at the wooden planks forming the tabletop. My fingers probe the crevices, my nails digging into the soft wood. "It was easier than believing the truth."

"Sometimes it's hard to find the truth, Brynda. Besides you were only a child when your mother died. Truth might look a little different from the perspective of an adult."

"I wish that were so, but facts are facts. I can't wish this away. Much as I'd like." I swallow the hard lump in my throat. "You were right. Momma didn't commit suicide, but she wasn't killed either. I was there with her. She was upset. Mr. Munson came to see her that afternoon. They fought. What I found out today"—I place my hand on the box containing my mother's letters—"is that they were having an affair."

Howard starts to protest, his mouth opening like a fish trying to breathe out of water, but I hold up my hand to stop him. "I didn't want to believe it either. But it's all here in her letters."

I lay the shoebox between us. "She started drinking after Munson left that night. The TV was on. Armstrong was landing on the moon, and all my mother could do was cry and cry. Sometimes when she got like that I'd seen her take some pills and feel better. So I got some medication from the cabinet in her bathroom."

I rub my palm along my jean-clad thigh and press it hard against my kneecap. "She took them all. I don't know what I gave her. I didn't mean for her to take all of the pills, just pick out the one she needed." I roll my hand over, stare at my open palm. "But she took them all."

Howard sits stone still, like the statue of Abraham Lincoln. I still can't look him in the eye, but I hear his breathing, shallow and nasal.

"She never woke up, Howard." I close my hand into a fist, as if still trying to grasp the meaning of it all. "And I never told anyone that story." My throat fights the emotions clogging it. I rub my hand down the length of my neck, lick my lips. "I was scared. I thought I'd get arrested or something. Obviously when I grew older I knew that wasn't the case, but still . . . I couldn't tell anyone what I had done. I've lived with the shame and guilt all these years, but it's time we both faced the real facts. I've spent my life scared someone would find out the truth, but I was just running from the truth myself. And at some point, you can't run anymore."

When I finally dare a look at him, tears swim in his misty blue eyes, and I reach forward to cover his hand with my own.

He pats my hand. "Brynda"—the words scrape out of him like a knife over a rock—"your mother made her choice. Both you and I have to accept that. She may not have been sober or of sound mind, but she had a choice to push away those pills, or take just one or two."

Pressure builds behind my eyes.

"Right?" He gives my hands a tender shake. "You have to let go of the guilt. It's not your fault. Let it go."

I can only nod. After a while I open the box, and together we read about my mother's life, her love for a man who never returned that love and simply used her for his own pleasure, and her desperation to make things right for her daughter. The tears we shed are of understanding, sympathy, and loss . . .

And we gather them together between us and let them wash away the heartache we've both lived with for too long.

LONG AFTER HOWARD RETURNS to the hotel, I sit in the park, stare up through the tree branches at the darkening sky, the rising moon. Tiny leaves look black against the pale moonlight behind them, creating shadows across what looks like a smooth marble surface. But I've seen the moon through a telescope, in pictures brought back from the original moonwalk, and I know the shell is rugged and fierce. Perspective changes everything. It would seem that an up-close-and-personal look would reveal all one would need to know, but in my mother's death, distance provided the best picture, like a Bev Doolittle painting, morphing from one image to another.

As the soft, pastel light filters down through the trees creating shadows around me, I feel a baby's breath brush of the wind against my cheek. What would be good about my mother dying? Maybe I'm wrong in asking that particular question. So, what would have been good about her living? She was bent on turning Barry away from his wife, getting him to marry her, and be a real father to me. But he had other children with Sylvia. He didn't need or want another child. Would that have been good for a growing girl? Would watching my mother become more desperate and despondent by the year have been beneficial? So maybe . . . just maybe there was some reason for all that happened. Maybe someone was watching out for me, protecting me. Maybe it's only the consequence of bad decisions that led to a tragic end for my mother. Maybe God simply allowed it to happen, as He allows each of us our own decisions.

Thoughts of my mother sift and churn inside me. At one time she must have had hope. Maybe when she fell in love with Barry Munson. Was it when she carried me inside her? Did she believe her life would turn out happy? Did she have faith in something larger than herself . . . in God? And if so, when was the moment that she lost that faith, that hope, that belief that all would turn out for the best? Was her faith chipped away each time Barry didn't show up to meet her? Was her faith eroded by sleepless nights while tending to a baby? Or did it snap like a dry twig the moment Barry slapped her? When he walked out her door for the last time? When I offered her pills to ease the pain that could never be eased?

Of course, I could see now that my own fledgling faith was blotted out the night she died. I didn't know what to hope in, believe in, or place my faith in at that point. And so I chose nothing. But is that any way to live? I never fully trusted my first husband. It wasn't anything he did or didn't do. It was me, the black hole in my soul that no one person could locate or navigate. I've risked my life too often in a devil-may-care manner, but I don't want my life to end with regrets and broken dreams.

Or like my mother's.

I pull my knees to my chest, rest my head on my bony kneecaps that I feel through the soft, faded jeans. For a moment I close my eyes. But the darkness unnerves me. The great unknown. But is it really unknown? Do I truly believe there is nothing else to this life . . . or after? I don't know about aliens or planetary alignments or cosmic projections, but I do sense there is something . . . *Someone* larger than the universe. My mind has trouble grasping the boundaries and depth of that Someone, and yet . . .

I believe as Howard does, that God put all this together: the stars and continents, asteroid belts and riverbeds. From the colossal to the infinitesimal, microscopic scientific discoveries yet to be made, there is order. All of this didn't come from random explosions of stars or solar systems evaporating. And while all of my answers don't fall into sudden place with answers aligning them . . . it's a start.

Maybe this is the decision Aunt Lillie sensed I was about to make. This time, when I close my eyes and offer a prayer that

I hope the God of the universe will hear, I'm not afraid. "Help me understand . . . show me the way."

No Godlike finger stretches through the sky like a jagged flash of lightning and taps me with sudden clarity, but a peace washes over me like a refreshing cool breeze. It feels like when I was seven and Momma took me to swim in a neighborhood pool. She held me in her arms until I relaxed and stretched out flat along the surface of the chlorinated water. The cool liquid framed my face and buoyed me, muffling the sounds of other children playing and somehow magnifying Momma's voice: "Trust me. I won't let go." I opened my eyes and looked into her smiling gaze. The undulating water rocked beneath and around me, lulling me away, but still I felt her hand on my back, not allowing me to drift too far from her side.

Now, another hand settles on my shoulder. "You okay?"

I blink open my eyes, not startled, simply subdued and calm, lulled by a distant memory and the hope of tomorrow. Sam stands beside me, the moon behind him bright and full, his hand on my shoulder solid and secure. I lean against him, letting my head rest against his arm.

He sits beside me. "What can I do?"

Suddenly I know the answer, what I must do with my new-found awareness. "Will you baptize me?" The look on Sam's face makes me laugh. "Surprised?"

"I'm realizing you are full of surprises."

"So, are you gonna make me ask twice?"

"I'm not really a pastor anymore."

"Did they revoke your ability to marry, bury, and baptize?"

"No."

"So?"

Standing from the picnic table, he holds out a hand toward me. I place mine against his palm and feel his fingers fold over in a solid embrace.

On our way back to the hotel, questions start to cloud out my reasoning. "Where can we do this? The bathtub? Or maybe we should wait, find some place in Austin?"

Sam doesn't answer, just walks straight through the lobby. When I see the sign pointing in the direction of the pool, I understand. It's an outdoor pool, with bushes clinging tight to the metal fence surrounding the decking. Sam kicks off his shoes and unbuttons his shirt. I tug off my boots and decide the rest of my clothing is best left in place. I wade into the cool water, my jeans clinging to my skin, my shirt billowing outward from my body.

Leading me toward the middle of the shallow area, Sam takes both my hands in his and looks me right in the eye. "You're sure about this?"

I nod.

"Okay then." He steps to my side and takes my hand in his, places an arm around me. "Bryn," his voice is louder than I expect, as if it's ricocheting off the water, "do you believe in God, the Creator of the universe?"

I glance around us, feel fireflies gathering in my stomach, but no one is at the pool. We are alone. And does it really matter if there was an audience or congregation? I stare up at the night sky. Stars glitter like angels' faces staring down upon us. The white disk of a moon glows like a night-light breaking through the darkness, leading me to this place. It's the pull of God upon my heart, like the effect of the moon on the ocean, that has brought me here.

"Yes." The firmness of my own voice surprises me. My hand tightens on Sam's, and he squeezes assurances back. Emotions well up inside me and I look to him, waiting . . . because I'm not sure what to expect next.

"Do you believe Jesus is who He said He was, God's only Son and our Savior?"

Flannel board pictures from my few days in Sunday school flutter across my mind in a succession of stories that for so long were only that . . . stories. But now their truth sinks deep into my soul.

"Bryn?" Sam prompts.

"Yes." My voice ripples outward into the night, like the circles of water surrounding me.

Sam's grip on me tightens, and his words flow over me like water. "I baptize you, Brynda Seymour, in the name of the Father, Son, and Holy Spirit." One hand settles at my back, the other lifts toward my face. "Don't worry, just lean back, I've got you."

My heart swells. I cup my hands around his forearm. "You know what you're doing?"

"I haven't drowned anyone yet." Smiling he leans me back into the water, closing his fingers over my nose. Water engulfs me, welcomes me. Then I'm rising out of it. The first thing I see is Sam's half-moon smile.

THE FOLLOWING DAY SAM takes me to the airport. He's staying with Howard in DC for the upcoming television interview, but it's time for me to go home, to pick up the pieces of my life. In a few days I'll pick up Sam at the airport. Where we'll go from there, I don't know, but it won't be the end. I'm learning I don't have all the answers. I never will. But I'm able to look at myself in the mirror, see stars reflected in my eyes, glimmering with hope and a newborn faith.

"You're sure you're okay?" He pulls the rental car over to the sidewalk for passenger drop-off.

"Yes. Some answers aren't what we want to hear or find, but sometimes that's all there is. I've been running, Sam, for a long time. I need to learn to be still."

He reaches over and takes my hand in his, entwining his fingers with mine. "And I've been doing the opposite. It's time I start to move forward with my life."

"What does that mean?" I study the differences in his tanned fingers and my pale ones.

"For us?"

"Yes."

He rubs his thumb along my palm, pressing, kneading, arousing. "It means I want to see you again. Would that bother you?"

My fingers tighten, curling over his knuckles—then I give him a watery smile.

"Come on. We don't have to have all the answers today, just faith that we'll know when the time comes." He opens the door. "You don't want to be late for your flight."

I meet him at the trunk. He pulls my suitcase out and sets it at my feet, sliding the handle out. Before I can take it, he puts his arms around me and pulls me close. "This isn't the end." He cups my jaw, his thumb testing the seam of my lips. "It's just the beginning."

"But what about that one person who makes you complete? Weren't you talking about your—"

"You. You're my blue moon." He dips lower and slants his mouth over mine. It's a tender, sweet kiss of promise that awakens something long-buried in my soul. I wrap my arms around his neck and hold tight, safe for a moment longer. Overwhelmed by the emotions he rejuvenates inside me, I push away. It's time to go. I'm not sure where this will end, but I know the path ahead seems smoother than the one we've traveled so far.

A shadow blocks the sun momentarily. A throat clears. Together Sam and I turn toward a man wearing a black suit, a narrow tie, and a white, starched shirt. His clean-shaven face is serious and stern. "Sam Walters." His voice sounds automatronic. "Brynda Seymour." He doesn't ask if that's who we are, he simply states our names. "Come with me, please."

Sam's arm tightens against my waist. "Why?"

"My agency has some questions for you."

"And what agency is that?" I ask.

He slips on a pair of dark sunglasses and turns his gaze to me. "I could tell you, but you wouldn't recognize it. Just come."

My gaze locks and melds with Sam's . . . and then we both begin to laugh. Maybe Howard's conspiracy theory has more merit than either of us believed. Maybe not. But after all that's happened, I do know this—sometimes a leap of faith gravitates us back to reality. And other times . . .

It sends us soaring into unexplored space.

Dear Reader,

Taking a leap out of an airplane is not my idea of fun, however, that's often just what God has in mind for us. Thankfully that's not literally God's will. Taking a leap of faith requires trust that the parachute will open or that God's waiting arms will catch us. So often the difficulties of life act on us like gravity, pulling us down, weighting us with doubts and guilt when God wants to lift us above our troubles and help us soar. When I wrote this book, that's what I had in mind for my characters—learn to trust and rely on His strength. By defying gravity, Bryn would learn to place her life solidly in God's hands and His peace and joy would buoy her through difficult times. As I was writing this book, I faced some very difficult days. My father was in the hospital for several weeks. Watching his illness worsen and saying good-bye when he passed away was a free fall of emotions, but I felt the support and strength of God's peace lifting and carrying me those days, weeks, and months. The situations my characters faced were different than my own personal ones, but the source of strength was the same. I hope this book will help you see beyond your everyday troubles, however great or small they might be, to the possibilities and hope that lie in Jesus Christ.

Thank you to each of you who have written me about how my books have touched you. Your words inspire and encourage me to keep writing on the days when I feel more like a chicken than an eagle. I love to hear from readers. You can contact me through my Web site, www.leannaellis.com, where I try to blog on a regular basis. Or if you're on Facebook, you can find me there as well. If you have a hankering to learn more about my crazy life and future books, you can join my e-newsletter.

Blessings,
Leanna